Opposites
attract

D0356101

"Are you afraid of me?"

"That's the second time you've asked me. Of course I'm not." Mairi did, however, take a step back, simply as a precautionary measure.

Logan Harrison was much too close. Too large and much too, well, manly. She could smell him, and that disconcerted her even more than realizing that he smelled of spices. Something his housekeeper sprinkled among his clothing?

Her face felt hot.

"I have to leave," she said, ducking around him and nearly sprinting down the hall. His majordomo moved quickly to avoid her but he wasn't fast enough. She ignored him as she opened the door herself and raced down the steps.

KAREN RANNEY

The Witch of Clan Sinclair

AVON

An Imprint of HarperCollinsPublishers

AVON BOOKS
An Imprint of HarperCollins*Publishers*
10 East 53rd Street
New York, New York 10022-5299

To Connie and Mike

The Witch of Clan Sinclair

Chapter 1

Edinburgh, Scotland
October, 1872

Nothing about the occasion hinted that it would change Mairi Sinclair's life. Not the hour, being after dinner, or the day, being a Friday. The setting didn't warn her; the Edinburgh Press Club was housed in a lovely brick building with an impressive view of the castle.

Still, possessing an inquiring mind, she should have somehow known. She should have seen the carriage pull into the street behind them. She should have felt something. The air should have been different, heavy with portent. Hinting at rain, if nothing else.

Perhaps a thunderstorm would have kept her home, thereby changing her fate. But on that evening, not a cloud was in the sky. The day had been a fair one and the night stars glittered brightly overhead, visible even with the glare of the yellowish gas lamps along the street.

A gust of wind brought the chill of winter, but her trembling was due more to eagerness than cold as she left the carriage. Straightening her skirts as she waited for her cousin to follow, Mairi wished she'd taken the time to order a new cloak—her old black one was a bit threadbare at the hem. She would like something in red, perhaps, with oversized buttons and a hidden pocket or two for her notebooks and pencils.

Her dress was new, however, a blue wool that brought out the color of her eyes and made her hair look darker than its usual drab brown. At the throat was the cameo that her brother and sister-in-law had given her on their return from Italy.

"We saw it and thought it looked like you," Virginia said.

She'd responded with the protest that it wasn't a holiday or her birthday.

Macrath had merely ignored her and pinned it on her dress. "The best presents are those that are unexpected," he said. "Learn to receive, Mairi."

So she had, and today she was grateful for the thought and the gift. The brooch enhanced her dress.

She didn't see, however, that the finely carved profile looked anything like her. She didn't have such an aristocratic nose, or a mouth that looked formed for a smile. The hairstyle was similar, drawn up on the sides to cascade in curls in the back. Perhaps that was the only point of similarity.

Fenella joined her in a cloud of perfume, something light and smelling of summer flowers.

Her cousin was a pretty girl, someone people noted even though she rarely spoke in a group. Fenella's blond hair created a halo around her fine-boned face, accentuating her hazel eyes.

Mairi had seen a swan once, and the gentle grace of the bird reminded her of Fenella.

In addition, Fenella was far nicer in temperament than she was. Whenever she said that, her cousin demurred, but they both knew it was the truth.

Fenella's cloak was also black, the severe color only accentuating her blond prettiness, while Mairi was certain that she herself looked like a very large crow. However, she wasn't going to be deterred by her appearance or any other minuscule concern on this most glorious of occasions.

She strode toward the building, clutching her worn copy of *Beneath the Mossy Bough* in her left hand, her reticule in her right. Her hated bonnet was atop her head only because Fenella had frowned at her in censure. Otherwise, she would have left it behind on the seat.

Before they could cross the street, three carriages passed, the rhythmic rumble of their wheels across the cobbles a familiar sound even at night. Edinburgh did have quiet hours, but normally only between midnight and four. Then, the castle on the hill above them seemed to crouch, warning the inhabitants to be silent and still, for these were the hours of rest.

She knew the time well, since she was often awake in the middle of the night working.

"Are you very certain this is proper, Mairi?" Fenella asked as they hurried across the street.

She turned to look at her cousin. Fenella was occasionally the voice of her conscience, but tonight nothing would stop her from attending the Edinburgh Press Club meeting.

"It's Melvin Hampstead, Fenella," she said. "Melvin Hampstead. Who knows when we will ever have the chance to hear him speak again?"

"But we haven't been invited," Fenella said.

Mairi waved her hand in the air as if to dismiss her cousin's concerns. "The whole city's been invited." She shook her head. "It's Melvin Hampstead, Fenella."

She climbed the steps to the top, opened the outer door and held it ajar for her cousin. Inside was the vestibule, a rectangular space large enough to accommodate ten people. Yellow-tinted light from the paraffin oil sconces illuminated the door at the end, guarded by an older man in a dark green kilt and black jacket.

At their entrance, he stood, folded his arms across his chest and pointed his gray-threaded beard in their direction.

"Is it lost you are, then?"

Mairi blinked at him. "I don't believe we are. This is the Edinburgh Press Club, is it not?"

"That it is, but you're a woman, I'm thinking."

"That I am," she said, clutching the book to her bodice. "We've come to hear Mr. Hampstead speak."

"You'll not be hearing him here," he said. "The meeting is closed to women."

The man didn't even look at her when he spoke, but at a spot above her, as if she were below his notice.

"That can't be true," she said. "Otherwise, it wouldn't have been publicized so well."

"This is the Edinburgh Press Club, madam. We do not admit women."

"I'm a miss," she said, stepping back. "Miss Mairi Sinclair, and I've a right to be here. I'm the editor of the *Edinburgh Gazette*."

"You're a woman by my way of thinking," he said. "And we don't admit women."

She had the urge to kick him in the shin. Instead, she batted her eyes ever so gently. She'd been told she had beautiful blue eyes—the Sinclair eyes—plus she was occasionally gifted with the same charm that Fenella effortlessly commanded.

"Are you very certain?"

Evidently, he was immune to both her eyes and her lashes, because he frowned at her.

"It's Melvin Hampstead," she said. "I adored his book," she added, holding it up for him to see. "If we promise to slip in, not speak to anyone, and simply stand in the corner, wouldn't you allow us to enter?"

"No."

No? Just no? No further explanation? No chance to convince him otherwise? Simply no?

She frowned at him, one hand holding the book, the other clenched tight around her reticule and the notebook inside. She carried her notebook everywhere, and the minute she could, she was going to record everything this man said, plus his refusal on behalf of the Edinburgh Press Club to allow her to enter.

"Is there a problem?"

She turned her head to find a man standing there, a bear of a man, tall and broad, with a square face and eyes like green glass.

"No, Provost Harrison, no problem. I was just telling this female that the Edinburgh Press Club did not allow women."

She'd listened to tales of Scotland's history from her grandmother, heard stories of brave men striding into battle with massive swords and bloodlust in their eyes.

This was one of those men.

He, too, was attired in a kilt, one of a blue and green tartan with a black jacket over a snowy white shirt. She could almost imagine him bare-chested, a broadsword in his right hand and a cudgel in his left. The sun would shine on the gleaming muscles of his arms and chest. He'd toss his head back and his black hair would fall over his brow.

There were men, and then there were men. One was male only because he wasn't female. The other was the definition of masculine, fierce and a little frightening, if her heartbeat was to be believed.

He braced his legs apart, folded his arms and regarded her with an impassive look.

She knew who he was, of course, but she'd never seen the Lord Provost of Edinburgh up so close. If she had, she'd have been prepared for the force of his personality.

If he meant to intimidate her, he was doing a fine job of it, but she would neither admit it nor let him see that she was wishing she'd thought to remove her cloak so he could see her new blue dress.

Nonsense. Was she turning into one of those women who couldn't be bothered with anything more important than her appearance?

Perhaps she should ask herself that question when she wasn't standing nearly toe-to-toe with the Lord Provost, with him looking half Highland warrior, half gentleman Scot. Or if she could have ignored his strong square jaw, full lips, and his sparkling green eyes.

"Is there a problem, miss?"

At least he'd gotten the miss part correct.

"No problem. But I don't understand why I can't attend Mr. Hampstead's lecture."

He raised one eyebrow at her.

"The Edinburgh Press Club does not allow women as members, I believe."

"Mr. Hampstead's lecture has been promoted throughout Edinburgh."

"For men to attend."

She could feel her temper rising, which was never a good sign. She had a tendency to do and say foolish things when she forgot herself.

She was very aware that there were inequities in society. For that reason, Macrath was the titular owner of the Sinclair Printing Company. For that reason, she signed her columns with either her brother's name or another male's. For that reason, she pretended Macrath was out of the office temporarily when men came to call to discuss a matter with the owner of the *Gazette*. She always took the information, made the decision, and wrote the supplicant with her answer, once more pretending to be her brother.

She had to hide behind a man to do her daily tasks, run a business, be a reporter, and publish a newspaper, but she'd never been faced with the situation she was in at the moment: being refused admittance solely because she was a woman.

It should have occurred to her, but because it hadn't, she felt the curious sensation of being blown off her feet.

"What does it matter that I'm a woman?" she asked. "Does Mr. Hampstead's lecture only appeal to men?"

Right at the moment, she didn't like the Edinburgh Press Club very much. Nor did she like the gatekeeper or the Lord Provost. Most of all, she didn't like the burning feeling in her stomach, the one that felt like humiliation and embarrassment, coupled with the knowledge that she wasn't going to win this skirmish.

Fenella evidently noted the signs, because she grabbed her elbow. "Come, Mairi, we should leave."

"I believe that would be the wisest course," the Lord Provost said.

She narrowed her eyes at him.

Did he think he was the first man to have tried to put her in her place? She was faced with criticism every day, and every day she had to deflect it, fight it, or ignore it.

"I would have thought, in your position, that you would speak for all citizens of Edinburgh, not just the men. Or is it because I don't have the ability to vote that you dismiss me so easily?"

He didn't say a word, the coward.

"Your silence indicates that you can't dispute that."

His lips curved in a faint smile. "On the contrary, my silence might be wisdom instead. I have found that it isn't wise to argue with those who are overemotional."

The breath left her in a gasp. "You consider women to be overly emotional?"

"I do not address women, miss. Only you. The club is a private organization, not one funded by or for the citizens of Edinburgh. I have nothing to do with its workings. I am simply a guest. Had I the authority, I would allow you entrance."

She smiled. "Then you do think women should be admitted."

"I think it's the only way to silence you."

She almost drew her foot back, but a soft sound from Fenella stopped her.

"Thank you, sir," Fenella said, stepping in and preventing Mairi from responding by grabbing her arm and pulling her toward the stairs. "We'll be on our way."

In her daydream, she sailed past the Lord Provost with dignity and poise while he wistfully stared after her. The truth was somewhat different. She left, but when she looked back, he was grinning at her.

Logan Harrison watched as the woman went down the steps, glancing back at him from time to time.

She had high cheekbones stained with pink and a chin that looked stubborn enough to double as a battering ram.

He smiled at her frown, which made her scowl even deeper.

He normally avoided angry women, but something about her made him want to annoy her further, just to see how fast her temper rose.

Her eyes blazed at him and her lush mouth was thinned in irritation. As he watched, she said something to her wiser companion. She evidently didn't want to leave. She'd probably be content to argue with him all night.

He rarely had the opportunity to argue with people. Gone were the fevered discussions of his earlier political life. He was at the point now that people respected his position too much to counter his pronouncements.

They practically backed out of the room.

Although he was the Lord Provost of Edinburgh, he wasn't God. Granted, his position dictated that he was also the Lord Lieutenant for the city, which meant he greeted members of the royal family—some of whom did think they were God.

"Who is she?" he asked. Robertson glanced at the woman then back at him.

"A Miss Sinclair, sir. She claims to be the editor of the *Edinburgh Gazette*."

"Does she?"

He knew the paper but he made a mental note of her name. She claimed to be its editor? Another interesting facet of the woman, one that had nothing to do with the fact that she had an arresting face and a figure that hinted at lushness beneath her cloak.

He watched as she entered the carriage, regretting that circumstances wouldn't allow him another chance to continue their discussion.

"He had no right to insult me," Mairi said as she entered the carriage.

"He didn't insult you," Fenella said. "If anyone did, it was the Edinburgh Press Club. They're the ones who refused to allow women."

"Next you're going to tell me it's the way of the world and I should simply accept it."

"Men are stronger," Fenella said.

Mairi glanced at her. "And smarter, I presume?"

Fenella didn't answer.

It was one thing for a woman to be treated with disdain by a man. Another thing entirely, Mairi thought, for another woman to feel the same. Unfortunately, Fenella wasn't alone in her thoughts. A great many women believed that men were stronger, smarter, more capable of being leaders. Let them protect women, and women—frail and helpless—would be the better for it.

She shouldn't be so critical of Fenella. Her cousin was nothing if not loyal. Despite not being a fan of Mr. Hampstead, Fenella had donned one of her better dresses, had her blond hair curled in ringlets, and came with her tonight.

"His eyes are green," Fenella said, sighing. "I do wish my eyes were that color."

Mairi turned to look at her cousin, surprised. Fenella was not the type to long for something she didn't have. Nor was she the type to notice a man's appearance. Or at least she never had in the past.

"Your eyes are lovely," she said, and it wasn't a lie. Fenella's hazel eyes had the ability to change color depending on what she wore. Tonight they appeared a soft brown.

Her own eyes were a deep Sinclair blue. Her brother and sister had a similar shade. If she wished to be different in any way, it would be that her hair wasn't a simple brown, but light and blond like her cousin's.

However, wishing to be different was a waste of time.

"I didn't notice his eyes," she said.

The lie embarrassed her. Of course she'd noted his eyes. And his face, looking as if it had been hewn by God's axe.

"He's entirely too large."

Fenella glanced at her.

She frowned at her cousin's smile.

"Well, he is. I prefer a man who's less imposing."

"He was certainly that," Fenella said on a sigh.

"I'm surprised he didn't throw us down the stairs."

Fenella's eyes widened.

"He seemed very polite, Mairi."

Mairi nearly threw her hands up in the air.

"I wanted to hear Mr. Hampstead. Not go all agog over a man."

Fenella's face turned a becoming shade of pink, and Mairi knew she shouldn't have said what she had. Her cousin had a delicate nature, one that required diplomatic speech. She always had to rearrange the words she was going to say before talking to Fenella, for fear of offending her or hurting her feelings.

"You have to admit he is a handsome man," her cousin said. "He's tall and has such broad shoulders. And his mouth . . ." Fenella sighed again.

"What's wrong with his mouth?"

"Oh, there's nothing wrong with it," Fenella said, sounding as love-struck as a silly girl. "He looks like he's about to say something shocking." She glanced over at Mairi. "Or kiss you."

Rather than just sit there and listen to Fenella wax eloquent over the Lord Provost, she pulled out her notebook and began to write down the conversation as she remembered it. Thankfully, she had a very good memory from years of practice recalling tidbits and snippets of information.

She didn't want to miss a minute of it.

Chapter 2

"**I** would talk to you," Robert said when she and Fenella arrived home.

"Could it wait?" she asked, striding through the kitchen still smelling of tonight's dinner of mutton and onions. She'd taken time off to hear her favorite author speak, reasoning that she could write about the lecture for the paper. Since she couldn't do that now, she had to find something else for the new edition.

Fenella moved past her, smiling apologetically as she whisked a maid from the room. At least there wouldn't be any witnesses to this dressing down. Normally, Robert didn't care where or when he criticized her.

After Macrath had purchased a home far from Edinburgh, he wanted her and Fenella to join him. She refused to leave the city, so they'd compromised. He purchased a large home for them, and instilled Robert, their second cousin, as chaperone and financial advisor, and their driver, James, as spy.

Mairi had told her brother that she and Fenella were capable of protecting themselves, however weak and defenseless he thought they were. Macrath had only smiled and done as he wished.

Robert was her daily trial.

The man's face bore evidence of each of his years, the last few making their mark with more impact. The pockets beneath his eyes sagged more each day, as if his face couldn't bear the weight of his skin.

His beard, thin and pointed, made his face appear even longer and accentuated the down-turned corners of his mouth.

His hair had thinned considerably in the last year, but he still maintained the notion that no one but he could tell, wrapping long strands around the top until they covered most of his bald pate. He was endearingly vain about his hair, but seemed not to notice when he'd splotched ink on his cuffs or shirtfront.

He was a private man, one who occupied a large room on the second floor surrounded by those items he'd brought from Inverness. For most of his life he'd lived with his sister, the woman dying shortly before he came to Edinburgh. No doubt Robert was another cause of Macrath's, another person who'd been helped from a bad situation by her brother's effortless kindness.

She only wished Robert had gone to some other distant relative.

But for all his dour appearance and personality, Robert was a man of great joys. He loved growing things. When he was not hunkered over the *Gazette*'s books, laboriously entering and grumbling over each expenditure, he was in their garden, transforming it into a place of beauty. Even in winter he was busy, readying the hardy shoots in the shed built for him, and laying out the beds in plans he worked on almost every night.

Now he frowned at her, the area above his nose folding into three vertical lines.

"No, it cannot wait," he said, blocking her way to the

stairs. "You need to explain these new expenses. Why are you spending so much on paper?"

She sighed inwardly. He'd seen the invoice for the newsprint. She knew, from previous harangues, that nothing she said would stop Robert's fussing. She simply needed to wait him out.

"I should take over ordering your supplies."

She pushed back her irritation. "That's not necessary, Robert," she said.

"It is if you're determined to put the Sinclair Printing Company in debt."

She circled him and nearly raced up the stairs and to her room before he could manage another word. But his glare followed her, making her wish he knew her better. She'd never put the paper in jeopardy. But she had no choice. Their paper supplies were running low. Did he think it was possible to print a newspaper on air?

Once in her room, she pulled off her cloak, settling down to work. If she had her way, she would have replaced her secretary with a long, broad table so she could spread a layout on it. But the minute she arranged for it, Fenella would have just had it removed.

"You work too much," Fenella would have said. A comment Mairi heard often. "You need to have a place of peace to rest."

Fenella was the one who gifted their home with personal touches. She acted as their housekeeper, conferring with Cook over menus and recipes. Soft sheets and towels graced their rooms, and dishes of potpourri were everywhere, the scent dependent on the room.

Here in Mairi's bedroom it was something spicy with cloves and cinnamon, reminding her of apples and autumn. In the spring the scent would change, and she'd smell roses. Because of her cousin there were porcelain figurines on the fireplace mantel, and upholstered chairs with tassels. Mairi would have been just as comfortable with a bare room and a bed, but she appreciated Fenella's efforts to make their home both beautiful and comfortable.

Fenella also trained the four maids on their tasks, managed the laundry, and oversaw the purchases for the house, presenting the bills to Robert.

Her cousin was very careful with money, and whenever Mairi presented the monthly expenditures for the paper to Robert, he held Fenella up as a paragon of thrifty virtue.

She doubted her cousin had ever been lectured on frugality.

Pushing back the embarrassment she'd suffered at the Edinburgh Press Club, as well as her irritation over Robert's lecture, she undressed, washed, and donned her nightgown, pulled from a drawer smelling of oranges.

Sleep, however, would have to wait until after she worked. Grabbing the sheaf of submissions, she sat and began to read.

Early on, she'd realized that the *Edinburgh Gazette* would have to change from what it had been in her father's day. Once, they printed six pages of legal notices, bankrupts declared or adjudicated, debt announcements, and official proceedings at Parliament. If the paper was going to attract subscribers, she knew it had to offer more content for people, ranging from information about citizens of Edinburgh to housekeeping tips.

The only thing she didn't write about was politics, reasoning that the numerous larger papers handled that topic better than she could.

She wrote three columns herself, each signed with a male pseudonym. But she also accepted submissions from other writers. Her newest idea, to begin in the new year, was to serialize a novel, something that had been done successfully in England for decades. She could only afford a fraction of what a London paper might pay a writer, but could offer something the other papers didn't: opportunity. She was more than willing to hire a woman writer.

If she had the money, she'd employ a few full-time reporters and take on the job of being solely the editor of the *Gazette*. That was for the future. For now, she'd continue to be the chief writer for both the paper and the broadsides they printed three times a week.

She selected two columns from the ten she read and wrote acceptance letters to the writers. Tonight, it irritated her even more than usual to sign Macrath's name.

One day, perhaps, she'd be able to use her own name as the proprietor of the *Edinburgh Gazette*. People would know that she was responsible for the success of the paper, that she was a woman of influence.

When would that ever happen?

The Lord Provost had looked at her like she was a beetle, one he'd found on his shoe and quickly dispatched.

Why had he looked down his rather bearlike nose at her? Very well, perhaps his nose wasn't bearlike, but the rest of him certainly was. He was entirely too large a man. When she was standing next to him she felt almost tiny, and she was tall for a woman.

He epitomized those minor irritants she'd experienced all her life. Now they gathered in a ball and sat, like lead, in the pit of her stomach.

What was wrong with a woman running a business? And the newspaper was as much a business as a millinery shop.

She hadn't heard anyone say she couldn't buy Melvin Hampstead's book because she was a woman. Why, then, wasn't she good enough to hear his lecture?

If she was competent enough to be editor of the *Edin-*

burgh Gazette, why couldn't she be a member of the Edinburgh Press Club?

Why wasn't she treated with the same respect as a man,
especially if she could do a man's job?

She never asked for help moving the reams of newsprint
into place. She might not accomplish the task as quickly as
a man, true, but she did it nonetheless.

Nor did she ever ask a man to write her columns, or
gather the information for the broadsides she wrote. How
many of the men who purchased their broadsides were
aware that a woman had written them?

Perhaps that's why she felt the insult at the press club so
acutely. She'd fought inequity all her life but never lost a
battle face-to-face the way she had tonight.

She'd been treated like a beggar at a feast. Go away,
don't bother us. How dare you think yourself the equal
of us?

The injustice of it made her seethe.

More and more women were daring to stand up and announce their displeasure with a society run by men. Josephine Butler's campaign against the Contagious Diseases
Acts was a model for women who believed their gender
was being treated unfairly.

Strides were being made each day. Look at the Married
Women's Property Act passed just two years earlier.

How did she change her own circumstances? It seemed
to her that she could either continue to be treated as shab-
bily as she'd been tonight or act as an instrument of change.
Standing in front of the Lord Provost and demanding that
he treat her better hadn't accomplished anything. He'd
only smiled at her.

There was a newly formed organization—the Scottish
Ladies National Association—that was taking up women's
causes, one of them suffrage. She could almost imagine

herself standing at a podium, imploring a crowd of women before her to vote for anyone other than the Lord Provost.

A few minutes later she caught herself staring off into the distance, then brought her focus back to finishing the letters.

Once they were done, she pulled out a blank sheet of her stationery. She knew exactly to whom she'd write, one of the founders of the SLNA, a woman who lived in Edinburgh.

When she heard the hall clock chime midnight, she pushed back her fatigue and continued writing. A half hour later, after reviewing her letter a dozen times, she sealed it and went to bed, only to lay there staring up at the ceiling.

Normally when she couldn't sleep, it was because she was caught up in worry about their subscription numbers. Tonight, however, she was on fire with ideas.

Would it be enough to just volunteer to assist a group? What could she do to awaken the women of Edinburgh?

She rose from the bed, walked to the window, and pulled open the drapes. A flagstone path, showing gray and black in the moonlight, led to the garden. A copse of trees stood on this side of the lawn. Saplings speared upward from the ground like arrows, the mature trees guarding them like protective mothers.

No wind shivered the leaves. They were perfectly still and waiting. Death could not be as silent as this night.

She was abruptly and painfully lonely.

Pushing that emotion aside, she walked back to her secretary, lit the lamp and sat.

If she couldn't write about the Hampstead lecture, she would write about something else: the Right Honorable Lord Provost of Edinburgh himself. She wouldn't put it in a column. Instead, she'd make him the subject of one of their broadsides.

Without hesitation, she began to write a poem. She finished it only a few minutes later.

> When shameful Vice began our streets to tread,
> And foul Disease reared his deathlike head,
> When the fate of sacred womanhood was profan'd,
> And fair Edinburgh's character was stain'd ;
> Then (by the Grace of God) Harrison came,
> (Ye residents of Edinburgh tremble at the Name!)
> He showed himself to our admiring sight,
> Indeed a burning and shining light.
> Yet weep my friends for more's the pity.
> He did not labor to clean the city.
> He doth not strive to cure the profane
> Or clean the vice and scrub the stain,
> No, Harrison dared show his face,
> Only to keep a woman in her place.

She added a small essay to the poem, explaining the situation and adding that the time for women to stand up and come out of the shadows had arrived. Otherwise, men like Logan Harrison would forever try to keep them from achieving their rightful place in society.

Smiling, she put the poem down, consulted her watch, and decided that she could sleep for a few hours. Then she'd head for the paper and begin her campaign to win equality for women.

She couldn't wait to hear what the High and Mighty Lord Provost thought of that.

Chapter 3

Logan liked working at dawn. Whenever he had something to accomplish, he did so in those quiet morning hours when there were few interruptions and his mind was clear.

In the dawn hours, the council chambers were dimly lit by a few sconces along the corridor. Other than one other representative and a doorman, whose task it was to secure the building and check for fire, he had the chambers to himself.

The hall smelled faintly of camphor, and he wondered if it was something used to clean. Even so, that agreeable scent had no chance against the odor of the gas lamps.

The carpet was crimson, embroidered in a Celtic pattern along the edges. Whoever had designed this newest iteration of the council chambers had decreed that all things Scottish must be featured, just as nothing could be used that hadn't been made in Scotland.

The furnishings were finer than in most bureaucratic offices. The occasional bench was finely carved wood, the landscapes on the wall of various scenes around Edinburgh. Even at dawn he had the feeling that this was the center of the city. Here, decisions were made that would affect thousands of people.

Where once the city had thrummed with political intrigue, now it puttered along slightly behind its Glasgow sister. They were being jerked and yanked into the future with a reluctance that was curiously Edinburghian.

As Lord Provost, he was dealing with topics that had never touched the desks of his predecessors: steam versus horse power, the stench and sanitation of Leith, and the eternal construction in New Town.

He hesitated before the double doors that marked his office. A bench sat on each side of the doors, and a sconce sputtered to his right, illuminating the brass plaque inscribed with his name.

Each morning, he felt a pinch of surprise when looking at it. Each morning, he hoped he was worthy of the honor. People depended on him to be wise and just, to think of their welfare. He never forgot that.

His secretary, Thomas, was seated at his desk when Logan opened the door. His own desk was larger and wider and set in the center of the window with a view of the castle. Thomas's desk was aligned against the south wall. Although the office was spacious, befitting the Lord Provost, at times it felt suffocatingly small.

Thomas was not only responsible for those activities mandated by his position, but served as his social secretary as well, attending to those matters of a more social or ceremonial nature. He was rarely without Thomas, the night before being one of those occasions.

His secretary possessed a narrow face and long, thin nose. Despite the fact that he was forever munching on a snack he squirreled away in his pocket, Thomas was almost cadaver thin. Even with his penchant for biscuits, Logan had never seen a crumb on any of his papers.

If Thomas had any flaws at all, it was his nose. That offending feature was always twitching or sniffing. When the two of them worked late, the nights were punctuated by sounds: a quick rustle of paper in his pocket, a surreptitious nibble, and a sniff.

Thomas was a human rat.

But he was a damn efficient secretary. Logan didn't know if he'd be able to perform all his duties without the man. All in all, he had very little free time, and what he had was devoted to another task—that of finding a wife.

According to Thomas, the fact that he'd been elected to represent his ward as a single man was astonishing. Thomas also thought that if Logan wanted to advance, he had to give some thought to marriage. Since more than one political mentor had given him that advice, Logan was beginning to think there was some merit to it.

His three brothers were married, and all of them seemingly happy. In record time they'd given him a dozen nieces and nephews.

For the last decade, he'd never had time for courtship. He probably would have continued thinking that but for one thing: he was giving thought to running for Parliament. A wife would be a political advantage, as much as not being married might prove detrimental.

Logan nodded to the Queen's portrait, a habit he'd formed when first taking up his position a year ago, then settled behind his desk.

"Was the lecture worth the time, sir?" Thomas asked.

"It was, for the most part."

Strange, that during the lecture he'd seen the Sinclair woman's flashing blue eyes and stubborn mouth. More than once he had to drag his thoughts back to the author's words.

Several men engaged him in conversation afterward. He allowed himself to be dragged into a discussion of the new royal infirmary and the talks about the Edinburgh

Academy Cricket Club, but he begged off meeting Hampstead himself. He preferred some mystique to exist between himself and the writers of the books he enjoyed, the same reasons he hadn't met Mr. Dickens during a similar lecture four years ago.

Now, he pulled out a piece of paper on which he'd jotted a name. "Find out what you can about her," he said.

Thomas stood and came to his desk, taking the paper from him. "The *Edinburgh Gazette*? It isn't a very large paper, sir. Not like *The Scotsman*."

"I want to know everything you can find out about its editor."

Thomas nodded, not asking any more questions.

Logan knew, just as the sun was rising in the east, that Thomas would make a thorough job of discovering anything he could about Mairi Sinclair.

At dawn, Mairi dressed, donned her cloak, and was on her way to wake her driver when she found him in the kitchen.

The room was warm, smelling of sausage and scones. James was finishing what looked to be a fine breakfast of black pudding, two slabs of sausage, and a few fried eggs. Abigail, one of the maids, was flitting around the table like a butterfly only too aware of its short life span. Any trace of scones had vanished.

Abigail personified sunlight. Her smile was always in place, her brown eyes sparkling. Her blond hair was kept braided and tucked beneath her cap, tendrils occasionally escaping to frame her round face.

James was tall and spare, with a shock of brown hair that was unkempt even after he'd combed it. His Adam's apple was prominent. She often found herself staring at it in fascination, wondering if it hurt him to swallow. When he smiled, like now, he looked more like a boy or a brownie in coachman's garb than a fully grown man.

Bemused, Mairi watched the two of them for a moment until James glanced in her direction.

"You'll be wanting to get to the paper, I imagine," he said, standing.

Abigail nodded to her, smiled, then busied herself clearing up the dishes. Did Cook know that Abigail had taken over her duties? Mairi decided she wasn't going to ask.

"I'm sorry," she said. "I know it's early."

"Don't fash yourself," he said, grinning at Abigail and then at her. "I've already readied the carriage."

Evidently, she was becoming a creature of habit.

Although they lived close enough to the paper that she could have easily walked there, Macrath had given orders that a driver was to be at her beck and call. Her relationship with James had never been employee to employer. He was a cross she must bear, and she was his task.

At least he wasn't as annoying as Robert.

Once at the paper, she sent James home. Since Allan lived above the paper, she was safe enough. She didn't need a duenna. Having Allan there was a reassurance she hadn't had six months ago. Back then she had worked on her own and sometimes with Fenella as a companion. But the newspaper finally provided enough income to hire a pressman with talent like his.

Unlocking the door, she entered the front office, then walked down a long hall, turning up the lamps as she went. Entering the pressroom, she hung her cloak on a peg by the door and pulled the poem from her reticule.

She read it through once more with a critical eye. Only when she was satisfied did she move to the frame beside the press. There, aligned in military precision, sat all the letters she needed to compose the broadside, along with symbols and spaces.

If she'd had the time, she would have ordered a lithograph carved of the Lord Provost, a pose with his bearlike arms stretched out to protectively enfold all the male inhabitants of Edinburgh while leaving the women huddling in a group to the side. But that would require time—and expense—she didn't have.

Her fingers flew as she began to typeset what she'd written, the click of metal against metal the only sound in the silence. In hours the broadside would be hawked through the streets of the city, sold for a penny apiece. The idea that what she thought would be conveyed to hundreds of Edinburgh citizens never failed to amaze and fascinate her.

The pressroom was a cavernous space devoid of any but the barest amenities. Two high-placed windows let in the dawn light, coloring the beige walls pink. She hadn't bothered to light the brazier in the corner, but she had donned her fingerless gloves. The walls were covered with wooden bins and shelves overflowing with paper. She'd plundered those files often enough to know what each contained even if they weren't labeled.

The woodsy scent of paper vied with the odor of the chemicals used to clean the press. Added to that was the ever present smell of ink. Would her skin be saturated with the odors after a lifetime of work here?

She'd spent her childhood in this room, had grown to womanhood doing exactly what she was doing now, setting type, preparing to work the press. Every memorable event in her life had somehow involved this exact place.

She'd learned to read here, by placing the metal letters in their boxes.

She'd come here after her father's death because this was the one place she'd always seen him. Sometimes she could almost feel him with her, whispering in her ear. "No, lass, there you've misspelled a word. Go back and change it. Always check yourself."

Here she'd been spurned, not far from where she stood. Calvin had held his hat in his hands, explaining with earnest embarrassment how his parents didn't think her suitable for their only son.

When Macrath had gotten word that his ice machine was a success, she'd celebrated with him here, toasting him with whiskey until the room had spun. She wasn't sure if it was an abundance of laughter and joy that had made her dizzy or simply the spirits.

Until her brother's success, when Macrath moved them into a substantial house, they had all lived in the cramped rooms upstairs. Now, half of them were used for storage except for Macrath's old room, which Allan now occupied.

Mairi heard a sound down the hall. Grabbing a rag, she wiped her fingertips, greeting Allan as he came into the room holding two steaming cups. She took one, biting back her smile at his shiver. A native of Dumfries, Allan had started complaining about the cold in September. She wondered how he'd like Edinburgh come spring.

The dazed look in his brown eyes was normal. Allan didn't wake easily, rarely speaking until nearly noon. His beard and mustache were always well trimmed, unlike the brown hair that flopped over his brow. He was forever brushing his wrist over it as he worked the press. He was only her height, but his shoulders were broad, his arms heavily muscled from years of manipulating a printing press.

Today, Allan wore his normal attire, so familiar it might have been a uniform: a blue shirt with sleeves rolled to the elbows, and dark blue pants.

She'd never seen anyone work a press as quickly as he did, not even her father. Allan could produce twice what she or Macrath did in the same time frame. Plus, he was a near genius at figuring out which bolt or screw was loose or needed to be replaced, and which part should be oiled.

"I had a visit from your cousin last evening," he said.

"Fenella?" she asked, surprised.

"No, Robert." He shook his head. "He wanted to know if I'd be willing to work for half my wages."

She bit back her irritation. "I hope you told him no."

Allan smiled. "He's a crafty old badger. He started making noises about how he could fire me if I didn't come cheaper."

"I'm the only one who can fire you," she said, making no attempt to hide her annoyance now. "And I've no wish to do that. Robert will simply have to grumble. Still, I'm sorry he bothered you."

She didn't care if Macrath had installed him to be her chaperone. Badgering her pressman wasn't included in Robert's duties.

"I've written a broadside," she said after taking a few sips of her tea. Before she handed him the paper, she told him about what had happened the night before.

"Is it wise, do you think?" he asked, reading it. "It's the Lord Provost."

"I may not be able to vote, Allan. I may not be able to do a great many things, being a woman, but my voice has not yet been fettered."

"Still, he's the Lord Provost," Allan said.

"I'm not insulting the position, merely the man. If he hadn't appeared, I might have been able to convince the doorman to let us in."

Allan only bent his eyebrow in response.

"Very well, I might not have," she admitted. "But he

certainly didn't do anything to assist us. He's the Lord Provost. He could have done something. If he believed in treating women equally, he could sway countless people. He'd no doubt even be heard in Parliament."

"There are rumors he wants to run for election there."

Surprised, she glanced at Allan. "How do you know that?"

"Gossip," he said. "I hear it occasionally."

"Well, you should tell me," she said. "Gossip makes for readership."

Before she could ask, Allan moved the stack of paper below the press, guided the finished blank into the housing and locked it into place. The press was old and needed to be replaced, but Allan was a genius at repairing it every few days.

After carefully rolling ink over the blank of the broadside, he rubbed off the excess. Placing a page on the press, he moved to the large iron wheel and turned it in a practice run. The plate descended to the page and back up again. Opening the press, he peeled the printed page away, handed it to her, and waited.

After reading it through quickly, she gave her approval.

She glanced at the brooch pinned to her collar. She had three hours to produce five hundred sheets. Allan, even working at moderate speed, could do that easily.

"The provost could make things very difficult," Allan said.

"How? By demanding that we not publish the truth? That would only get us more publicity."

"Is it the truth?"

She turned and looked at Allan. He was fully awake now, his brown-eyed stare direct and unflinching.

"Yes, it's the truth," she said, wishing she didn't feel on such shaky ground.

Perhaps the provost couldn't have changed the rules, but he could certainly have been more gracious. Nor did he have to smile at her like that.

She nodded just once, hoping Allan wouldn't question her further.

Chapter 4

Fenella hadn't been able to see her lover for a whole day. Her *lover*. The word skittered up her spine and curved her lips in a smile.

How shocking she was, but no more so than Mairi had been. Or a hundred, thousand other women, she suspected.

How decadent she was, almost wicked. People would think so, and they would probably comment among themselves. "Did you know Fenella has taken a lover?" They might as well say, "Did you know that she has embraced her downfall with such joy?"

Allan was her lover, and the secret ached to be spilled and shared. Allan, her beloved, who slipped away when he could to see her, who made the very air shimmer with joy.

No one noticed that she was out of sorts all day, or how close she was to tears. Not even the maids, with whom she had more dealings than anyone, seemed to think anything was amiss.

Fenella closed her eyes, listening to the night and the sound of barking dogs. For whom did they bark? Each other? Or did one of them mourn a fallen master and the others simply join in to share his grief?

She willed Allan to her with a thought. *Beloved, come*

soon. She'd wait for another quarter hour and if he wasn't here reluctantly head to her room.

Sometimes he couldn't get away, but when he could, Allan walked from the paper, meeting her in the garden. If circumstances permitted, she accompanied him back to his room, where they were guaranteed privacy and passion.

If she were lucky, she'd see him tonight. She would be able to talk with him. She'd raise her hand and put it on his face and trace the contour of his smile with her thumb.

She missed him so much she ached with it.

The creak of the garden gate alerted her.

Gathering her cloak close, she flew along the flagstone path, and when Allan grabbed and held her, she laughed against his chest, his coat smothering the sound.

A moment later his mouth warmed her lips and set her heart quivering in her chest.

"I thought she would never leave," Allan said.

She placed her hands on his chest, worried that his coat wasn't thick enough against the cold.

"Can we go back to the paper, then?"

"Can you get away?" he asked, as he did every time.

She nodded. "Everyone thinks I've retired to my room. I've a headache again."

"Poor sick sweetheart," he said, kissing her once more.

She muffled her laughter.

"We have to tell her," Allan said. "I don't like all this secrecy."

"I know, I know," she said, patting his chest. "But I'm all she has."

He stepped back. "So you'll stay with her for the rest of your life, then? Simply because you feel sorry for her?"

She smiled at the thought of anyone feeling sorry for Mairi. Her cousin was such a sweet person but people didn't notice that about her. Instead, they only saw Mairi's passion. She was never just irritated, she was incensed. She never felt badly for someone, she wept for them. She wasn't interested in a cause, she was engulfed in it.

She'd always been that way, even as a child. But Fenella knew that if Mairi hadn't been so intense with her emotions, and so spirited, she might not be standing in the garden of a home far lovelier than the one in which she'd once lived.

"I owe her so much," she said. "She took me in, made me a sister."

Mairi had given her a home after her parents died, only months apart: first, her father of a heart problem, and then her mother, of pneumonia. Mairi had taken her hand at her mother's funeral, marched over to Macrath and announced, "Fenella is coming home to live with us now."

At the time, her cousins had been as poor as she, but at least there were three of them. The idea of being part of a family, of not being alone, was so heavenly that she'd started crying right then and there. She knew it hadn't been her tears that convinced a much younger Macrath—barely more than a child himself—to take her in, as much as Mairi's stubborn insistence that she was one of them.

Since then, she had truly become one of them. She was as much a member of the Sinclair family as Mairi or Ceana or Macrath.

How could she make Allan understand?

After Calvin, Mairi had walled herself off from people. She no longer trusted as easily. Nor was she as generous in spirit. She eyed other people with more caution, as if waiting for them to disappoint—or worse—hurt her.

She'd narrowed her world until it became only the *Gazette* as a source of pride and Fenella as her only friend.

The best thing, she thought now, was to tell her about

Allan, and quickly. Mairi would simply have to understand why she hadn't mentioned her feelings before. What she felt for Allan was special and hers. She hadn't even wanted to share it with her cousin.

"She'll have to make her own life," he said. "Without you."

She wrapped her arms around his neck. The night was cold but she didn't care. Even here, in a knifing wind, it was heaven as long as Allan was with her.

"Give it a little time, Allan," she said. "We've only known each other for a few months."

"I knew the minute I saw you," he said. "It was the same for you."

She nodded. She'd come to the paper to fetch Mairi for some errand or another, and her cousin had introduced her to Allan.

She was used to being ignored, which was why she was so shocked when he had said, "You're so beautiful."

Stunned, she only stared at him.

"I'm sorry if I was rude," he said.

She shook her head, bemused by his grin.

"It's just that I needed to say it. I imagine you hear it all the time."

She'd blushed in response, and he'd stared at her. At that moment she'd felt beautiful. Whenever she was with him, he made her feel that way.

That day had abruptly changed, become sunnier, and each day afterward had been the same.

Whenever she saw him, she was different, as if air was trapped in her stomach, buoying her up, making her feel strangely light.

She found reasons to call on Mairi during the day, made excuses to go to the paper. Some days Allan was so busy he could only spare her a quick grin. Sometimes Mairi was out and they had time to talk.

She'd learned of his apprenticeship. She told him of her early life in Leeds. They liked the same kind of books, wanted to see more of the world. Each had a sense of humor that meshed well with the other.

Love crept up on her unaware.

One morning she looked at him and suddenly the world was different. Spring was all year long and happiness alternated with misery as her predominant emotions.

They'd been in each other's arms the night he asked her to marry him.

Allan was right. She had to talk to her cousin.

As Logan sat in his library at home, signing letters that would be posted the next day, Thomas recited the guest list for the night's entertainment.

As usual, Thomas was concise, listing the names of the invited guests, their occupations and interests. Logan was expected to remember as many details as possible, so as to be charming and gracious when being introduced to the fashionable citizens of Edinburgh. At least their host had been gracious enough to provide the list. That way he had some warning who would be in attendance.

According to Thomas, who had once uttered the comment after imbibing a few too many whiskeys, Logan was on stage at all times. The only time he was exempt from being a politician was on the privy and asleep.

Occasionally, he wondered if Thomas remembered that slurred advice, but thought not.

Marriage, a relatively recent event for Thomas, had changed the man, causing him to smile more. He could even be heard to hum a tune from time to time.

What about him? Would marriage change him? A thought that kept Logan staring at the letter in front of him. To what? A tamed and domesticated cat? Would he purr for his wife?

He was damned happy as it was.

As he finished signing the last of the correspondence, he sat back in the chair listening.

Finally, Thomas ground to a halt.

Logan asked a few questions, made mental notes, and was satisfied that he was prepared.

"I've the dossier you wished, sir," Thomas said, retrieving a piece of paper from the back of his file and pushing it across the desk to Logan.

"The dossier?"

"On the Sinclair woman, sir."

He nodded and began to read. Mairi Sinclair did work as the editor of the *Edinburgh Gazette,* one of the newspapers he read on a weekly basis.

"She owns the paper?"

"No, sir. It's owned by her brother. She manages it, however, and is evidently responsible for its day-to-day operation." He consulted another sheet of paper. "She is also responsible for three columns, the most prominent of which she writes under her brother's name, Macrath Sinclair."

That was a surprise. He looked forward to reading that column with each edition of the paper. The fact that Mairi Sinclair was the author left him with a discordant feeling. The woman who'd been so argumentative at the press club also possessed a fine mind and a cohesive way of marshaling her thoughts.

He handed the dossier back to Thomas. His secretary would dutifully file it in a place where it could be easily retrieved. As for him, he'd had years of perfecting his memory. He'd recall everything he needed to know about the woman.

"I'll be ready shortly," he said, standing.

"I'll have your carriage brought around, sir," Thomas said.

After he left, Thomas would return home to his wife, sleep only a few hours, and be back at his desk at the council offices at daybreak.

Logan dressed in a black evening suit with a white shirt and embroidered vest. As he fixed his cuff links, he thought about the Sinclair woman. She lived only a few blocks away, with the *Edinburgh Gazette* building somewhere in the middle. One of three children, she was orphaned when she was sixteen and had never been married. She wasn't a young woman right out of the schoolroom, but had probably been forced to grow up quickly.

Experience was sometimes a greater teacher than age.

Who was Macrath Sinclair, that he'd given over control of the family newspaper to his sister? Who was Mairi Sinclair that she'd accepted it?

He discovered that he very much wanted to know the answer to both questions, in direct violation of his common sense. The Sinclair woman was aggressive and argumentative, not the type who should interest him.

As he left the house, the cold dried his eyes and burned the inside of his nose. The air smelled of approaching snow. He'd once loved Edinburgh in the winter, when a dusting of white frosted the craggy edifice of Castle Rock. Now, he noted the men, women, and children over the fires in Old Town and his love of the season faded in light of their misery.

He knew too much about the problems of the city to see only its beauty. Edinburgh was a dual creature, steeped in history and bedeviled by current problems.

They stopped in front of the Drummonds' magnificent home in Old Town, his carriage waved ahead of the others.

The four-story red brick structure dominated a square filled with waiting vehicles, an indication of the popularity of the Drummonds' entertainments. Ribbons of glittering windows lit up the house, and as he left his vehicle, he could hear the orchestra playing a lively waltz.

His own home was not nearly as ostentatious, but he hadn't the Drummond fortune. Still, his rise had been what most people would call meteoric. Twenty years ago he was apprenticed to a bookseller on Leith Walk. Five years later he accumulated the funds to open his own stall and then his first bookshop. He'd never considered politics at the time, until he became irritated by the slow movement of the city council. He hadn't imagined that his election would be so easy. Nor that he'd be elected Lord Provost a few years later.

The constant need to be affable and attentive was draining, however, and never more so than on nights like this when he was swept along on a tide of greetings, smiles, and handshakes, or claps on the shoulder.

He was a servant of the city and that knowledge never left him. He was to serve Edinburgh like a faithful steward, care for her people and her problems, and perform his duties as capably as he could.

Still, there were nights like tonight when he felt that Edinburgh was a jealous mistress and clung to him with talonlike fingers lest he stray.

When someone called out, he turned to greet an acquaintance, their conversation interrupted by the sight of Barbara Drummond, looking resplendent in a pale yellow gown.

"How pleasant you look," he said, which wasn't overstating the matter. Her blond hair was arranged in almost a Grecian fashion, upswept and tucked up in the back. Little bows held up drapes of fabric on her dress. Her long white gloves were immaculate and festooned with a dizzying number of buttons.

She smiled at him charmingly, acknowledging his appreciation. The great-niece of a duke with a merchant father, she was one of the women on his list of acceptable candidates for wife.

Whoever he married would need to be a companion, a helpmate, and conscious of his position at all times. She must always be an asset, be personable, kind, and able to remember people's names, their children's names, and other pertinent details. She might even slide into Thomas's role from time to time, giving him information about those people he'd forgotten.

She would, above all, have similar political beliefs.

"How lovely to see you, Provost Harrison," she said, her brown eyes warming.

Extending a hand, she placed it on his arm, and indicated the staircase leading to the ballroom with an inclination of her chin.

He was doomed to dance tonight.

He forced a smile to his face. On the whole, he preferred almost any occupation to that of dancing. But like most personal thoughts, it wouldn't be voiced.

Once he'd finalized his choice for his wife, then perhaps he could be more open about himself, more honest. Or was he, like Thomas thought, to be on a stage for the rest of his life?

Chapter 5

Mairi only employed two boys, but each did the work of a dozen hawkers.

Bobby had a perpetually dirty face, like he'd rubbed his cheeks on a soot-covered building on his way to the paper. His nose was red and delightfully rounded, and his brown eyes sparkled with mischief. She thought he was a successful hawker because his grin and his joyful air intrigued people. On even the dourest day in Edinburgh, Bobby was smiling.

Samuel was taller and slimmer, with a long face that probably wouldn't change much as he grew. He looked like a man of importance who passed judgment on others. She wondered what he would become, being one of innumerable children growing up in poverty.

She paid them their commission and added in a little bit besides. Bobby had a new sister, and Samuel's father was ill. Granted, she would have to explain to Robert, and he would grumble, not understanding that generosity was sometimes its own reward.

After the boys had pocketed the coins, she gave them tea and fed them treats she'd requested from Cook. Today it was rock biscuits, and the boys fell on them as if they were starving. She didn't know how much either boy had to eat, but it was obviously never enough.

When they were satiated for the moment, she began to ask them questions. Bobby had Macrath's talent for listening. He, too, came back to the paper with information about what he'd overheard, tales people were talking about on street corners and in pubs. She took notes of his comments so she could tailor the next broadside to mirror those topics on the minds of Edinburgh's citizens.

One day, she was certain the *Edinburgh Gazette* would be famous throughout Scotland. Until then the income from the broadsides helped defray most of their operating expenses.

She often published broadsides of a salacious nature, simply because they sold well. People hungered for the bizarre, the tragic, and the risqué. Even more than that, they loved gossip and intrigue. She was determined to give them all of that.

Still, today was the first time they'd sold every single copy of their broadside so quickly.

"I'll see you tomorrow," she said, and the two boys nodded.

Bobby's grin would charm the paint off a canvas. She smiled back at him, and resisted the urge to ruffle Samuel's hair as he passed.

Perhaps the two boys would be as close as she ever came to having children of her own.

She walked into the pressroom to talk to Allan.

"I'm off now," she said over the sound of the press. "Do you need anything anywhere?"

Allan smiled and shook his head.

Gathering up her cloak and gloves, she prepared to do battle with the November cold. Eyeing her bonnet, she decided to leave it behind. The hated thing wouldn't make her warmer, and it would act as an inducement for the wind to catch it and tug at the ribbon beneath her chin. Better for it to remain here.

At the last minute she changed her mind, grabbed it and wrapped the ribbon around her wrist. She might go somewhere she needed it.

When she went out reporting, she never knew where she would end up. Reporting was like pulling a thread. She almost never saw where the thread ended, but the beginning was lure enough.

She traveled down Cockburn Street, the cobbles wet in the sleet, and hesitated at the base of Warriston Close. The steps were shallow but seemed to go upward forever. In the gloom of a November afternoon, they were draped in shadow, not yet illuminated by the gas lamps.

Instead of climbing the steps, she went around the long way, continuing on Cockburn Street.

Beneath the Royal Mile were places where Edinburgh citizens had lived and died in the sixteenth and seventeenth century. She always felt like she was walking over a graveyard, as densely populated as the burial ground on Calton Hill.

She turned left, heading upward toward the castle again, then following another street around to St. Giles Cathedral.

Named for the patron saint of Edinburgh, the cathedral was undergoing restoration, something the Lord Provost was responsible for starting. She hadn't been able to see inside, but Bobby had told her that all the old galleries and partitions were being removed to create one single space. Evidently, the provost had also planned and financed the new stained glass, one section of which sat in a wagon covered by canvas.

Strange, that she knew so much about the Lord Provost but had never met him until the other night. After the success of the broadside sale, perhaps she should reassess her stance about not delving into politics.

Walking on, she finally reached her destination.

Donovan's Bar was known as a place where many of Edinburgh's magistrates and elected officials frequented, since it wasn't far from the City Chambers. Mr. Donovan was one of her best sources for what was happening among the important people in Edinburgh. Sooner or later every man stopped in for a pint or a dram at Donovan's. Once a confectionery shop, the bar still looked like a shop from the outside, as most of Edinburgh's taverns did.

As she did whenever she called on him, she knocked on the rear door, familiar enough with the alley that the location didn't disturb her. Perhaps she didn't have the sensibilities of most women. Or perhaps she'd simply had to ignore them over the years. The stench of ale and whiskey wafting from the empty barrels stacked against the building made her grateful for the gusty November winds. From inside the tavern came the rhythmic drone of conversation, waves of sound reaching her whenever an inner door was opened.

Mairi was welcome to stand at the back door, a fact that started to grate on her only recently. She'd never seen the interior because women didn't frequent Donovan's Bar. She'd been told it was one large space. A U-shaped station sat at the head of the room, with spirit barrels mounted high up against the wall. From his vantage point, Mr. Donovan could see the majority of his patrons. Just when she thought she couldn't bear the cold one minute more, Mr. Donovan opened the door and peered outside.

Despite his sixty years, he was a man of erect posture and sturdy gait. Experience showed in the depth of his gaze and good living in the folds of his face. His normally affable expression was in evidence now.

"Now you'll be having me thinking terrible thoughts about myself all day, lass, making you wait for me," he said as she shivered and thrust her gloved hands into the slits of her cloak.

"It's all right, Mr. Donovan. Your customers come first."

"As they do, lass, as they do."

"Do you have anything you'd like to share?"

She never asked Mr. Donovan to betray a trust, knowing how vital that was between a merchant and his customers. Over the years, however, he had provided her enough information that she could hint at activities soon to occur in Edinburgh. She wasn't necessarily the first person with the story, but she prided herself on the fact that she got the details correct.

"Naught happening of much interest, lass. The government commissioners on the pollution of rivers are meeting in Leith. Had a few of them here, fussing about who's responsible for the sewage of the water of Leith and such. But you're not interested in that."

Nor did she think her readers would be interested in sewage.

"But I do have news you can use. Mr. MacTavish is getting wed again."

MacTavish was a wealthy merchant, a well-known figure in Edinburgh. The fact that he had outlived a great many wives always sparked talk. His previous wives had died either of ill health or in childbirth. Within months of the funeral, however, he always had another young woman picked out for his bride.

"What does that make now?" she asked. "Five?"

Mr. Donovan shook his head. "This one will be number six. It's a Burns girl from Glasgow. I've heard the Lord Provost is thinking of doing the same."

"Truly?" She hadn't heard that from her other sources.

"His secretary stops in here almost every night. I learned it from him."

"I would have thought a secretary would be more discreet," she said.

Mr. Donovan nodded. "Aye, lass, I thought the same, but maybe he has a reason for telling tales. It could be the provost himself wants the news known."

"Why would he do that?"

Mr. Donovan laughed. "He's much sought after by the ladies. Maybe the notion that he's interested in taking a wife will calm the women of Edinburgh."

She'd never heard of the provost being so irresistible to the opposite sex. The man was entirely too large, too forceful, and he had a way of smiling at someone that simply stripped the words from her.

She was not going to ask, for fear of appearing too curious, but thankfully Mr. Donovan didn't need prodding.

"The Drummond lass is rumored to be Provost Harrison's pick."

She knew of the Drummonds, of course. A wealthy and accomplished family, they were renowned throughout Scotland. Most of Scotland's history featured a Drummond from one side of the family or the other.

They chatted for a moment or two more before his glances toward the interior hinted that he needed to attend to his customers. She made her farewells then, thanking Mr. Donovan as she always did and promising him a supply of next week's broadsides for distribution to his customers.

Donovan's Bar was located off the Royal Mile, and in this same area she had three other sources. Perhaps one of them could tell her something more exciting. She certainly didn't need to hear anything further about the Lord Provost and his potential bride.

Leaving the narrow wynd, she headed uphill. She loved this part of Edinburgh, but then she loved most of the city. Every part of her home was infused with history, some of it bloody and most of it tragic.

For hundreds of years Scotland had fought against oppression. Now, they'd learned to live with it, absorbing the English into their borders. They'd even charmed an English Queen until Victoria rhapsodized over the beauty of Scotland.

English accents were as common as Scottish ones on the streets of Edinburgh. The English purchased homes in Scotland or visited often, buying souvenirs to take home and display in England.

In the end, would the lines between the two countries blur? She couldn't believe that would ever happen, not as long as a true Scottish heart still beat, but there were things each country could learn from the other.

She rounded the corner, her gaze caught by a group of men dressed in long coats and wearing gloves and hats against the November cold. They were a prosperous looking bunch, intent on conversation. In the middle of them, as if she'd conjured him up simply with her thoughts, was Logan Harrison.

He wasn't wearing a hat, his black hair ruffled by the increasing wind. Here, the gusts reached out to snatch at her hem and travel down the back of her cloak, a reminder that she'd stood in one place for too long waiting for Mr. Donovan. If she didn't hurry, she'd get a chill.

She wasn't going to get sick staring at the Lord Provost like one of those fascinated women Mr. Donovan had mentioned.

He glanced at her at that moment, their gazes meeting across the cobbled street. Her stomach clenched.

She was not afraid of the man.

Nor was she overly impressed with him. A great many men looked like Highlanders of old. Granted, he was taller and broader than the men around him, but perhaps they were simply short and thin.

He was studying her carefully, even as he spoke to someone at his side. Was he commenting about her? She doubted it when no one turned to look at her.

Had he read the broadside yet? Evidently not, because his expression was agreeable, not angry. She might even call him handsome if she wasn't so irritated at him.

She nodded to him. To her surprise, he nodded back.

A moment later he strode across the cobbled street with the intent of a man with a destination in mind.

Her.

For a frozen second she debated turning and walking as quickly as she could in the other direction. Or simply gathering up her skirts and making a dash for the next wynd.

She was wrong. He'd read the broadside and was going to make his opinion known publicly. He was going to dress her down right here on the street as the men watched.

He stopped in front of her, nodded his head in lieu of tipping a nonexistent hat, and then confused her thoroughly by smiling at her.

Perhaps he was more handsome than she realized, especially when he was smiling. His green eyes were gleaming and his face ruddy from the cold.

"Miss Sinclair. It's a raw day, isn't it?"

She hadn't felt anything for the last minute, the temperature not as important as anticipating the confrontation with him.

"It is cold, but it's November in Scotland."

"Aye, that it is."

Had she amused him? Why were his eyes twinkling at her?

Gathering her cloak around her throat, she forced a smile to her frozen face.

"I should be about my work."

"And what would you be doing out on such a raw day?"

The comment grated on her.

"My job, Lord Provost."

"What would an editor of the *Edinburgh Gazette* do on the streets, Miss Sinclair?"

"I'm not merely an editor, Lord Provost. I also write columns and do the reporting for the paper. Otherwise, all the *Gazette* would publish would be legal notices. Who would subscribe to us then?"

"Indeed," he said, his smile still in evidence. Was he impervious to the cold? Weren't his lips numb and his teeth freezing?

She felt as if her nose must be bright red. Hopefully, it wasn't running. She slipped a hand up to her lips, breathing on her glove.

"And you, Lord Provost, why would you be out and about and not in council chambers?"

"We had an inspection of the gradient of the street," he said. "A company is claiming that steam power will effectively power tramways in the city."

"Do you agree?"

"I'm not certain," he said. "Steam power might be against the Edinburgh Tramways Act we passed last year. Besides, I see the possibility of accidents through failing brakes. It's not a chance I'm willing to take with the lives of the citizens of Edinburgh."

She was going to have to examine the act in more detail. Perhaps she should write a column about the future of Edinburgh, including the Lord Provost's opinion on steam trams. Perhaps the man was simply averse to progress.

That, she could most certainly pass along to her readers.

"But I've kept you too long," he said, reaching out and wrapping her scarf around her throat, a gesture that held her silent and surprised. "You're beginning to shiver. However, it was a pleasure to see you again, Miss Sinclair."

"I'm quite used to Edinburgh's winters," she said. "It's my home."

He smiled again. "How odd that we've never met before now."

The fact that she had thought the same was annoying.

"Not that odd. I do not cover politics. I prefer to report on things that matter."

His smile didn't slip one degree. Instead, she seemed to have amused him again.

"I shall keep your words in mind, Miss Sinclair, and endeavor to matter today."

She wanted to say something wickedly wise, words that would impress him with her capacity for repartee. Nothing, absolutely nothing, came to mind, and she was forced to simply nod, watching as he walked back over the street, his long coat flapping around his legs. She'd never been rendered speechless around anyone.

He was an imposing man and a bothersome one. He'd either seen the broadside and wanted to confuse her or hadn't yet read it.

She only wished she knew which one it was.

Turning, she made her way to her next source, a shopkeeper near Princes Street.

She could feel Harrison's eyes on her all the way up the street. Twice, she stopped, and twice told herself to keep walking. She would not turn around to see if he was still there. What disturbed her was not the sensation that the Lord Provost was watching her but the fact that her heart was racing at the thought of him doing so.

The Drummonds had two daughters. Which one was he going to marry?

She would bet next month's income from the paper that none of the Drummond girls ever wondered about their futures. Nor would they be concerned about the plight of women in Scotland.

Perhaps she wasn't being fair. She had a habit of pre-judging people sometimes, especially when she felt lacking or not as accomplished as the other person. When that happened, and she noted it at the time, she made a concerted effort to correct her behavior.

Both Drummond girls could be suffragettes for all she knew.

She doubted it, however. They were probably the type who would simper around Harrison, playing coy and delicate and helpless. He would like that type of female.

He probably thought it beneath him to be challenged by a woman.

No, he hadn't read the broadside, she was certain of it. She smiled into the wind, anticipating when he finally did.

Chapter 6

Today's council meeting had been contentious. Just when Logan thought the clamor might die down, a male representative of the Scottish Ladies National Association was allowed into council chambers.

When he read the petition handed to him, presented by a man who otherwise looked intelligent, he only stared at it.

"The SLNA wants to march through the streets of Edinburgh?" he asked, biting back his irritation and attempting to sound calm and reasoned.

"Yes, Provost Harrison, in order to demonstrate to the good citizens of Edinburgh our just cause."

He put the petition on the long table in front of him. "Have you traveled through Edinburgh lately, Mr. McElwee?"

The man held his ground, smiling back at him. "Indeed I have, sir, and I understand your concerns about congestion. The SLNA wishes to hold the march at a time both convenient to the council and when we would be most visible to the citizens."

Logan glanced to his left, then his right, meeting the stony features of his fellow councilmen. "We will take it under advisement, Mr. McElwee."

The man nodded. "When might you make a decision, Lord Provost? The ladies are most anxious."

"Have you no concern for their safety?" he asked. "Or are you not aware of the number of disturbances during each of the SLNA meetings?"

For the first time, McElwee didn't look as sanguine. "We are indeed aware, Lord Provost, which is the reason why we wish to march. If the inhabitants of Edinburgh truly understood our goals, I believe we would be able to marshal their support."

Two women had been badly hurt last week, and just a few days ago a group of men shouting epithets had advanced on women leaving one of the meetings.

One of his predecessor's most memorable acts had been to adopt a dog and, when he died, have a statue erected in his honor. While Logan knew he would, no doubt, be remembered by posterity as the man who oversaw the destruction of Edinburgh by a war of the sexes on the Royal Mile.

"The ladies will simply have to petition other cities in the interim," he said.

A half hour later he parted from his fellow council members. After giving instructions to the secretary recording the meeting, he made his way to his office, only to be waylaid by McElwee. The man stepped out from an alcove and stood in the middle of the corridor, effectively blocking his passage.

"Mr. Harrison, if I might have a moment," he said.

"Now is not the time to press your case, Mr. McElwee. I believe you already did a sufficient job of that in council chambers. As I told you, we will take the matter under advisement."

"What would it take to convince you, sir, that the SLNA should be given the opportunity to educate and inform?"

"There are plenty of ways they could educate and inform, Mr. McElwee, that wouldn't put them in jeopardy. We could not guarantee their safety."

"We do not wish to be safe, sir. We wish to be heard."

Logan folded his arms, staring at the other man. "We? How did you find yourself involved in a group of women?" Raucous women at that, who were determined to press their case to others who didn't want to learn or listen.

"There are numerous men who belong to the SLNA, Mr. Harrison. Those men who realize it is the nineteenth century, time enough for women to take their rightful place alongside men." He eyed Logan with narrowed eyes. "You're a director of the Scottish Society for the Prevention of Cruelty to Animals, are you not?"

"I am."

"A pity you do not care as much for the plight of women as you do a cart horse, sir. I'll tell the ladies that we would be better served to go to Glasgow or Aberdeen. Perhaps their governments are more enlightened."

With that, McElwee turned on his heel and strode down the corridor.

Logan walked back to his office in contemplative silence. Had the man been correct? Had he never considered the plight of women?

He entered his office, grateful to find it empty for once. Normally, he was surrounded by people who just wanted to add one more thing to a discussion, ask a favor, or deliver an invitation.

Even Thomas was absent, a fact for which he was grateful.

He closed the door behind him, wishing it had a lock, and settled into the chair behind his desk, turning slightly so that he could see the view. Edinburgh Castle hunkered on the hill, reminding everyone that this was a royal place, the capital of Scotland, the home of intrigue. What better place to march?

What would Edinburgh citizens do in response? Some of the men might jeer. Some would no doubt feel threatened. How would the women react? Perhaps half of them would be shocked, or maybe the majority of them would applaud.

Thomas entered the office without knocking, but then he thought Logan's office his domain.

Logan ignored him.

He didn't know many women. His mother had died when he was nineteen after a long illness. His sisters-in-law were all pleasant women but he had the impression that he terrified them. None of the three had ever initiated a conversation with him. Instead, they stood in the background staring at him like he was a beast in the parlor.

He supposed they were happy. Whenever he visited his family, his brothers were the same boisterous bunch, laughing and boasting as they always had. They were his brothers and they hadn't changed, although he might have.

Strangely enough, he enjoyed going to their houses more than them coming to his home. They weren't the same people when they came visiting. His brothers were as silent as their wives.

Would his sisters-in-law wish to march through Edinburgh? Or would they be appalled at the idea? Were they eager to vote? Or was that something they left to their husbands? Were they more concerned with their children than their rights?

He heard Thomas rustling papers behind him and wished he could banish the man for a while. Only in his home was he allowed any true privacy, but even that had to be dictated and enforced. No visitors. No slipping into his library to ask if he wanted coffee or something to eat. No bringing domestic problems to his attention.

Mrs. Landers ensured that his library was sacrosanct. She was also one of the few women he knew well.

Even the women on his list of potential wives weren't personalities as much as commodities, and that realization would have shamed him had he not understood they did the same to him. Did he earn enough to support them and a family to come? Was he of sufficient social bearing? Criteria that was perfectly acceptable and understandable.

But who were they as people? Did Barbara Drummond care about the plight of women or was she more concerned with her own life? Did Olivia Laurie want to engage in politics or did she consider the whole idea beyond her?

"The SLNA wants to hold a march through the middle of Edinburgh," he said without turning.

"Do they, sir?" Thomas said, his voice without inflection. Thomas, from his tone, didn't give a flying farthing.

He nodded. "They want to call attention to the organization, and educate the citizens of Edinburgh on the causes of women."

"Causes, sir?"

"Voting. Women getting the vote."

"Why should women get the vote, sir? They would only go to their husbands to be told who to vote for."

He glanced at Thomas. His secretary wasn't a bigot; he was repeating those tenets he'd been brought up to believe.

"You aren't supporting that, are you, sir? Most men don't want women to vote."

"Why is that? Or is that even a correct assumption? I don't believe I've ever asked one of my companions his feelings on the matter. Have you?"

Thomas looked from left to right, then down at his papers, almost as if he were torn, wanting to answer in the affirmative but being loath to lie in case Logan questioned him further.

He took pity on his secretary. "Perhaps in the future," he said, "you might ask some of your associates how they feel."

"I will, sir," Thomas said.

"How do you feel, Thomas?"

"Me, sir?"

"Do you wish your wife could vote?"

Thomas's eyes showed too much white. "I've never given it much thought," he said.

A tactful answer, but then Thomas was a man with just the right answer for the right moment. He was the quintessential political being, someone who gave advice after weighing both sides and choosing the best option. Not necessarily the right thing to do but the most expedient.

Once, he would have considered himself fortunate to have a man with Thomas's instincts working for him. Lately, however, Thomas was a barnacle on his backside.

The world wouldn't end if he said the wrong thing at the wrong time or chose a position that might go against the mainstream. What was wrong with trying to convince others? What was wrong with being independent of thought and action?

According to Thomas, it would be a death knell to his political ambitions.

Even those were coming under scrutiny, but only his own. He wasn't up to sharing his dissatisfaction with Thomas and being lectured hourly.

Thomas fumbled with his papers, withdrew one and advanced on his desk.

"I debated showing this to you, sir," he said.

He extended his hand. "What is it?"

"A broadside, sir. Written by the woman you asked me to investigate."

He scanned it quickly, then read it slower.

Now, Mairi Sinclair—there was a woman who would march through Edinburgh and say to hell with anyone who tried to challenge her.

Logan held the broadside in his hand and extended it the length of his arm. It didn't get better at a distance.

Strange, he'd never been the subject of a broadside. She thought him a misogynist, did she? A man whose only intent was to keep women subservient to men?

When had women ever been subservient to men? They simply lived in a different world, one not occupied by meetings, negotiations, and conciliations. Their lives were concerned with fashion and gossip, filled with friends and laughter.

However, he'd enjoyed the columns she'd written under her pseudonyms. A test there, and one he'd spectacularly failed. He'd thought her a man. Nothing she'd written had sounded overtly feminine.

"I think someone should suggest she keep her opinions to herself, sir."

"I don't need a keeper. Or a protector, Thomas."

Thomas's face grew even more ratlike as his mouth pursed tightly.

Standing, Logan walked out from behind his desk, still clutching the broadside. He strode to the window and looked down at the square, finally turning and addressing his secretary.

"Give me an hour or two," he said. "There's nothing pressing on my agenda, is there?"

"You said something about wishing to talk to Miss Drummond's father, sir."

That could wait.

Logan's every movement was dictated by expectations. Everyone's but his. He countered his momentary irritation with the thought that he'd wanted this life, had done everything he could to obtain it. If the fit sometimes chafed, it was little enough to pay for the privileges of his rank.

"I need to take care of this matter," he said.

"Sir, are you going to call on Miss Sinclair?"

He bit back his impatience and answered Thomas. "If I am?"

"Wouldn't it be better to delegate the task to someone else?" Thomas asked. "That way you wouldn't be accused of consorting with her type."

Exactly what was her type? He realized he wanted to know, a comment he didn't make to the other man.

"No, I think I'll make the time to speak with her myself."

Thomas nodded, his mouth twisted in a disapproving downturn. "Very well, sir, I'll call for the carriage."

"I don't need you accompanying me," Logan said.

Thomas frowned. "Are you certain, sir?"

Certain that Thomas was a constant and unremitting shadow? Certain that he was growing tired of the man's omnipresence? Certain that he could breathe without Thomas sharing his air?

All he said was, "Yes, I'm certain."

Perhaps it would have been better to have had a witness to the confrontation with the Sinclair woman, but he was surfeited by witnesses, by chaperones, by people constantly following him.

He made note of the fact he was having that thought fairly often.

A quarter hour later he was in front of the Sinclair Printing Company. He'd passed this building countless times, and never thought about it. Of yellow brick, it was neither an excessively prosperous appearing structure nor one that looked like it suffered a financial hardship. Somewhere in the middle, like most of the businesses he frequented, run by civil people who wanted a decent life.

The lettering on the wooden sign above the door read: THE SINCLAIR PRINTING COMPANY, ESTABLISHED 1843. Beneath it were the words: THE EDINBURGH GAZETTE.

Nowhere did it feature the words "incendiary broadsides" or "scurrilous opinions offered for a penny." Or even "bad poetry featured here."

He took his time leaving the carriage.

Mairi Sinclair's name wasn't mentioned anywhere. Nor had she signed the broadside. Wasn't an author normally proud of his authorship? Unless, of course, it was libelous. In that case, she was right not to have signed her name.

He opened the door, surprised when no one greeted him. He left the front office, walked down a narrow hall, and found himself in a cavernous room smelling of paper and something sharply chemical—the ink? The sound of metal slapping against metal from the press in the center of the room was loud enough to drown out any conversation between the two people working there.

One of them was a stranger, a bearded man with a shock of brown hair who operated the press. The other was almost unrecognizable as a woman at first. Her hair was tied back and a full black apron stretched from neck to ankle. A smudge of ink marred her cheek, and as he watched, she rubbed the back of her gloved wrist on her forehead.

She didn't look like an anarchist.

But she didn't look like any of the women he knew, either.

He advanced on Mairi Sinclair.

Chapter 7

Mairi grabbed a stack of printed pages, placing them on one of the long tables against the wall, and returned to the press. As fast as Allan was turning the wheel, they would have the paper printed and assembled in an hour or two.

Allan was curiously silent this afternoon. Twice he started to say something, and twice stopped himself.

She could only wonder if he wanted to talk about the broadside about the Lord Provost.

Fenella had made her opinion known well enough.

"Are you sure that's the wisest thing to do?" she had asked when Mairi told her what she'd done. "Won't some people retaliate against the paper?"

"They may," Mairi said. "Then again, maybe they'll notice the *Gazette*. Perhaps we'll get more subscribers because of it."

Fenella communicated more with her gestures than any person Mairi had ever met. Compassion was visible with a simple look of her hazel eyes, curiosity with a tilt of her head, and anger in the stiff stillness of her face.

When she only pursed her lips in disapproval, Mairi turned away, disappointed.

And there he was.

The Lord Provost of Edinburgh stood in the doorway, dressed in a long coat over a severe black suit. His face was firm and fixed, his green eyes as cold as the deepest loch.

She took a step backward then chastised herself for doing so.

She should have realized he would come in person. He wasn't the type to send a member of his staff to complain about the broadside. No, the Lord Provost was the type for confrontation. He wasn't long-suffering, and she doubted if he ever turned the other cheek.

No, he'd stand toe-to-toe with any opponent, even her. Most especially her, since he'd already done so once.

She deposited another armload of papers on the table. Only then did she face him again, removing her gloves and tucking her hands under her arms.

She didn't look away, refusing to allow the man to intimidate her.

Allan stopped turning the wheel of the press. Gradually the noise level diminished. At least she didn't have to raise her voice to be heard.

"People are not allowed in the press room," she said. "It's a dangerous place."

He didn't say a word, only continued to stare at her.

Her pulse raced and her palms felt damp. Were her legs trembling? Nonsense, she was not afraid of the man.

Slowly, he withdrew something from an inside pocket, unfolded and held it up with two fingers, almost as if he didn't want to be contaminated by it.

She knew it was her broadside.

"Did you write this?"

"Yes," she said.

When one eyebrow arched upward, she frowned. Had he expected her to deny it?

"I thought it quite clever myself," she said. "A bit of doggerel, perhaps, but I was pressed for time."

"Does your brother know what you've done?"

She couldn't speak for the rage bubbling up in her chest. Who was he to call her to task like that, then remind her that Macrath was the real owner of the paper?

She turned to Allan. "If you'll give us a few minutes," she said.

"Are you sure, Mairi?"

She nodded, grateful for his protective impulse. She doubted, however, if Allan would have been a match for Harrison.

When he'd left the room, she turned to the provost again.

"Do you go about threatening people all the time?"

He smiled, an expression that had the effect of startling her, since it reminded her that the man was too handsome for his own good.

"I'm not threatening you, Miss Sinclair. I'm just asking if the owner of this paper was aware of the actions of his employees."

She wasn't an employee and the fact he'd called her one made her doubly angry. She studied the press, wiped off a smear of ink with a rag located nearby, and glanced at the first sheets of the newspaper set aside to dry before being folded. Another stack was ready for distribution the next day.

He evidently didn't like being ignored.

"How can I get in touch with your brother?"

"Do you use that officious tone often?" she asked. "Does it work most of the time? Do people bow and scrape before you?"

"Or to you? Has the power of the press gone to your head, Miss Sinclair?"

"Shouldn't people be able to point out to their elected officials when they're in the wrong? Or are you too high up on your pedestal to hear us?"

"I thought you didn't involve yourself in politics? Or is it only defamation?"

"I haven't defamed you one bit," she said. "I merely told the truth."

"Your version of it."

"If you don't mind," she said, looking pointedly at the press, "I'm very busy. I'll send word to my brother that you wish to speak to him. But I doubt he'll care. He's a very busy man who doesn't waste his time."

She wasn't just Macrath's employee. Her brother didn't take any interest in the paper and was only a figurehead she used when she must.

Right at the moment, however, she was annoyed to have to stand behind Macrath.

Why should she?

Harrison took two steps toward her, and she almost moved so the press was between them. She would have felt safer had she done so. Instead, they were toe-to-toe, so close she was forced to tilt her head back to look at his face. Another intimidation gesture of his that only ratcheted up her temper.

"My brother has nothing to do with the running of the *Edinburgh Gazette,* Lord Provost. If you have any complaints, bring them to me. I'm responsible for the broadside and for the paper."

His smile changed subtly, shifting the expression in his eyes to calculation. She had the oddest thought that the Lord Provost was a more dangerous man than she'd first thought.

"Are you responsible for calling me a bully, Miss Sinclair?"

"You were a bully, Lord Provost."

"My title is not my name, Miss Sinclair. You may refer to me as Mr. Harrison."

She was sharply aware of him. He was lightning, bright, hot, and frightening. His gaze was direct, difficult to maintain, but she willed herself not to look away.

"Thank you for the lesson in etiquette. However, I believe that I have quite a few names for you. None of which would please you any more than being addressed as Lord Provost. Misogynist, officious, just to name two."

He took another step closer until her foot was sandwiched between his. His breath smelled of mint and his coat of sandalwood. Perhaps he had a housekeeper as assiduous as Fenella.

"You know quite well that I didn't refuse you admittance to the press club. Their rules did so. You know quite well that I did not attempt, in any way, to keep you from the lecture. Or, as you so eloquently wrote, put you in your place. Although the idea has merit."

She stepped back, folded her arms and regarded him with what she hoped was a placid look. Inside, her stomach was churning and words bubbled in her mind, demanding to burst free.

"And how do you think I should be put in my place, Lord Provost? Chains? A gag, perhaps?"

"A chaperone," he said.

"A chaperone?"

"Someone who could help you restrain your speech. The idea of a gag has merit. A bodyguard, perhaps. Someone who could keep you from those events where you are certain to be banned."

"You could have used your influence," she said, breathless with irritation. "You could have convinced the press club to allow me entrance. Instead, you merely fell back on the excuse that it was the organization's rules and not yours. You are, Lord Provost, the worst kind of coward."

He leaned forward until his nose was only inches from hers.

"And you hide behind pseudonyms, Miss Sinclair. You are at turns Macrath Sinclair, Donald MacTavish, or Grant Cameron. Who's more afraid?"

His deep voice skittered along her spine, enough that she didn't pay attention to his words at first.

"What?" She glared at him. "Did you just call me a coward?"

He didn't answer, merely folded his arms in a pose to mirror hers and regarded her.

"I am not a coward."

As if she'd said nothing, he continued, "Besides, why should I convince them to admit you? You would, no doubt, have criticized the lecture, found fault with the club's decor, fussed at the fact only whiskey was served, and generally been difficult."

"All I wanted was to hear what Mr. Hampstead had to say," she said, feeling an absurd desire to defend herself. Why she should want Harrison to have a better opinion of her, she didn't know. "I liked his book very much."

He unfolded his arms. "It was a tedious hour," he said. "You would have been bored."

"I doubt you know me sufficiently to decide if I would have been bored, Harrison. I never got the opportunity." She frowned at him again.

His smile had completely disappeared, replaced by a predatory expression in his eyes. He truly didn't like being challenged.

She relished a good argument and it was evident the Lord Provost didn't. How boring it must be to have everyone bend to your will so easily.

"Will you cease in your efforts to impugn me?" His charming smile was back in place.

She wasn't surprised at his change of tack. The man was a master of manipulation, something she hadn't known until now. He pushed at people until they had no choice but to submit to him. If that didn't work, he tried something else.

No doubt most people melted beneath the force of his personality.

She was not, however, most people.

Taking another step back, she said, "Thank you for visiting. I trust you don't need me to escort you to the door."

"Do not write about me any further, Miss Sinclair."

"Or?" she asked, wondering if she was daring a mad dog to bite her.

"Or I will have to take other measures."

"Such as?"

He studied her for a minute, the seconds ticking by on a clock measured by her heartbeats.

Finally he moved to stand close to her again.

"I find it reprehensible to threaten women," he said. "Even a woman as annoying as you."

"If I'm annoying," she said, speaking past the constriction in her throat, "it's because you've pushed me to it."

"Do you not take responsibility for your own actions, Miss Sinclair? Do you, instead, blame others for your deeds?"

"I take full responsibility, Lord Provost, for any action I've taken against you. Not my brother. Not anyone else. Blame me."

His hand reached out and in a gesture so strange she was frozen in disbelief, he removed the scarf that she'd tied around her hair. It was dangerous working near the press without taking precautions since her hair could easily get caught in one of the gears.

"Then I shall, Miss Sinclair," he said, his voice rough.

"What a pity I'm not a magistrate. I would decree a punishment severe enough for the crime."

He dropped his hand and stepped away. Only then could she breathe again.

"What punishment would that be, Lord Provost?"

He didn't answer, only smiled. In the next moment he left the room, and it was like the wind stopped blowing. The sudden silence made the space around her feel hollow.

She bent to retrieve her scarf, feeling absurdly dizzy. Grabbing the press wheel, she stared at her white knuckles until her heart stopped galloping and her breath returned to normal.

Chapter 8

"Yes, Mrs. Hargrove, I understand your concerns. I must repeat, however, that the *Gazette* did not intentionally insult Provost Harrison."

"He is a great man, Miss Sinclair. A credit to Edinburgh. We are fortunate to have him. Your brother should have known that. I'm disappointed. Very disappointed."

Mrs. Hargrove was wrapped up against the cold in a frayed black coat that hung below her ankles and looked to have belonged to her late husband. Along with a succession of multicolored knitted scarves, she wore a black bonnet from another decade, adorned with blowsy black fabric flowers that needed desperately to be dusted or replaced.

Despite her penury, the septuagenarian stopped into the paper every week to purchase either a broadside or the newest edition.

"Yes, ma'am," she said, dipping her head in a gesture of subservience.

She walked Mrs. Hargrove to the door. When she saw James pull the carriage to the curb, she grabbed her cloak, deciding that something must be done.

She marched into the press room. "I'm leaving," she told Allan.

He only nodded, not saying a word about the number of people still outside.

"I'll put a sign on the door that we're closed," she said. That way, he wouldn't be forced to stop tinkering on the press.

He only nodded.

When she told James their destination, he raised his eyebrows. She readied herself for an argument, but to her surprise he only shrugged.

A few minutes later they were parked outside Logan Harrison's home.

That morning a gear had shattered on the press. They wouldn't be able to publish any broadsides or the weekly edition of the paper until the part was available.

Fenella was acting oddly around her.

She wasn't sleeping well.

None of which she could lay at Harrison's feet.

But the other? Yes, he was most definitely responsible for that.

Between fielding questions and hearing complaints, for two days she hadn't been able to get much work done. Long lines of people had appeared first thing in the morning and they didn't stop coming until dark, all of them complaining about the broadside she'd written about the saintly Lord Provost.

For the first time in her life, she dreaded going to work. Nothing she'd ever written or reported had created as much ire as that poem.

They'd lost twenty subscribers, and they only had three hundred to start. She was never going to make a success of the newspaper this way.

Why had she never realized that, to the citizens of Edinburgh, Logan Harrison was nearly a saint? She hadn't lied to him. She had never, at least not until meeting him, been involved in politics. But surely she should have known about his reputation. According to the people who had come to the paper, he was concerned about people's welfare. He enacted reforms. He ensured that each individual who had ever come in contact with him—and from the number of people in her office, that was a great many— remembered him not only for his generosity of spirit but also his charm.

Was she the only person in the world who hadn't been charmed by the Lord Provost?

She wished she'd never encountered the man.

But the very last straw had come this morning when she visited Mr. Donovan, only to have the man nearly slam the door in her face.

"I've nothing for you today," he said, his chin jutting out.

He was turning back to the interior of the tavern when she stopped him.

"I haven't seen you for a few days, Mr. Donovan. For you not to have any information is odd."

"Would you be having me make up things, then?" he asked, frowning. "Like you do?"

That's when she knew.

"The Lord Provost told you not to talk to me, didn't he?"

"A finer soul you'll never know. I'd watch your words before you start imagining stories about him."

Logan Harrison had evidently threatened Mr. Donovan, and probably most of the men who'd been too busy to speak with her in the last two days.

Tucking her notebook into her reticule, she frowned back at him. "You'll not be advertising with me either, then?"

"I'll not," he said, his gaze focused on the neighboring building, the yard of which adjoined the alley.

"I never wrote anything untrue, Mr. Donovan. You know I don't do that."

He finally looked directly at her. "I used to think that, Miss Sinclair. I wonder, now, if being a woman has changed your thinking."

It was beginning to, in ways he probably didn't realize. His prejudice, and that of the other men, was cementing her resolve.

She was declaring war on stupidity.

All these years she'd been very careful to act behind the scenes, to allow Macrath to be the figurehead. He was more than willing to cede the power to her and intervene when it was necessary. But now she no longer wanted anyone, even Macrath, to fight her battles for her.

Yesterday she'd received a letter from the Scottish Ladies National Association. The woman had written:

> *Miss Sinclair, it is imperative that women such as you, in positions of power and influence, come out to support other women. I am gratified to know another woman in publishing, as my dear friend Mary Louise Booth is the editor of* Harper's Bazar *in New York . . .*

The letter writer went on to ask her to speak publicly. Until this morning she had every intention of writing the woman and telling her she couldn't possibly do so. Her forte was in the written word. Besides, she wanted to remain in the background.

That was before the meeting with Mr. Donovan. Now she was determined to go through with it.

Just as intent as she was in stopping Logan Harrison.

His house was of deep red brick trimmed in black, with a peaked roof and three rows of small paned windows. On either side of the black door was a brass lantern now flickering a yellow welcome against the gray sky.

Stately and magnificent, the house lorded it over the rest of the neighborhood. She had the sudden and inexplicable image of the emblem of Scotland itself, a lion rampant, right paw raised, claws extended.

She should have brought Fenella with her. Or Abigail at the very least. But either woman would probably have tried to talk her out of confronting the Lord Provost.

If he were a gentleman, she wouldn't be here. She'd sent him a letter, asking him to call on her at the paper. While she would have preferred to meet him on her home ground, the man had ignored her. She was forced to go to him, either to his office or his home. She'd chosen the house simply because there would be fewer people present.

Her humiliation was already at grandiose levels.

The carriage door opened and James stood there.

"Are you certain about this, Mairi? Do you think it wise?"

"Probably not," she said.

She could admit that writing the broadside had resulted in consequences she hadn't considered. Logan Harrison had to be persuaded not to continue to punish her. Otherwise, the *Gazette* would go bankrupt.

If she had to apologize, she would.

James shook his head, but he didn't say anything as she left the carriage.

To her surprise, he accompanied her across the street and stood at the bottom of the steps.

"I'll just wait for you here," he said.

She clasped her reticule in her hands and faced him. "Do you never grow tired of minding me?" she asked.

A sliver of a smile curved his lips but he didn't answer.

"Will you tell Macrath?"

"Mr. Sinclair doesn't want to know what you do each day. I only inform him of circumstances that might prove important or a danger to you and your cousin."

"Would this be one of those circumstances?"

He only smiled at her.

With a roll of her eyes, she turned and went up the steps, her gaze intent on the crimson velvet curtains behind the sparkling glass of the nearest window.

The brass knocker was in the shape of a wolf's head, with its open jaws revealing very sharp teeth.

She grabbed the wolf's snout and let the knocker fall.

Logan's favorite room in his house was the library, a place where those books he loved were featured among those things he treasured. Bits of his past sat on the shelves along with items he'd discovered on his travels: a bowl from the set of china his mother had loved, purloined from his sister-in-law and now used to hold potpourri scented with oranges and cinnamon; a bit of coral he'd taken from a Spanish shoreline; a corner of crumbled brick from a thousand-year-old Italian church, and a shard of stained glass from the same church, given to him by the priest in remembrance of his visit.

Periodically, Mrs. Landers would go through his shelves and straighten the books, but he'd invariably take one out and lay it down on his desk. Or make his own sort of order through the stacks. He never organized by title or author, but by subject or interest. Did he like the book? Did it make him smile in some way? Incite a hunger or a need for further knowledge? Those books were always closest at hand.

He often worked in his library, finding it a more peaceful place than his office in council chambers. There, anyone was liable to knock on the door and ask for his time. Here, only two people did so—his majordomo and his housekeeper—and neither bothered him without a good reason.

When Rutherford interrupted him, he was surprised.

"You have a visitor, sir."

Rutherford's grayish face was arranged in a disapproving look. His shock of thick white hair was never in disarray. His suit was never marred by a speck of lint; his shoes always bore a mirror shine. He was the perfect majordomo, as proper as a Queen's servant.

Logan had the feeling that he often disappointed Rutherford.

Now the man's mouth was turned down and his eyes narrowed so much, Logan was surprised the man could see.

"A visitor?" He'd dismissed Thomas an hour earlier and he wasn't expecting anyone. "Who is it?"

"A woman, sir," Rutherford said, trembling with disapproval. "Who was quite rude when I stated I would have to announce her."

He put down his pen, made a neat stack of his correspondence, and placed it on the left side of his desk.

He didn't know any woman who would call on him at his home. No, he knew one who might dare.

"Does she have brown hair and piercing blue eyes?"

"She has an aggressive manner, sir, and was quite ill-mannered. I believe she does have blue eyes and unremarkable brown hair."

"Show her in, Rutherford," he said, wondering at the surge of anticipation he felt.

Rutherford nodded, his mouth looking even more grim as he bowed, stiff with dignity, and left the doorway.

He heard footsteps, sat back in his chair and waited for her.

She didn't disappoint.

Mairi Sinclair stood in the doorway frowning at him in much the same manner Rutherford had only a moment earlier. This time, however, Logan smiled.

"Why aren't you wearing a bonnet?" he asked.

"I hate them. Why do you care?"

"I'm curious."

"About me? Shall I be overjoyed that the Right Honorable Lord Provost evinces some interest in the hoi polloi? Mark this as a day of—"

"Forgive me for interrupting you, but why are you here?"

She stared at him.

Did no one ever stop Mairi Sinclair in mid-tirade?

"It's not fair to use your position to try to intimidate me," she said.

He settled back against the chair. "All I asked was why you were here."

She huffed out a breath. "I don't mean now," she said. "I meant in the last two days."

"What have I done in the last two days?"

She had the most remarkable eyes. They animated her face. Angry, she was even more impressive. Her cheeks were pink, her eyes flashing, and that full-lipped mouth thinned.

"My sources refuse to speak to me," she said. "My revenue has dropped to what it was five years ago. I've lost subscribers. You can't threaten my sources. You can't tell people not to talk to me."

"Have you had dinner?" he asked.

She stared at him as if he'd lost his sanity. Perhaps he had.

"Would you care to eat dinner with me?"

"Of course not."

"You don't break bread with your enemies? Sometimes, it's the best way to form an accord."

Her eyes darted around the room. "Am I supposed to form an accord with you?"

"Take the opportunity," he said.

"I'm not here to eat with you, Harrison."

"No, you're here to chide me for something I haven't done."

Her words had evidently seared her tongue because she didn't speak.

"Come have dinner with me. A peace offering, if you will."

"It wouldn't be proper."

"Who's to know? You're already here."

"My driver. Your staff."

"My staff is the essence of discretion. Would you like me to talk to your driver?"

Her eyes blazed at him. "Why is it that men think they can do something a woman can't do? If I wanted my driver's discretion, I would certainly be able to convey that to him."

"Then will you?"

One hand fluttered in the air as if to dismiss him with a gesture. He liked seeing Mairi Sinclair annoyed, and somehow inviting her to dinner had done just that.

"It's not a large meal," he said. "We're having potato soup. Do you like it? It's my favorite."

He stood and came around his desk.

"You're wearing a kilt again," she said.

He was still wearing a black jacket atop a blue and green kilt, his sporran hanging from a gold chain. His stockings were white, the cuffs of which were lined with the same blue and green tartan. He'd been required to open a hospital this afternoon and people liked seeing him in formal regalia.

"Are you wearing anything beneath it?" she asked, tilting her head back to smile thinly at him. "Custom would dictate not, but I can't envision the Lord Provost bare-arsed for all to see. What if a wind blew?"

Her smile was edged with daring, as if she expected him to be shocked by her comment.

"Why don't you see, lass?"

He shouldn't have been surprised when her smile broadened and she took a step toward him, but he was.

Her hand stretched out, trembled just a little as she touched his hip.

His smile faded.

Silence stretched between them, marked by the soft whir of the mantel clock.

She gathered up the material of his kilt with one hand. When her fingers touched his bare leg, he felt a current passing between them. Did her fingers scorch his skin or was that only foolishness?

His eyes never left hers.

In a second she would touch him, yet he didn't pull away or caution her.

She moved her hand, her fingers trailing over leather.

Her eyes widened.

So did his smile.

She jerked her hand back.

"It's a truss of a sort," he said.

Clasping her hands together, she stared down at his sporran. Covered in rabbit fur, it was adorned with three large tassels, each bearing an identical crest, that of his office.

"Have you been injured?"

His laughter swept through the room like a wave.

"No, but if I didn't wear one, I'd be bruised."

She frowned up at him.

"I'm large enough that I can't be swinging about," he said. "Now, shall we go in to dinner?"

While she looked a little dazed, he bit back his laughter, took her arm and headed toward the dining room.

Chapter 9

Dear God in heaven, what had she done?

She'd touched a man.

She'd only touched one man in her life. Calvin had been so surprised at her exploration that he'd drawn away. She'd been disappointed and more than a little embarrassed at his reaction. Wasn't discovery part of love? She'd found out, not too much later, that she was the only one who'd been in love. He'd only felt lust or maybe not even that.

What did Harrison feel?

Amusement, she decided, looking at his face. His eyes were dancing and his mouth was pursed. Was he trying not to smile?

A truss? What on earth did that mean? He was too large to be swinging about?

Her face warmed.

If she'd been the innocent she should have been, she wouldn't have known anything about a man's anatomy. How, then, did she pretend a virtue she no longer possessed?

"I'm not a virgin," she said as they left his library and walked down a wide hallway. The moment the words left her lips, she was horrified. Turning to him, she took a step back, one hand in the air between them.

Why on earth had she said such an idiotic thing? He didn't need to know whether or not she was a virgin. That information should be held in reserve for the man she married, if she ever married.

"Just in case you thought I should be shocked," she said, floundering for some reasonable explanation for her verbal excess.

"That's good to know," he said, the smile finally escaping from its mooring to make his face even more attractive. "I'm not a virgin, either."

She nodded, so humiliated she would have been grateful if the floor opened up beneath her. Instead, it stayed firm as rock.

At the dining room door he stepped aside so she could precede him.

What was she doing even thinking of eating a meal with Harrison? But here she was, being led to a chair like she had no will of her own. Maybe that, too, was because of him.

The dining room was as richly appointed as the rest of the Lord Provost's home. A long mahogany table sat atop a patterned carpet of emerald and pale green. Two sideboards sat on either end of the room with a fireplace occupying a third wall, the black mantel elaborately carved with thistles and berries.

She only had a moment to note the plaster frieze on the ceiling and the lovely painting of a bowl of fruit before he pulled out the chair for her.

She sat, bemused.

He was a single man. She was a single woman. The very fact she was here, in his home, was untoward behavior. Now she was eating a meal with him? What would James think? He was certain to tell Macrath about this episode, if not Robert.

"You look as terrified as a rabbit in a trap, Miss Sinclair."

She blinked over at him. Not one word came to mind. Perhaps that was for the best, because the door on the far wall swung open and a woman of middle years entered the room.

Stopping abruptly, she looked from Harrison to Mairi, and back again.

"You'll be having company, then," she said with a jerk of her chin toward Mairi.

Harrison nodded but didn't offer any explanation. Nor did the woman seem to need one. She simply went to the sideboard, gathered up extra silver, and arranged it before Mairi. A goblet and water glass were taken from the hutch, set in front of her knife, and seconds later a butter dish and charger were in place as well.

The minute the woman left the dining room, she was replaced by two other females. One carried a large white tureen. Another held a tray on which there were various serving dishes.

Mairi stared down into the bowl she'd been served. The soup smelled and looked wonderful, thick and butter-colored with chunks of potato, onions, and beans.

She was already here plus it had been a very long time since lunch, and that had consisted of only a piece of dry bread with mustard and a bit of ham.

The soup tasted as wonderful as it looked. She closed her eyes after the first mouthful, the better to savor it. Half the bowl was gone by the time she glanced over at the Lord Provost again. When she did, it was to find him smiling at her.

"It's my favorite," he said again.

"I can see why. It's wonderful."

"I'll have my cook give you the recipe."

"Thank you, that would be very nice."

Now they were conversing as pleasantly as if they had just met and knew nothing about each other. As if she hadn't touched his truss after his dare.

"You don't look as frightened. I'll have to remember that in the future. Keep you fed and you won't be afraid."

"I'm not afraid," she said, putting her spoon carefully down on the side of the bowl. "Do you think I'm afraid of you?" She allowed herself a small laugh.

"My error," he said, sipping at his wine. He sat back in the chair, his green eyes intent over the goblet.

She sat back as well, grateful that she'd had a chance to eat some of the soup before the battle began. She rubbed her fingertips over the napkin in her lap, not at all surprised at the tight weave of the linen. The Lord Provost evidently liked fine things.

"Why didn't you agree to meet with me?" she asked.

He frowned at her. "Meet with you?"

"I wrote you a letter," she said. "I delivered it to council chambers myself and asked that it be given to you."

He shook his head. "I never received it."

"Have you truly not tried to keep people from talking to me?" she asked.

He studied her over the rim of his goblet. When he finally put it down on the table, he blotted his lips and looked at her again.

"I have not."

"Can I have your word on that?"

"Miss Sinclair, if I were the type of man to do such a thing, what makes you think my word could be trusted?"

Not quite an answer, though, was it?

"No," he said in the face of her silence, "I haven't. However, it's entirely possible someone on my staff did. Even so, I do not absolve myself of responsibility. I am responsible for the actions of those I employ."

Now was the time for her to apologize for her own behavior, but she remained stubbornly mute. She was not quite ready to concede anything to the Lord Provost. Nor was she willing to admit he was as charming as everyone believed.

The look in his eye said he was capable of being as wicked as anyone. She had proof of that. Her fingers still tingled from touching him.

"I will ensure that the matter is investigated. No one will say a word against you, Miss Sinclair. Can I say the same about you?"

She glanced over at him again, then focused on the painting on the wall. The artist was very skilled, enough that sunlight seemed to be dancing on the cobalt blue bowl.

"I see no reason to bring up your name," she said. "Unless you act in a matter unbefitting your position."

Why was he smiling at her?

"I shall attempt to be circumspect and proper at all times. And you?"

Was he referring to that moment in his library? Was she blushing? *Please don't let her be blushing.* That would simply be too much.

His smile was at once teasing and tender, an expression that no doubt caused women other than her to think of laughter and seduction in the same breath.

She was not going to be attracted to the man.

She forced her lips into a straight line, banished the thought of smiling, and met his eyes.

"I can't promise to be circumspect and proper at all times, Harrison. Not when the time has come for women to make a little noise, to demand their rightful place in society."

"By marching?"

She frowned at him. "I don't know what you mean."

"That's a welcome surprise," he said.

Was he trying to be cryptic? If so, he was succeeding.

"I don't see anything surprising about a woman wishing to be treated more fairly," she said. "Or being able to vote."

"Why that cause? Why not draft horses or child labor?"

"Are you saying that women shouldn't vote?"

He shook his head. "Not at all. I'm merely curious."

"Until meeting you," she said, "I would have been content to be the editor of the *Edinburgh Gazette*. Now I want to be more active in women's causes, and the most important of those is the vote."

He sat back in his chair, folded his arms and stared at her.

"And you would lay that transformation at my feet?"

"Men with whom I've done business in the past have pulled their advertising. They have refused to speak to me as a reporter. Solely because I dared criticize an elected official."

"It was your decision to publish that broadside, Miss Sinclair. Shouldn't the ramifications for it be on your head?"

"Yet you should be exempt from criticism?" she asked, picking up her spoon again. She was probably going to be ushered out of his house at any moment. Why shouldn't she continue her dinner?

He didn't say a word as she finished the rest of her soup. Where had he learned that silence was intimidating?

"One day," she said, placing her spoon on the edge of the bowl, "women will run for office, too."

He just looked at her, his green eyes intent, as if he'd never seen anyone quite like her. It was altogether possible that he hadn't.

She took another sip of the wine he'd poured for her, wondering if it had gone straight to her head. Her pulse raced and she felt deliciously light-headed.

"Do you dance, Miss Sinclair?"

Her eyes widened at the question.

"Do I dance? Yes, I do."

"Let me rephrase the question if I may. Do you enjoy dancing?"

Her eyes narrowed. "No, but does it matter?"

"Absolutely not," he said, beginning to eat his soup again. "People will have you dance whether you wish it or not, won't they?"

She nodded.

"It's a ridiculous occupation when you think about it, moving around a dance floor to music."

"Like a trained bear," she said.

"Exactly."

Why were they suddenly in accord? For that matter, why was her skin feeling so tight and her face still so warm? She really should leave.

The longer she was near him, the greater the danger she was going to say or do something else idiotic.

"I hear congratulations are in order," she said, hearing the words with something akin to horror. Was she two people? Why bother having a speck of intelligence if she was going to say anything that flew into her mind?

"Why is that?"

She took a sip of her wine, wondering if she should tell him that she'd also tasted whiskey. Did she want him to think her shocking?

How much more shocking than telling him she wasn't a virgin?

"Aren't you getting married?"

"Who told you that?"

"One of my sources," she said, unwilling to expose Mr. Donovan.

"He's a poor source, then," he said.

"So you aren't marrying the Drummond girl. Which one are you interested in? They're both blondes, are they not? Do you have a preference for blond-haired women?"

He sat back and regarded her somberly. Not a hint of his smile remained, only that chilled gaze of his. As a weapon it was very effective.

She almost shivered.

"I would appreciate it if you wouldn't carry tales," he said. "Especially if they involve an innocent like Barbara Drummond."

Now she truly did wish to apologize, but she reached over and plucked a roll from the tray in front of her, and busied herself buttering it.

"So you do prefer blond-haired women. Must they have a certain color eyes?"

"Why are you so interested in my preferences, Miss Sinclair? I might ask the same of you. What interests you in a man?"

A tall, broad Highlander who grins like the devil and whose eyes are glittery shards of emeralds.

She wanted to slap herself.

"Perhaps looks don't interest me at all," she said, taking a bite of the roll.

"You're a more cerebral type, is that it? The physical appearance matters nothing to you as long as the man is intelligent."

"I can't say that," she said. "There's something to be said for a certain type of animalistic attraction."

"Which is why you're no longer a virgin."

She felt her face heat. Why had she told him that?

"Another area of disparity in our society, Lord Provost. A man is expected to be experienced, while a woman is castigated if she does the same. Does it not make you wonder with whom the man is getting his experience?"

"I don't believe I've ever thought about it, Miss Sinclair."

She sat back, her roll forgotten, and studied him.

"One could only wonder about your experience, Lord Provost. The family maid? A kindly neighbor? A paid companion, perhaps?"

"A wonderfully wise widow in France," he said. "I learned a great deal from her."

She had the feeling she'd met her match in the art of dueling words.

"I hope you and Miss Drummond are very happy," she said. "No doubt she has all the qualities you are looking for in a wife."

He studied her without speaking. An interesting experience, being the subject of Harrison's stare.

"What would those be?" he finally asked.

She propped her chin on her hand in violation of table etiquette and pretended to consider the matter.

"Well versed in politics, I would think," she said. "Agreeable, certainly."

He didn't say a word, which was a disappointment. She expected—or wanted—him to challenge her assessment.

"She would think you brilliant," she added. "That's almost understood, I think."

"Of course," he said.

"Tact," she said. "The ability to tell someone to go to perdition while smiling."

"A good memory."

She dropped her hand. "Why?"

"To remember the names and occupations of all the people I meet from day to day. A good hostess as well. I would be expected to entertain more with a wife."

She nodded.

"All in all, whoever she is must be very talented. Must she play a musical instrument?"

"Not required."

"Must she know how to cook or merely supervise a staff?"

"Staff alone, I think."

"All that's left is appearance," she said. "And you've already indicated a preference for blondes." She was tempted to ask about the woman's figure, but decided she'd tweaked his nose enough on the subject.

He took a sip of his wine, watching her over the rim. "And your criteria for a husband? Would it not be fair to share it?"

She shook her head. "I'd rather talk about Edinburgh's gardens or the weather. Or even your plans for the coming holidays."

"I always spend the time with my family," he said. "I've three brothers, all married. All with an incredible number of children."

"I've heard from countless people in the last few days how charming you are."

"But you don't find me so?"

She smiled brightly. "Actually, you are. Although there are times when you forget and become something else entirely."

"Perhaps it's you, Miss Sinclair, that brings out the 'something else entirely' in me," he said, staring at his wine as if transfixed by the ruby color.

She smiled at him, seeing the glint in his eye and recognizing it for what it truly was, a declaration of war.

How quickly his charm had vanished.

Perhaps it would be wise to leave before Harrison lost that tenuous hold on his temper. How she knew he was barely able to keep it in check was another thing she would think about later, when she was safely away.

Standing, she placed her napkin on the table, then walked to the door, intending to leave before he stood.

She wasn't quite that fast.

He moved to block her exit.

"Thank you for dinner," she said, "but I must leave. Please convey my appreciation to your cook."

"Mairi," he said, speaking her name in a way she'd never before heard, drawing out the syllables as if there were hills and valleys between them.

This time she did shiver.

"I shall not mention Miss Drummond's name," she said. "Nor will I use yours. I trust you will inform your staff that my sources aren't to be intimidated."

"How agreeable you are all of a sudden. Are you afraid of me?"

"That's the second time you've asked me. Of course I'm not." She did, however, take a step back, simply as a precautionary measure.

He was much too close. Too large and much too, well, manly. She could smell him, and that disconcerted her even more than realizing that he smelled of spices. Something his housekeeper sprinkled among his clothing?

Her face felt hot.

"I have to leave," she said, ducking around him and nearly sprinting down the hall. His majordomo moved quickly to avoid her but he wasn't fast enough. She ignored him as she opened the door herself and raced down the steps.

Chapter 10

Logan returned to his library, sitting at the desk that was a gift from his mentor, the previous Lord Provost who'd educated him on all things political. Logan had been born, Dennis McDaniel said, with a knack for making people believe in him.

"Trust is one of the most difficult commodities to attain, Logan. If people feel it for you, never scorn or waste it. If you do, you'll never get it back."

Perhaps his instinctive abilities and his mentor's advice had gotten him elected to council and then on to being Lord Provost. To Parliament—that had been his dream and why the perfect wife was such a necessity.

Then why was he staring at the calendar of his engagements for the next week, not seeing anything but fiery blue eyes and a mouth pursed in temper?

Mairi Sinclair should not even be a thought. He shouldn't recall anything she said. Or the look on her face when she stormed into his house, all bluster and blue eyes.

He'd wanted to kiss her, and the need to do just that had startled him into doing something even more foolish: daring her to touch him.

He had the idea that no one challenged Mairi Sinclair.

Contrary to her accusations, he hadn't advised anyone to avoid her. Unfortunately, he wasn't as sure of Thomas's actions. Had his secretary let it be known that cooperating with Mairi Sinclair wouldn't be seen as wise? Thomas was the master of the veiled threat, the whisper campaign, and the unspoken insult.

He'd make a point of talking to the man.

Had Thomas also intercepted her letter? Or had it simply gotten lost in the general confusion that sometimes reigned in council chambers?

He picked up his pen and studied it, seeing her face before him. She smiled quickly, the flash of humor on her face mirrored in her eyes. Just as easily, she could catapult into temper, her lips thinning while her eyes blazed fire. But when she left his house it had been with a strange and disconcerting expression on her face.

What made Mairi Sinclair afraid?

Her mind intrigued him. Twice, tonight, she'd surprised him. Once, when she'd taken his dare and touched him. Had she known how much he wanted to grab her with both hands and haul her up into his arms for a kiss? The second time, she'd asked about Barbara Drummond, and he'd been so startled by her knowledge that he was curt. How had she discovered he was planning on marrying?

Perhaps he'd underestimated her talent at reporting.

"She's gone, then?"

He looked up to find Mrs. Landers in the doorway.

Mrs. Landers was as thin as his cook was plump. Her features were angular; her face long and ending in a pointed chin. Even her eyebrows seemed elongated, stretching from over her nose nearly to her temple.

Her hairline began only an inch above her brows. If he hadn't overheard her conversation with a maid where she bragged about her healthy head of hair, he would have thought it a wig in a perpetual state of sliding too close to her nose.

Each emotion shown on her face and was capable of reshaping her features. A smile shortened her nose and widened her mouth. A frown elongated her chin.

She was, as most housekeepers probably were, an imminently practical woman. She instituted economies that saved him money, advised him on the staff with more insight than Rutherford, and took great care with his possessions.

She was also one of the most softhearted women he knew. She once hesitantly asked if she could take advantage of his library, and he'd been pleased to give her that freedom.

More than once, when returning home early, he discovered her reading in the wing chair beside the window.

"A very touching story," she said on the last occasion, replacing the book on the shelf and moving out of the room before he could engage her in conversation. He hadn't looked at what she'd been reading, but now he wished he had, wanting to know more about the women in his life. Perhaps if he were more enlightened he wouldn't be as confused.

Now she was looking down at him, her forehead crinkled in a frown, further reducing the space between brow and hairline.

"She's a lovely girl," she said.

"Yes, she is." Any other time, he might have looked down at his desk, at the piles of papers stacked to his left. Mrs. Landers would have immediately understood that he wanted to work and would leave him. Tonight he didn't do that.

"She runs the *Edinburgh Gazette*," he said. "Have you read it?"

"I have, and the broadside she wrote about you." She smiled at him.

The strangest thing happened. He felt the tips of his ears grow hot as if he were embarrassed.

"Did you really try to keep her out of the club?" she asked, her tone more friendly than chiding.

He shook his head. "No, but I doubt she believes that."

"Then you'll just have to keep trying to make her see your point of view, won't you?"

She sent him a toothy smile, then strode toward the door. "I'll bring your coffee in, then, shall I?"

He nodded, a little bemused at the thought of trying to convince Mairi Sinclair of anything.

However, it might be interesting to try.

James didn't say a word when she entered the carriage an hour after she left him. But he gave her a look that indicated he was definitely going to inform Macrath.

She lay her head back against the seat, staring up at the silk above her.

Why had she said what she had? Why had she touched him? Why had she felt so strange around him? It was bad enough him witnessing her humiliation at the hands of other people, but to do it to herself hardly seemed fair.

What was it about the man that had her opening her mouth and all sorts of secrets spewing forth?

Words had power and she wielded them well. At least she had until meeting the Lord Provost. Around him she was lucky to string two words together and do so without slavering.

Nor had she ever realized the power of presence. The sight of Harrison dressed in his kilt, looking like a civilized barbarian, took her breath away. He left no doubt of who was in charge.

She certainly hadn't been, even of her own mouth.

What sort of silly and frivolous woman was she, to be so impressed by a man's appearance?

Or perhaps it was simply his smile that affected her so strangely. Or the way he had of looking at her, as if she were more important than anything else in the universe.

She'd gone to Harrison's home for the purpose of demanding he stop whatever he was doing. The result had been dissatisfying since he refused to admit he'd done anything.

He could charm the feathers off a bird. All it took was one smile, starting slow and finally reaching his beautiful green eyes. Or a touch of his hand, gentle and almost tender, proving that he knew his own strength and never used it against someone smaller and weaker.

Was she becoming delirious about the Lord Provost? No, she was not that much of an idiot.

Yet something about the man pushed her close to the edge of decorum. She'd been irrational and foolish, losing her objectivity and falling into the trap of allowing emotion to dictate her actions.

He'd been very protective of Barbara Drummond. Was he in love with her?

Love was a silly reason to marry, all in all. Love involved your loins first, then your heart. Neither area was renowned for reason or judgment.

What she was feeling now was not jealousy. She didn't care who Harrison married. Why should she be concerned?

If she were to marry—an occasion that had never been in her mind much after Calvin—she'd choose a man similar to herself, someone who valued words, who was curious, who always wanted to know the answer to why. With any luck, he'd be handsome and physically appealing, not a great bear of a man who overpowered her with his presence. He would have a wonderful sense of humor, seeing the ridiculous aspects of life. He would be ambitious and want to succeed at whatever endeavor he chose. He would, above all, believe in her, demonstrate his loyalty to her, and cherish her. In return she would honor him above all men, care for him, and share her thoughts with him.

Love would be subjugated beneath practicality.

When they arrived home she thanked James as she left the carriage, knowing he would wait until she climbed the steps to the front door before pulling around to the stables. Having lived above the newspaper for years, she understood why Macrath had opted for a large home. But the house, with its three floors, twenty-two rooms, and a dozen fireplaces, was too big for the four of them. Eight people, if you added the maids.

Still, it seemed petty to complain about the luxury in which she lived. Macrath had derived a great deal of joy from providing for all of them. The least she could do was be silent and thankful.

Opening the door, she stepped inside, grateful for her work schedule. No one in the household would think it was odd if she were later than usual. She could attribute it to a dozen different things, all having to do with the paper.

"You missed our meeting."

She jumped when Robert emerged from the darkness at the bottom of the stairs.

Placing a hand over her thumping heart, she looked at the man. "You startled me."

"You missed our meeting."

Every week, on Wednesday night, Robert insisted on going over all the bills again with her. Since he never let an amount go unchallenged, either with the vendor or with her, the meeting was not necessary. Even so, she always set aside some time for him to rail at her once again, since doing so seemed to give him pleasure.

Tonight, however, she'd gone to see the Lord Provost.

"Can't it wait, Robert?"

"Not unless you're determined to ruin the company your father built."

She really needed to talk to Macrath about him.

"Very well," she said, pulling off her gloves. "Let me make this short for you. I erred. I spent too much. I was wrong. There, our meeting is done."

"You do not treat this with the solemnity it requires, Mairi."

She sighed. "I am not wasteful, Robert. You seem to forget that all of the money I'm spending is money I've earned."

"Because of your father's company."

Had he never paid any attention to how many hours she put in at the paper? Even when she didn't feel well, she was at work. She often took her meals at the kitchen table while she wrote notes to herself or finished up a broadside. Did he think she didn't worry about what she was doing or how to increase subscribers?

Evidently not, or he wouldn't level that disapproving stare on her.

"You're paying those boys too much."

"I am not cutting the hawkers' wages," she said, not bothering to tell him that she suspected it was the only income their families had in some lean weeks.

He looked as if he would say something but only shook his head.

"I owe it to your father to keep your habits in check. And to Macrath."

She was most definitely going to talk to her brother.

Without giving Robert another chance to comment, she walked away, hoping he didn't follow her into the kitchen.

Grateful that the kettle was full, she made herself some tea. She sat at the table, staring down into her cup. Fenella purchased the most wonderful blend of teas. This one was what they drank at night, a fragrant, lightly colored tea that smelled like flowers and had a delicate taste.

What did it matter what she drank? After the incident at the provost's house, she doubted she would sleep anyway. Even now she could close her eyes and see Logan's teasing smile.

The door opened and she sighed inwardly, readying herself for another battle with Robert. Instead of the older man, however, Fenella stood there.

"We need to talk, Mairi," she said.

"Has Robert been fussing at you, too?"

Fenella shook her head, coming to sit opposite her.

"I know exactly what you're going to say," Mairi said before her cousin could speak.

"You do?" Fenella asked.

"I've been rude and inconsiderate. I should have sent word that I wasn't going to make dinner."

"We don't hold dinner for you most nights, Mairi. You're often working."

"I know," she said, staring down into her cup. "I wasn't working tonight. I was at the Lord Provost's house."

"You were?"

Mairi nodded. "You can't say anything to me that I haven't already said to myself. I've been a fool in a dozen ways."

"You have?"

"I don't know what's happening to me," she said. "I'm a blithering idiot around the man."

She made herself meet Fenella's eyes. "About tonight.

I should have let you know but I had no idea I was going to stay. One moment I'm in his library and the next I'm eating soup."

At Fenella's silence, she continued. "I should have been prepared, but Harrison was entirely too charming."

"Was he?"

"No man should be that charming," Mairi said. "Especially him. He should be forced to wear a sign, something to warn an unsuspecting woman."

"I would never have considered you an unsuspecting woman, Mairi."

"See? That's exactly what I mean. I went there to demand he stop trying to ruin the *Gazette,* and before I knew it . . ." Her words trailed away. She was not going to tell Fenella about reaching under Harrison's kilt.

"How is he ruining the *Gazette*?" Fenella asked, her eyes wide.

Mairi stared down into her almost empty cup, took a deep breath, and told her cousin about the reversals they'd suffered in the last two days.

"Was that entirely wise, Mairi, accusing him?"

She shook her head. "No. Not wise at all. Nothing I've done around the man has been wise. I can't even talk around him."

She looked over at Fenella.

"There's something almost wicked about the man. If I believed in such things, I'd think him enchanted. One of the wee folk transformed into the Lord Provost."

Fenella smiled.

"I would very much like to say that I handled myself with comportment and decorum. I don't think that's true at all."

"What is the truth?" Fenella asked, tilting her head to one side like an inquisitive bird.

"He's very handsome," Mairi said. "He has a way of looking at you that makes you want to spill all your secrets to him or tell him things you never dreamed of revealing to anyone."

"Do you?" Fenella asked, wide-eyed. "Did you?"

Mairi sighed again. "I came very close. I have to stay away from him, that's obvious. Very far away from him."

"Whenever I hear a woman talk about a man in such a manner," her cousin said, "I think it's because she's attracted to him. Are you attracted to the Lord Provost?"

"Yes. No. Perhaps. I don't know." She shook her head. "All those answers and maybe more."

Fenella's hazel eyes gleamed. Reaching across the table, she patted Mairi's clenched hands.

"I think you're attracted to him and have been from the very beginning."

"I hope not," Mairi said. "Nothing can come of it. He and I are opposites in every way. He's an annoying man who has little use for women."

"How can a man be charming and annoying at the same time?"

"I don't know, but he can. I think it's better to avoid him at all costs. From this moment on there is no Lord Provost of Edinburgh. Logan Harrison does not exist."

"Are you certain it's wise to make such a rash statement?"

"It's not rash, just practical. I need to devote myself to the paper. I've allowed myself to be too distracted lately."

"Mairi . . ." Fenella began.

"I know, Fenella. I know. I need to pay more attention to my work. I've even been impatient with Allan."

"About that, Mairi—"

"Men are not worth the trouble or the aggravation. Any woman who devotes her life to a man is a fool, and I'm most definitely not a fool."

"He isn't Calvin, Mairi."

The words were said gently, but Mairi felt her stomach clench nonetheless.

"I know he isn't."

"Just because you had one bad experience doesn't mean it would happen again."

"It doesn't mean it wouldn't," she said. "Right at the moment, I don't want to think about attraction or love or anything remotely like that."

She looked up at her cousin.

"Thank heavens you're more sensible than that, Fenella."

Fenella smiled, but remained silent as she left the room.

Chapter 11

Thomas had alerted Logan to the meeting tonight. His secretary had offered to attend in his stead, but he'd waved Thomas home. Tonight was Thomas's first year anniversary, and Logan didn't want to interfere with the occasion. Besides, it would do him good to see the Scottish Ladies National Association in person. He had yet to allow their petition to be voted on in council. Perhaps this meeting would give him a little more insight into the character of the group.

To his surprise—and why should he be surprised, when she was at the center of his thoughts lately?—Mairi Sinclair was the featured speaker.

Nearly a quarter of the large audience was men. Evidently, they found something of value in the SLNA. His curiosity grew along with his discomfort about being recognized.

Since he didn't want to give the audience members the idea that he approved of the organization's purpose or even this meeting, he pulled Mrs. MacPherson aside and explained that he was here personally and not in his position as Lord Provost.

Mrs. MacPherson smiled at him, revealing a charm that some much younger women would do well to emulate.

"I have just the spot for you, Provost Harrison," she said.

She led him to an alcove not far from the entrance to the ballroom. From here he could easily see the stage as well as the audience, yet be hidden from their view.

"We call it the nest," she said, "for girls who are not old enough to attend a ball. Here they can sit and watch the proceedings without being seen."

He thanked her, and once again she smiled, her beauty evident despite her age.

Mairi was already seated, along with two women he didn't know. She stared out at the audience dispassionately, as if she were bored with the proceedings. He wondered if that was the case or whether she was just better, in a public forum, at hiding her feelings.

She didn't try to mask what she felt around him.

Mairi sat on the straight-back wooden chair on the back of the stage hoping her panic did not show to the audience. Her face was arranged in a rictus of composure; she could feel the strain in the muscles of her jaw. Beside her were two women to whom she'd been introduced but whose names she couldn't remember now.

She was lucky to be able to recall her own at the moment.

Tonight she had dressed in dark brown, not because it was a color that favored her, although it did. The shade was also sober, making her appear more like a matron than a single woman.

Sound carried very well in the ballroom where she sat, a necessity for the small orchestra normally arranged on this stage. She could hear bits of conversation, scraps of talk between the audience members, none of which referred to her or even the topic for tonight's speech.

No one had told her that the gathering would be quite so large.

There were at least two hundred people here. She had thought a few dozen would attend. At the most, perhaps fifty. Instead, Josephine MacPherson's ballroom was filled with a sea of chairs, now occupied by people slowly turning to stare at the stage where she sat.

If they were expecting her to faint, they were going to be sorely disappointed. She'd never fainted in her life. Now might be the ideal time, however. Her hands were cold, her breath shallow, and her pulse was racing so quickly she wondered if she would even be able to speak.

Mrs. MacPherson, the woman hosting this meeting of the Scottish Ladies National Association, was moving to stand at the front of the stage. The woman was well known in Edinburgh, being a philanthropist of sorts. The widow of a wealthy cotton mill owner in Glasgow, she'd moved to Edinburgh to be closer to family. In the last year, she'd embraced the cause of women's equality with open arms and reticule.

A fine web of wrinkles covered her face, but you didn't think of age when talking to Mrs. MacPherson as much as humor. Her mouth was always curved in a smile, and the expression in her soft blue eyes was filled with wisdom and understanding. Her crown of brilliant white hair made her appear taller and younger than her seventy odd years.

Her voice, soft yet resonant, calmed the audience immediately. People leaned forward to hear her better.

The SLNA had been turned down for every hall they wanted to rent for the occasion, which was why they were meeting in Mrs. MacPherson's ballroom. Still, it felt a little odd to be delivering an address on such a serious topic when above her was a mural featuring scantily clad gods and goddesses cavorting among the clouds.

She was abruptly reminded of Logan Harrison.

The very last person she needed to be thinking about was the Lord Provost, especially since she was trying to compose herself.

Someone had a liking for fresh air and opened the windows along one wall despite the fact that it had only just stopped sleeting. The cold dampness seeped into her skin and made a disaster of her hair. Why was she concerned about whether her hair frizzed? People had not come here to see her. Instead, they wanted to know what she thought. At least, she hoped they did.

She looked down at her notes, realizing she couldn't focus on what she'd written. She'd spent hours rehearsing her speech and couldn't remember one single point.

A smattering of polite applause sent Mairi's stomach to her toes. It was time. She would have to stand, walk the few feet to the front of the stage without tripping and falling.

Moving to Mrs. MacPherson's side, she thanked the woman for her kindness and the fulsome introduction. She hadn't heard a word of it, and hopefully Mrs. MacPherson hadn't expanded on her qualifications too much.

She cleared her throat, looked out at all the faces staring back at her, and realized she couldn't address this many people. She could, however, talk to one person, so she selected one in the third row, a young woman who'd untied the ribbon of her bonnet as if it chafed her under the chin.

Mairi had done that so many times she felt an instant kinship.

"I was born Mairi Anne Sinclair, in Edinburgh. I have always been proud to call myself a Scot. My family has lived in Edinburgh for as long as there was a city."

She straightened her shoulders.

"When I was a little girl, I was conscious of the fact

that my brother and I were different. Not only in the way we looked and how we wished to play, but in our futures.

"My father assumed my brother was going to run the paper when he got older. I was going to marry and have children. I didn't see anything wrong with that future, but it hasn't come to pass. There was no other option for me. That's what I was told. That's what I was shown."

She cleared her throat again.

"When my father died, and my brother no longer expressed an interest in the paper, I took it over. I became the editor of the *Edinburgh Gazette* and worked very hard to ensure the paper survived. I worked in a job that was considered a man's position. I did the job well even though there were many times when I had to pretend to be a man."

She saw many women nod their heads.

"I'm here tonight to tell you my story. To explain that I am like a great many women who have taken on jobs that are not considered proper for our sex. None of us, I believe, want approbation for our actions. We do not wish to be lauded for what we are doing, only to be allowed to continue to do it."

The room seemed to grow quieter, as if she'd caught their attention.

"But we are not martyrs to our cause. We do not wish to toil in anonymity and merely be grateful to be given a chance to earn a living. What we wish is to be treated like any other citizen of Edinburgh, of Scotland. We want to matter. We want to be able to choose, to take our place with other citizens.

"Right now, if I disagree with a politician, I have no recourse. If I am married, I might try to convince my husband of my thoughts. If I am not married, I am disenfranchised. I am invisible. I am one of the anonymous people who labor in the shadows.

"It is time for women to stand in the sunlight, to say to every single man, 'Look at me. I count. I matter. I think, therefore my thoughts should be heard.'"

She hadn't much practice in public speaking. Logan could tell that from the moment she opened her mouth. Instead of the husky voice he remembered so well, her tone was high-pitched and almost shrill.

If she would accept his help, he could give her some advice. He'd given a thousand speeches in his life.

He found himself listening to her words, not the way they were delivered. She spoke simply, telling the audience who she was, neither elevating herself nor claiming false modesty. Her reasons for wanting the vote were sympathetic, her arguments well thought out.

He wasn't against the vote for women. What rankled him was when a group demanded that the status quo be overturned without due deliberation. Or claimed that he had deliberately deprived them of their rights. He'd done nothing of the sort. Nor had any other man of his acquaintance. If they were guilty of anything, it was of following the law.

If the women of Scotland believed they deserved the vote, there was a way to change the law. Petition the government, convince representatives, sway Parliament, anything constructive.

It occurred to him that perhaps he'd misjudged the SLNA, because it looked as if they were attempting to do just that. Mairi's speech was impressive. Her words were capable of winning over the men and women in the audience.

Four men suddenly appeared in the doorway behind him. Dressed as workmen with short coats, scarves knotted at their necks, and hats pulled low over their foreheads, they began speaking loudly. Their language was so foul that several of the women turned and glared, outraged, at the intruders.

He didn't have a good feeling about this.

One man would have been bad enough, but four men hinted at the beginnings of a mob.

In the last several weeks, the SLNA gatherings had served as galvanizing points. Several people, both men and women, had been injured.

If he wasn't mistaken, a brawl was about to begin.

He slipped out of the alcove and headed toward the back, intent on assisting the two burly men wearing the MacPherson livery.

Mairi was conscious of noises in the back of the room, a commotion she deliberately tried to block out as she finished her speech. But a man's voice rose louder than the others, causing her to break off in mid-sentence.

She'd first heard those words from a hawker her father employed. The poor lad couldn't speak for swearing, and her father finally had to let him go. Only after much coaxing would Macrath tell her what the words meant, and even then she stared at him, disbelieving.

"Why would they make swear words from a lady's parts?" she asked.

Her brother had shrugged, red-faced. "Some men do, that's all."

The idea that a man might only think of her as different sections confused, then angered her.

A man shouted something she couldn't understand. He was challenged by another male, and in seconds they were pummeling each other. Two other men joined in as people in the back of the room began to stand, moving away from the scuffle.

It looked as if she wasn't going to get the chance to finish her speech. Nor did she have to worry about questions from the audience, even though she'd been told to expect them. No one was remaining around to ask her anything. The ballroom was emptying fast.

Somewhere in the back of the room a woman screamed, and both of her companions on the stage stood, following the rest of the crowd.

At least a dozen men were fighting now, and as she watched, a half dozen more joined in.

Her breath was tight, her thoughts disjointed. Should she escape as her companions had? The answer was taken from her when a man raced down the center aisle, heading directly for the stage. She took a few cautionary steps back just as he was caught by the collar by one of the men she'd met this evening. The two of them went at each other, the heavy thump of fists hitting flesh making her step back even farther. The grunting, swearing, wet slap of blows and the ugliness of it all made her sick.

She wrapped her arms around herself, trying to stay composed.

She was instantly back in her childhood when they'd been one step up from the poorest inhabitants of Old Town. Their father had worked hard for his meager living. Being the proprietor of a struggling newspaper had meant they sometimes did without. They'd never known how poor they were until later, after their father died and Macrath was the head of the family while still little more than a child. Then, they'd worried about their next meal, shoes with holes, and threadbare clothing.

She knew what it was like to be pointed out and laughed at, to feel her stomach sour with anxiety at the thought of having to go to the shops or anywhere where someone might see her.

Once Macrath had become wealthy, no one mocked her. Not until today.

What had she done to deserve such treatment?

She'd dared to tell the truth.

Chapter 12

The audience disappeared from the ballroom and down the stairs like water spilling over stone. None of the other members of the SLNA lingered to give her commiseration or congratulations. Even Mrs. MacPherson had disappeared in the wake of the fight.

She wished Fenella hadn't been indisposed this evening. She needed moral support, or a sounding board if nothing else. The speech had been a disaster, and that was a surprise since she thought it started so well.

Should she simply consider it practice? Surely after tonight it would be easier to speak in front of a large group. Or would she be causing a riot each time?

Why had those men insisted on calling her names? Why, because she wanted to become the editor of the *Gazette* in truth, instead of always hiding behind Macrath? Why did that idea—or the idea of a woman doing what she wished—enrage them?

Did they hate women?

None of the women she'd met in the SLNA movement had ever said anything derogatory about a man. In fact, she'd met a great many men who actively supported the organization.

She respected the men in her life. First, Macrath, who was an example of someone dedicated to achieving his dream. He used that same determination in his personal life as well. Then, her father whose memory warmed her heart. James, Robert, and Allan were all men whose presence added to her life. The only male who hadn't acted in an honorable manner was Calvin.

Even the Lord Provost, as much as she might hate to admit it, was a man to admire.

She stood at the head of the steps, wishing that the mass of people milling around the bottom of the staircase would leave. She didn't want to endure their compassionate looks. Nor did she wish to encounter any of the men who'd spoiled her speech.

Turning, she walked in the opposite direction, hoping to find the servants' stairs. Instead of leaving from the front of the house, she would slip out the back, find her carriage, and avoid the crowd.

Humiliation was a bad enough emotion to feel alone, but she didn't want to be forced to pretend she was fine when it was obvious she wasn't. Tears were just beneath the surface and she wasn't the type to cry easily. Her face felt warm. Her hairline was damp and itchy and she wasn't even wearing that despicable bonnet.

A few minutes later she found the stairs, descended them to find herself in an alcove beside the kitchen. When she asked a passing maid for directions to a back door, the girl didn't seem surprised at the request. After thanking her, Mairi made her way outside.

The earlier sleet might never have happened. The skies were sprinkled with glittering stars as the wind caressed her face, bringing with it the crisp threat of snow and, below that, the heavy smell of wood smoke. Moonlight spilled over the landscape, transforming the hedges to rounded humps and the grass to a gray swath leading to the gas lamps on the street.

People clustered in small groups in front of the portico, their words indecipherable and their voices only a faint drone. She clung to the shadows, hoping to escape detection. From where she stood, behind a row of hedges, she didn't see James, but there were a great many carriages in line.

The sound of conversation drifted away as she walked farther, following the drive. The trees cast shadow ghosts over the lawn, the wind making the branches dance a disjointed jig.

She didn't know the shadows were real until the men were almost on top of her. Her heart skipped a beat as she waited for them to pass. Instead, the three of them stopped a dozen feet away, each man hefting something in his hand.

"So you'd have a woman be like a man, would you? Can you fight like a man?"

She was tempted to respond to him, but some kernel of caution kept her silent.

"A fine sight you are, out in the cold by yourself. No man to protect you?"

She turned to walk back toward the house, but they were suddenly in front of her.

"Let me pass," she said, clasping her hands beneath her cloak.

When they only laughed, she strode forward, expecting them to give way. They didn't. Instead, the largest of the three shoved her with both hands.

She staggered but didn't fall. Taking a few steps back, she measured the distance to the house. Could she make it to safety? If she screamed, would one of the drivers come to her aid?

These men wanted to hurt her, and no one had ever wanted to hurt her before.

"Let me pass," she said again.

Something struck her on the arm, the blow so unexpected she cried out. Before she could question why he'd thrown something at her, another man raised his arm. The rock struck her shoulder. She turned and began to run but she wasn't quick enough. Another rock hit her back. A fourth clipped the back of her calf.

Panic gushed from her pores.

She was being pelted by rocks, each the size of her palm. The blood roared in her ears.

Suddenly one of the men was at her side, then in front of her.

She screamed in pain when a rock struck the base of her throat, only to be pummeled by more rocks. She fell to her knees, hands over her head. The world rained rocks. Then she was on the ground, her knees drawn up.

Someone shouted, but the words were meaningless. She heard running footsteps and cowered.

Fear was a sharp sword, cutting a hole through her courage, bloodying her mind. She couldn't think, could only feel, the pain demanding its share of her attention.

She huddled on the cold ground, waiting to be struck again, her breath coming in harsh gasps, blood bathing the side of her face. She was trembling, her teeth almost chattering. She was colder than she could ever remember being, as if the blood chilled in her veins. Even her heartbeat slowed, seeming to come from a deeper place.

A shape towered over her, making her jerk in fear.

"Mairi?" He knelt beside her. A voice as soft as velvet murmured in her ear. "They're gone."

What was Harrison doing here?

She couldn't bite back her moan when he helped her stand, and when he raised her in his arms she should have protested.

She was not going to whimper.

"I'm here," he said. "It's all right."

She wasn't sure it would ever be right again.

"You?" she asked as he strode into the darkness with her in his arms. "Was it you?"

"Was I stoning you? Daft woman."

He opened a carriage door, laying her on the seat. A second later he reached up and opened the window.

"Get us out of here," he said to the driver.

She needed to tell him about James. She had her own carriage. She couldn't be seen in his carriage, not unescorted. People would talk. All thoughts that flitted through her mind and back out again, pushed away by pain.

"Where were you struck?" he asked, kneeling beside her.

He unbuttoned her cloak, pulling it apart.

When he began to open the placket of her bodice, she made an effort to grab his wrist. "No."

"Yes," he said, easily twisting her hand free. "I need to know whether or not to take you to a physician. You might have been badly injured."

"Home. Take me home."

He didn't answer, merely continued to open her bodice. A second later he was pulling down the top of her shift.

She dug her nails into her palms, closed her eyes and pretended she was home in bed, a delusion that lasted until he prodded the area below her throat. Clamping her mouth shut so she wouldn't sob, she turned her head away and prayed he'd soon finish.

"You're going to have a bad bruise," he said, placing his fingers gently over the area. "But it will take a physician to determine if anything was broken. Where else were you struck?"

She kept her eyes closed.

"So fierce," he murmured.

She wasn't feeling very fierce. She was feeling wounded and incredibly frail.

Slowly, she did an inventory of her injuries. Her chest hurt so much it was painful to breathe. Her cheek was bleeding and one of the rocks had struck her back.

"My chest," she said. "My back."

"Your face," he said gently, touching her jaw with the edge of his thumb.

"Home," she said. "I need to go home."

"Be still," he said.

She really should have protested. She should have told him that she was more than capable of caring for herself. That was hardly the truth, though, was it?

For now she kept her eyes closed and let him be the strong one.

"I feel so guilty for not accompanying Mairi," Fenella said, snuggling closer to Allan. They sat in his bed in the room that had once been Macrath's.

"Is it that you feel guilty?" he asked. "Or guilty because you don't feel guilty?"

She pressed her forehead against his arm and smiled.

"Probably the latter," she said. "But I knew tonight I would be free to see you."

"I've been there for six months, Fenella," he said. "I've proved myself reliable and a good worker."

A somber note in his voice warned her.

She sat up, glancing at him in the candlelight.

"Yes, you have. Mairi talks fondly of you."

Allan had purchased the candles that sat on the grate before the brazier and the small table beside the bed. She'd taken the curtains from the room that used to be hers and hung them on the small window. The room smelled of the verbena potpourri she'd brought from the house. Together, they'd transformed the small room into a haven.

She told him of the years she lived across the hall in the room she'd shared with Mairi and Ceana. How they'd all despaired of making ends meet, but refused to talk about their fear. They'd been inventive in their cooking, the kitchen they once shared now used by Allan to make his meals.

They hadn't purchased any new garments for years, making do with each other's clothes, turning hems, collars, and cuffs. For all their penury, the years had been pleasant ones, surrounded by people she loved and who loved her.

"You can survive most things as long as you have love," she had once told Allan. His answer had been to kiss her, and all thoughts had flown from her head.

Life had changed in the last few years. They no longer had to worry about their survival. Mairi's focus had never wavered, however, remaining on the *Gazette*.

And hers? Until meeting Allan, she'd been content to keep house for Mairi and Robert, concentrate on the duties of each day, offer comfort and coziness in exchange for what she truly wanted: her own home and family.

She wanted a man to love, someone with whom she could share her life. A man who would sleep close to her at night and hold her in his arms.

She didn't want to change the world. She didn't want to redress any wrongs. Nor did she want to inspire anyone else unless that inspiration came from the way she lived her life.

Nor was she altogether sure that she wanted to vote.

Mairi was always so certain of what she wanted. So much so that sometimes that determination was difficult to be around and to match. When Fenella wasn't as certain, other people thought her submissive and retiring. She knew she wasn't at all. She just didn't have as much passion as Mairi.

Until she met Allan.

"I will talk to her tomorrow," she said. She leaned toward him, putting her arms around him. "She needs to know."

He nodded.

"In the meantime, I'll write Macrath," he said. "That's the proper thing to do."

"What will you tell him?" she asked, feeling her heartbeat escalate.

Allan pressed a kiss to her temple. "That I love you without measure. That my greatest wish would be to have you as my wife. That I'll provide for you all the days of your life."

She raised her hand and placed her palm on his cheek. The candlelight flickered on his face, adding shadows and hollows.

"Then write to him, my dearest Allan," she said. "Tell the world."

"Not the world," he said. "Only Mairi."

She smiled and promised, then sealed her word with a kiss.

Logan had mastered his emotions for a good many years. Being in politics meant he needed to maintain a discipline and a distance from issues. He couldn't react to things simply because they tugged at his heart or engendered his pity. He needed to look at the bigger picture. What was better for Edinburgh? What was better for Scotland?

Right at the moment, however, he didn't give a flying

farthing for Scotland, Edinburgh, his district, or any of the myriad sad cases brought to him daily.

Someone had hurt Mairi.

He was almost disappointed that the men had dispersed at his arrival. They weren't the same ones Mrs. MacPherson's men had cornered in the back of the ballroom.

Mairi moaned as the carriage hit a rough patch of pavement. He remained kneeling at her side, protective of her in a way he hadn't expected to be. He didn't want to take her back to her home until he was certain she wasn't badly injured. Knowing her recalcitrance, she'd refuse to see a physician on her own.

She was still trembling, and he feared she was in shock. He removed his own coat and tucked it around her. Once in his house, he'd place her in front of a roaring fire, give her hot tea, and try to find some way to reduce her pain.

He'd never felt as helpless as he did now.

Slowly, she turned her head and opened her eyes, her blue eyes cloudy with pink as if she wept inside.

"Why?"

Why was he tending her? Why was he taking her to his house? Why had she been stoned?

He opted for the latter and answered with the truth, softened a bit due to her pain.

"It's happened at more than one SLNA gathering. A bunch of men feel threatened and they hurt those who can't fight back."

She nodded, closed her eyes and turned away, her fist still resting on her chest. He wanted to reassure her, so he did, with promises that sounded trite and as insubstantial as air.

"I'll have the authorities look into it," he said. "We'll find those responsible."

She nodded again.

"I'll make sure of it."

A soft smile curved her lips.

Did she think his promise ludicrous? He found the idea of being ridiculous to her distasteful.

"How is the pain?"

She made a humming sound but didn't speak otherwise.

Now was not the time for recriminations, but did she think her position as editor of the *Edinburgh Gazette* made her somehow impervious to danger? Why wasn't she taking care to keep herself out of harm's way? Hadn't anyone at the SLNA told her about the women who'd been attacked? If not, they were as guilty as the men who assaulted her.

He kept watching her, holding her hand in wordless comfort. Her face was pale, and she bit at her bottom lip as if to keep any sounds from escaping.

Was her pride so unflinching? God forbid she allow anyone to see her in a weak moment.

If she weren't in so much pain, he would have told her what he thought about her going out without a companion. Where was her driver? Why hadn't she waited for her carriage under the portico like the other guests? Why was she standing in the shadows away from other people?

What would've happened if he hadn't been looking for her? That was the question that disturbed him the most. If he hadn't arrived, she might have incurred worse injuries than those she'd already suffered.

Or they might have killed her.

That thought stripped the breath from him.

How much longer until they arrived home? Less time than he feared and longer than he wanted. His driver stopped in the back. A good decision, since it would shield him from prying eyes when he carried Mairi inside.

Before he did so, he gave his driver instructions to Dr.

Thorburn's home. The hour was late, but Mark wouldn't hesitate to come in an emergency.

He lifted Mairi gently, his mouth tightening when she moaned. Any other woman would have screamed in pain. She grabbed his jacket, keeping her eyes shut, biting her lips.

Slowly, he walked from the alley into the back of the house, where Mrs. Landers met him.

"Dear heavens," she said. "What is it, Mr. Harrison?"

"She's been injured," he said.

"It's the young lady, isn't it?"

Of course she remembered Mairi from the night she ate dinner with him.

Who could forget Mairi Sinclair?

"I need some hot water," he said, then changed his mind. "No, a brick, warmed in the stove, then wrapped in flannel."

Mrs. Landers nodded, turning and giving directions to a maid as he walked down the hall and into the parlor.

Here, he entertained those individuals who weren't comfortable calling on him at his offices. More than one political favor had been granted or asked for in this room. More than one hint had been made that he would be an ideal candidate to run for Parliament next year.

He'd pictured his wife sitting here in the parlor, occupied with her needlework, as he practiced his speeches. She'd critique him as to delivery, perhaps question him on his points, and act as helpmeet and advisor. To her, he would confess his uncertainties when they came and his irritations when they filled him.

He'd imagined them talking and laughing in this room, enjoying morning tea or evening libations.

He'd never thought that Mairi Sinclair would occupy the settee or that any other vision would pale beneath his concern for her.

He laid her gently on the cushions, moved another pillow to place under her head. Before anyone else arrived, he knelt at her side, pulled her bodice apart, frowning down at the rapidly darkening skin at the base of her throat.

Was the injury to her back as fierce looking? Or her arms? The wound had stopped bleeding, but dried blood coated her cheek. He raised her slightly, so that her uninjured cheek rested against his shoulder. Propping a pillow behind her back, he tried to make her as comfortable as he could, taking the time to refasten her bodice.

In a matter of moments Mrs. Landers appeared with the wrapped brick, handing it to him. He carefully placed it against Mairi's chest. The heat should ease some of the pain until Dr. Thorburn arrived.

"Begging your pardon, Mr. Harrison, but how was the lady injured?"

He hesitated, wondering what to tell his housekeeper. Finally, the decision was made for him by habit. He never told a lie when the truth would suffice.

"Miss Sinclair gave a speech tonight, Mrs. Landers, on why women should be given the vote."

Mrs. Landers didn't comment, which surprised him. He glanced up at the older woman, to find that she was frowning down at Mairi.

"She was attacked by some men who thought she shouldn't be speaking about such things."

"Ignorant bastards."

Startled, he glanced at his housekeeper again.

She met his gaze. "Begging your pardon for the language, Mr. Harrison, but don't you feel the same? Why shouldn't women be able to vote? We can do everything else. We cook for you. We clean for you. We wiped your faces when you were drooling as babies, and other places, too. We brought you into the world. You'd have us pretend we can't do all that and more?"

"Are you a suffragette, Mrs. Landers?"

"I'm a woman with a mind, Mr. Harrison."

"Another for the cause," Mairi said faintly, looking up at his housekeeper.

He squeezed her hand, praying for Dr. Thorburn's swift arrival. One more male in the household—even temporarily—would not be amiss. Especially since he had the sudden and surprising thought that he was outnumbered by strong women.

Chapter 13

The parlor was such a pleasant place that Mairi was curious if Mrs. Landers had decorated it or if someone in Logan's family performed the task. She doubted the Lord Provost had anything to do with selecting the fabrics or colors.

Instead of the overbearing crimson that seemed so in vogue, the parlor walls were covered with pale blue wallpaper with a tiny white and brown stripe. The two matching settees were upholstered in a blue to match the wallpaper, and the chairs upholstered in brown velvet.

A gold framed portrait over the mantel was of a severe looking older man with mutton chop whiskers and a sober mien. He wasn't smiling, but the look in his eyes made her think he wished to. Was the painting of Logan's father or another relative?

The tables were all heavily carved mahogany, and each of them shone with the care they'd been given. A faint smell of lemon permeated the room. Was it because of the furniture polish or had Mrs. Landers put lemon peel in the potpourri?

The ferns in the windows seemed a feminine touch as well, along with the small porcelain statues on the mantel and pierced urns on the hearth.

"You were very lucky, Miss Sinclair," Dr. Thorburn said. "I've seen strong blows stop the heart. You could have collapsed and died right there."

Mairi sat on one of the settees, buttoning her bodice with trembling fingers. Shouldn't there be a rule that a doctor could not converse with a patient until she was completely dressed?

"As you can see, I'm very much alive," she said.

"And hurting a great deal, if I don't miss my guess. Take that medicine," he said, pointing at the bottle he'd placed on the table. "It might give you bad dreams, but it will take away the pain."

She nodded and smiled politely, acting the part of the good patient. The minute he left the room, she was going to drop his bottle of laudanum in the rubbish. She'd taken it once before and it had given her more than bad dreams. She'd been sick for a week.

"The blow to your back is not as severe as the one to your chest, but you'll have a great deal of bruising there, as well as on your face. I don't like the look of your left arm, either. You weren't hit anywhere else?"

She shook her head, carefully sitting back against a pillow. She would have protested the examination by a strange physician—one handsome as the devil and a friend of Logan's—had she been feeling better.

"You were speaking at a rally?"

"Hardly that," she said. "A meeting at Mrs. MacPherson's home."

"An SLNA meeting," he said.

She nodded.

"You would be better served expounding on the necessity of women's health. Corsets will shorten your life."

The idea of not wearing her corset was so novel that she didn't comment. She made a mental note to discuss corsets at a later date with Dr. Thorburn. Perhaps it was something her readers needed to know.

"Have you been friends with Mr. Harrison long?" she asked.

"Ever since he opened his bookstore," he said, beginning to pack up instruments in his black bag. "I used to frequent it often."

"His bookstore?"

He glanced at her curiously. "Didn't you know? He owns Blackwell's."

She knew Blackwell's and frequented one of its three locations often. Blackwell's? Logan Harrison owned Blackwell's?

What kind of reporter was she that she hadn't known that?

She felt like she'd been asleep until meeting Logan. How had she missed him or his reputation in Edinburgh? Now she discovered he was a successful man of business like her brother. Perhaps that's what made Harrison feel so familiar.

Nothing more than that.

To her surprise, Dr. Thorburn didn't ask any questions about her relationship with the Lord Provost. She'd expected them and had already prepared an answer. He had simply been attending the lecture at which she spoke and had rescued her.

Dr. Thorburn pointed to the green bottle again.

"I urge you to take the medication, Miss Sinclair. Otherwise, you're going to be suffering."

She nodded and smiled, emulating a perfectly conformable woman.

"Do I have your promise?"

She didn't want to lie to the doctor. She hoped he wouldn't push the matter.

"Thank you for helping me," she said. "I would like to talk with you about corsets at a later date."

He only shook his head, gave her a stern look, and left the room.

A moment later she sat on the edge of the settee, or tried to, before she collapsed back against the pillow.

She felt as if a carriage had run over her. Her leg ached. She closed her eyes and tried to marshal her will. Even though she was in pain, she needed to get home.

Logan would send her home in his carriage, of course, the act of a considerate man. He'd been exceptionally kind earlier. He'd been tender, and that had not only been disconcerting, but dangerous. The man had charm along with a wicked smile. Plus, he was decidedly attractive in a way that was bothersome. She really didn't want to spend any time thinking about him.

Nor did she want to spend hours in recollection of his every expression and comment.

She had much more important tasks to occupy her time.

Fenella would be worrying. James would be frantic. What would he be thinking when he was unable to find her? What would Robert say?

No, she simply couldn't wait any longer. She had to get home.

First, she had to sit up. That's all.

She turned her head and eyed the bottle of laudanum.

Closing her eyes, she thought about it for a moment. Perhaps if she just took a spoonful of it. Or less than that. It would take away the pain while not being enough to make her sick.

"You're very lucky, the doctor says," Logan said, entering the room carrying a tray.

She glanced over the contents as he placed it on the table in front of her. A teapot, cups, and three plates of treats sat there. The chocolate cake looked delicious, as did the biscuits and scones.

"Why are you offering me sweets?" she asked. "Are you trying to bribe me to do something?"

"Doctor's orders," he said, grinning. "You are to have something sweet and some strong tea. That will keep you from becoming sick after taking the medicine."

"My stomach is fine," she said. "It's everything else that hurts."

"And you're not going to take the laudanum," he said.

She slitted her eyes at him. "How did you know that?"

"Because I feel the same way. Hate the stuff."

He sat in the chair opposite her. To her surprise, he poured her a cup of tea and brought it to her.

Since he was being such an impeccable host, she had no other choice but to take it from him.

"I don't like how it makes me feel," she said. "All woozy and not in control of my functions."

"Is it necessary for you to feel in control at all times?"

She considered the question for a moment, then nodded. "Yes, I believe it is."

"Another thing we have in common," he said.

"You've been very kind," she said, eyeing him over her cup. Every movement hurt, even the small lift of the cup to her lips.

The tea was hideous, an odd green color that had a very strange taste, something she normally wouldn't have drunk. Because she was a guest, however unwilling, in his house, and because he had served it to her, she sipped at it and tried not to make a face.

"I can't help but wonder why you are being so solicitous," she said.

"Am I not allowed to be a kind person, Miss Sinclair?"

"You are excessively kind," she said, willing to concede that point. From the beginning, Logan Harrison had a reputation for being a considerate man, one who genuinely cared for his constituency.

Plus, he was a man of his word.

Her sources had practically genuflected to her when she'd seen them. Even Mr. Donovan had unbent enough to invite her into the back room of his tavern, an invitation he'd never previously offered. She accepted, of course, anything but stand in the freezing wind.

She was probably a loathsome person to be annoyed that the rumors of Harrison's sainthood were true.

Did she want him to be mean and unkind?

"You've been very kind," she said again. "I would like to go home, however. My household is no doubt concerned, and my driver has been looking for me, I'm certain."

"After Dr. Thorburn arrived, I sent my driver to find yours," he said. "I've no doubt your household is concerned, but they know where you are."

Ice settled in her stomach.

She closed her eyes, forced herself to take as deep a breath as she could manage before opening her eyes again.

"What on earth did you tell him?"

"Your reputation is intact, Miss Sinclair. I explained that you had been delayed, that you and several other members of the SLNA were meeting with me at my home."

"A lie?"

"I have found that it's advantageous to twist the truth in certain circumstances. This is one of them."

"Now that is something I would expect a politician to say."

"Are politicians the only ones who ever lie?"

She gave that question some thought, even though the answer was immediate. "Of course not. It's just that your lies are so much more important. They involve greater numbers of people. Plans and organizations and money."

"I have never lied in the conduct of my job, Mairi. I will

guarantee you that. I have, however, lied in a social setting. Unfortunately, more often than I would prefer. But when a woman is preening for compliments, what am I to do? Tell her that instead of looking delightful in that new dress, the color doesn't flatter her? Have you never done the same?"

She really didn't like the way he turned questions back on her all the time. She always felt as if she were drowning conversationally around him, when she'd always been able to tread water with anyone. Why was Logan Harrison so different?

He stood and walked to the sideboard, turning his back to her. When he returned to the chair, he was holding a glass filled with an amber liquid.

"I've tasted whiskey before."

"I'm sure you have," he said, sipping.

"You're not going to ask me if I wish any whiskey?"

"I am not."

"Why, because it would be unladylike? A woman isn't supposed to drink whiskey?"

His frown was really quite extraordinary and very off-putting. If she hadn't witnessed it before, she might have been intimidated by it.

"Given the events of the evening, I could understand how you might feel that way, but not all men are like those who hurt you. Not everything a man says or does is designed to subjugate a woman."

She took another sip of her tea, wishing it didn't taste quite so green.

"You're right," she said.

One of his brows arched upward, as did the corner of his mouth. She wondered if they were connected somehow.

"I'm capable of identifying my own mistakes, Lord Provost."

She took another sip of the tea. Although she didn't like

the taste of whiskey, she thought she might prefer it to this concoction.

She yawned, covering her mouth with her hand. To her surprise, Harrison stood, placing his glass on the table beside the chair. In the next instant he was raising her legs up on the settee and covering them with a throw. She really should have protested but it felt so good to be warm that she didn't say a word.

"I didn't do anything," she said. "Why do they hate me so much?"

"You scare them," he said, surprising her by raising her to sit up a little.

"I'm not scary."

"But you are," he said, sitting at one end of the settee and arranging her so that she leaned against him. One arm was around her, holding her in place, almost like an embrace.

She really should protest.

"You're a sincere woman with a message. Granted, you need to work on your speaking skills. But what you had to say was scary enough to them."

"What do you mean, my speaking skills?"

"I've had a lot of experience speaking in public. I'd be happy to coach you."

"Why are you being so nice to me? I don't like you."

"Ach," he said, humor lacing his words. "That's the first lie you've told tonight, Mairi."

"I don't care how nice you are to me," she said. "I'm not reaching under your kilt again."

"There you go again, another lie."

She really didn't know what to say to him. Silence might be the best recourse. Besides, he was so warm and comfortable that she could easily fall asleep. But she knew she couldn't fall asleep in the Lord Provost's arms. Not in his house.

What a foolish time to weep.

He drew her back to him, gently cradling her. Her tears felt like acid on her cheeks but they wouldn't stop. Embarrassed, she tried to turn away, but he wouldn't let her.

"I'm not the crying kind," she said.

"I know."

"I never cry. You'll think I'm a fool."

"Never. I know you better than that."

"You don't know me at all."

"Oh, but I do," he said. "I know you feel as if you have a calling. That you want to enlighten the populace, and inform them of what goes on around them. I know you care for the paper like ink is in your blood. I know you're impatient and want perfection from yourself and others you deal with. I know you have a temper and it sometimes slips its reins. I know that life has not been particularly easy, but you don't whine. Nor do you demand that anyone owes you anything beyond fairness."

Tears brined her throat and made it raw. She wanted to lay her head against his chest, breathe in the scent of him and forget the rest. He made her sound much more noble than she was.

"I have to leave," she said.

"I know."

She started to place the cup and saucer back on the tray, but the act of moving in a certain way made her gasp. He took the cup from her and put it on the table.

She looked up to find him peering down at her, his green eyes direct and focused.

"You put something in my tea," she said, the effort of speaking almost beyond her.

"I did," he said. "I'll not lie to you, Mairi. It will ease your headache."

"How do you know I have a headache?"

"Your eyes," he said, placing his palm gently on her forehead.

She liked the touch of his fingers through her hair and closed her eyes to savor the sensation. A moment later she was drifting off to sleep.

Minutes, or hours, later she awoke to feel his arms around her.

"Shh," he said, when she would have roused. "Go back to sleep, Mairi. I'll care for you."

What a lovely promise. How wonderful to feel so cosseted.

That thought alone should have sent her scrambling for home.

Fenella made it back to the house with only seconds to spare, noting the strange carriage as Allan kissed her good-bye.

She entered the house but didn't immediately close the door. She stood in the darkness at the bottom of the steps, her hand on the latch.

The carriage didn't move away. Instead, the door opened and a man emerged. A second later she gasped, because she recognized the Lord Provost in the light of the gas lamp.

She also knew the woman in his arms.

Fenella flew out the door and down the walk.

"What happened?" she asked, reaching Mairi's side. She reached out and touched Mairi's arm, her cousin's wince making her jerk her hand back.

"She was injured," the Lord Provost said.

"I'm fine," Mairi said faintly.

"You're hardly fine," Fenella said.

"Right now she needs to get comfortable."

She nodded, racing ahead of Harrison, opening the door and leading the way to the parlor.

"Oh, Mairi," she said, shocked at the sight of her cousin.

The Lord Provost placed Mairi on the settee and would have spoken, but Mairi shook her head, a gesture that, from her tight-lipped look, caused her pain.

Fenella sank to her knees in front of the settee.

The hair at Mairi's temple was matted and one of the white cuffs of her dress was spotted with blood. She suspected the other dark stains were blood as well but it was difficult to tell with the brown fabric.

"Someone took offense to my words," Mairi said slowly.

"They struck you?"

The provost told the rest of the story, leaving Fenella suffused by guilt. If she'd been there, if she'd attended the lecture, Mairi wouldn't have been alone and attacked. Instead, she'd been with Allan, luxuriating over her own downfall.

What kind of terrible person was she?

The provost still stood beside the settee. He looked rather like a dragon, if a dragon had been transformed to a human dressed in a black greatcoat. His eyes were green, so intent they looked like they could shoot fire.

She wondered if the men who'd attacked Mairi knew that they'd acquired an enemy.

He pulled a bottle out of his pocket and handed it to her.

"It's laudanum. She won't want to take it but a little will dull the edge of the pain."

She nodded, wondering how he knew Mairi so well. Even as a girl she hated to admit she didn't feel well.

"She's not to exert herself. Or climb stairs," he added. "She's to rest."

He turned that dragon stare on Mairi, who calmly met it with her own look. Fenella had the distinct impression that the two of them had acquired the ability to converse without speaking. Right at the moment, they were fussing at each other.

"I'll send word to Allan," Fenella said. She'd tell him about the events of this evening. Their own plans would have to wait until Mairi was well.

"I will take a day or two, that's all," Mairi said, her gaze not veering from the provost.

He only shook his head, gave Fenella a few more instructions, and glanced at Mairi once more. Again, that unspoken communication, one that made Fenella feel as if she were invisible and most certainly unnoticed.

Standing, she walked the provost to the door, thanking him for his kindness.

"I'll call on her in a few days," he said, looking back at Mairi. "Don't let her do too much."

She bit back her smile. She wasn't capable of stopping Mairi from doing anything she wished. Her cousin was a wild wind against which she was only a sapling.

But she nodded, closed the door after him, and set about caring for Mairi.

Chapter 14

"Would you like another cup of tea, Mairi?" Fenella asked, tucking in the throw around Mairi's feet.

"I'm sloshing in tea," she said.

She really should have remained in her room, but she was tired of her own company. The parlor had seemed a likely place to sit and read.

Fenella, however, was surfeiting her with kindness.

"What about some scones? Cook has just taken them from the stove."

"Perhaps in a bit," Mairi said.

"I could build up the fire."

Mairi wrapped her arms around her waist, forced a smile to her face, and looked up at her cousin.

"I'm fine, Fenella, truly. Go do what you would do if I weren't home."

Being home during the day was such a unique event that they both had difficulty adjusting to it over the last week.

The men who'd attacked her had never been found, but she discovered them every night in her dreams. Her imagination had furnished them with shadowed faces, taloned fingers, and tall, hunched bodies. They screamed obscenities at her as they threw boulders, and she collapsed bleeding and in agony at their feet.

Each night she awoke sweaty and trembling. For the first time in her life she was afraid, and it enraged her. She wanted to be able to direct her anger toward a person or a tangible object. There was no one, except for the men who'd escaped detection. They could be anyone, even one of her sources. She could know them, do business with them, even talk to them from day to day.

She hated that idea. She couldn't look at the world with constant suspicion.

For days after the attack she'd hurt all over. Raising her arms over her head had been excruciating. So, too, turning in a certain way. Gradually, however, her pain had eased. As soon as the bruising faded she'd return to the paper and forget about the whole horrible night.

She doubted if she'd be able to forget Logan's tenderness, but memories like that were more troublesome than helpful.

So much so that she was almost grateful when Robert opened the sliding door, interrupting her thoughts. Her gratitude lasted only long enough for her to see the sheaf of papers in his hand.

He stared at her and she sighed, knowing they were about to have another one of his conversations. At least Robert didn't treat her as if she were fragile.

"Are the ether supplies depleted? Must you buy the most expensive ink, Mairi? And the parts for the press. Are they entirely necessary?"

"Yes," she said. "If the press is to run. It's old, Robert, and it needs to be repaired often. If we could buy another press we wouldn't have to spend so much in repairs."

His eyes narrowed at that suggestion.

"You spend money like it's air," he said, a comment she heard often enough she could repeat it along with him.

If he could give her a suggestion that was worthwhile, she wouldn't hate their encounters so much. But the newsprint she used was common enough, neither the worst grade nor the best. Ether was required to clean the type. Otherwise, the ink accumulated until the print was smudged. The ink was perhaps a little pricier than most, but it worked better with the old press. The parts were necessary, although she would admit they'd had to replace too many gears lately.

"Your father was a frugal man."

She'd heard that statement before, too.

"You could rent out parts of the building."

That was a new suggestion. She eyed him with interest.

"And charge your pressman rent for his room."

She frowned at Robert. "His room is part of his salary."

"You pay him too much."

Her elderly cousin was lamentably out of touch with the cost of wages lately. He was still budgeting for thirty years ago.

"The income of the paper has suffered in the last week."

"That's because I haven't been working," she said. "As soon as I go back to reporting the news and writing broadsides, our income will increase."

When he finally left the room, she sighed in relief. When Fenella appeared again, intent on hovering over her, she stood, the motion making her bite back the gasp a pain.

Fenella was instantly at her side.

She needed to get away. She needed to get out. She needed, most of all, to be alone.

"I'm going to the garden."

"It's much too cold," Fenella said. "There's snow on the ground."

"I won't be gone long," she said, gathering up the blankets on the settee. "Just a few minutes of fresh air."

"Shall I come with you?" Fenella asked.

"No," Mairi said. "I'll be fine. Truly. Just a few minutes of fresh air." And solitude.

"Are you very certain?"

"Very certain."

She escaped from the parlor before Fenella could say another word. Or worse, insist on accompanying her.

Fenella stared after Mairi.

Nothing she did seemed to make any difference. Mairi was still too quiet, too reserved, in a way she'd never been.

If Fenella had been set upon and attacked, she knew she would no doubt have acted the same. Still, it wasn't like Mairi to be so reclusive.

She had remained at home for nearly a week, refusing to see anyone, even Allan. She'd relayed what information needed to be shared through Fenella. One of the women from the SLNA called on her, and Mairi asked Fenella to tell the woman she was not at home.

"I'm not up to seeing anyone, Fenella," she said in a curiously flat voice.

"I'm sure she's here to console you, Mairi. Don't you think that's worth a few moments of your time?"

Mairi hadn't answered, only stared out the window of her bedroom.

At least she'd come down to the parlor in the last few days. That was a step in the right direction.

She turned as Abigail appeared at the door.

"There's a man here, miss," the maid said, bobbing a curtsy. "I think it's the Lord Provost. He wants to see Miss Sinclair."

A few minutes later Fenella smiled at their visitor, inviting him into the parlor.

When Harrison entered, he dwarfed the room. She did wish he would sit and stop looking so fierce.

She would have taken his hat but he wasn't wearing one. Before she could offer to hang up his coat, he spoke.

"I've come to see Miss Sinclair," he said, his smile lighting his face.

What a handsome man he was. The thought pinched, feeling disloyal to Allan. Shouldn't she consider him the most handsome man in the world?

"She isn't seeing anyone," she said, wondering if she should offer him tea or coffee.

How on earth did she entertain the Lord Provost?

"I must insist," he said, his tone cooling.

If it were up to her, she'd take him to Mairi right this moment.

"She's refusing to see anyone," she said. "Even her pressman."

One of his eyebrows ascended upward.

"How is she?"

"She's healing," she said. "Today is better than yesterday and so much better than last week."

"But she isn't seeing anyone."

"No."

"Is she taking the laudanum?"

She suspected, before she shook her head, that he knew her answer.

"Is she sleeping?"

Now that was a question she hadn't expected.

"I don't think she is," she said, surprising herself by answering him. Was she violating Mairi's privacy in doing so? She hoped not, but something was wrong and maybe Harrison could help her cousin.

"I want to see her."

She didn't know how to convince Mairi. She eyed him. Just how stubborn was the Lord Provost?

"Mairi's in the garden," she said. "But she would never forgive me if I took you there myself."

He nodded. "I understand."

Thankfully, it seemed as if he did. She watched as he turned and left, grateful that he was as stubborn as her cousin.

Of course the latch to the garden gate was frozen solid, defying Logan's attempts to open it.

The garden wall, however, didn't look that high. He followed it midway to the front of the house. Here the bushes weren't as deep. He wedged himself next to the wall, found a foothold, and lifted himself to the top.

Thankfully, the Sinclairs hadn't reinforced their wall with spikes or wrought iron. He threw his leg over, feeling the rough surface tear at his trousers. If his constituents could see him now they'd label him a loon. Worse, a man not in complete control of his faculties.

Had he been quite sane since meeting Mairi Sinclair?

He eyed the expanse of lawn beneath him. The garden was larger than he thought, and his quarry nowhere in sight. Had he climbed the wall at the same time she decided to return to the warmth of the house?

The flower beds looked as if they had been piled high with mulch before the snow obscured them. He was surprised at the number of plantings as well as the careful paths between what must be a spectacular garden in the spring and summer. He was startled to see a large fountain not far away, but blessedly not beneath him. He was willing to climb a garden wall but not break his fool neck.

He was losing his mind.

He made the jump with only a slight jar to his pride as he caught his coat on an ice-encrusted rosebush.

He could just imagine the headlines from her paper: Lord Provost Offends Citizen's Privacy. She'd probably write a poem about him crawling over the wall like a spider with clawed hands, bulging eyes, and a mouth filled with rotting teeth.

If that didn't frighten the children of Edinburgh, nothing would.

"There is, I take it, a reason you're invading my garden."

He turned to see her sitting there in a puddle of fading light. She was bundled against the chill with a cloak and two striped blankets but still looked miserable, like one of the children in Old Town huddled against a wall.

Her face was drawn and too pale, making the blue and yellow bruise on her cheek even more shocking.

He remained in place only because of years of training at standing on stages, behind podiums, answering questions and being shouted down. Otherwise, he would have gone to her, picked her up and sat down again with her on his lap. Only then would he have gathered her in his arms.

Did she understand that there were times when she needed to be protected and perhaps pampered a little, too?

"It's too cold for you to be sitting in the garden," he said.

"Thank you for the information. Is that why you jumped over the wall? I don't need a guardian. Too many other people are more than willing to put themselves in that role."

He bit back his smile. She was testy. That was a good sign. At least she wasn't quiet and hurting.

"You're still not well," he said.

"I haven't been sick. I was injured, not bedridden. What are you doing in my garden?"

"Coming to see you."

"I don't want to see you."

"That's what I heard."

"But you jumped over my wall and now you're here despite my wishes."

He hadn't exactly jumped, but he didn't tell her that. He only smiled. Even bruised and battered, she was indefatigable.

"You're an impossible man," she said, narrowing her eyes at him. "Are you that way with everyone or is it only me?"

He regarded her for a moment and then gave her the truth.

"I think it's mostly you," he said. "Something about you makes me want to get nose-to-nose with you. I enjoy arguing with you although I can't say it's a normal preference. In fact, I don't feel that way around most women. With any other woman."

"How fortunate I am," she said.

"Why don't you want to see me?"

"Vanity," she said so quickly he knew it was a lie. She lined up her excuses like toy soldiers, always at the ready, self-protection at its finest. "I'm not looking my best."

"You don't give a flying farthing about your appearance," he said, marching up to her.

Her eyes widened as he bent down and placed both hands on either arm of her chair.

He wanted to smile when he should have offered comfort, but he never acted the way he should around her.

Up close, her bruising was worse. He wanted to soothe her in some way, take away the pink in her eyes that spoke of too little sleep.

"I could shout and someone would come running," she said. "They'd escort you out of my garden."

"I'll be leaving soon in any case. I came to see how you

were faring. Once you tell me, I'll take myself off. Are you still in pain?"

"I'm not going to tell you. You'll drug me again."

"Which means you are. Where?"

She didn't answer but she also didn't protest when he repositioned the scarf closer around her throat. She was going to take a chill if she sat out here much longer.

He should be about his work. He had the voluminous paperwork of the Edinburgh and Leith Sewerage Act to study. The river was in bad condition, worse than it had been before the passing of the act. He'd been petitioned to bring the matter before the Government Commissioners on the Pollution of Rivers who were due to visit Edinburgh this week.

He had a full schedule, subject to last minute appearances by constituents, royal appointees, or commissions whose sole mission in life was to clog council meetings with their own personal projects.

Still, he wasn't leaving until he got his answers.

"Tell me how you feel."

When she remained stubbornly silent, he smiled.

"You haven't been producing any broadsides lately," he said. "My reputation hasn't been assailed once. I came to reassure myself that you are well. I'm staying until you tell me."

Her eyes snapped at him. "Do you invade people's homes to check on each of the citizens of Edinburgh? How fortunate we are to have such a caring Lord Provost."

"Thank you," he said, studying the darkness beneath her eyes. "Why haven't you been sleeping? Is it pain? Or have you been having nightmares?"

"How do you know?"

"It's what's normal in this case. Especially for a woman like you."

She scowled at him. "What does that mean?"

"You're used to coping with situations on your own, handling matters. When you can't, it must be frustrating. Frustration has to be expressed in some way, such as being unable to sleep and being rude."

"Rude?"

"Argumentative," he said with a smile. "Belligerent. Antagonistic. Are you that way with everyone or is it just me?"

She frowned at him again but didn't answer, choosing, instead, to stare pointedly at the house. Was she summoning someone to her rescue with the power of her thoughts? If anyone could do it, it would be Mairi Sinclair.

Why did she feel so singular, unique among his acquaintances? Why did he anticipate seeing her, when it would've been so much wiser to ignore her presence, even to pretending she didn't live in the same city?

She argued like any councilman he knew, cogently and yet with a challenge. A tilt of her head, a glimmer of smile, her blue eyes lighting on him and then away—they all fascinated him.

He wanted to frame her face in his hands to study it in more detail, find the reason he was bewitched. Although her mouth was lush and inviting, he'd never been enthralled because of a mouth before. Her deep blue eyes were beautiful, her lashes thick and long. Not once in his life had he ever been so intrigued by a woman's eyes that he acted the idiot. Her figure, hinted at by the very proper clothing she wore, was enough to fuel his dreams, but not sufficient to render him foolish. Her mind was quick, her words sharp and biting or sweet and kind.

He realized what it was, finally. It was the whole of her,

the totality of Mairi Sinclair that ensnared him from the first.

Her smile made him want to laugh.

He had the strangest thought that she was freedom. She was a breath of wind in a stuffy room, a Highland chill after a heated summer. She was everything that shocked him, startled him, and was alien to him.

Being with her made him feel alive and more himself than at any other time.

He leaned closer until their faces were only inches apart.

"Why don't you want to see me, Mairi?"

Why didn't she want to see him?

Because he weakened her. Because seeing him standing there, hatless, his cheeks bronzed by the cold, his eyes twinkling at her, was just too much.

He made her want to cry.

He made her want to lean into him and let him protect her again.

She wanted to kiss him, and wasn't that senseless?

"Does it matter now? You've burst in where you weren't wanted."

"You could offer me tea and hospitality," he said.

"I have no intention of doing that."

He only nodded, still too close. "I didn't think you would."

Why should that remark annoy her so?

How, for that matter, had he known she hadn't been sleeping well?

"Why are you sitting out here in the cold?"

"I wanted a little solitude," she said. A remark that made the corners of his mouth turn up.

What an impossibly handsome man he was.

"I wish you'd leave," she said. "You can use the gate this time."

To her disappointment, he straightened. He smiled at her, showing white, even teeth, the grin of a predator. She had the sudden thought that she was his prey. Shouldn't that have made her call out for James or Robert? Instead, she remained silent.

"I'll leave if you go inside," he said. "Besides, I want to see you walk."

"You want to see me walk?"

He nodded, the smile slipping from his face. "Your leg was injured. How is your chest?"

She looked at the gray and unremarkable winter sky, wishing a lightning bolt would strike him. Very well, not a direct strike, but perhaps something close enough that he would be startled or would flee.

No, Logan Harrison would never run away from anything.

"I know where I was injured," she said. "I'm fine. I'm healing well. I'm cared for with the greatest concern. I'm absolutely sotted with kindness."

"It's loathsome, isn't it?"

To her surprise he was smiling at her again. The expression should not be able to lighten her mood but it strangely did.

She nodded. "I do wish people would go away," she said. "Fenella is the kindest person. She's too kind. She's forever hovering. Are my pillows plump enough? Do I want something to eat, drink, read?"

"Is it difficult to be grateful?" he asked.

She sighed. "I'm forever apologizing. I shouldn't have spoken at the meeting. I shouldn't have put myself in danger. The only reason I haven't had to apologize for

being at your house is because no one knows about that."
She frowned at him. "You won't say anything, will you?"

He shook his head.

She lay her head back against the chair. "Good."

"Will you go inside now?"

"Yes, since my nose is numb. I was going before you
suggested it."

He only grinned.

"Did you really come just to see how I was?"

She shouldn't have asked the question. She knew that
the minute it left her mouth, but he didn't ridicule her
for it.

Instead, he extended both of his hands. She unwrapped
her arms from beneath the blankets and placed her fingers on his palms, feeling his heat against the chill of her
skin.

"I am going to be fine," she said, allowing him to pull
her up. "Truly."

"I'm glad," he said.

He was standing much too close.

"I would hate for my nemesis to be ailing in any way."

"Am I your nemesis?" she asked faintly.

"I've never thought so, but I believe that was your intent."

"You're an obstinate man," she said. "Much too used to
getting your own way."

"Not with you, though."

"No, not with me."

Then why was she standing there, close enough to feel
his breath on her forehead, close enough to see the pulse
pounding in his neck?

Reaching up, she gathered his muffler, ensured his
throat was covered, the mirror of his earlier gesture.

The man changed her. He made the air feel charged like
just before a thunderstorm.

When she turned and walked away, leaving the blankets in a puddle on the lawn chair, she was conscious of his gaze on her. She refused to limp. But the ache in her chest wasn't caused by her assailants. No, that was something else entirely, and all because of Logan Harrison.

Chapter 15

"**I** must admit, Mr. McElwee, that I've been unable to get your comments out of my mind."

Frank McElwee nodded and took a sip of his whiskey.

The Lord Provost's office consisted of two rooms. Attached to Logan's office was a small parlor where he sometimes entertained guests. More than one concession had been made in this room, more than one arrangement for the betterment of both parties.

The two men sat in the two chairs arranged in front of the fireplace. Each man held a tumbler of whiskey and both stared at the fire as if the answer to their mutual problem was to be found in the flames.

"I was very surprised when you asked me to come and speak with you this afternoon."

Logan sat back. "I've a personal reason, Mr. McElwee."

The other man glanced at him. "That's how it normally starts, sir. A woman in your life will challenge all you hold dear. She'll demand that you open your mind and your eyes. Look at her life. When you do," he said, smiling into his tumbler, "it's amazing what you see."

"What do you see, Mr. McElwee?"

"A life wasted, sir."

Startled, Logan looked at his visitor.

"Let us consider that a woman is equal to a man in intelligence and heart." McElwee held up a hand to forestall objections Logan had no intention of making. "Then, you quell that spirit and muzzle that intelligence. It's a form of slavery, sir. The deliberate restraint of another human being."

He'd never considered the matter in that light. "And you think your march through Edinburgh will help cure that?"

"Not one iota, Mr. Harrison. Abolition did not happen in a day or a year. It was a painstaking process of illuminating the situation, gaining supporters and advocates, moving one step at a time."

Logan nodded. He'd done the same with his campaign against reformatory dormitories. The law stated that juvenile offenders should be incarcerated no matter the infraction. To his mind, jailing children would lead to a life of crime, but it had taken a great deal of effort to convince his fellow councilmen that the law was too harsh.

"Perhaps you could allow yourself to be convinced on the side of women."

"Mr. McElwee, is there not some other way they can achieve their aims without being strident?"

McElwee sat his tumbler down on the table between them. He studied Logan for a long moment. "For years, women have been polite. They have petitioned. They have suggested. At no time did they demand to march or even raise their voice. Why should they not now make some type of noise?"

He realized he didn't have an answer.

"Can you not support them in their quest? All they want, sir, is to be treated with the same dignity as a man. It seems not too much to ask."

McElwee leaned forward.

"I've asked someone who's very influential in Edinburgh to join us, Provost. With your permission, of course. I didn't wish to invite her without your approval. She's waiting in the carriage. Shall I bring her here?"

"Please do," he said. "I'm open to discussion on the matter."

He stood, walked to the window, wishing he were home. He'd be sitting in front of a fire, contemplating his life, thoughts that were troubling at best.

Mairi Sinclair would be at the forefront.

She'd bewitched him. Whatever spell she'd chanted, whatever potion she'd given him, somehow Mairi Sinclair had played the witch and enchanted him.

He'd never before been so fascinated with a woman. She was contrary, opinionated, fierce, and determined. Probably the closest to his own personality than anyone he'd ever met.

Around her, his thoughts were rash and improvident. He wanted to be reckless. With her, he felt free.

He missed her. His schedule had been brutal in the last week but he thought of her often. How was she faring? He'd sent her a note but she hadn't written back. He would call on her tomorrow, and if she didn't agree to see him he'd simply climb over the garden wall again.

If she hid in her room, he'd find which window was hers and toss pebbles at the panes.

He'd act the idiot so she would have to see him, if for no other reason than to chastise him for his behavior.

How the hell did he court someone who'd bewitched him?

"Lord Provost," Mr. McElwee said from behind him. "I'd like you to meet Miss Mairi Sinclair."

When Mr. McElwee asked her to accompany him to the council offices, Mairi considered the matter for all of five minutes.

Now, standing in the doorway, she knew it wasn't to get a look at the provost's offices or meet his secretary. She couldn't care less about the man sniffling behind her or the luxurious appointments of the large room or this smaller parlor.

No, the reason she was here was because of him. The man standing at the window, the one walking toward her with his eyes bright and his lips hinting at a smile.

It wasn't fear she felt in his presence but anticipation.

"Miss Sinclair and I are acquainted," he said, coming to stand in front of her. "Thomas will take your cloak." He held out his hands as if to strip it from her himself.

Mr. McElwee was looking at her curiously. Did he wonder why she hadn't mentioned that she knew the provost? Or was she betraying something by her expression?

Her cheeks felt warm but that could easily be the blaze of the fire after the cold of the afternoon.

The fact her heart was racing so furiously, however, was not due to the weather.

He was dressed in severe black again, the white of his shirt attesting to the skills of his laundress. At least he wasn't attired in his kilt, although she didn't see how she could ever forget that sight.

She sat on one of the two chairs in front of the fire, watching as he carried a straight-back chair in from the other room. She hadn't expected him to do something like that himself. A moment later he introduced her to his secretary, another gesture she hadn't anticipated.

Thomas Finly didn't seem pleased to meet her. He nodded, looked down his long nose at her, then vanished as quickly as he could, leaving behind a palpable chill.

Had the Lord Provost told his secretary something about her? Was that the reason for the man's obvious disapproval?

She wasn't given much time to consider the matter because Logan closed the door to his office, returning to where she and Mr. McElwee sat. She was having difficulty reconciling the official Lord Provost to the man who had climbed her garden wall then so solicitously wrapped a blanket around her and held her when she was in pain.

They seemed to be two different men. Or perhaps the pose of Lord Provost was only surface deep. Could the kind and considerate man be the true Logan Harrison? Or was it just the opposite?

"You didn't tell me you knew the Lord Provost, Miss Sinclair," Mr. McElwee said, disapproval lacing his tone.

"It is not an acquaintance of long standing, sir," Logan said. "But I'm more than happy to meet with Miss Sinclair again. As you said, she is a well-respected woman in Edinburgh. A quite accomplished one, too."

She felt a rush of warmth from his words.

"I'm sorry we have no tea, Miss Sinclair."

Was he remembering that night in his house when she told him she'd sampled whiskey?

There was nothing to be gained, however, by trying to be shocking now, especially in front of Mr. McElwee. Besides, Logan had already seen her at her worst. Perhaps it was time for him to see a better side of her.

"I would like to add my words to those of Mr. McElwee," she said, folding her hands one atop the other. "I hope you consider our proposal to march through Edinburgh. It will bring some attention to our cause."

"I have heard of women being attacked because of your cause," Logan said.

Thankfully, he didn't go into detail or mention her by name. Mr. McElwee was aware of the incident but he didn't know of Logan's involvement.

"More attention might bring about more danger," he added.

"Has any just cause been without risk, Lord Provost?" she asked. "Any time you change something that has been in place for a great many years, there are people who are frightened of change, who want things to remain the same."

"By people you mean men," he said.

"By people I mean men." She glanced at Mr. McElwee. "Most men do not want change. Some men, those more intelligent, see the reason for it.

"Scottish women have a reason to be dissatisfied with the current law," she went on. "They are citizens of Edinburgh, Mr. Harrison. But they are not given the same privileges as women in England. Why is it, for example, that English women can vote yet Scottish women cannot?"

"I didn't know you had an interest in politics, Miss Sinclair."

She warmed at the look in his eyes, a reminder of their earlier conversation.

"The Municipal Franchise Act," she said. "Women who head households in England can vote in local elections. It doesn't apply to Scottish women. Why is that?"

"Because it is an English law, Miss Sinclair."

Under the silky accent were shards of glass.

"Why haven't you proposed a Scottish law? Is it because you do not care about the plight of Scottish women?"

To her delight, she could tell she'd flummoxed him.

Mr. McElwee's frown kept her from saying more. Evidently, she was to fawn a bit more and argue less.

Very well, she could fawn a little. She smiled brightly at Logan then deliberately batted her eyelashes at him.

He only stared at her. She wondered what words trembled on his lips.

They were constrained by the presence of the earnest Mr. McElwee, who was glancing between the two of them as if they were a puzzle he needed to piece together.

For the rest of the meeting, Logan kept his attention on Mr. McElwee, only glancing at her from time to time. Whenever he did, his gaze seemed to scorch her. She couldn't help recall what it felt like to be held in his arms.

How foolish she was being. The inhabitants of Edinburgh were correct in calling their Lord Provost a genuinely kind and considerate human being. He had their welfare at heart. Everything he'd done for her was simply a natural extension of his character.

He would have treated any other woman the same.

Finally, the meeting was done. Logan agreed to consider the matter and promised to consult with other councilmen.

"It's a fair hearing we're asking for, sir, that's all," Mr. McElwee said.

"You'll get it," Logan said.

They stood and said their farewells. At the door, Logan turned to Mr. McElwee and said, "Would you mind if I spoke with Miss Sinclair alone for a moment? I have a message from a mutual friend to give her."

Mr. McElwee nodded, making his way into the other room.

Before she could understand what he was doing, Logan pulled her behind the half-closed door.

"What mutual friend?" she whispered.

"Are you well?" he asked. "Your bruises have faded, but the other injuries?"

Her face warmed.

"I'm fine."

"Did you get my note?"

"Yes," she softly said.

"You didn't answer."

"No." What could she have possibly said? *I held your note in my hands for an hour. I held it, telling myself you'd touched it. Here's where your fingers had rested.*

How foolish she was around him.

"Did you miss me, Mairi? I missed you."

That had her widening her eyes in surprise.

"Did you think I wouldn't admit it?" he said. "I told you I'd never lie to you."

She would have said something scathing to him in reply, but nothing she thought would have been the truth.

I didn't miss you at all. Oh, she had, in so many ways.

I thought it delightful not to have to speak to you. How many other men were so, well, challenging?

I didn't think of you once. Probably the most egregious lie of them all. He'd been at the front of her mind every day.

Silence, therefore, was a better recourse.

"I've been very busy," he said, taking another step toward her. "Otherwise, perhaps I would have invented a reason to call on you."

"Lord Provost business and all that," she said, stepping back prudently.

One more step toward her.

She retreated.

They danced without touching, a step back, one forward.

She narrowed her eyes at him.

He smiled at her.

She was finally in the corner without room to move.

Reaching out, he pushed a tendril of hair away from her cheek.

"You've no scar. Good."

"You really shouldn't talk about my scars," she said.

"Too personal?"

She nodded.

"I've seen your shift."

"You really shouldn't talk about that, either," she said, grateful for the surge of irritation she felt. That was all it was, of course, the reason her body felt on fire. Even her lips were hot.

"What about the other places? Any scarring there?"

She almost said, God help her, the words that trembled on her lips. She almost said, *Why don't you see for yourself?*

The man tempted her to idiocy.

She wasn't herself around him.

He leaned close to her, so close she pulled back.

"You can't kiss me here," she said, panicked. "Mr. McElwee's on the other side of the door."

He chuckled. "Why, Miss Sinclair, you shock me. Why would you think I'm about to kiss you?"

He was staring at her mouth. Now he was stroking his finger across her bottom lip as if priming her for his touch.

"Do you fear a kiss or anticipate one, Miss Sinclair?"

Both, but that was something she most definitely wouldn't say. She hadn't lost her mind to that degree.

"I've got to leave," she said, glancing in the direction of his office.

He stepped back, allowing her to escape. She could only wonder as she made her way to Mr. McElwee's side what would have happened had the man not been there.

A quick glance in Logan's direction made her think he was considering that question, too.

Chapter 16

Mairi felt like she was sinking into the ground as she walked. Each step was more difficult than the last, as if her feet weighed a hundred pounds. Her head was bent, her eyes intent on the darkened path from the street to the door. She'd asked James to drop her off in front of the house because she didn't have the energy to walk through the garden.

In one hand, she held her proper bonnet. She should have left it in the carriage, but Fenella would ask about it and she'd have to retrieve it. A trip to the carriage house seemed impossible when she was so tired she could have dropped to the ground where she stood.

Her crusade to become involved with the SLNA had taken all her time for the last two weeks, not to mention money she hadn't expected to expend. Because she was the editor of the *Edinburgh Gazette,* the SLNA thought she would be more than happy to print anything they wished in the way of pamphlets and announcements. Free, of course. Not only was the expense becoming burdensome, but the time required to typeset all of the materials and print them meant she was working even longer hours.

If the paper were making enough money, she would

have hired another pressman. But it wasn't. Nor was it going to as long as she was giving away so much work.

She'd received a letter from one of the principals of the SLNA in which the woman had been compassionate about her injuries while counseling her that the path would be a difficult one. *People will revile you,* she stated, *but you must prevail at all costs. The more women who speak the truth, the faster we will awaken the populace to justice.*

But was being injured a criterion? If so, she might have to reassess her participation in the SLNA.

She wanted to be the editor of the *Gazette* without having to hide behind her brother. She wanted to be able to go places and do things without being limited because she was a woman. She wanted to be able to choose her own elected officials.

But the cost might be higher than what she'd originally thought.

She begged off giving any more speeches. She didn't know if she had the courage to stand on a stage and wait to be heckled and jeered again. Nor was she entirely certain that she was brave enough to attend a meeting. She'd accompanied Mr. McElwee to the council offices one additional time, to call on a councilman he thought might be influential in their cause. To her disappointment, she hadn't seen Logan. Nor had he contacted her in all this time.

Twice, she thought she saw him in a carriage in front of the paper, but he hadn't stopped, nor had he turned his head and acknowledged her.

Was she pining for the man? How utterly ridiculous.

The house felt deserted even though there was a lamp lit in the foyer for her. Although it was full dark, it wasn't that late. The quiet was absolute, however, as if the house inhaled every extraneous noise.

December would soon be upon them, a month that always felt like a tunnel of darkness to her. Only a faint flicker of light at the end promised spring, her favorite season. Spring was the time of hope, of renewal, something she almost desperately craved at the moment.

She called out for Fenella. When her cousin didn't answer, she removed her cloak, left it and her bonnet in the foyer, and walked to the kitchen in the back of the house. A cozy room, it was twice that tonight, with the stove warming the space and the lamps casting a pleasant yellow tinge over the cupboards and floor.

Three of the maids, still in their serviceable blue dresses and aprons, were sitting around the rectangular kitchen table, all of them intent on a paper Robert held in his hands. At her appearance, he folded the sheet into a square, clasping his hands atop it.

"Where is Fenella?" she asked, curious about what he didn't want her to see.

"In her room," Robert said. "She has another headache."

Robert was often testy. She'd learned to ignore it unless she was irritated herself. Tonight was going to be a challenge to keep her mouth shut.

"I've laid out a place setting in the dining room, miss," Abigail said. "I'll bring your dinner to you now if you wish. Or would you rather have a tray in your room?"

Robert wasn't looking at her. Instead, his head was bent and he was staring down at his clasped hands.

"I'll eat in a little while," she told Abigail. "What is it you don't want me to see?" she asked, sitting at the end of the table.

Hannah and Sarah stared down at the table just like Robert. Since Abigail was the only one who looked at her, she addressed her question to the maid.

"What is it?"

Abigail looked to Robert, who only sighed heavily.

"Is it bad news? Has something happened to Macrath?" She held her breath as Robert turned to look at her, his bloodhound eyes sadder than normal.

Her heart clenched, and even as she readied herself to hear the worst news, she wondered how she would be able to bear it. Macrath was her anchor. She and her brother didn't always agree, but she respected his judgment, his strength, and his character.

"It's not Macrath," Robert said, his voice thick with his accent. For some reason, he always sounded so much more Scottish than she. Was it because he hailed from Inverness?

"Virginia?" she asked. Had Macrath's wife fallen ill again? He shook his head.

"What is it, Robert?" she asked, a little calmer since it wasn't bad news about Macrath and Virginia.

"It's nothing," he said, but he glanced down at the paper.

She stretched out her hand and he sighed again, extending the paper to her slowly.

"It's not the first one, miss," Abigail said.

Robert's quelling look had no effect on Abigail.

The girl simply frowned back at him. "She needs to know, Mr. Robert. It's a letter, miss, left on the doorstep, and it's not the first one."

She opened the letter, conscious that everyone at the table was watching her.

She read quickly, scanning the words as she normally did, absorbing the meaning. Only after a moment did she begin to feel what it said, realizing that what she was reading was tantamount to a broadside. A vile broadside filled with such profanity that she skimmed over the words. She'd been called such things the night of the SLNA speech, but she'd rarely read the words.

One section more than the others stopped her. She looked at Robert, but his impassive gaze was impossible to decipher. None of the women said a word.

"This isn't the first one?"

"No, miss," Abigail said.

"How many?" To her dismay, her voice was quavering. She steadied herself, determined not to allow anyone to see how horrified she was.

Someone hated her.

"How many?"

Robert didn't answer, so she looked to Abigail.

"This is the second," the maid said. "I threw the first one away. Beg pardon, miss, but I thought it was rubbish and rubbish it is."

"You'll stop now."

She glanced at Robert, thinking he was talking to Abigail. Instead, he was looking straight at her.

"Stop what?"

"Trying to be a man," he said, slapping his hands flat on the table. "The newspaper's not a woman's job. Give it over to Allan."

In all these years, Robert had never once indicated his disapproval of her. Granted, he had grumbled at her expenses on a continual basis, but she'd put that down to his personality, not to his dislike of her work.

He'd never come out and said the words "not a woman's job."

The one place she expected support was at home. People could say what they would to her in public. They could come to the newspaper office and complain about the *Gazette*'s stand on this or that or about her reporting. When she entered the door of her home, she expected to be greeted with kindness and care.

She stood, taking the letter with her.

"I think I've changed my mind," she said to Abigail. "I believe I will have a tray in my room."

With that, she turned and left the kitchen, the taste of betrayal as sharp as acid on her tongue.

Fifteen minutes later she changed her mind, slipped from the house and made her way to the stables.

She knocked on James's door over the carriage bay, stepping back when he answered it only seconds later.

"I need you to take me somewhere."

"Now?"

She nodded, knowing he was going to fuss.

"To the Lord Provost's home."

"I'm not sure that's wise, Mairi."

"It probably isn't," she conceded. "But it's something I need to do. And you need to keep it to yourself. I don't want anyone to know about this."

He didn't answer her, the glitter of his eyes in the light of the gas lamp warning her well enough. James was not a man to challenge. Macrath would not have put him in her household if he was easily cowed.

When James still didn't speak, she placed her hand on his arm.

"Please," she said, the first time she'd asked a favor of him.

"I like Cook's tarts," he said. "The ones with the apples."

"I'll see that you have a dozen of them every day if that's what you want."

"Not a dozen," he said. "One or two saved back for me. Maybe with some clotted cream."

"You'll have it," she said, smiling.

Soon they were parked in front of the house. Darkness gave the Lord Provost's home an even more overpowering air. Lights in the windows looked like bright eyes, and the wide portico with its brass lanterns an open mouth.

The hour was too late to make a social call. However, she wasn't going to lose another night of sleep because of Logan Harrison.

Instead of his majordomo, Mrs. Landers answered the door, and the woman's shocked face was an indictment of Mairi's actions. She shouldn't be calling on an unmarried man at night, alone.

"Is he here?"

Mrs. Landers stared at her.

"Well, is he?"

She was being rude in addition to being shocking. She took a deep breath.

"I am sorry, Mrs. Landers. Is Mr. Harrison at home?"

The woman seemed to shake herself out of her daze.

"He is. Returned just a few minutes ago from chambers."

Was the woman going to make her ask? Evidently, she was, because Mrs. Landers didn't open the door any wider. Instead, she stood there, her hand on the latch, her lips so thinned that her cheeks looked like plump apples.

"I would like to see him, Mrs. Landers," she said.

The woman looked as if she wanted to refuse.

Mairi slapped her hand flat against the door and pushed her way into Harrison's home.

Mrs. Landers followed her.

"He's an important man, Miss Sinclair. He's not to be disturbed."

Mairi made her way to the library. If he had retired for the night, she'd invade his bedroom.

Mrs. Landers stepped in front of her.

"You can't be bothering him."

"Does he overpay you, Mrs. Landers?" she asked. "Why

is everyone so eager to protect the man? Does he massage your feet at night? Has he hired your entire family?"

"That will be all, Mrs. Landers," Logan said from behind her.

Before Mairi had a chance to respond, he grabbed her arm, pulled her into his library, and slammed the door shut.

"A clue for your edification, Miss Sinclair," he said in a voice as chilled as the night, "the way to my housekeeper's heart is not to insult her."

She poked him in the chest with her finger. "You give them some kind of potion, don't you? I've heard about people hypnotizing other people. Is that what you do?"

He grabbed her finger. "What are you talking about?"

"Everyone I talk to adores you. They all have nice things to say about you. It isn't normal, Logan. You're an angel come to life. You frequent their establishments, you praise their businesses. You probably know the names of all their children."

"I'm the Lord Provost, Miss Sinclair. I'm expected to know my constituents."

She refrained from screaming only by a hair.

"You aren't wearing a bonnet again."

"You never wear a hat. But I doubt wearing something on my head will make all of Edinburgh love me."

He laughed. "All of Edinburgh doesn't love me, I can assure you. You should come to a council meeting one day and see that for yourself."

She made a mental note to do exactly that, dug into her reticule and produced the letter. She handed it to him.

"Tell me if you're responsible for this."

He took the letter from her and read it, his amusement vanishing.

"Do you actually think I'd use such language?" His

voice roughened. "Or direct those kind of comments to you?"

"What about that part?" she asked, pointing to the second paragraph. " 'A whore's behavior one would say. In dawn's light she crept away.' It's horrid poetry, by the way." She rolled her eyes when she realized she'd rhymed with the idiotic poem.

"While your broadside about me was a literary masterpiece," he said.

"It was better than this."

He threw the letter on the desk. "I didn't write it, and I'm more than a little annoyed that you would think so."

She didn't think she'd ever seen anyone as angry as he looked at the moment. His eyes positively boiled.

"You're the most infuriating, stubborn, ignorant woman I have ever known."

She reared back and glared at him. "I am not ignorant."

"Yes, you are," he said. "You're narrow-minded, fixated, prejudiced, and blind."

"I am not," she said, poking him in the chest with her finger.

He grabbed her finger and held it wrapped in his hand.

She made a fist of her left hand and punched him in the shoulder.

"What did you do before I came into your life?" he asked, releasing her finger.

When she frowned at him, he smiled.

"Who did you blame your problems on then? I am not the source of your troubles, Mairi, however much you would like to think so."

"Who else knew I left your house nearly at dawn?"

"Probably half a dozen people," he said. "No one from my house would have said a word. What about your own staff?"

"No one saw me," she said. No one she knew about or had seen. Only Fenella, and she wasn't responsible for the letter. She doubted Fenella even knew some of those words, let alone what they meant.

"It's a bunch of filth you would be better served by ignoring, Mairi."

"Would you ignore something like that?"

"Probably not, since I didn't ignore what you wrote about me. That, at least, was devoid of any profanity. Not to mention references to my anatomy."

"So you didn't write it?"

He shook his head.

"Nor tell your secretary anything about that night?" She suspected Thomas Finly did not like her. At least, his reception in Logan's office had been a chilly one.

"I did not," he said.

"Could Mrs. Landers have said anything?"

He studied her, eyes sharp as glass.

"Why are you so certain someone in my employ or my household did this, Mairi?"

His question stopped her cold.

She looked at the floor, her hands, anywhere but at him. The truth was there between them, and he knew it, too. His eyes softened when she finally glanced at him.

"Because I couldn't bear it if it was anyone I knew," she said softly. "It's so much easier to blame you."

"I didn't write it, Mairi, and I can vouch for the people in my employ. They didn't, either."

Could she say the same?

James had only asked about the SLNA meeting, how long it had gone on after they'd left Mrs. MacPherson's house. She'd looked at him blankly until remembering that Logan had told him she was with other members of the SLNA meeting with the provost.

Had James somehow known she was at Logan's house instead?

Would he have placed such a letter on their doorstep?

No, James would have simply informed Macrath of her actions.

Robert? He was too busy complaining about her expenses to fuss at her about anything else.

That left Allan, which was a horrible thought, one prompted by Robert's outburst. Give the *Gazette* up to Allan? She wouldn't give the *Gazette* to anyone, not even Macrath.

Yet Allan had ambition and talent. He'd come highly recommended and could have easily gotten a job at any printing company. That he agreed to work for her had been a blessing from the beginning. In addition, she liked him. She couldn't work so closely and for such long hours with someone without getting to know him.

"Or did you write it yourself as a reason to see me?" Logan asked.

She blinked at him, then pointed a finger at the letter on his desk. "That isn't an invention. I'm sorry you think so, Lord Provost. If I was to do something so foolish, it would be better written and without so many epithets."

"You called me Logan a moment ago."

"A moment ago you hadn't accused me of making up a reason to see you. Of all the idiotic ideas."

He bowed slightly, making no effort to wipe the smile from his face. "My apologies, Mairi."

"Miss Sinclair to you."

He took a step toward her until they were nearly nose-to-nose. Or they would have been if he hadn't been a head taller. He bent until they were eye-to-eye.

Why had she scampered to his house like an eager bunny? He was the wolf on his front door.

"I would hit you with my reticule, but you'd probably retaliate by writing something about how violent I am."

"I'm not the one who takes pen to paper when angry," he said. "And that's not how I would retaliate, Mairi."

"Oh?"

"I would do this," he said, leaning forward and placing his lips on hers.

Chapter 17

She couldn't breathe.

She'd been kissed before, but nothing like this. This was more than a kiss. It was as if she'd walked inside a bubble, one that was owned and dominated by Logan Harrison. This was an immersive experience, where her pulse raced and her heart pounded furiously.

She couldn't breathe, and of course she had to open her mouth beneath his and allow his tongue to cool her heated lips.

She gasped and he swallowed the sound, transforming it into a moan. Reaching up with both hands, she grabbed his shirt as if to keep him there. Or perhaps to keep herself upright because her knees were suddenly weak.

Her ears were buzzing. Her eyelids fluttered and caution wound through her with a faint but insistent voice.

Open your eyes. Don't succumb.

Why shouldn't she? Logan Harrison was retaliating, and what strength did she have against him?

Poor defenseless woman that she was.

Where had her reticule gone? Had she dropped it to the floor? No, there the string was, around her wrist. She should strike him with it. He would release her then.

He angled his head to deepen the kiss and her toes curled.

Oh, dear God. She was breathing his air and he was breathing hers. Their hearts seemed to beat in rapid tandem. She made another moan, deep in her throat, and he gently bit her bottom lip.

Her body was heating. Everything was warming. Delight shot through every limb, tingled her fingers and made her insides molten.

If he let her go right this minute, she would fall, she was certain of it.

"Are you ravishing me?" she asked faintly when he ended the kiss.

Swaying toward him, she curled her fingers into his shirt.

"If I am, it's a mutual ravishment," he said, his voice rough.

Was there such a thing? Was she capable of ravishing him?

"Shall I walk you to the door, Mairi? Send you home?"

She would have answered in the affirmative if he hadn't been placing little kisses along the line of her jaw, then her throat, his fingers stroking the back of her neck.

The world suddenly spun, but she wasn't dizzy. She was in his arms.

He really had to stop doing that.

As if he'd heard her thought, he laid her down. She was on the floor looking up at him.

Her eyes widened as Logan straddled her, taking her gasp of surprise as encouragement to continue unbuttoning her bodice.

Because of where he was sitting, her small hoop was being crushed, not to mention the damage to her petticoat and her silk skirt. She didn't have time to caution him about the state of her apparel when it was all too obvious he was trying to rid her of it.

"If you've any objections to being ravished, lass, now is the time to voice them."

She couldn't think of anything to say. A dozen rejoinders should've come to mind, but she just lay there looking up at him, more than a little bemused.

She should have screamed, if nothing else. Mrs. Landers would have come instantly to her aid.

"You're a woman of contradictions, Mairi Sinclair," he said, rearing back and looking at her. "Your lips are all full and wet, while your eyes are angry."

Her mouth had lost the ability to form words. Her brain had turned to oats. Only her hands knew what to do, and they reached up and gripped his arms. Not to push him away as much as keep him close.

He bent down, brushed a kiss over her lips, making her want more.

"I think your mind is forming a protest while your lips are urging me on." He kissed her again, a little deeper this time. "The only thing to do is to keep kissing you," he said. "That way, you won't be able to think."

She noted with a foggy thought that his voice sounded breathless. At least he was capable of forming words. She'd lost that ability at the first kiss, and it didn't look to be returning any time soon.

"Which is it, lass?" he asked.

The breath was still stripped from her, leaving excitement and mad laughter in its place.

She had no idea what he'd asked her. She needed a little time to consider this overwhelming reaction to his kiss, but when he would have drawn away, she gripped the back of his head and pulled him forward.

She was being seduced.

Oh, that was hardly the word, was it? Ravished was an apt description. Mutual ravishment might be more correct. Yet she suspected if she raised so much as her pinkie, he would have stopped. He would have gotten to his feet, left her lying there on his soft carpet wondering what had just happened.

Still kissing him, she pulled him to her, rubbing her hands from his shoulders to his hips, feeling the solid strength of him. The wool of his trousers was soft to the touch, covering hard muscle and bone.

She told herself to stop kissing the man, get off the floor, clutch her libido and her tattered dignity and back away. Her will, however, wasn't that strong.

When he finally broke off the kiss, her hand, independent of any wisdom or decorum, stroked over the curve of his buttock. She didn't look away. How could she, with those beautiful green eyes of his pinning her to the spot?

How she wished he was wearing his kilt.

"Do you have your holster on?" she asked.

His bark of laughter should have embarrassed her, but she only smiled at him.

"Well, what else would you call it?"

Instead of answering her, he kissed her again. As soon as his lips met hers, heat shot through her. He kissed like he smiled, with sincerity and purpose, charm and devastation. She loved kissing him, and that was the first sign of danger. When he slowly began to open her bodice, she let him, liking his touch and the soft strokes of his fingers over her skin.

He stopped long enough to pull the tail of his shirt from his trousers. He unfastened his cuffs and then removed his shirt, tossing it somewhere. In seconds, it seemed, he stood, ridding himself of the rest of his clothing.

The Lord Provost, undressed, was magnificent.

Kneeling, he placed his fists on his hips and regarded her.

She felt an absurd surge of delight at being confronted by this naked man. It was like she was two people: the wise Mairi, most often in place, and a new, wilder woman, daring and courageous, who appeared whenever he was near.

Wild Mairi laughed inside, her amusement as unfettered as a Highland wind.

He didn't move. Nor did he say another word, simply studied her in silence.

"It's a truss, and as you can see, I'm not wearing it."

He was long and hard and altogether impressive. She pressed the whole of her hand against him, and there was still more of him left uncovered.

She wasn't a virgin, but her one and only coupling with Calvin hadn't prepared her for this moment.

The firelight turned Logan's skin golden, bathed him in a faux dawn light, as if he were the first man, God's perfection.

His shoulders were broad and muscled to match the sinewy strength in his arms. His chest was sculpted in a fit of divine inspiration, so magnificent that he took her breath away.

She pressed her hand against the dusting of hair there, amazed that he flinched at her touch.

"Does being the Lord Provost require manual labor?" she asked. "You're quite fit for a politician."

"Have a great many politicians stripped bare in front of you?"

"You're my first politician," she said.

"But not your first lover."

She shook her head.

Did he expect her to apologize for that? Or even explain? If so, he was doomed to disappointment. She told herself that giving herself to Calvin was a sign of her love for him. Only later did she realize that she shared nothing with Calvin other than an appreciation for his form and face. His character hadn't been nearly as attractive.

Or perhaps she had come to that conclusion only after he rejected her, telling her that she wasn't feminine, didn't act like a woman should. Nor, according to Calvin, had his family approved of her.

No one looking at her now would approve of her.

But with Calvin she'd never been so wild and abandoned. She'd never wanted to laugh or be wicked.

Perhaps she would just pretend that this interlude, if that's what she could call it, was happening in a dream. She was not the woman who gripped Logan's bare shoulders with both hands and pulled him down for a kiss. She was certainly not the woman who opened her mouth to inhale his breath. Or who wiggled beneath his exploring hands as he nearly jerked her dress from her.

Her hoop went crashing into the bust of Aristotle in the corner. Her corset was draped across the top of the desk. One stocking was tossed too close to the fire, while the other went into the coal bin. She wasn't entirely certain where her shift went.

Neither of them seduced. Nor were they coy, charming, or gentle. They gripped and struggled, pushed, shoved, and wrestled with her clothing until, dear God, she was naked on the carpet in his office, the firelight and gas lamps revealing everything.

No secrets could possibly live in that bright pool of light.

She was losing her mind over this man.

She was not herself, so completely and fully not herself that she decided to embrace the strangeness of the moment and the experience. If she wasn't Mairi Sinclair, but a woman who'd heretofore hidden herself beneath layers of ambition and duty, then let her spring forth in all her glory, be Athena fully formed and garbed.

But Athena was the goddess of wisdom, never falling prey to passion.

Not once did Athena wish her breasts were smaller or perkier, or that her stomach was more taut. Or that she didn't have a scar on her knee from a fall as a child or a mark beneath her chin from the same tumble.

Yet from the way Logan was looking at her, he didn't seem to mind all her imperfections.

As far as his, there were none. He was, quite simply, perfect. He was everything any woman could want in a man.

Taking his hands, she pressed his palms to her breasts, wanting to be touched.

She placed her fingers around his cock, gently cradling it, feeling it quiver in her hands. She'd never known that a man's member could react so vibrantly from a touch.

"Why not? It's part of me," he answered when she said as much. "It's not a separate entity, like some men would have you believe. At the moment, I'm very much reacting to you."

"Are you?"

Her smile was no doubt laced with pride. Why shouldn't she? He trembled in her hands, and his eyes darkened as she stroked her thumbs down his length.

He frowned, tracing his fingers just below her throat.

"You're still bruised."

"It doesn't hurt," she said. Reaching up, she pressed her fingers against the furrow between his brows. "You're very intimidating when you're irritated, Lord Provost."

He lifted her until she sat up. Then he looked at her back, her arms, inspecting her.

"Are you certain this doesn't hurt?" he asked, flattening his hand against her chest.

She shook her head.

She didn't want him examining her. Instead, she wanted his fingers on her breasts. Or his mouth there.

"Or this?" he asked, stroking the bruise on her arm.

"No, Logan," she said.

She cupped his face with her hand. She, who dealt in words, was speechless. His green eyes sparkled with rage and the set look on his face was formed by anger. Not at her, but at the men who'd injured her.

A strange time to feel so protected, naked on the floor before his library fire.

She got to her knees, wrapping her arms around his neck, leaning into him.

"It's all right, Logan. Truly."

"I would not cause you pain, Mairi."

She closed her eyes. Where a moment ago she was adrift in pleasure so intense she felt as if she might faint, now her heart was filled with tenderness for this man.

"You couldn't," she said, sitting back on her heels. "Unless you dress and leave me. I imagine that would be painful enough to encourage me to write another broadside."

A corner of his mouth lifted in the beginnings of a smile. A Logan smile, full bore and accompanied by sparkling eyes.

"No last minute protestations? No screams for mercy?"

"Help me," she whispered, lying back and pulling him with her. "I'm being ravaged by a barbarian."

A golden bear who kissed the smile off her face, then lowered his head to her breasts, paying homage to each of them as if he'd never seen breasts before and was overwhelmed by the sight.

A month ago she'd been looking forward to a life of celibacy, and now she was being ravished.

She smiled.

She should castigate herself for being here, for welcoming him into her body, but she felt good instead of guilty. This felt right. His fingers and mouth placed her on the edge of bliss and his whisper nudged her over until she tumbled, laughing.

The second time they loved was sweeter, slower. His hands were no less talented and his mouth had learned her curves. His lips hesitated before touching her nipples, as if he knew how much she wanted to be suckled. He breathed against her throat, murmured her name at her temple, and drove her slowly mad.

Her hands clenched his shoulders, trailed from his waist to his hips to his buttocks, smoothing over his muscles in mute appreciation. She had thought him impressive clothed, but naked he was a work of art.

When she said as much, he laughed, flipping her over onto him as if she weighed no more than a feather.

"And I can see why you wear a leather harness," she said.

He laughed again, took her hand and placed it between them.

"Are you certain I'm not a disappointment?" he asked.

She shook her head, amused at his question. It was the first time he'd ever indicated that he was less than supremely confident. That it centered on his manhood surprised her, because it quite simply was magnificent.

She could have played with him all day, testing the limits of his resolve and his stamina. She wanted to stroke him from his testicles to the mushroom shaped tip, walking her fingers around him.

Even shocking him by bestowing a kiss there.

The hiss and pop of the dying fire were sweet accompaniments to her soft moans as she lifted herself over him, talented in this act in a way she'd not expected.

She lay over him, watching his shadowed face. No one else had eyes like his, so intent, so dangerous. She rose up and then lowered herself to him, daring him to stop her, to protest her domination. He smiled, the expression surging into the core of her just as she lowered her body. She filled herself with him, feeling both daring and afraid at the same time.

His face changed and he put his hands on her hips, gripping her tightly and pulling her to him.

"Mairi," he said. Just her name, but it was summons enough.

It simply felt right to keep her eyes on his as they pushed each other to bliss, only closing them when she was overcome by pleasure.

Then she was crying out, answering him with his name as he surged into her, filling all the empty spaces.

She collapsed onto his chest, her knees on either side of his body, her hot cheek pressed against his. Pressing her hand against his chest, she felt the pounding beat of his heart, a match for hers. He stroked her back, let his hand fall to cup her buttock.

She'd never felt anything like what she'd just experienced with him. Even more confusing, she'd never known that such passion existed.

Sinking down into his kiss and his arms, she slowly returned to herself with a feeling too much like regret.

Chapter 18

Mairi awoke sotted from sleep, fighting to surface as if it wanted to drag her back down to a land of dreams. She was rested, completely and totally for the first time in weeks. The feeling was so delicious that she stretched slowly, marveling at all the different sensations she was feeling.

Her fingers touched something warm and human, a masculine arm dusted with hair.

Her eyes flew open to meet his. Logan's hair was tousled, his morning beard giving him the appearance of a ruffian. No, a marauder with his own broadsword below the sheet.

She closed her eyes again.

How could a man who looked so uncivilized be the Lord Provost? For that matter, what was she doing in his bed?

"Good morning," he said, his voice rough and holding an undercurrent of humor.

She slowly made an inventory with spreading fingers. She seemed to be entirely covered by the sheet, even up to her shoulders.

Opening her eyes, she nodded at him. Words were simply impossible at this moment.

He smiled and the sun was here in this room. A feeling of such warmth raced through her that she couldn't help but smile back.

Good morning?

Her gaze flew to the windows. The dawn light slipped between the curtains, a clarion call that she was in dire straits indeed.

She closed her eyes again. This was not a dream. She could keep her eyes closed for a year but when she opened them she'd still be here, not in her own bedchamber.

How was she going to extricate herself from this situation? Not only did she have to leave Logan's bed, but she had to leave his house.

She opened her eyes again. He was still smiling at her.

"How did I get here?" she asked. The last thing she remembered was falling asleep on his chest.

"I carried you."

Her face felt hot. She closed her eyes again since it was easier to imagine his smile than actually see it.

"And my clothes?"

"They're here as well."

"My reputation is ruined," she said.

"Is it?"

"Are you always going to respond with a question to my question?"

"Do I do that?"

She slitted open one eye.

His grin made the morning seem even brighter.

"You know quite well my reputation is ruined."

"Are you going to announce on a broadside that you were in my bed all night? Unless you do, I don't see why your reputation would be in ruins."

"Because my driver's outside, and he's been outside all night. Surely someone saw him."

"Are you so famous that people would note your carriage and your driver immediately?"

She frowned at his smile.

"Very well," he said, "I'll phrase it in a statement. I doubt people would know the carriage was yours. Nor have I done anything, lately, to attract the attention of the press. Present company excluded, of course. But I can't see you putting anything in the newspaper about last night."

She closed her eyes. "If I did, your popularity would soar."

His laughter echoed through the room. She opened her eyes again.

"But only if women got the vote."

"Are we back to that again?" he asked, then chuckled. "This may be more difficult than I thought, phrasing everything as a statement. So, we're back to politics again."

She raised up on one elbow, taking care to drape herself modestly with the sheet. A bit of foolishness, since he'd seen, stroked, and kissed every inch of her body.

"Is it politics?" she asked, then waved her free hand in the air when he smiled at her. "I'm allowed to ask questions, especially when I'm curious about you, and the way you think."

"I'm not allowed the same curiosity?"

"Everybody knows what I think," she said. "Especially if you read the *Gazette*. You, on the other hand, are a very pleasant Sphinx. Inscrutable, unknowable."

There was that grin again.

Very well, she knew everything there was to know about him, or nearly so, after last night.

She should have been shy when he rolled with her until she was draped over his body, supporting herself with her arms on his chest. He arranged the sheet so it covered both of them.

"I would much rather talk about anything else," he said. "Such as how you scream when you find your satisfaction."

"I don't," she said, feeling warmth infuse her cheeks. Was she blushing?

"Yes, you do," he said, smiling. He touched the tip of her nose with one finger, then trailed it up to the corner of her eye and then the temple before tracing the curve of her ear. "A very ladylike scream. Perhaps a little yelp."

"Now I sound like a puppy."

"You called me a bear last night," he said.

"Is that an insult? You're very bearlike," she said.

"Am I?"

"And you snore," she said, rubbing her palms against his chest. She needed to rise, find her clothing and get dressed. Somehow, she had to find a way to face James and silence him about last night.

Perhaps she could hire a pastry cook to serve him. Or make the quarters over the stable a little more pleasant.

"You have the oddest expression on your face right now," he said. "Half embarrassment, half calculation."

She lowered her forehead to his chest to breathe against his skin.

She really didn't want to leave his bed or him. That was such a confusing thought that she tucked it away to examine later.

What should she say to him? Thank you?

"I have to leave," she said.

"Yes."

A simple assent and that was it. The interlude was done. Dawn had arrived and with it some measure of sanity.

One thing she'd discovered: she knew with certainty that he hadn't written those letters.

If Logan had an issue with her, he would come out and tell her straight to her face. Oh, he would be wearing a charming smile while he did so, but the words would be direct and to the point. There would be no prevarication or doubt about what he meant.

She looked at him, reached out her hand and cupped his cheek, wondering at the sudden tenderness she felt.

What they had done was wrong by society's rules, by moral laws that dictated how she, as a woman, would behave. She'd occasionally questioned why a man was not held to the same standards of virtue and chastity as a woman, but it had been a mental exercise. She'd never thought of gleefully disobeying everything she'd been brought up to believe because of pleasure.

Last night she was someone else, not the person she'd always known herself to be. That woman had been wild with desire, daring, and fierce. Her face warmed as she remembered things she'd done, words she'd spoken that now seemed so brazen.

The whole situation was shameless, and wishing herself gone was not enough. She had to rise from the bed, gather her clothes and dress.

She sat up, grabbed the sheet and, pulling it around herself, left the bed, surprised to find that all the scattered bits of her clothing had been carefully folded and placed on a chair.

Had he folded her knickers? The thought sent a tide of embarrassment sweeping through her. She'd much rather parade naked in front of him than contemplate him touching her undergarments, a thought that made no sense whatsoever.

She ducked behind the screen in the corner, thankful it was there, and arranged her garments, horrified to discover that her shift was nowhere in sight. She had no other choice but to announce that fact. Either that or leave her garments behind to be discovered by a curious maid. Or, God help her, Mrs. Landers.

Her face flamed.

"I seem to be missing an article of clothing," she said.

"Perhaps we left it in my library," he said, his voice muted. A door opened and closed, and she peered out from behind the screen to find him exiting his bathing chamber.

He was gloriously naked. He stood there with his hands on his hips, a sight to behold. She forced herself to look away.

"What are you missing?"

"Does it matter?" she asked, loath to actually speak the word aloud. It was one thing to have acted the harlot, quite another to be forced to describe her unmentionables. "Any lady's undergarments in your library will belong to me."

She heard movement. Hopefully, he was putting on his clothes. When she turned her head it was to find him standing there attired in a dressing gown and a smile.

"I'll go find your clothes, Mairi," he said, his eyes twinkling at her. He was close to laughing, just as she was close to hitting him with her fist.

When she heard the door close behind him, she darted into his bathing chamber, impressed with not only the size of the tub but the rest of the fixtures. The water was truly hot, and she hadn't heard a boiler clanking through the night as hers did at home.

Retreating behind the screen again, she pulled on her stockings and pantaloons. When she heard the door open, she steeled herself for his teasing, but he didn't say a word, merely draped her shift over the top of the screen.

She wanted to ask where it had been, but decided that curiosity, in this case, would only lead to more embarrassment.

As it was, her face would never revert to its normal color. She would forever have pink cheeks. Nor would she ever be able to look him in the eye again. Not when her shift had no doubt been draped over his desk.

What had gotten into her?

Logan.

She choked off her laughter. He had corrupted her. Until last night she'd been demure and utterly proper, or nearly so.

"Would you like breakfast?" he asked. "It's a little early," he added, "but my staff is used to my rising before dawn."

"Good grief, no," she said. "I want to leave before anyone else knows I'm here." It was bad enough she had to encounter James.

In a matter of minutes she was ready. Her hair was a mess, but she was decently dressed.

The sooner she left this house and got home, the better.

She emerged from behind the screen, thankful she'd left her bonnet in the carriage. She had nothing else but herself to worry about. Her reticule was placed on the chair and she grabbed it, desperate for something to say, anything to bridge the awkwardness. What was worse was that he didn't look the least uncomfortable standing there at the window dressed only in his blue silk robe.

What a sight he made, with his black hair tumbling over his forehead and his chin firm as he parted the curtains to stare down at the street. Everything about him was perfect, and she was so far from perfect that last night should have been an aberration.

Instead, it was a memory she would have for the rest of her life. How could she forget something as joyous and exuberant as making love with Logan Harrison?

"Good-bye," she said.

He turned his head, his smile gone, only the intent look in his eyes remaining.

"I'll walk you to the door, Mairi," he said, making her name something lovely and fluid on his lips, almost like a caress.

She wanted, suddenly, to kiss him. But if she did, that kiss might well lead to something else. How much wiser she'd be to simply leave.

Chapter 19

James was asleep inside the carriage.

The morning was frosty with curls of chilled fog winding around her legs. Last night had been cold, but James had remained at his post.

Her conscience scraped at her.

She hesitated before opening the door. What could she say in explanation? There was nothing more to be done than to face the situation as it was. As her father used to say, nothing ever came of trying to avoid a problem.

This was most definitely a problem.

She opened the carriage door, watching as James awoke with a suddenness that surprised her. One moment he was deeply asleep or feigning it well, and the next he was staring at her.

She entered the carriage, sitting opposite him.

"What do you want to forget about this?" she asked.

"To keep quiet? I don't think there's enough food in the world, Mairi."

She was afraid of that.

"You're going to write Macrath, aren't you?"

He remained silent. Perhaps that was better than a lie.

"Very well," she said. "Write my brother and tell him

anything you want. Tell him the truth. Everything I've done."

"It's my job, Miss Sinclair. I'm to let him know anything that affects your well-being."

She was not an infant. Nor a toddler who needed to be guided not to cross the street in front of a carriage. Yet her actions of the night before were hardly those of a mature, rational woman, were they?

Still, she was annoyed both at James for being so intent to fulfill his tasks and Macrath for assigning them to him. What would her brother have thought if she'd announced *he* needed a keeper?

James opened the door again, but before he could slip from the carriage, she reached out and placed her hand on his arm.

"I'm sorry," she said. "I was inconsiderate. You shouldn't have had to spend the night sleeping in the carriage."

She wasn't going to apologize for any of her other actions.

Besides, she wasn't truly sorry that she'd wholeheartedly participated in passion. How could she regret something she would recall for the rest of her life? Last night was a memory to tuck away like a precious letter in a beribboned box. She'd open it once in a while in the future, to recall when she felt desired, when she'd acted with abandon and little sense.

Surely everyone had a memory like that? She couldn't be the only foolish woman in existence. Or certainly not the only one in Logan Harrison's world.

He'd held her tenderly at the door, pressing a kiss to her forehead. He'd gently said her name but added nothing more. No promises, reassurances, or hints about the future.

She was most definitely not disappointed. He hadn't hinted at a continued relationship and she didn't want one.

Last night, as delightful a memory as it was, would stand as an instance of her impulsiveness. If she were to be taken seriously as a reporter and an editor, she would have to act in a manner that inspired confidence and approbation. She would not long for the Lord Provost. She would not be his momentary mistress. She would not be in thrall to him.

He was going to offer for one of his women and become a bridegroom.

To his credit, James didn't say another word, but he glanced at her as he left the carriage and mounted the driver's perch.

She didn't look back at Logan's house. If he was still in the doorway, she didn't want to know. She didn't want to see him again. Doing so wouldn't be wise, and she'd always tried to have a modicum of common sense.

None of which she'd demonstrated since meeting Logan. She'd acted like a fool from the very beginning.

Did every woman have a man like that in her life? One who would talk her into behavior she'd never otherwise condone? Did every woman know a man who only had to look at her in a certain way to warm her blood and send her heartbeat singing?

She fervently hoped she was not alone in her stupidity.

Her cheek and chin were tender where his night beard had abraded her skin. Her breasts felt full, and unexpected soreness in other places reminded her of an active night.

She couldn't be around him anymore. Whenever he was close and bent his head, she would think he was about to kiss her. She'd be instantly aflame, her lips parting, her toes curling in response before he ever touched her. Her palms would grow moist when he smiled, and other parts of her body, quiescent and obedient until now, would tingle in absolute and unfettered delight.

Was he right? Had she only used the letter as an excuse to see him again?

What a foolish woman she was if that was the case.

Yes, she would see Logan from time to time throughout Edinburgh. She might even talk to him again, face-to-face. When she did, she would be agreeable and as charming as she knew how to be. She would talk to him about the weather. Later, after he'd selected his bride, she'd congratulate him on his marriage. Still later, she might note that he was a father.

A man with Logan's ambition was no doubt going to rise far in the world. Of course she'd be sure to mention any future achievements. She could even feature him in a column in the paper. Or if he attained some greater rank, she would do a special edition to honor him.

All her life, she tried to think ahead, to take a cautious path, see the hurdles she needed to conquer. Around Logan Harrison emotion always got the better of her. Circumstances simply happened. She, who so prided herself on her intelligence, lost it in his presence.

There, the truth, as unpalatable as it was.

Nothing had been the same since the day she met him. He'd turned her life upside down. She'd acted the idiot around him. She'd found herself in impossible situations, doing insane things, making outlandish remarks.

It would be a relief to avoid him from this moment forward. She wasn't going to think about him or his soon-to-be wife.

She had no right to be jealous, and it served no purpose whatsoever to be sad.

His habit of rising at dawn was proving to be decidedly unhelpful.

Despite the early hour, his staff was already moving about. He could hear them beyond the baize-lined door. No doubt he'd already been seen dressed only in his robe, escorting Mairi to the front door.

He'd kissed her there, with the door open to the cold November morning. His breath had transformed into clouds. He'd wanted to utter improvident words that were no wiser on this morning than his actions had been the night before.

Don't go. Stay with me today. We'll sit together in the garden, wrapped up in our coats, watching as the leaves freeze on the trees and the gray morning gives way to a slate-colored afternoon. We'll talk and I'll tell you foolish thoughts that ricochet around my mind even now. How I was as a boy, my bookstores, what I want to do with my life. I'll learn of the paper, how it drives you, what you wish for your life as well.

But he didn't say anything. He remained silent, giving her a quick hug before releasing her. She walked away from him, stood at the side of her carriage for a moment before opening the door and entering.

Feeling a discordant tug on his emotions, he wanted to stop her, coax her back into his house, talk to her about a hundred different subjects. Ask her opinion about a dozen different items before the council. Instead, he turned, slowly mounted the stairs and went to his room.

There, he closed the door, leaning against it, telling himself it wasn't wise to walk across the room to the window, where he could see her one last time. Like a boy in the throes of his first love, he nonetheless did, placing his fingers against a pane of glass, willing her to turn and look up at him.

A last smile was all he wanted. Or her saying his name in that way of hers, as if she couldn't decide whether to be sarcastic or charming and the result was a mixture of both.

He wanted to hear her laughter again. Or that startled, abortive sound when her own body surprised her.

She'd been as swamped by passion as he, and the sheer surprise of it startled him.

What kind of situations was she going to put herself in, walking through the wynds and closes of Edinburgh? He wanted to caution her to be more careful, to know that daylight could be as dangerous as darkness.

Mairi Sinclair, however, was a force unto herself. She would say or do whatever she wished. She'd go wherever she wanted and there was nothing he could do about it.

He wanted to tether her to him in some fashion, but knew he couldn't. A sense of powerlessness fell over him like the fog that rose as her carriage pulled away. As if the wheels churned up a cloud and she simply disappeared into it.

Or maybe she'd never existed at all and his memories of the night before had been merely wishful thinking.

James didn't pull to the front of the house. Instead, he drove around to the stables in back, letting her out before pulling the carriage into one of the bays.

She left him, opening the gate to the garden. The shape of it was a square with a copse of trees plopped in the middle. Tall brick walls bordered the property on three sides, with the back of the house forming the fourth side of the square. At the rear of the garden was a wooden gate with a carved archway over the top, the design of Celtic letters spelling out a bit of whimsy: SEE THE BEAUTY IN ALL THINGS.

She picked up her skirts, walked the flagstone path along the mulched beds prepared for winter, past the fountain drained and filled with sand lest it crack in the cold.

In the summer, sunlight sparkled through the trees, teasing her to come and walk slowly through the garden, smelling all the various blossoms. Now, remnants of fog clung to the grass, being blown away by a wind that chilled her ears and neck.

Perhaps she should have engaged in some subterfuge, hidden herself in the shadows and crept into the house.

No doubt everyone in the household knew she had been gone all night, and if they didn't know now, James was certain to tell them. The maids would look at her and no doubt titter behind their hands. Fenella would be shocked. Robert would lecture her on her duties to the Sinclair name.

Very well, she'd brought disgrace on the family. Why weren't men judged in the same fashion as women? She doubted that anything would happen to Logan because of last night even if his staff had happened to see her. No one would consider him fallen. No one in his employ, not even Mrs. Landers, would look sideways at him.

She approached the kitchen door slowly, took a deep breath and opened it, expecting the whole household to be standing in the kitchen waiting for her.

To her great surprise, no one was there.

A kettle simmered on the stove, but the room was empty.

Had she been fortunate beyond belief?

The wonder of the night before wouldn't be ruined by recriminations. No one would fuss at her.

She didn't need lectures. She knew very well what she'd done. She'd acted the part of a loose woman. She'd been no better than a doxy. There, she'd excoriate herself in the absence of anyone else. She'd been loose. She'd not respected herself or her position as editor of the *Gazette*. She'd been tossed to the carpet and had not once screamed for help. The only screaming she'd done had been another type entirely.

Now, she needed to forget last night and get on with the business of living. Her real life, not the one she'd allowed to happen for a few hours.

Her steps, loud on the polished wood floor, sent caution hurtling through her. She stopped and unlaced her shoes and removed them, carrying them in one hand while the other held her bonnet.

She made her way to the back stairs without seeing another soul, only to look up to find Fenella standing at the top of the steps.

Her cousin stood there in her wrapper, her arms folded, her chin jutting out. Her hair was wrapped in strips of cloth, the only way Fenella could coax a little curl into her hair. The whites of her eyes were curiously gray, as if she hadn't slept all night.

Had she kept Fenella up all night with worry?

Shame raced through her, not simply for her actions of the night before but now, standing a few steps below Fenella and not wanting to go farther.

Taking a deep breath, she prepared herself to give her cousin an explanation.

Chapter 20

"**A**re you going to tell me where you were last night?" Fenella asked, her hazel eyes dark and flat like a stone.

"I was at the paper. We had a large order of brochures to print," she said.

"You're lying."

Surprise held her mute. She disliked lying to anyone, and lying to Fenella seemed doubly wrong. But to be called on it was even stranger.

Fenella had never once doubted her word.

"You weren't at the paper," her cousin said. "You weren't at the paper, because I was."

She stared up at Fenella, not understanding.

"Allan and I were there. In his room."

Every thought flew out of her mind. In the stillness, she stared at her cousin, a curious bubble of silence surrounding them.

"We wanted a place to be alone."

Should they be having this conversation so close to Robert's room?

Mairi walked down the hall, opened Fenella's door and waited until her cousin joined her. After Fenella entered, she closed the door softly, trying to marshal her thoughts.

"Are you saying that you and Allan . . ." She couldn't finish the sentence.

Had the world turned on its axis? Fenella, shy and quiet and unassuming, was as guilty as she of aberrant—and some might say abhorrent—behavior?

And with Allan, which made it only worse. She wasn't at all certain Allan was to be trusted.

"Yes," Fenella said. Twin splotches of color bloomed on her cheeks.

"Fenella, how can you do such a thing?"

"I find that a little incongruous, Mairi, since you're tip-toeing through the house holding your shoes. Where have you been?"

Fenella sat on the edge of her bed, one arm wrapped around a bed post, her gaze direct and unflinching.

Mairi looked away, inspecting Fenella's vanity. Sparkling bottles and pots sat on a lace doily. Not a speck of dust could be found. The lamps were pristine; the windows shone, as did the mirror. Her embroidered bed linens matched the immaculate antimacassars on the reading chair. Fenella's room was always neat, always smelled of roses, and was always a haven, at least until now.

"Allan asked me to marry him," her cousin said, further surprising her.

Her world was upside down. Nothing was making any sense.

"I love him, Mairi. You have to know that. I want your blessing but I'll marry him without it."

She abruptly sat on Fenella's reading chair.

"I know you're hurt. I know you thought I would always live here, but I want my own home, Mairi. My own family."

She could only blink at her cousin. "I'm not hurt," she said. "I just never thought about you leaving."

Fenella's smile was kind and strangely maternal, as if

she were Mairi's mother, accepting her daughter with all her sins and loving her regardless.

"That's because you don't really notice people, Mairi. You don't see them. It's only the paper for you."

"That's not true."

"Isn't it? You don't go anywhere unless it has something to do with the paper. You don't socialize. You don't entertain. Everything is centered around the *Gazette*."

Since she hadn't noticed that Fenella was interested in Allan, there was nothing she could say to that criticism.

"I've written Macrath," Fenella said.

Was the whole world in communication with her brother? She was certain Robert complained about her weekly. James was no doubt going to regale Macrath with her exploits, and now Fenella? What was Macrath, some sort of puppet master who dictated the actions of everyone in the household?

"Are you certain you know Allan as well as you think you do?" she asked, and then told her about the letters.

"You think Allan would have done something like that?"

"I don't know," Mairi said. "I hope not but I don't know anyone else."

Fenella stood, moved to the other side of the room, as far away as she could get.

"Don't do anything to him, Mairi, or I'll go to Macrath about that, too."

She didn't know whether to be hurt or angry. Fenella's words stung.

"You wanted to know what I was doing tonight, Fenella? I was making new friends," she said. "I was with the Lord Provost. With Logan."

Fenella stared at her. "All night?"

"Yes," she said.

Fenella's wide-eyed glance goaded her, but she wisely

refrained from telling her cousin more. Let her guess that she and Logan were lovers, if that word adequately described what Logan was. He was like a thunderstorm and she parched earth.

"Mairi, is that wise?"

"No wiser than your relationship with my pressman," she said.

Suddenly, she wanted to guard her emotions and her thoughts, keep them hidden from her cousin. She wanted to tell Fenella that she would be fine. Perhaps she would even take another lover after Logan, become known as the very shocking Miss Sinclair. No one need worry about her or chastise her because she was more interested in ideas than people.

She willed her lips to curve into a smile, and banished even the thought of tears.

Without another word, she retreated to her bedroom. Once inside, she dropped her shoes and her bonnet, flattened herself against the door, both arms outstretched like a living barrier. No one would breach her privacy. Not a person in the household would dare.

Fenella's words felt like arrows that had found a perfect target. Maybe her cousin was right. She'd been so single-minded in pursuit of her own goals that she'd never noticed other people close to her.

What else had she missed?

Allan loving her cousin, for one.

She'd never seen hints of their relationship, and she should have. She most definitely had not been aware of what was going on in her own world.

At least the world of the Mairi Sinclair she'd known herself to be a few weeks ago. Who was she now?

She unbuttoned her cloak and draped it over the end of the bed before sitting beside it.

Perhaps the *Gazette* had always been the reason she attended an event. Because she was probably too direct and less charming than she should have been, people did not gravitate to her in social settings. Only two reasons prompted them to do so: they wanted to be featured in a column or pass along some information to the public. People did not, however, want to become friends with her. Tell Mairi Sinclair something of an intimate nature? You might as well run through Edinburgh shouting the story.

Fenella was her only friend, someone she trusted implicitly.

Hurt sat like a lump in her stomach.

She hadn't closed the drapes the night before, and dawn thrust broadswords of pink and blue from a rising sun. A new day, one in which she was mired in a bone deep confusion.

"**Y**ou're late," Mairi said when Allan finally entered the pressroom a few hours later.

He only nodded in response, which surprised her. She expected him to say something in defense of himself, but he merely donned the apron to protect his clothes from the ink spatter, and moved to the press.

"Do you hate working for a woman?" she asked.

He glanced over at her and frowned. "Have I given you reason to think so?"

"That's not quite an answer."

He jerked the tie of the apron into a bow and answered her, "No, I don't hate working for a woman."

"Do you hate working for me?"

"What's this about, Mairi?"

His pleasant, agreeable face was folded into a frown. She realized that she'd not often seen him out of sorts.

"Would you tell me if there was something you didn't like?" she asked. "If there was something that made you angry?"

"I told you I thought the broadside was a bad idea."

He had, but he'd still helped her finish it.

She didn't want him to be responsible for the letters. Not for Fenella's sake but for her own. She liked him; he was a good worker, and she'd grown accustomed to the feeling of safety she felt around him.

"Do you think running a paper is woman's work?" she asked.

To her surprise, he smiled. "Not until I met you," he said. "But you seem to enjoy it and the *Gazette* is a good paper. One with a future."

"Do you really think so?"

He nodded. "Have I done something, Mairi?"

She wiped her hands on the rag beside the press, walking to the line of shelves. She studied a few of the crates as if she were looking for something. She needed the time to come up with the right way to broach the subject.

"I've been getting letters at home," she said. "I've only seen one, but there have been two, I understand."

"What kind of letters?"

"The kind you don't want to read aloud," she said. "Not highly complimentary of me."

He frowned. "Does it have something to do with your SLNA work?"

"Perhaps. Or the broadside I wrote. Or a column. Or simply because someone doesn't like me."

The idea that it could stem from her work with the SLNA appealed to her. If someone could assault her for what she said, then it was certainly possible for someone to write her nasty letters for the same reason.

At least that way the letters wouldn't be from someone she knew.

"And you thought they came from me?" He rotated the wheel of the press, studying her.

"If I did, I wouldn't be leaving you in charge."

"In charge?" His eyebrows drew together. "And where would you be going?"

"To Drumvagen," she said. "I need to see my brother." She also needed to escape Edinburgh, but that wasn't a confession she'd make aloud.

Moving to the other side of the room, she pulled the apron off her head, hanging it on the hook where it belonged. She turned and studied him in the light from the windows.

How many nights had they worked together? How many times had they laughed over something or discussed the news? He knew her as well as anyone, because he knew the Mairi of the *Edinburgh Gazette*. Here at the paper she was her truest self.

Please, God, don't let her be wrong. If he was responsible for the letters, she didn't think she could bear it.

Sometimes, however, she had to believe. When circumstances were against her, when people urged one way of thinking, she had to listen to her own counsel. Something told her that Allan hadn't written those letters, and she was going to act as if he were innocent.

She turned and looked at the board where she pinned their next projects. Two broadsides were due as well as the next edition of the *Gazette*. In addition, three brochures and notices of meetings had been promised, for free, of course.

"We'll do the notices, and the brochures can wait until I return. We'll postpone the next edition as well."

He nodded, turning the wheel of the press. The clacking

sound was strangely reassuring, as if the press was happily talking to her.

When Macrath had purchased Drumvagen and wanted her and Fenella to move to his new home, she'd asked him, "What would I do if I left Edinburgh?"

He hadn't an answer for her. But they'd both known she was talking about more than the city. Edinburgh was her home, but the Sinclair Paper Company was her life.

If she could stay in this room, she'd be happy. But that's what Fenella had accused her of, wasn't it? Everything in her life had narrowed to the *Gazette*.

Until, of course, Logan Harrison.

She hadn't thought of the *Gazette* last night, or her reputation, or subscription numbers, columns, or broadsides. Instead, she'd been a woman enthralled, captivated, and enchanted.

Reason enough to want to flee Edinburgh as fast as she could.

"**S**he's gone?"

Fenella clasped her hands together, prayed for composure, and addressed a very irritated Logan Harrison.

"She's left Edinburgh."

She'd never seen anyone's face turn to stone the way his did.

"Where has she gone?"

Should she tell him? Or keep Mairi's privacy?

"She's gone to visit her brother," she said, the decision having something to do with the intensity of his gaze. "At Drumvagen. Would you like her address?"

"I know it," he said. This time his smile was more genuine. Or perhaps it was simply because the ferocity had left his eyes. "How long will she be gone?"

"A fortnight," she said, although it was little more than a guess.

The idea that her cousin had engaged in an illicit relationship with this forceful man was startling.

The day was too cold and blustery to stand here with the door open. She invited him inside, wondering if Cook had baked that morning.

To her relief he declined.

"Thank you," he said, nodding at her again. Then he turned and left, heading for the stately carriage on the curb.

Was the Lord Provost in love with Mairi? Is that why he seemed so surprised at the news that she'd left Edinburgh?

If so, she could certainly understand his bewilderment. Love made fools out of everyone.

Even men like the Lord Provost.

Going to Drumvagen was like stepping back in time. Macrath's home crouched at the edge of the sea, sufficiently far from any train depot that the only way to get there was by carriage.

Normally, the drive took four hours. Today, however, the distance seemed to fly by as quickly as the time. The skies were clear with no hint of snow and the winter winds subdued.

As they were nearing Drumvagen, Mairi reached up and opened the grate, calling for James to stop.

The carriage slowed. She gathered up her skirt, wishing she hadn't chosen to wear one of her better dresses, but she hadn't planned on walking through the Scottish moors.

Ellice sat on an outcropping of rock. She might have been a statue, she was so still. The girl's shoulders were slumped and her head half bowed, staring at a clump of gorse.

There was something so abject about Ellice's posture

that Mairi could neither ignore her nor pretend she was invisible.

Although there was no relationship between them, even that of marriage, she liked the girl and felt they were friends. Ellice was her sister-in-law's sister-in-law. Virginia had been married before Macrath, and her husband had died. Ellice was the eighteen-year-old sister of that first husband.

After Virginia and Macrath married, both Ellice and her mother had come to live at Drumvagen. The arrangement had worked out well for the two English women, at least on the surface. But it was almost as if the gods, having seen how happy Virginia and Macrath were, wanted to add spice to their lives. The spice, in this case, was Virginia's former mother-in-law, Enid, Ellice's mother.

Mairi grabbed her skirts with both hands, watching the ground for stones and holes. She didn't want to scrape the leather of her new shoes or twist an ankle.

At her approach, Ellice turned and smiled.

"Sometimes prayers are answered," she said.

"I've never been the answer to a prayer," Mairi said.

"Not specifically you," Ellice said. "Anything that could resolve the situation."

The past two years had been eventful and difficult for the younger woman. Ellice had lost her older sister, nursed her mother back from deep grief, and moved from London to Drumvagen. Her entire life had changed, the circumstances enough to make her sad or even angry.

Ellice had been neither.

Instead, her wide brown eyes studied everything, and she watched people with great interest, rarely commenting until her opinion was solicited. Even then her thoughts were measured and considerate, as if she had a mental filter through which all her words flowed.

When Mairi first met Ellice on the occasion of Macrath's wedding, she'd been amused by the girl's incessant curiosity. She was placed in service to help answer a few of Ellice's innumerable questions about Drumvagen, Macrath, the family, Scotland, and a dozen more subjects.

Lately, however, Ellice had been less curious or perhaps just more restrained. She wondered if it was because Ellice had been told that no one approved of a curious woman.

She went to stand in front of the girl. "Are they at it again?" she asked.

Enid, having been the mistress of her own establishment in London, was expected to play the part of cherished family member. In doing so, however, she was no longer able to dictate the rules of the household, supervise the menus, or approve expenditures. Such a change in roles might have been difficult for anyone, but Enid had found it impossible. Not because she disliked Virginia but because her battles weren't with her former daughter-in-law.

Enid despised the housekeeper, Brianag.

Brianag reciprocated in kind.

"I've never seen any two people so ill suited to be in the same room," Ellice said. "I try to leave when that happens."

Whenever they were in earshot of Virginia or Macrath, Enid and Brianag maintained a perfectly agreeable tone while sniping at each other. The minute Virginia or Macrath left the room, voices were raised and the sniping turned to all out war.

For hours each woman nominally tried to ignore the other. Then something would set one of them off and the battle raged.

Ellice swept her skirts away from a rock strangely shaped like a footstool and Mairi dusted off the surface before sitting.

"What is it now?"

"Food," Ellice said, tapping at one of her bodice buttons. "Mother says she can no longer tolerate Scottish cooking. Brianag served her haggis for breakfast."

Mairi laughed, hating haggis herself. "So what did Enid do?"

"She told Brianag that we come from a long line of English witches and she was going to recite a spell."

"A spell?" That sounded a little desperate, even for Enid.

Ellice sighed. "Mother's running out of threats. Most of the time, Brianag just laughs at her. This time Brianag told Mother that she was going to kirk to pray for her, then tell Macrath that she'd have nothing to do with an ungodly woman in the house. She refused to serve her dinner."

"I admire your mother," Mairi said. "Brianag is frightening."

Ellice glanced down at her. "The most frightening person I've ever known," she said. "If I were a child, I'd have nightmares about her."

"Has she done anything to scare Alistair?" she asked, speaking of her nephew. He was nearly three now, and no doubt spoiled, but such a darling child that it didn't seem to matter.

"She dotes on him. So does Mother. I think that's what started the whole thing this time. Mother said something or did something that violated one of Brianag's superstitions. I think we need a list of things we should or should not do," Ellice said, staring off toward the ocean.

"Even if you had one," Mairi said, "I doubt it would matter."

"Is it because we're English?"

"No," Mairi said. "It's because you're there. I'm as Scottish as Brianag. But we clash as well."

The woman was phenomenally devoted to Macrath and would hear nothing bad ever said about him. Unfortunately, she felt the same way about Drumvagen and Scotland. Even a mild comment such as, "It's a cold day today, isn't it?" would result in a glower and a mumbled threat along the lines of refusing fuel for the fire. "We'll see how cold you'll be then."

Her brother, unfortunately, had almost as much devotion for Brianag. Whenever Mairi complained to him, Macrath would shake his head and say something along the lines of, "She's very well respected."

Was it respect or fear? Was the rest of the staff as cautious about the housekeeper as she was?

Whenever she broached the subject of Brianag to Virginia, her sister-in-law got a wild look in her eye as if she wanted to escape the room immediately. She couldn't blame Virginia. She probably had that same look.

She turned her head, looking toward Drumvagen, now hidden behind the pines. She really wasn't in the mood for more drama, but it seemed as if she had no choice.

Standing, she held her hand out for Ellice. "Come on, we'll face them both together."

Ellice sighed again as she plucked at her left cuff with her right hand. "She's my mother, but she can be very trying."

An apt description, but she decided not to say that to the girl.

"Brianag can be as well," she said.

Ellice allowed herself to be pulled from her perch and accompany Mairi back to the carriage.

December in Scotland could be dreary. The mornings were gray and often the sun didn't burn away the clouds, leaving the afternoons the same. The days were short, with snow in the air and sometimes on the ground. So far this year they'd been spared, but it was only a matter of time until everything was coated in white.

Drumvagen, however, was an oasis of green, the massive house surrounded by tall pines. Built of gray brick only slightly darker than the white-flecked ocean to her right, the house was square, with four tall towers on each corner. The dual staircases in front curved from the broad portico to the gravel approach, welcoming a visitor like outstretched arms to Macrath's magnificent home.

Because they were family, James pulled around to the back of Drumvagen. Before they were out of the carriage, Mairi heard the shouting.

"Macrath and Virginia are at Kinloch Village," Ellice said. "The two of them have been going at it all day."

Mairi had the uncharitable thought that at least Brianag was fussing at Enid and not her. Normally, the housekeeper didn't have any qualms about telling her what to do and how to do it whenever she visited Drumvagen. If Brianag was focused on Enid, perhaps she would be left alone on this visit.

As they left the carriage, approaching the back entrance, she realized why she could hear them arguing so well. The two women stood in the middle of the laundry yard.

"You're a harridan!"

"At least I'm not a tumshie Sassenach," Brianag replied more calmly.

They were probably close in age, but in appearance they were opposites. Enid was short and plump, and Brianag tall and thin.

Mairi had the strangest notion that if they were chess pieces, Brianag would be the queen and Enid the pawn. That didn't mean, however, that anyone should underestimate Enid. The Dowager Countess of Barrett had kept her own establishment after having been widowed for a dozen years, negotiated a marriage for her invalid son and, when faced with penury, revealed the true extent of her manipulative powers.

Brianag, on the other hand, was rumored to be a wise woman, dabbled in healing, and was knowledgeable about anything to do with Kinloch Village and its environs. She also had a very bad habit, when irritated, of retreating to a peculiar type of Scottish the locals spoke, which meant that the servants understood her but no one else did.

The two women were well-matched in temperament, will, and determination. They were also very tiring to be around.

She and Ellice exchanged a look.

"Awa and bile yer heid," Brianag said, catching sight of them. She smoothed her apron down with both hands and smiled.

The sight of Brianag smiling was daunting indeed.

Drumvagen's housekeeper was as tall as Macrath. Pink cheeks adorned her square face. Her nose was knifelike, too narrow to fit well on her face. Two vertical lines were etched between her deep-set brown eyes, giving her a glower even when she was in a good mood, a rarity for Brianag.

Her hair, brown threaded with gray, was normally arranged at the back of her head in a severe bun, but now several tendrils escaped, giving her an uncharacteristic disheveled appearance.

Her mouth was thinned in a smile as she approached them. Mairi didn't trust that expression because Brianag had never hesitated in conveying how she felt, and her feelings did not lean toward affection.

"Mairi," Enid said before Brianag could speak. "How delightful that you're here." The Dowager Countess of Barrett, short, stocky, and determined, nearly skipped to reach her first.

Enid's face was plump, her face, although lined, appearing younger than her years. Now a triumphant smile curved her lips as she enveloped Mairi in a fulsome hug.

Brianag frowned impressively.

Ellice's eyes twinkled as she moved away, leaving Mairi in the middle of the two women.

She had the thought that perhaps Edinburgh, with all its complications, might be a calmer place than Drumvagen.

Chapter 21

Mairi's reluctance to talk to Macrath was like walking through a wall only she could see. She had to talk to herself all the way to her brother's library.

She loved Macrath and she respected him as well. When their father died, she had worried about the burden placed on his too young shoulders, but her brother had taken up the responsibility, providing for all of them. Not once had he complained about the addition of another mouth to feed when she'd impulsively adopted Fenella. Nor had he ever hinted to their cousin that she wasn't welcome.

Macrath had taught her, by example, what it was like to face adversity, which is why she pushed through the wall, entered the room and went to sit on one of the chairs at the other end, a warm and comfortable spot in front of a blazing fire.

He joined her, and for a moment they simply sat and watched the flames.

They'd shared some difficult years together, enough experiences that she was reasonably certain what Macrath would say about the recent activities in Edinburgh.

Standing, she walked to the window, staring out at the view of the wind-tossed sea. In turn, she went to stand in front of his desk, then to the bookcase that hid the passage to the beach.

Macrath and Virginia had shown the grotto to her last year. When she'd made the comment that the stone window was a lovely place to sit and while away the afternoon, Virginia blushed, making her wonder if her brother and his wife had done exactly that.

Since marrying Virginia, her brother's blue eyes, a shade matching her own, had never been so filled with humor or his lean face as relaxed. As a boy he'd been fueled by ambition. He wanted to create an empire and a clan. Now that he had the empire and was working on the clan, he'd lost his impatient edge. He was calmer and more patient, especially with his son, Alistair.

Yet it wasn't just Alistair who had the ability to bring a smile to his face. When Macrath was with Virginia, even his stature changed. His body curved as if to cover and protect her. Earlier, Mairi had interrupted them on the staircase, and he'd had his arm braced against the wall while he kissed his wife senseless.

Recalling that, she felt a twinge of envy and regret, the scene bringing back memories of the evening in Logan's library. Perhaps it would be better not to remember that night. Or Logan, for that matter.

"What's wrong?" Macrath asked.

She glanced at him. "Why would anything be wrong?"

"Because it takes a pry bar to get you out of Edinburgh," he said, smiling. "You whine about leaving the paper, about not being able to report, a dozen excuses that keep you chained to the *Gazette*."

"I do not whine." At his look, she sighed. "Very well, I whine a little."

"So what's wrong?"

"Nothing. Everything."

"Why do I think you need to confess something?"

She came and sat beside him again. Staring up at the ceiling, she wondered exactly how much to tell him. Macrath was incredibly protective, despite the fact that she was two years older.

"Start at the beginning," he said.

"I haven't the slightest idea where that is. When you left Edinburgh? When you left James and Robert in charge?"

"Not in charge," he said. "Merely there for your protection."

She turned and sent him a look that resulted in his smile.

"I wasn't trying to constrain your independence, Mairi. I really wanted them there simply for your protection. A single woman is not safe living alone."

Since she'd proved him right in that regard, she didn't have a rejoinder.

"How much has James told you?"

He took a sip of his whiskey and placed the glass on the table. "I haven't met with James." He raised one leg, resting his ankle on his knee. He looked relaxed and not at all anxious. She hated to disturb his calm.

She told him the story of the broadside, why she'd written it, and the resultant financial impact. Throughout her recitation, Macrath remained silent.

"Do you expect me to criticize you, Mairi?" he asked when she was done.

"I expect you to be disappointed."

"I agree that you could have picked someone a little less influential."

"He deserved it," she said. At least, she'd thought so at the time. Several weeks had clarified the magnitude of her mistake.

"I can never be disappointed in you, Mairi," her brother said.

"It's a wonder I haven't bankrupted us," she said. "I've been a fool, Macrath."

He sat and sipped at his whiskey, attentive and aware. Somehow, his patience made this meeting more uncomfortable.

"I also decided that I should become more active in society," she said.

"Which probably doesn't mean attending more balls," he said dryly.

"I gave a speech about my thoughts at the SLNA. I think women should be given the vote."

He didn't say anything, which made her glance at him. He was still smiling, that contented expression making her partly happy, partly envious.

"I don't think it's fair that women are treated a certain way because they're female. Or being told that it's none of my concern because I'm a woman. I detest being patronized."

"Have I ever patronized you?"

She shook her head. "You're remarkably fair," she said. "Marriage has mellowed you."

"I was fair before I married Virginia."

"You're calmer since you've been married. Not as driven."

"Oh, I'm as driven," he said. "I'm just happier." He smiled at her. "You should try it."

She blew out a breath. "To care for a male is not my sole concern in life."

"Is there something wrong with caring for a male?"

Since his question was so blandly voiced, she answered him.

"No, not in the context of a rich, full life. But not in lieu of having a life. Can you imagine me doing nothing more than being a wife? 'Would you like more potatoes, husband? Could I bring you some whiskey, dear?' I'd be bored in a day."

"No doubt you'd be printing broadsides in your attic and distributing them when you hung the clothes out to dry."

His crooked grin sparked her laugh.

"Don't you ever want to fall in love, Mairi?"

The fact that her brother was asking her about love was strange enough. That she wanted to answer him added to the discordant feeling.

"Love seems a fine thing for men. Less so for women. Take servitude to a man and wrap love around it, and it seems justifiable and even pretty."

"A man cares for a woman, protects her, shares what he has with her. Wrap love around it, and that, too, seems justifiable. Or maybe it's enough to simply love with no thought to anything else. Is love strong enough to stand on its own and exist for no other purpose but to be itself?"

"How philosophical we've gotten, Macrath, and I don't have the answer for you. All I do know is that love is probably not for me. Purpose is."

He didn't speak.

She turned and faced him. "I've always been able to do what I wanted to do, but I had to resort to subterfuge or outright lies in order to do it. Maybe I'm tired of not being myself. Or of hiding behind you."

"Then do it."

Annoyed, she stared at him. "It's not quite that easy," she said.

"Or maybe it's easier than you know. Make the *Gazette* yours completely, Mairi. Change it to fit you. Stop hiding behind my name. You've done a phenomenal job with the newspaper. You always have. You cared more about it than I did. Sometimes, I think you cared more about it than Father."

"Don't say that, Macrath."

"Why not? If he were here, I think he'd say the same thing. You have almost a missionary zeal, Mairi."

She felt her face warm at his praise.

"You've always been the very best brother," she said.

"I'm not trying to flatter you. I'm telling the truth. But the same zeal that makes you so good at your job, Mairi, can also narrow your judgment. Take a step back from time to time and reevaluate why you're doing something."

"Are you talking about the broadside now?"

"And other things."

"Like love?" she asked. She shook her head.

He smiled. "The broadside was an error in judgment, Mairi. But errors like that can be fixed. Just don't make the same errors about your life. Permanent mistakes."

She stood again, walking to the window. "Sometimes I let my emotions get the best of me. Before I know it, I'm in the middle of another situation of my own making."

Turning, she faced him. "Do you ever question yourself, Macrath? Did you ever think you weren't good enough for all the things you wanted to do? Or not up to the challenge?"

"No," he said with a smile. "They were my dreams. They fit me. Yours will fit you."

"Will they? I wonder. I want people to know the name of the *Gazette*. I want to have influence."

He stretched out his feet. His boots weren't the cleanest, but this was his house. If Macrath wanted to track mud through Drumvagen, that was his business. She would have done anything other than incur Brianag's wrath.

"Then do so," he said.

"I always thought I was brave," she said.

"You are."

She shook her head. "No, Macrath, I'm not."

She wasn't going to tell him about the attack on her.

"I know that women who have spoken out have been the targets of violence. I don't want to be singled out in that way."

"Nor do I want you to be. Can you not do something else equally as important, but be less visible?"

"I've been printing thousands of brochures and announcements for the SLNA," she said. Would he criticize her for that? Would he question her expenditures as vigorously as Robert had?

When he didn't, she asked, "Why did you hire Robert? Was there no one else you could have installed in the house to oversee my expenses? Someone who was less dour, who smiled from time to time?"

"I thought he would be of help to you. Give you advice when you needed it."

Surprised, she glanced at him. "Well, he doesn't give me any advice. He does, however, make me explain every time I've purchased something."

Macrath's eyes narrowed. "I never asked him to do that, Mairi. He sends me a monthly accounting, but I never asked him to put you in that position. Why don't you just tell him it's none of his concern?"

She threw her hands up in the air. "Because I thought that's exactly what you wanted him to do."

"I have more faith in you than that," he said. "If I didn't, I wouldn't have left you and Fenella in Edinburgh."

"You wouldn't have gotten us out of Edinburgh," she said. She folded her arms, and tapping her foot against the wood floor, pretended an interest in the view.

Winter had a grip on Edinburgh, but here it was still waging a war for dominance. The waves were foamed with white to mirror the sky. A snow sky, most people would say. Would she be snowed in at Drumvagen? Perhaps it would be a blessing if she were.

"You've created a home here. Drumvagen's a magnificent creation, and you did it."

"Not alone, Mairi. Any more than you create the paper alone. You need help."

"Speaking of which," she said, sighing deeply, "Fenella's in love with Allan, my pressman, and the best one I've ever seen."

"Is that a problem?"

"No, I guess not. I just hate to see a man turned to idiocy because of love."

He laughed, startling a smile from her. "Are you saying that because of me? Was I an idiot? Am I still?"

She turned and faced him, dropping her arms. "No, you weren't. And he isn't, either."

Perhaps she was the only one in the family who was idiotic about love. That thought was so startling she decided to push it aside to think about later.

"Fenella said she had written you. Did you get her letter?"

Macrath sat back, sipping his whiskey leisurely. If a question confused him or he wanted time to think about it, he simply didn't answer. She didn't think he ever lied, and wished she could say the same. He simply didn't speak until his thoughts were arranged in a certain fashion.

The only person who could alter his habit of being a stone wall was Virginia. With her, he was impulsive and sometimes rash. Look how quickly they had married. For that matter, look at Alistair. He was most definitely Macrath's son, born a year before their wedding.

"I haven't received hers," he finally said. "But I did get a letter from Allan. I've no objection to them marrying. Do you?"

"No," she said. "He's been an excellent employee. Fenella is in love and he seems to feel the same."

"Yet you still have reservations."

Surprised, she glanced at him.

"It isn't about Allan and Fenella," she said, determined to tell him the rest of it.

She pulled the letter from her pocket.

"I received this the other day," she said, handing the letter to Macrath. "It's one of two. Abigail threw out the first."

He read it through, then folded it.

"May I have it?"

"Why? I don't want it," she hastened to explain, "I'm just curious why you do."

"Something about it bothers me. Either the way it's written or the handwriting."

She nodded, watching him tuck it into his pocket.

She didn't have any objection to him taking the letter. She wished she could hand off the rest of her problems to someone else.

"You have a nest of wasps in your home, Macrath," she said, staring out the window.

Below them, on the headland, Brianag and Enid were at it again, shouting at each other so loudly their words could be heard through the windows.

"Or maybe not a nest. Two very loud wasps. Do they think no one can hear them?"

"Yes," Macrath said, coming to stand beside her. They also think Virginia and I don't know about the discord they cause. "I've had visits from every inhabitant of Drumvagen at one time or another. When I'm not here, Jack and Sam inform me of what's going on. It seems we have a war at Drumvagen."

She nodded. "You need to do something about them."

He nodded. "I do, as you need to do something about your own situation." He patted his pocket. "I don't like this."

"Neither do I," she said, compelled to agree.

"Promise me you'll stay safe."

She nodded. "But I won't be a hermit, Macrath, and I won't be boxed up in the paper's offices."

He grinned at her. "But you will continue to let James accompany you wherever you go."

She nodded. Her brother didn't need to know about her concerns about Allan. Nor did he need to know anything about Logan Harrison.

Since he didn't want to bother Mairi's cousin again, Logan stopped in at the Sinclair Printing Company a few days later.

The young man manning the press was a surly sort. At first he refused to tell him anything except that Mairi wasn't in the building.

They faced each other, Logan standing in the doorway, the other man with a wrench in his hand, glaring alternately at him and the press.

"Are you in charge when Miss Sinclair is not here?" Logan asked.

"I'd be asking why you want to know."

He would have to tell Mairi how loyal her employee was and how annoying. But a Scot was often like that, suspicious until coaxed into friendship.

"I don't wish her ill," Logan said. "I just want to know if she's returned to Edinburgh."

Allan didn't say anything for a few moments, intent on removing something from the press. When the gear clattered to the floor, Logan retrieved it, noting that one of the teeth had broken.

He handed the gear to Allan, who glared at it with the same ferocity he'd turned on Logan.

"I'll have to send for the part," he said, looking as if he wanted to kick the press. "It was old twenty years ago. We need a rotary press, not this ancient thing. I've been putting it back together every day for the last seven months."

"You're new here, then?" Logan asked. "Are you new to Edinburgh, too?"

Allan scowled at him. "Again, why would you be wanting to know?"

Logan debated for a moment, then gave the man the truth. "I find I'm interested in what Miss Sinclair does. Since you work here, I'm also interested in you."

"Yes, I am new to Edinburgh," Allan said, grabbing a rag and wiping his hands. "It's a good place for a pressman to work."

"They call us the Athens of the North," Logan said, smiling. "We've a great many newspapers and publishers."

Allan nodded. A moment later he lifted his head and stared straight at him.

"I know who you are, Lord Provost. I remember the first time you were here, trying to put the fear of God in her. I'm thinking it's a good thing she left Edinburgh for a while, and I'm thinking it would be a good thing for you to stop inquiring about her."

"And I'm thinking it would be a good thing if you kept your advice to yourself," Logan said, taking a few steps toward the man until he faced him across the press.

Allan threw the rag on a nearby table and rested his hands against one of the supporting bars.

"I'm in love with her cousin," Allan said. "I'm stupid with it. Enough to see it in the face of another man."

Logan didn't respond. Politics had taught him the value of silence. Never more important than now, when words had been stripped from him by surprise.

"She's not here, and I don't expect her today," Allan

said, directing his attention to the press once more. "If you come tomorrow, I might be giving you the same answer." He looked up. "Or maybe not."

Logan ran his hand over the large wheel. The cool metal beneath his fingers seemed to warm to his touch, as if the press were a living creature, one seeking a source of heat.

He could almost feel her hands here, remembering when he entered the press room that first day and she'd been attired in a leather apron and a scowl.

"How long?" he asked. "How long do you think she'll be gone?"

Allan straightened. "However long Mairi wants."

The answer was right before his face. If he wanted to see Mairi, he'd have to find her first.

Chapter 22

"There's a carriage coming up the drive," Brianag said at the door of the parlor.

"A visitor? Who?"

"Are you the Queen of England now? If you want to know who it is, go to the door yourself."

Mairi closed her book, praying for patience. With each passing day, Brianag grew even more disagreeable.

Or perhaps it was because she was bored beyond belief. The time away from Edinburgh dragged. She'd caught up on all her reading, spent hours in contemplation of what Macrath had said, and exhausted entirely too much time thinking about Logan.

Every time she tried to write, she'd find herself staring off into space. She found it difficult to keep her train of thought. She was forgetting tasks, names, and other information that she normally remembered with ease.

She noticed the looks between Macrath and Virginia and was so envious her stomach hurt.

She put down her book and stood. Maybe a visitor was just what she needed.

When Brianag left the room, stomping down the hall, Mairi stared after her. How did Macrath tolerate the woman?

Drumvagen startled him. Logan had known Macrath Sinclair was a wealthy man. He just hadn't expected a mansion in the wilderness. Set among the pines, hugging the cliff above the ocean, Drumvagen was a masterful piece of architecture, the equal to anything he'd seen in Scotland or England.

The sweeping grand staircases were no doubt meant to impress. Here, you are in the presence of power, they seemed to say. Or money. Or taste. Or a dozen different attributes, all designed to awe.

He was, but he wasn't cowed. When his driver entered the circular drive, the oyster shells crunching beneath the wheels, he only felt anticipation.

At the door, instead of a majordomo, a woman with a regal bearing greeted him. She was attired in a long skirt of tartan wool, a white blouse with a clan brooch pinned on her chest.

When he asked for Mairi, she made a sign with her fingers, grumbled something, and turned to stomp off into the house. When she didn't come back, he entered and shut the door behind him, only to hear her return.

"Well, are you coming?" she asked.

Now, there was a woman who could intimidate him.

He bit back his grin and followed her.

A few minutes later Brianag returned to the parlor with the very last person Mairi expected to see at Drumvagen.

Logan stood there attired in a black coat, his hair mussed by the wind, his cheeks ruddy from the cold.

"You can't be here," she said.

"Why can't I?"

"You're the Lord Provost. You can't go sallying forth all over Scotland."

"Sallying forth?" he asked, his grin too white and charming.

"Who is doing your job?"

"I'm allowed a few days to myself from time to time," he said.

"What are you doing here?"

"Perhaps there were things I needed to see near here."

"Name one."

"Kinloch Village," he said easily. "The villagers have made significant inroads in correcting the erosion on the cliff side."

He had to have done some research to know that. Or he could simply be lying. She didn't know what the villagers were doing.

"I could go on and on about the fishing trade, if you wish, or perhaps I simply felt the need for a drive."

"A four hour drive in the winter?"

His grin faded. "I came to see you, Mairi."

Her heart was beating a rhythm that was alien to it, making her breathless.

"Again, why?"

"Perhaps I missed you."

She folded her arms and glared at him. Quite easy to do, since she was frightened by his appearance and it was easier to be angry than afraid.

He speared his hands through his hair. Logan was as adverse to headwear as she. He really should take more care, however, since he was often out of doors. He'd be warmer wearing a hat.

She stopped herself in mid-thought, turned and walked toward the windows.

He would meet Macrath and Virginia. He would effortlessly charm them, she was sure. She had to explain his presence somehow, and she knew Macrath would never accept that the Lord Provost of Edinburgh was simply driving round Scotland in the snow and ice.

He'd come to see her.

Should she be feeling this surge of excitement? Probably not. She should, instead, be measured and calm, restrained and proper. Above all, she should not recall how he only had to raise his eyebrow for her to fall to the floor.

"My brother will want to know why you're here."

"A neighborly call," he said.

She glanced over her shoulder to see him smiling lightly.

"Don't tell him we were lovers."

His smile faded. "Any other woman would be overjoyed that I went out of my way to visit, not question me on my tact."

"Then go and see her. Give her my best regards."

He came to stand behind her, so close that if she turned she'd be in his arms. She most certainly wasn't going to turn.

The wind blew the waves away from the shore in a fan shape, unfurled and flirty. The day was overcast, no hint of sun showing through the pale gray sky. Her mood had been the same until he'd come.

"Mairi."

He mustn't say her name like that, rolling his r's. He mustn't use that tone of tenderness, either.

"Why did you leave?"

"Does it matter?"

"I find it does," he said. "You've been on my mind."

She turned, taking the precaution of stepping back. When he didn't say anything more, she shook her head.

"I shouldn't be. Any more than you're on mine."

His smile was sudden and almost the match of the hidden sun.

"You're a very important man. Surely you have more

important things to do than chase me throughout Scotland."

"At the moment I can't think of one."

"Don't you have meetings to attend? People to impress? Laws to enact?"

"We can consider this a meeting," he said. "We can enact a law stating that it's imperative you consider me impressive."

She rolled her eyes. "You can't be here. We were unwise. Foolish. Improvident."

"I agree."

"It can never happen again."

He didn't say a word.

"I will not be your doxy."

Still nothing from him. Just that annoying smile.

"Why did you leave Edinburgh?" he asked.

"I wanted to visit my brother. Since you've never met my brother, you don't have that excuse, Logan."

She glanced at him to find that his smile had slipped. Instead, he was looking at her somberly, studying her as if to divine her thoughts. Should she tell him what she was thinking? If she did so, it would be the ruin of her.

He made the day brighter. He caused her stomach to churn, her heart to beat too fast.

She was excited, overjoyed, and terrified.

"You don't believe women should have the vote," she said.

She would have talked about the weather if it would keep him from looking at her in just that way.

"I don't believe I've made my views known on the matter."

"That's a politician's statement if I've ever heard one."

"Like it or not," he said, "I'm a politician."

"You used to be a bookseller."

"I still am that as well. Blackwell's is, to my great satisfaction, a growing concern."

"All three of them."

"All three of them," he said.

"Does everything you do have a golden touch?"

"Evidently not, or you'd be falling into my arms."

She frowned at him. Her frowns had been known to subdue most people, but the only effect on Logan Harrison was to make his smile wider.

What was she going to do about him? Worse, what was she going to do about her reaction to him? Her heart was still beating fast, her lips dry.

"As you can see, I'm very well. I'm simply visiting my brother. Now that you've found me, you can return to Edinburgh as quickly as possible."

Hopefully, before her brother or sister-in-law knew he was there.

Unfortunately, it was about five minutes too late. Mairi heard the footsteps with resignation. This situation was about to get worse, much worse.

She stepped away from him just as Virginia entered the room.

"Brianag told me we had a visitor," she said, smiling.

From the moment she met her sister-in-law at Virginia's wedding to Macrath, she'd thought Virginia one of the most beautiful women she'd ever seen. Her face, a perfect oval, was dominated by light blue eyes, so clear and guileless it seemed as if her soul shone through. Her black hair surrounded her face like a frame for an exquisite painting.

She smiled often and laughed as much. She was joy given life.

Now she walked into the room, brightening the space with her smile.

"Logan, I'd like you to meet my sister-in-law, Virginia

Sinclair. Virginia, this is Logan Harrison. The Lord Provost of Edinburgh."

Virginia's eyes widened a little but she didn't express her surprise in any other manner.

"How lovely that you've come to Drumvagen," she said. "We are so out of the way most people don't visit."

Just like that, Logan was welcomed. His coat was taken, refreshments were ordered, and the three of them sat in the parlor as if the air wasn't thrumming around them.

Before Logan could say anything, such as he was just leaving, Virginia smiled brightly and said, "But of course you'll stay for dinner, will you not?"

Mairi glanced at him but he only smiled at her as if he were enjoying the entire situation.

"I anticipate meeting your husband," he said. "I've heard a great deal about Mr. Sinclair."

She sent him another look, but Logan ignored her, exchanging smiles with Virginia.

Mairi wanted to close her eyes and magically transport herself somewhere else. Anywhere else, even back to Edinburgh.

Logan stood at one side of the fireplace with Macrath on the other. He was taller than her brother, with a build that made Macrath looked almost frail in comparison. She had the disloyal thought that Logan could pin Macrath easily in a brawl.

Dear God, don't let it come to that.

With any luck, Logan would keep silent about what had happened in Edinburgh. Would he?

If Macrath was surprised by the arrival of so august a personage as the Lord Provost of Edinburgh, he didn't betray it by word or deed. Instead, he was himself, only more so. More affable, more relaxed, and more intense in the looks he sent her. She was under no illusions. The minute Logan was out of earshot, she was going to be interrogated, she was sure of it.

She sat in silence as Macrath and Logan talked about some obscure act in Edinburgh. When he had her brother become so politically minded? For that matter, when had Logan become a courtier?

This was the man she'd heard about, the one who smiled so charmingly, who laughed at the right time, and complimented his hostess until Virginia blushed. Each of the maids tried to catch his eye, and even Brianag had softened toward him.

Mairi almost threw her hands up in the air in exasperation.

Since it appeared as if Logan had been accepted into the bosom of the family, she was surprised they didn't enter the smaller, and more intimate, family dining room.

But Ellice had been escorted into the formal dining room by Logan, following Macrath and Virginia. Mairi was accompanied by Enid, who was curling her lip in preparation for yet another battle with Brianag.

The first course was Kinloch skink, a fish soup that was one of Macrath's favorite dishes. She couldn't help but remember the potato soup she'd eaten at Logan's house. From his quick glance, he remembered as well.

Would this meal never be done?

"How is it that you know Mairi?" Virginia was asking.

Mairi met her brother's eyes, then shifted her gaze to Logan.

"She wrote a scurrilous broadside about me," he said easily. "I objected, naturally."

Virginia looked over at her.

"It's true," she said, placing her spoon on the edge of the bowl. "I did."

Since that part of the story was common knowledge, she didn't have any reluctance to comment on it. The rest, please God, let the rest remain a secret.

"Of course I was mistaken. The Lord Provost is the epitome of all things good and proper."

Macrath shot her a look, and she almost stuck her tongue out at him.

Logan laughed, further charming all the females at the table, including Enid, but with a sole exception—her. She was not going to be charmed by the man again.

Look what had happened the last time. She'd been charmed right out of her clothes.

Virginia looked like she was striving to come up with another topic. Because Mairi felt some measure of compassion for her sister-in-law, she decided to participate in the conversation.

"I am attempting to convince the Lord Provost that women should be treated with some degree of equality," she said. "He is reviewing the matter."

Macrath stared at her. Logan smiled. Virginia's eyes were wide.

"Isn't that so, Provost Harrison?"

"I've always believed there are times when women should be on top," he said.

Mairi almost choked on her wine.

"You said your housekeeper has a reputation for being a healer," Logan said, turning to Macrath.

Her brother nodded. "She does. Do you have need of her services?"

"A small rash," Logan said. "A carpet abrasion, I believe."

She sent him a fulminating glance, which he promptly ignored.

"Tell me, Mrs. Sinclair," Logan said, looking at Virginia, "how do you feel about kilts?"

She was going to kill him.

Virginia looked from Logan to Mairi. A slow smile blossomed on her face. "I believe there's no more stirring a sight, Mr. Harrison, than a Scot in a kilt."

"Are you all right?" Ellice asked, leaning over and touching Mairi's hand.

Mairi smiled at her. "I'm fine," she said, pasting a determined smile on her lips. She avoided the looks of the other people at the table, namely Logan and Macrath, both of whom glanced in her direction.

"You will stay the night," Virginia was saying, to her horror. "After all, it's beginning to snow."

Even the weather was conspiring against her. What kind of horrible person would she be not to offer him hospitality? Of course he had to stay. With any luck, a blizzard wouldn't keep him trapped at Drumvagen for a week.

The thought was enough to make her close her eyes.

For the rest of the dinner she was silent. Everyone else laughed and joked, but Mairi decided it would be better if she simply retreated from the field of battle, especially since it was obvious Logan had won that skirmish.

Macrath took one look at his wife, shut the door to their suite, and swept her up into his arms.

"Were we as foolish?" he asked.

"Oh yes," she said. "Perhaps a little more so."

"I refuse to believe it. Mairi's not herself," he said. "I've never seen my sister so . . ." His words trailed off.

Virginia laughed. "She's ten times herself. I've never seen her more annoyed. Or alive, for that matter. You aren't going to talk to her about him, are you?"

Now, he pulled back and looked at her.

"Why not?"

"Two reasons. We didn't exactly act in a virtuous manner, Macrath. We are not shining examples of how to behave. Mairi would pin your ears back for your hypocrisy. Secondly, she's madly in love and not at all happy about it."

"Maybe I should include that in the Sinclair motto," he said. "The Sinclair Clan: struggling against love."

"Oh, but the end result is so worth it," she said, laying her cheek against his chest and sighing happily.

Dinner had been a disaster.

What was worse, every time she caught Virginia's eye, her sister-in-law smiled.

Was it as obvious as that? Did the whole world know how easily Logan could reduce her to foolishness?

Mairi waited until Drumvagen settled down around her. Only then did she open the door of her bedchamber, a guest room that had been permanently allocated as hers, and slip down the corridor to the room Logan had been given.

One tap on the door was all it took before it opened and she was inside. She stepped back before he could get the wrong idea, keeping the door halfway between them.

"Aren't you supposed to be in Edinburgh being Lord Provost?" she whispered.

"Yes, I am," he whispered back. "But would you have me be rude and refuse your sister-in-law's gracious invitation?"

"Yes." The word came out as a hiss. "You have to leave."

"I was planning on doing so tomorrow morning," he said, folding his arms and leaning against the door. "Of course, if you wish, I can always leave now. In the dark. In the snow."

"There was no need to come to Drumvagen."

"You left Edinburgh without a word to me."

She stared at him, wishing he were more than a shadow in the darkness.

"Am I required to obtain your permission for whatever I do?"

"Not permission, lass. Only explanation. You were gone when I called on you. I was concerned."

"You called on me?" she asked. "Why?"

"Maybe I missed you."

She was almost as frightened of him now as she was of the men who'd attacked her. They could only wound her body. Logan could shatter her heart.

"How is your search for a wife going?" she asked.

He placed his finger on her cheek, trailed a path to her chin, then tapped it lightly. "Did you come to my room to ask me that, lass? Or is it more you're looking for?"

She took a step back.

"I've been thinking of your kisses," he said. "Wondering if I imagined them. Would you care to give me a taste?"

She shook her head.

His laugh would wake all the inhabitants of Drumvagen.

When she said as much, he chuckled. "Perhaps they're awake already. Perhaps they're doing what I would like to."

He took a step toward her, and she took a step back. Irritated, she stood her ground when he took another step in her direction.

"Have you always been a satyr?" she asked.

"I've been remarkably celibate until you," he said. "I've not been able to get that night out of my mind, however."

She was not going to tell him she felt the same.

"This is my brother's home," she said.

"And so you'll not be indulging in wickedness, is that it?"

"That's it exactly," she said, both grateful that he understood and a little disappointed that he didn't try to convince her otherwise.

"Not even a kiss? You could pretend that you and I are just friends. Perhaps old friends who have not seen each other for a while. It will start very friendly, almost passionless. If you want to deepen it, you'll need to let me know."

"I don't think that would be the wisest idea," she said, knowing how volatile they were around each other.

"What about an embrace? I will hold you in my arms, loosely, like this," he said. Suddenly he was there, enveloping her like a cloud. His arms wrapped around her, but loose enough to give her room to escape.

He bent his head, rested his cheek against her hair. "I'll just hold you like this," he said. "Feel you pliant in my arms and wonder what you would feel like in a nightgown and wrapper."

"Please," she said, and it was the one word she hadn't expected to say, the one word that silenced him.

Long moments later he dropped his arms and stepped back. "Perhaps it would be best if you said good-night now," he said. "And leave me."

She didn't want to. Did he know how much she didn't want to?

But she did, finally, turning and nearly scurrying down the hall before she could change her mind and stay.

Chapter 23

In the morning Mairi slipped out the back door, heading for one of her favorite spots at Drumvagen, the gazebo.

At dawn Drumvagen's forest had been a wonderland of icicles and ice encrusted branches. Now the air was slowly warming and the incessant drip, drip, drip on the decaying leaves was an oddly sad sound, as if the trees wept.

Drumvagen was easily ten times the size of her Edinburgh home. Macrath must have plans for filling it with children. Since he'd already begun at that task, she didn't doubt he'd be successful.

Until Macrath married, she'd never felt odd about being his older, unmarried sister. After Calvin rebuffed her, she hadn't given much thought to marriage. Or perhaps she'd known, somehow, that she wasn't the type to settle down to a union of wedded bliss.

She wasn't, as Calvin had said, "conformable." She didn't fit in. She wasn't like other women. She'd considered that a badge of honor. Seeing her brother so happy, knowing that his love for his wife had added to his life, made her examine her own in greater detail. Was she missing something by being so independent? Were other people happier?

She was happy. Or if not happy, she was certainly content, at least until she'd met Logan. She enjoyed her work, wanted to get to the paper every morning. She enjoyed pulling together the various stories people submitted, including those she paid to use from her small staff of reporters. She thought she'd done a good job with the paper.

Was it enough?

She'd never before asked herself that question.

"I was told I might find you here."

She didn't turn, didn't face him. How could she, when she'd come to Drumvagen to escape him?

"I thought you would have left this morning. At dawn," she said. "Without a word to anyone, satisfied that you'd done what you came to do."

"What was that?"

She held tightly to one of the pillars of the gazebo, feeling the wood give beneath the pressure of her fingers.

"To make me miserable. To make me question my own mind. To make me regret."

"All that? What an insensitive boor I am."

Because his voice was laced with humor, she finally turned.

She shouldn't have looked at him.

Logan in the early morning made her remember. He hadn't yet shaved and his chin was bristly. His eyes were red, as if he, too, hadn't slept well.

"Who told you I was here?"

He walked toward her, clad in his black greatcoat, his boots making a crunching sound on the ice and snow. "Your brother's very surprising housekeeper. A surly woman, isn't she?"

That forced a smile from her.

"Brianag is one of the most disagreeable people I've ever met. Why Macrath puts up with her I've no idea. But he tolerates her and the Countess of Barrett. Together the two of them are misery. They are forever quarreling, but Macrath tolerates it."

His smile was too tender. She looked away.

"Perhaps he practices tolerance."

She blew out a breath. "My brother is not a saint. I think he does it for his wife. Virginia would be sad if Enid was forced to live somewhere else and she'd feel guilty if Brianag left Drumvagen."

"Your brother must love his wife very much."

She did not want to talk about love with Logan.

Thankfully, neither did he. But his next question was just as bad.

"Did I make you regret that night?" he asked. "Is that why you came to Drumvagen?"

Yes. No. Perhaps. Yes.

She steeled herself to look at him again. "I wanted to see my brother."

"Which necessitated a trip in the middle of winter."

"Yes."

"Do you lie to everyone or only to me?"

"I normally don't lie to anyone," she said, releasing her grip on the wood and thrusting her hands inside her cloak.

"Do you regret that night?"

"Must you keep asking that question?" she asked.

"Yes, I must."

Lying would be safer than the truth. Honesty would bare her soul, lay herself open to his derision.

"No. I don't," she said, finding that, unwise or not, she didn't want to lie to him.

"Neither do I," he said. "Although I should. It would make you less enticing."

She glanced at him again. She'd never been called enticing before, especially by such a handsome man. But he knew her better than anyone, didn't he? He'd seen her naked and abandoned on his library room carpet and in his bed.

If Logan Harrison thought her enticing, then she must be.

She wanted to bat her eyelashes at him, simper a little, perhaps coo at him as she'd seen other women do in public around men. She was lamentably lacking in the social graces as defined by predatory females.

Dear heavens, was she feeling predatory about him?

Perhaps she wasn't the prey after all.

To test him, and perhaps herself, she went and sat on the bench built into one of the gazebo's walls.

"Am I enticing enough that if I invited you to take me here, would you?"

His laughter startled her.

"Have you a penchant for freezing your arse off, Mairi? I prefer a different place for my loving."

She was feeling quite warm now and she was certain her cheeks were flaming. This business of seduction was more complicated than she considered.

"Then come to my room," she said. "We'll have an afternoon of loving."

There, the whole of it. She wanted him to touch her, to please her. She wanted to kiss him, to lose herself in joy with him. Did that make her a ruined woman or just a foolish one?

"No."

Surprised, she reared back. "No?"

"I'll not take advantage of your brother's hospitality by seducing his sister beneath his nose. Come to my house and you'll get all the loving you can handle."

How had this situation been turned on its head? Instead of testing him, she was the one being dared.

"Once was quite enough," she said.

"It was more than once."

Should he look so proud of that fact?

"I'm not afraid of you."

His smile abruptly disappeared. "I should hope not. Why the hell should you be?"

He should immediately apologize for his language. When he didn't, she frowned at him. He frowned right back.

"Have I ever given you reason to fear me?"

"No," she said.

He took a step into the gazebo. "Is that why you said 'once was enough'? Were you afraid of me?"

"No, but—"

He didn't give her time to explain. Instead, he gripped her arms and hauled her up to face him.

She disliked having to look up at him. Nor was she all that pleased to discover how angry he was. His eyes glittered; his mouth was pressed into a thin line, and a muscle on his cheek flexed.

"Of course I'm not afraid of you," she said, deliberately looking away. Facing him was difficult. Facing him while confessing her reaction to him was nearly impossible. "If anything, I'm afraid of myself around you."

He didn't let her go. Instead, he took a step closer until even the chilled air couldn't seep between them.

He warmed her just with his presence. The thought of what he could do to her, how much pleasure he could bring her, heated her even further.

"Tell me what you mean."

"What do you want from me, Harrison? Haven't you enough women falling at your feet? How is your search going for a wife, by the way?"

"I've given it up. Tell me why you're afraid of yourself."

He'd given it up?

He leaned closer, his mouth hovering only an inch over hers. She closed her eyes, wishing he would kiss her.

He didn't.

"Tell me, Mairi," he said.

Very well, perhaps she would. Perhaps the truth would bring one of them back to his senses.

"I want to be abandoned with you," she said, looking him straight in the eye. "I want to be naked. I want to seduce you. I want to do all the things all the forbidden books I've secretly read say happens between shocking women and experienced men. I want to wear you out until you can't rise from the bed."

"Good."

He wasn't supposed to say that. Nor was he supposed to smile at her like she'd pleased him.

Logan Harrison was an immensely dangerous man.

She gripped his coat with both hands, lowered her head until her forehead rubbed against the wool. He bent closer, his breath warming the curve of her ear. He smelled of spices and the cold.

Oh, dear, what was she going to do about him? Staying away from him was the best solution, but they didn't seem to be able to do that, did they?

She didn't step away, but rather, placed her hands on his chest, her nails curving into his coat. She closed her eyes, hearing the sounds of the forest around them, the melting ice, the chilled breeze causing the branches to clack together. From somewhere came the rustling sound of a small foraging animal.

He didn't speak. Nor did she.

She wanted to weep, and she rarely did. Her chest felt heavy, as if her heart weighed five times what it should. Her breath was tight, her lips thinned in an effort to hold back words of wisdom. Words such as, "Let me go." Or, "Please go away."

She ran from Edinburgh and he followed her. She invited him to her bed and his honor marched to the forefront, shaming her. When she expected him to tease her, he only tenderly held her in his embrace.

What was she going to do about him?

She was going to be wise for the first time. Slowly, she stepped back, holding up her hand when he would have reached for her again.

"I think you should leave," she said. "Go back to Edinburgh."

"Is that what you want?"

No. Yes. No.

She nodded.

He smiled, another expression that touched her heart. She wanted to place her fingers on his lips, banish the expression, but that would be as useless as wanting him to be less handsome or forceful.

Logan Harrison would not change.

Nor could she, even though at this moment she felt a tinge of regret that she'd never be a proper wife for him. Someone else would have to be politic and demure. Some other woman would have to brush his hair back from his brow, counsel him to wear a hat to keep his head warm, or always tell him he was right regardless of whether he was or not.

Another woman, reared with obedience and docility, would be the perfect politician's wife.

Not Mairi Sinclair, too outspoken and too independent.

She slid around him, leaving the gazebo without another word, taking the path back to Drumvagen and keeping herself from running only because he was watching.

"**H**e's gone, you know," Virginia said, entering her suite of rooms.

Mairi put her book down. "I know."

She'd watched his carriage leave Drumvagen. Part of her had rejoiced at his departure. A greater share had wept at the loss of him.

"He left us a lovely note," Virginia said, coming to sit beside her on the settee. "He's a very charming man. Macrath quite likes him."

"You sound very English this morning," she said. Virginia's accent always amused her, especially since her sister-in-law was an American.

Virginia smiled. "I've been told that I'm sounding quite Scottish lately. My *r*'s are rolling, and I picked up a few words of the Gaelic."

"God forbid you ever sound like Brianag," Mairi said.

Virginia laughed.

They sat in companionable silence for a few minutes.

"Have you ever thought yourself a fool?" Mairi asked.

Virginia laughed again. "Is it a man doing that to you? The Lord Provost, for example?"

"Yes," she said. "And I think he knows exactly how he affects me."

"Oh, they always do, the brutes. Somehow, they never seem to worry about it."

"Most of the men I know are supremely confident. They know exactly who they are in the world." She glanced at Virginia. "I don't. I haven't the slightest idea where I fit in or what I'm to do or how I'm to do it. I know what I want, but I don't know if I can achieve it.

"When I was a little girl, my goal—my only goal—was to grow up. And then the older I got, the more I became aware that I was supposed to become a wife and mother."

"Aren't those normal goals for women?" Virginia asked.

"Of course they are. But for all women? I doubt I will ever marry, since it's been so many years since I was of a marriageable age."

Virginia made a sound like a snorting laugh. "Don't be ridiculous, Mairi, you're not too old to marry. Granted, you're no longer a schoolgirl, but you're certainly not a spinster."

"I've always detested that word, spinster. Bachelor is a much better sounding word. Every time I hear the word spinster, I think of a skinny, gray-haired woman hunched over her cane, frowning at the world and shaking her fist.

"And what is a bachelor?" Virginia asked with a smile.

"A portly man sitting back with his feet on a footstool, enjoying a cigar and a glass of whiskey. There are no children running about underfoot. He has no complaints from a wife, and he is thoroughly enjoying his solitary life."

"Do you?"

Mairi looked down at the toes of her shoes peeping out from beneath her skirt hem.

"If you had asked me that a few months ago, I would've told you that my life was complete."

"But now?"

"Fenella is getting married. I'll be alone in the house with my elderly second cousin, who can't think of anything nice to say about most people."

"I've often wondered why you haven't married."

"Macrath didn't tell you about Calvin?"

Virginia shook her head.

She wasn't surprised. Macrath kept other people's secrets as well as he kept his own.

"Calvin was my first love. I thought, until recently, that he broke my heart. Now I wonder if I was ever truly in love with him."

When Virginia didn't respond, she continued.

"I think I was a great deal more trusting before I knew him than I am now. Or perhaps I was more childlike. I used to talk with Fenella about when the two of us would get married, how our children would grow up together. Our husbands would be men of influence, and friends, of course. We'd have houses close together and go shopping and do errands."

"I can't imagine that you envisioned that future for yourself, even as a child."

She considered Virginia's comment for a moment. "I think, at the time, I did. But I loved working at the paper. I loved almost everything about it." She glanced at her sister-in-law. "Except sweeping the pressroom." She smiled.

"Even setting type was fun. The process of printing the newspaper was one that fascinated me. I loved helping my father, looking at the folded editions and knowing that my own labor went into it."

"How did Calvin fit in?"

"He was a friend of Macrath's. Perhaps not a good friend, because Macrath was always too busy for friendship. An acquaintance, shall we say. He came around the paper often enough that we became friends. When he asked Macrath for permission to call on me, I was excited."

She smiled in remembrance of her own innocence.

Resuming her story, she said, "Calvin continued to call on me even after I decided to become the editor of the paper. I don't think he was happy about that, but he didn't say anything at first. I was so busy I didn't notice that he was calling on me less and less."

"That's a sign, don't you think?" Virginia asked. "I couldn't imagine not noticing when Macrath wasn't around."

Mairi smiled again. "I think I still believed I was in love at that point. At least until he told me he didn't think I was acting in a proper fashion."

"Because you were running the paper?"

She nodded.

"He told me that his parents didn't approve of me, that his friends thought he was a fool to consider marrying me."

Virginia reached over and clasped her hand over Mairi's, a wordless show of support.

"I think I knew, right at that moment, that I would have to make a choice about my life. Either I was going to be able to do what I truly enjoyed, what I was good at, or I was going to have to act completely different in order to attract a man."

"I think Calvin was a coward. You're a strong woman," Virginia said. "But strong women still want to be loved."

"He told me, essentially, that I was not proper enough to be his wife."

Virginia startled her by laughing. "What a fool he was, and how much better off you are without him in your life. Logan, however, is a different story, isn't he?"

"I've never met a more arrogant, stubborn man."

"I'm guessing that you've acted as yourself around Logan, yet he certainly seems attracted. Is he the reason you asked if I've ever considered myself a fool? The answer is oh, dear heavens, yes. Perhaps even now. Most of my thoughts are about your brother. He occupies a great deal of my mind and my heart."

"That's hardly fair, is it? Do you think you occupy that much of his mind and heart?"

Virginia smiled. "Yes, I do."

Logan occupied too much of her mind and heart as well.

How could she possibly tell anyone that she was very much afraid she'd done the worst thing in the world, fallen in love with Logan?

"Does passion strip your wits from you? Are you supposed to forget everything but him?" Or consent to be taken on a library floor, laughing with delight?

"Yes," Virginia said. "If you're fortunate."

She turned to face her sister-in-law.

Virginia smiled. "Being in love is a lovely type of insanity."

Mairi shook her head. "He makes me do things I'd never do."

"Are you talking about coercion?" Virginia asked, her smile fading.

Only if passion could be considered coercion.

"When I'm around him something happens. I want to kiss him senseless. I want to do things I never think about with any other man. It's just him. It's only him. I don't think of anything other than him."

"Here's where I'm supposed to counsel you on your reputation," Virginia said. "And urge you to consider your position."

"Are you?"

Virginia smiled again. "No, because you are smart enough to do what's right for you."

"I wish I felt the same. I don't know what to do."

"Macrath has taught me that love makes anything possible."

When had her brother become so wise? Or maybe she was just excessively foolish.

"**I**'ve come to ask you about my sister," Macrath said.

James looked up from where he was repairing a piece of tack and nodded.

Macrath went to the bench where James sat, joining him. The stable was a warm and active place, even on this wintry afternoon. The horses blew loud snorting breaths, their hooves stomping the ground. As they worked at the end of the building, two stable boys found something amusing. Their laughter made him smile.

The stable wasn't far from the building he'd erected as his work room and laboratory. There, they built the biggest of his ice machines, behemoths developed for ships transporting foodstuffs across the oceans.

At the moment, however, his aim was to develop an ice machine that could be used by every household, thereby enabling people to get ice whenever they needed it. To that end, he had Jack and Sam working on a smaller model. Each successive iteration of the Sinclair ice machine was more compact than the one before.

He'd hired another man in the last year, someone who was adept at mechanical design. Ian could draw anything Macrath imagined, allowing him to instantly decide if an idea he had for a new device would work.

Drumvagen was getting crowded, when for so many years the place echoed around him. Now he had associates and friends here. Most importantly, he had family.

Family required a great deal more work, which was why he was sitting here in silence, trying to find the words to ask James what, exactly, Mairi had been doing.

What he hadn't expected was for James to shock him.

"Mairi's no' actin' like a lady, sir. Not with her spending the night at the Lord Provost the way she has. Twice, I figure." James glanced at him.

Macrath stared at the stall ahead of him, at the plume of air from a young mare's nostrils. The horse pawed at the ground as if eager to be gone from this place. At the moment, he felt the same.

"Did she tell you she was attacked?" James asked.

Their gazes met. "No, she didn't mention that."

"Aye, the night she gave the speech," James said, and proceeded to tell him the whole of it. "The Lord Provost's man came and found me himself," he said. "I was to go home and not worry about Mairi, since she'd gone to speak with him with a few other ladies."

Macrath glanced at him. "But you didn't believe that?"

"I knew it wasn't true, sir. I'd been looking for her myself. No one else was missing but Mairi, and everyone was talking about how the Lord Provost himself had rescued her." He shook his head. "Some people seem to think they're invisible, sir, that just because they don't want to be seen, they won't be."

"So she spent the night with the Lord Provost?"

James nodded. "And a time after that as well."

Macrath leaned his head back against the timbered wall behind him and told James about the letters.

When he was finished, James stared straight ahead.

"I've no idea who would do that, sir. But I think a woman would be behind it."

Surprised, Macrath looked at him. "You would, why?"

"Because a man would come right out and say something direct. It's women who hint and threaten all delicate like."

He couldn't say that he agreed with James, but the idea did have merit.

Right now he needed to figure out a way to get Mairi to mitigate her behavior. Not only for her reputation but more importantly for her safety.

"I'd have you stick a little closer to her, James. Protect her from whatever threat she's facing."

"And what if she's a yen for the Lord Provost, Mr. Sinclair? What am I to do then?"

The two men stared at each other, leaving Macrath with two thoughts: life around his sister was never dull and maybe Logan Harrison was exactly what she needed.

Chapter 24

As long as Virginia and Macrath were around, the house was peaceful. The minute the two of them went into Kinloch Village or were occupied with tasks, Enid and Brianag were at it tooth and nail. More often than not, Mairi joined Ellice on a walk.

Today they'd bundled up against the cold and escaped to the woods.

"They have to stop one of these days," Ellice said.

"They haven't yet and I doubt they will," Mairi said. "Some people actually enjoy arguing," she added, then wondered if she was one of those. Granted, there was something exciting about entering into a debate with Logan. Thinking about it, her pulse raced and she had an absurd wish to smile.

What was he doing now? He certainly wasn't walking through the woods, shivering with the cold.

"I do get tired of their constant disagreements," Ellice said.

"Would talking with your mother have any effect?"

Ellice shook her head. "I know my mother. She may smile and be very polite, but she's the most stubborn person on earth. Brianag is the same."

Mairi motioned toward a fallen tree trunk. She didn't even care about the state of her skirt, merely sat herself down, arranging the soft hoop around her. Her cloak, normally thick enough for an Edinburgh winter, was no match for the wind coming off the ocean. Her lips were numb and her face stiff with cold.

She had lost the ability to smell anything a half hour earlier, unless it was the cold.

"I'm going home tomorrow," she said. "You're the one who's going to have to endure them."

The *Gazette* had never gone for more than two weeks without an edition. Plus, she had broadsides to publish as well as the rest of the printed material for the SLNA she'd agreed to do.

"You remind me of my sister," Ellice suddenly said, coming to sit beside her.

"I do?"

"Oh, not in appearance, although Eudora was regal looking and so are you. It's just that Eudora had a way of getting things done."

She had never thought of herself as regal looking, but didn't say so to Ellice.

"You must miss her a great deal."

Ellice nodded. "It's easier being here," she said. "Eudora was never at Drumvagen. It's not like the London house, where I saw her everywhere. I think it's better for Mother, too." She smiled, an expression that brought out the beauty of her brown eyes.

She truly liked the girl. Ellice deserved better than to be placed in the middle of squabbles between her mother and Drumvagen's housekeeper.

"You need to come to Edinburgh to visit me," she said.

Ellice's eyes widened. "Truly? I should enjoy that

above all things. I love Drumvagen, but in London there were so many things to see and do. Is it the same in Edinburgh?"

"I would venture to say that there is more to see and do in Edinburgh than there ever was in London."

When Ellice smiled at her, she tempered her Scottish pride a bit. "Or at least the equal of London. Perhaps you can even return with me. I'll talk to Macrath today. He can talk Enid into anything."

Mairi entered Macrath's library later that day, taking the chair in front of the fire instead of the one beside the desk where he sat. She wasn't going to feel like a penitent in front of her brother.

"I'd like to take Ellice back to Edinburgh with me."

"Ellice?"

She nodded. "The girl deserves a change of scenery. And a little less bickering." She frowned at him. "You need to do something about the two of them, Macrath."

"What do you suggest I do?"

He looked helpless, and she felt a surge of fondness for him. He'd always been the most competent person. She hated for him to be at the mercy of two harpies.

"I don't know," she said, wishing she had an answer. "But think of something to keep them occupied other than making everyone at Drumvagen miserable. In the meantime, I'm going home."

"Before you leave," he said as she stood and was making her way to the door. "Let's solve another problem, shall we?"

She glanced over her shoulder at him.

"I've talked to James."

Oh dear.

He stood, coming around the desk and advancing on her.

"Why didn't you tell me about the attack on you?"

"Because I knew it would upset you," she said. "Because I don't bleat about my problems and I wasn't about to come running to my little brother."

"By two years, Mairi, that's all."

They'd had this conversation often enough for it to be annoying now.

"A little consideration, Mairi, that's all I ask. I would have liked to be informed."

"You would have come to Edinburgh," she said, "when your family needs you here. You would have insisted that I come to Drumvagen to live. We would have fought about it and neither of us given way. Isn't it better to learn after the fact?"

He frowned at her. She wanted to tell him that he wasn't nearly as intimidating as the Lord Provost of Edinburgh, but perhaps it wasn't wise to bring up Logan at the moment.

"Why do I need to write you at all, Macrath, when you have your spies on me? Robert eternally fusses at me about money, and James about the rest of my life. I'm surprised you don't know every detail of my days."

"James is to look out for you, not be your nanny. And Robert's position was never designed to be a taskmaster."

"Tell Robert that," she said.

He leaned back against the desk, folding his arms and studying her.

"How did Harrison come to rescue you?"

Her mouth fell open, and she closed it with a snap. She hadn't expected that question. Everyone in her household knew she'd been attacked. They hadn't known about Logan's role.

What had James told him? Or had Logan said something? No, he'd given his word.

"Does it matter now?"

"Are you in love with the man?"

Another question she hadn't expected. She headed for the door.

"Mairi."

She turned and looked at Macrath again. "You ask too many questions, Macrath. I don't have answers for you."

"Or for yourself?"

Her brother was becoming a little too perceptive for comfort.

"Can Ellice come with me?"

"Yes," he said. "I agree that she needs a change of scenery."

She nodded, slipping out of the room before he could comment further.

Macrath sat at his desk, his attention on the fire. The cold had made conditions inside his laboratory unbearable, so he'd given his men the day off. Tomorrow they'd make inroads on finalizing the new design. For now, he had to solve the problem he'd been avoiding for months.

He'd taken Enid and Ellice into his home because they were family to Virginia. The assimilation had been difficult for the older woman, and he wasn't certain about Ellice's feelings. She was so quiet and self-effacing that if he asked her, she would probably say something like, "I'm quite happy, Macrath," even if she were weeping.

From the beginning, however, Enid and Brianag had clashed. Now he had to do something.

He summoned a maid, gave her instructions and watched the flames while he waited.

When the knock came, he stood, walked around the desk and opened the door. Brianag and Enid were standing on the threshold.

Without saying a word, he returned to his desk, standing behind it. How long would they remain there before one of them gave way? The answer was two minutes. Then Brianag tilted her head, nodded toward Macrath, and stepped slightly to the right. Enid sailed into the room with a small triumphant smile.

"Ladies," he said, gesturing toward the chairs on the other side of the room.

Neither sat. Instead, they stood in front of his desk, Brianag taller, Enid short and squat. Both women were equally determined.

"We need to solve this problem," he said. "It's one that affects everyone living at Drumvagen." He looked at each of them in turn. "You're making everyone miserable with your quarreling."

Once more he gestured to the chairs in front of his desk, and this time they sat.

Brianag looked directly at him, her gaze flinty. Enid studied her fingers with the same fascination Alistair had exhibited as an infant.

He could send Enid back to London, but she didn't have funds of her own to live a London life and had too much pride to take an income from him. He wasn't going to fire Brianag. She'd made Drumvagen his home.

"What started this war?" he asked, wondering if either would answer him. When the silence stretched thin, he shook his head. "Then what escalated it? You were occasionally amenable to each other in the past, but in the last few months you've been sniping at each other constantly. Why?"

Enid was the one to look away.

"I need an answer," he said, wondering if they realized how irritated he was becoming.

"The laundress ruined my brooch," Enid said softly.

"Ach, and don't you have enough nonsense to wear?" Brianag said. "You, with your brooches, your rings, your earrings."

He sat back in the chair. Could it be this easy? Could they be jealous of each other?

"How did that happen?" he asked.

"Carelessness," Brianag said. "The woman thinks the world waits for her, that we're all here to do her bidding." She turned and glared at Enid. "We've no lady's maids waiting on you here."

"I left it pinned to my dress," Enid said. "I didn't know the laundress was going to wash it." She sent a fulminating look toward Brianag. "But you didn't even let me talk to the woman."

"Talk? You were shouting at her."

"Why shouldn't I shout?"

"Because she's part of my staff, not yours. If she's to be shouted at, I'll be doing it."

Macrath shook his head again, leaned back in his chair, folded his arms and regarded both of them.

"It wasn't just any brooch," Enid said in a small voice. "It was my mourning brooch for Eudora. It held a lock of her hair. Gone now."

Brianag looked stricken, a rare occurrence to catch her in a moment of regret.

"Bessie lost her husband recently," she said. "She would have seen it if she hadn't been mourning herself."

The two women shared a look, not of accord, but a measure of understanding.

Before they could get back to carping at each other, he said, "You've been working at cross purposes ever since

Enid arrived. You, Brianag, have an intimate knowledge of Kinloch Village and the other villages beyond it. People respect you. I might even go so far as to say they revere you in certain ways."

Brianag nodded, a small smile indicating that she approved of his comments.

"But Enid is the Dowager Countess of Barrett who managed her own staff in London. Have you never considered that the two of you working together could accomplish a great many things?"

Enid sent a look toward Brianag, one that he could only interpret as incredulous, while Brianag was staring at him as if he'd just sprouted two heads.

"Why not pool your knowledge? Why not write a book, perhaps, a guide to women who are managing their own households?"

"A book?" Enid said, her face taking on a rosy tint.

"A set of Scottish hints," Brianag said.

Before she could continue on a nationalistic theme, he interrupted. "Both countries, ladies. A Scottish and English book compiled from the wisdom of two women well versed in the art of homemaking. We own a printing company. It wouldn't be all that difficult to publish your book."

In fact, it would be a monumental undertaking, but he was willing to fund the venture if it would make Drumvagen a happy place again.

He'd given them enough to think about. If that didn't work, he'd have to come up with another way to end this feud that had turned his home into a battleground.

Now, to convince Mairi to form a publishing company. All in all, that was an easier task than getting Brianag and Enid to act in accord.

Logan was giving some thought to returning to Drumvagen to fetch Mairi home himself if she wasn't back today. He could just imagine her reaction. She'd verbally box his ears and then probably refuse to see him again.

No, perhaps it was better to simply remain patient. A difficult process when he was counting the hours.

He'd become a source of amusement for her pressman. Allan always greeted him with a smile and a comment.

"She's not here, Provost. Not today."

He usually spent some time with the man, getting to know him and Fenella, who appeared more than once at the paper.

As Allan said, he was stupid in love with the girl, and that was evident to anyone halfheartedly paying attention. She obviously felt the same for him, nearly glowing in Allan's presence.

He strode through the hallway, turned left into the pressroom, laughter lighting his way. When he entered, they turned to face him.

"I'm sorry, Mr. Harrison," Fenella said. "But she's not home yet. But I'm sure she will be soon."

Did he look as disappointed as he felt? Evidently he did because she came to his side, reached out and patted his arm in a curiously maternal gesture.

"She really will return soon. She's never gone more than two weeks without printing an edition."

The paper would bring her back to Edinburgh. The paper and not him.

He looked around the room, at the overflowing bins, inhaling the complex scents, and wondering why this place had such a fascination for her.

"She loves it, doesn't she?"

"She's a newspaper person, Provost," Allan said. "Ink's in her blood. She tells people about their world."

"And hides here," Fenella added.

Allan glanced at her.

"It's the truth," she said. "As long as she's reporting on something or writing a broadside, she's happy."

He didn't like them talking about Mairi when she wasn't here to defend herself, but most of all he didn't like what Fenella was saying.

He didn't want her content with her life. He didn't want her happy without him.

He'd been elected Lord Provost, the culmination of a goal. He was planning on a future in Parliament. Only recently had he realized that all his plans were somehow not enough. A certain woman of fiery temperament was what he needed to complete his life and add spice to it.

Perhaps he should take advantage of this time and marshal his arguments, prepare his courtship, and make strategic plans for when she returned.

He was in love, and damn it all, as stupid with it as Allan had declared himself to be.

The only difference was that the pressman's affections were returned.

The fact that he didn't know how Mairi felt was the one flaw in all his plans.

Chapter 25

"They're going to write a book?" Mairi asked. "And you're going to publish it?"

"No," Macrath said, grinning. "You're going to publish it."

Her eyes widened. "When am I going to have time to do that?"

"Make time," he said.

"I've plans of my own, Macrath." She'd been thinking about it over the last week.

She hadn't taken advantage of being in Scotland's capital by reporting on the political news of the day. Nor had she tried to convince readers of her own opinions and beliefs.

What if she did?

What if, instead of erring on the side of caution, and hoping to entice a broad group of subscribers, she narrowed the focus of the paper? What if the *Edinburgh Gazette* became the Edinburgh Women's Gazette? What if she used the paper to promote women's causes?

When she told Macrath her idea, he smiled broadly.

"Make it yours, Mairi. If you want to convince other people to your way of thinking, do so. If they're good ideas, people will side with you."

"Or they could cancel their subscriptions and the paper would be in financial ruin."

He smiled. "Not quite that," he said. "Not as long as people want to buy ice."

"I can't take money from you, Macrath."

"I don't see why not. You can consider me your financial backer. I am a contributor to women's causes."

She narrowed her eyes and looked at him. "You've never been interested in such things before," she said.

"I've never been married to an intelligent woman before," he said. "One who is going to have another child. I might well have a daughter. I want her to be treated with fairness and justice. You earned your place in the world, Mairi. Let me help you the rest of the way."

When had he become so aware of the world? Macrath normally fixated on his inventions to the exclusion of everything else. She had to find Virginia and thank her with a hug.

"Only if I need help," she said. "Only then."

"You'll need the money right away for the publishing company," he said, stubborn as always. "I think you'll make a success of your new venture, Mairi. Just make sure to protect yourself as well."

She wasn't sure if he meant the attack on her or guarding her heart. Either way, she nodded, kissed him and Virginia good-bye and entered the carriage, sitting beside Ellice.

The fact that Enid agreed to let Ellice travel to Edinburgh surprised Mairi. Especially since the girl was going to be in her company the whole time.

When she said as much to her brother, he smiled. "Enid has a cause. Her book."

They said good-bye to Drumvagen, heading toward Edinburgh with a three tiered mission: the first, to educate

Ellice about the capital of Scotland and the charm of Edinburgh. The girl would fall in love with the city, Mairi was sure. Secondly, to make monumental changes to the *Edinburgh Gazette*, and thirdly—a goal only an hour old—to publish books.

The idea excited her even though she didn't know anything about it. Surely, though, printing a book and printing a newspaper couldn't be all that different? Perhaps Allan knew something about the press required.

At the thought of her pressman, she sighed. She had to repair her relationship with Fenella.

While she was at it, she needed to solve the mystery of the letters.

She had a great deal to do, and all her tasks would keep her mind occupied. She wouldn't have to deal with thoughts of Logan.

Ellice fidgeted with her cuffs, stared down at her polished shoes, traced each button from her waist to her neck. Today she was dressed in dark brown, with white cuffs and collar. White piping edged her hem and down the placket of her bodice. Her bonnet was brown with matching flowers.

The color suited her, a dark backdrop for her perfect skin and brown eyes.

Mairi was wearing a dark blue dress, one of the serviceable dresses in her wardrobe. Her bonnet was somewhere, perhaps in her valise. Or she had probably left it at Drumvagen.

Fenella was the only one who fussed at her for not wearing a bonnet, although Logan had questioned her twice now. Of course, any woman of his acquaintance must be properly attired at all times.

Perhaps she should start wearing more colorful clothes. In the past, she hadn't been concerned about her wardrobe.

However, now she wanted to leave an impression, and not one of a drab spinster.

When had she started thinking she was doomed to remain unmarried? Had Calvin done that to her? Or had her own uncertainties after he'd spurned her caused her to reject the notion? Granted, her duties of reporting and being editor of the *Gazette* occupied her time, but there was more to life than work, even if that work had purpose. Hadn't Macrath proven that a man could have love, a family, and an empire?

If a man could have it, why not a woman?

Fenella was right.

"Thank you," Ellice suddenly said. "I can't tell you how much I appreciate your taking me to Edinburgh. I shall be the very best house guest. Anything you want done, I'll do."

She reached over and patted the girl's hand. "You don't have to do anything, Ellice."

"But I do, don't you see? I was dying at Drumvagen. It's a lovely house, and quite a wonderful place. But no one wanted to talk to me. Virginia was always busy either with Alistair or Macrath. Mother was occupied with her feud with Brianag, and all the maids were quite nice girls, but they were always worrying about talking too much."

Ellice rolled her eyes. "I've been known to go out and talk to the sheep. Or the horses or any animal that would stand still long enough to listen to me. But even they seem to have better things on their minds."

Mairi had never considered how Drumvagen might be isolating to the young girl. Even though Ellice was the sister of a deceased earl and the daughter of a dowager countess, she was doomed to remain in the Scottish countryside.

Edinburgh would look like paradise in comparison.

"I don't know much about dances and balls and such," she said. "But I'm sure there are some entertainments that would interest you."

Ellice's eyes widened. "Please tell me you're not hinting that I should marry. I haven't any wish to be married, at least not right away. It seems like I haven't had any time at all just to be myself."

Since she'd often felt the same, she didn't try to convince Ellice otherwise.

But marriage didn't seem such a terrible fate anymore, and wasn't that a strange thought to have? Were her feelings connected to Logan Harrison by any chance?

What would've happened if she'd never written the broadside about the Lord Provost? She and Fenella would've gone back home, and she would probably have fussed and fumed for a while. Would she have involved herself in the SLNA? If she had, and the same circumstances had occurred, who would've come to her aid? Not Logan. Perhaps no one would have, and the outcome would have been more dire.

If she'd never written about him, would she still have spent the night in his arms?

The scenery sped by as she contemplated the question and another one even more troubling: what if he married the Drummond girl?

How would she bear it?

" . . . don't want you to regret taking me to Edinburgh," Ellice was saying.

She came back to herself, smiled at the girl, and said, "I could never regret that."

Macrath had been very clever by allowing Ellice to come with her to Edinburgh. By doing so, he ensured that her own behavior was impeccable. She had to be a good example, which meant no more nights away from home.

Surely that wasn't a twinge of disappointment she felt?

She thought about all the things she could show Ellice. She would begin with telling her a little bit about Edinburgh's history, how the city was built on volcanic rock. The girl would see Edinburgh Castle first, of course, everyone did. She'd design a path, one that Fenella could explore with her, James accompanying them and acting as chaperone. They'd start at the castle, head down Castle Hill, past the water tank that looked like a fortress, and left to the Camera Obscura erected in 1853.

Yes, she could keep all three of them busy with an itinerary of sites to visit, which would give her enough time to work on her new idea for the *Gazette*.

"Let me tell you about the household," she said. "You've met James, of course. Our driver. And Fenella, but you know her, of course."

Ellice nodded.

"Then there is Robert. He's our second cousin, and he came to stay with us when Macrath purchased Drumvagen. My brother wanted a chaperone for Fenella and me. Robert also does the books for the Sinclair Printing Company," she said. He also lectured her incessantly about her expenses, but she didn't make that comment. There was no need for Ellice to know that she and Robert were forever at loggerheads.

To her surprise, Ellice asked, "Will we be seeing the Lord Provost again?"

The question brought her up short.

Had Logan made another conquest? Evidently so, from Ellice's blush. Did she need to warn the girl about him?

Don't look at him as if he were a Highlander of old, armed with a broadsword, standing with arms folded, legs braced, a stern look on his face. Whenever you do, don't let your heart be engaged, because such a man will only hurt you. He'll talk to you about heiresses and women who are proper to be considered as his wife. He will ask you what you want in life, and then give you a set of criteria for his, none of which you could possibly match.

As if she even wanted to be a wifely candidate of his.

She had to stop thinking about the man.

"No," she said. "We won't be seeing him again."

Ellice sighed. "What a shame. He's so attractive."

Especially in a kilt, but that was another comment she'd not make aloud.

The longer they traveled, the worse the weather. The sleet had claws, hitting the carriage windows, screeching against the panes.

She sat back against the seat, impatient to be home.

One of her first duties was to make peace with Fenella. Life was much more difficult when you had to consider the feelings of other people, people you loved, cared for, and never wanted to hurt.

She pushed away the image of Logan. The less she thought of him—and saw him—the better.

Life was perfect.

Macrath sat listening for a sound of discord. There was not a whisper of disunity. No glowering looks as Enid and Brianag met in the hall. No sniping remarks at dinner, when Enid made sure to tell him how her household had been so much more smoothly run.

Not once in the last day had Brianag entered the room with a complaint, only to stomp out when he refused to send Enid back to London.

Nor was there an indication of dissension about the

rearing of his son. Enid's English sensibilities had often clashed with Brianag's Scottish beliefs, but not now.

The pounding of footsteps alerted him. Macrath looked up just as his son barreled into the library to wrap his arms around his legs.

He bent and lifted Alistair up in his arms.

As a baby, his son had looked like him. As the months passed, Alistair became even more a miniature version of himself. His hair was black and tousled more often than not. His smile bore a resemblance to Virginia's, but his blue eyes were those of generations of Sinclairs.

"Go fishing, Papa," he said. "Go fishing today."

Alistair had started speaking early. His first word hadn't been "Mama" or "Dada." Instead, it was "Brianag," which made both Macrath and Virginia suspect the housekeeper had repeated it endlessly to the boy.

"Not today, I'm afraid. It's too cold. When it warms a bit, son."

"He doesn't understand the idea of the future," Virginia said, standing in the doorway. "Alistair is a creature of now, I'm afraid."

He strode to his wife, bent and kissed her, an activity their son tried to interrupt with hands that smelled of soap and jam.

Virginia smiled at him, reached up and trailed her fingers over her son's cheek and then Macrath's. "I don't think he likes to fish all that much. I think it's because he likes to be with you and have you all to himself."

"Pity you don't come fishing with me," he said.

"But I have you to myself in different ways," she said, her cheeks turning a becoming pink.

He laughed and kissed the tip of her nose.

"Fishing!" Alistair said.

"Aren't you a fine little despot," Virginia said, reaching out and taking Alistair from him.

"What you consider being stubborn, my love, is simply being a Scot."

His American born wife laughed. "I think you have the right of it," she said, in a credible Kinloch Village accent. "He's just like his da."

When he frowned at her, she laughed harder. His only recourse was to kiss her until amusement was the farthest thing from their minds.

No, life was good at Drumvagen, and he had his sister's idea to thank for that.

When he said as much to Virginia, his wife smiled at him again.

"It's you who gave them the notion of writing a book of recipes and housewifely hints. They're in Enid's suite making plans."

She put Alistair down on the carpet. He promptly went to the chest in the corner and pulled out one of his puzzles. Virginia plucked a few broadsides from the shelf to read. Mairi always kept her furnished with the latest from Edinburgh. Some women liked flowers. Others liked confections. Virginia loved reading broadsides, the more gruesome, the better.

"Even if we take a loss on the book," he said, "it's worth the expense."

She laughed, the sound of it carrying her through the library and spearing his heart. Was there any sound as beautiful as Virginia's laugh?

"Perhaps they'll surprise you, Macrath, and it will sell well."

"I don't honestly care," he said. "It's worth whatever it costs just to have a little peace."

He straightened the top of his desk, having learned from prior experience that it wasn't a good idea to have an inkwell where Alistair could get to it. He also put away his best pen in case his son decided to try to use it to draw again.

As he opened his desk drawer, he saw the letter Mairi had given him. To his discredit, he'd put it there and forgotten about it.

"Why are you frowning so?" Virginia asked.

"Mairi's been getting anonymous letters," he said.

"Has she?"

He extended the letter to her. Virginia uncurled her legs from the chair, stood and retrieved it. Taking it back to her chair, she sat and read it, her frown deepening as she did so.

"What has she done that's so terrible?" she asked, lifting her gaze to him.

He shrugged. "Written something that annoyed someone. Always a chance in the newspaper business. She went after the Lord Provost. That might have incited the letter writer. Or her involvement in the SLNA."

"From what I saw, her relationship with the Lord Provost isn't an adversarial one."

He needed to tell her what James had said, where little ears couldn't hear.

"Does the handwriting look familiar to you?" she asked.

"Something about it does," he said. "But I'm not certain what."

Virginia stood, crossing the room. Without a word, she grabbed a ledger from the shelf, bringing it back to his desk. Opening the book at random, she pointed to a page.

"Look at the writing."

"It's not the same," he said. "He's printed there."

"Not everywhere. Look at the letters. They match."

She was right. Why hadn't he seen it before? For that matter, why hadn't Mairi, unless she'd only seen the printing on Robert's ledgers? The next question, why had the man he'd hired to help his sister written something so vile?

Robert owed him an explanation.

"You'd better leave first thing in the morning," she said calmly, picking up the ledger and putting it back into place.

He sat back, watching her. From the very first moment, he'd known he could fall in love with this woman. Not once had he considered that the love he felt for Virginia might deepen and grow until it was a part of him, as important as breath or his beating heart.

She understood him and now she knew he felt he had to get to Edinburgh for Mairi's sake.

"Have I told you how much I love you?" he asked.

He stood and opened his arms. As simple as that, and she was there, smiling at him.

Fenella was an excellent hostess, making Ellice comfortable in the guest room, asking if there was anything the girl liked to eat. She even mentioned taking her around to see various sights in Edinburgh.

However, she barely spoke to Mairi and she never once looked in her direction.

Mairi waited until her cousin was alone in the dining room before approaching her.

"You're still angry with me."

Fenella didn't look at her when she answered. "Shouldn't I be? You accused Allan of something horrid."

"I don't think it was Allan. I don't know who it was."

Her cousin glanced at her.

"I want only the best for you, Fenella. I like Allan very much and I'll warmly welcome him into the family."

Reaching out, she enveloped Fenella in a hug. "I want you to be happy."

"Do you still suspect him?"

Mairi shook her head. "No," she said. "I don't." She was listening to her heart on that decision. She didn't want Allan to be guilty.

"Mr. Harrison will be pleased you're home," Fenella said. "He's inquired about you almost every day."

"Has he?"

She most definitely did not want to talk about Logan.

"Tell me, have you and Allan selected a date?"

Fenella spent the next five minutes telling her everything she and Allan had planned. Allan's brother, the last of his family, was traveling from Dumfries to meet her. The wedding was to be a small one, but the date had not yet been selected.

As she spoke, Fenella's joy was visible for anyone to see.

Mairi had never once been jealous of her cousin and she found the emotion uncomfortable now.

At dinner, she wasn't surprised to discover that Ellice was charming, amusing, and able to converse with both Fenella and Robert easily. She'd noted a change in Ellice the more distance she'd put between herself and Drumvagen. No longer was she quiet, almost shy, and certainly fearful. Was it leaving Drumvagen? Or was it coming out from beneath the shadow of her mother?

Robert looked at Ellice with approval. Of course, the girl didn't say anything shocking, was filled with praise about the house and its furnishings, and stated that she was excited to see more of Edinburgh.

He was less pleased with Mairi, who waited until they were served dessert to make her announcement.

"I'm changing the name of the newspaper," she said. "Well, not just the name, but the emphasis as well. The new name is going to be the 'Edinburgh Women's Gazette.' We're going to feature stories that would be of interest primarily to women. Even the columns will be slanted for women."

She looked at each face, noted Fenella's and Ellice's interest. She hesitated a moment before looking at Robert, but when she saw his eyes flatten to two brown stones, she wasn't surprised.

"It will not cost that much," she said, breaking a rule and discussing finances at the dinner table. "I have Macrath's blessing."

"What will happen to the current subscribers?" Fenella asked.

She'd already thought about that.

"They'll be given an opportunity to continue their subscription. If they object, then they will be taken off the roll."

"You'll have to refund the money," Robert said.

"Only on a pro rata basis," she said. "Thankfully, most of our subscriptions have come at different times throughout the year. We won't feel an immediate financial hardship if they all discontinue at once."

She smiled determinedly. "But I won't give them the opportunity to cancel," she said. "They'll be so impressed by the new paper that they'll not only renew, but convince their friends and neighbors to subscribe as well."

Robert abruptly stood, said good-night to Fenella while once more welcoming Ellice to the household. Pointedly ignoring Mairi, he made his way to the stairs. They could hear him stomping to his room.

"We don't feel the same, miss," Abigail said, gathering up the dishes on the sideboard. "As Mr. Robert, I mean."

She glanced at the maid.

"It's proud we are of you, all of us."

"Thank you, Abigail," she said, feeling a surge of warmth at the girl's words.

If she had to fight this battle in her own household, how much worse was it going to be among the citizens of Edinburgh?

Why did it suddenly seem more than she could accomplish?

Chapter 26

To Mairi's dismay, sleep wasn't easier in her own room than it had been at Drumvagen. Instead, she lay staring up at the ceiling illuminated by the bluish white glare of moonlight. She could hear Fenella and Ellice giggling down the hall, but gradually even the sounds of amusement faded, leaving only the sigh of the wind against the windows as company.

The hole in her chest expanded, growing larger and larger until she could envision a giant black space in the middle of the mattress encompassing everything, even her.

She missed him.

There, a confession she should have been too wise to utter even to herself.

He was close. Close enough for her to walk to his house if she was thoroughly foolhardy. In her imagination, she dressed and donned her cloak and her gloves, roused James from his room above the stable. She would caution him to secrecy, knowing that it meant nothing because he would tell Macrath. Now she simply didn't care. She would laugh at his threats and race to the carriage, waiting impatiently.

She wouldn't bother to explain herself to Logan's majordomo or Mrs. Landers. Instead, she would run up the stairs to Logan's room, throwing off her cloak and her clothes.

He would rise in his bed, surprised at her appearance.

Wicked and wanton, she would mount him, keep his head still for a kiss.

She'd take advantage of him, stroke her hands over his arms and chest, let her fingers dance along his skin, and incite shivers where she touched him. She'd inhale his moans and kiss him until he was senseless. Only then would she take him into her body and hold him there until the pleasure was so great she had to have her release.

The thought of being so abandoned was hardly restful or conducive to sleep.

After a while she sat on the edge of her bed, then went to her secretary, placing her hands flat on the surface where she'd written the broadside about him. If she wrote another about the Lord Provost, what would she say? What would she accuse him of? Stealing her sleep, perhaps. Infusing her mind with all sorts of wicked images, none of which she could easily banish.

She sat, laid her head down on her folded arms and sighed, thinking that she was sad sight indeed, a woman in thrall to a man.

Surely, though, men felt the same way. She would discount Calvin for the moment. He wasn't the epitome of all things good about men, being as disloyal as he'd been. Did Allan feel that way about Fenella? Perhaps one day, if she had enough courage, she would ask him.

Her father had loved her mother long after she died in childbirth. He spoke of her often, and whenever he did, it was with a smile.

Perhaps, in her reporting, she could ask the men with whom she conversed how they felt about their wives. She would use the information for a future column of the

Gazette. Surely women would be interested to hear what opinion husbands held.

She picked up her pen and jotted that idea down, along with another. She would ask Fenella her thoughts about love. What did it feel like? Was it a general ache in the body? Was it a burning sensation in the stomach? Was it a cacophony of thoughts that flew about in the mind like bats escaping from a cave? Was it the sudden inability to form a cogent thought?

Or was she ailing in some way?

Going to Drumvagen had not been the least bit relaxing. She'd been miserable there, and even more unhappy after Logan left.

Now, despite her plans for the *Gazette,* she wasn't as enthused as she should have been. Why wasn't the paper enough? Why was she so jealous of Fenella? Why did she feel so ancient when Ellice looked at her with admiration in her eyes?

Something must be done. She couldn't allow this malaise to continue.

One way or another, she had to revert to her normal self. The Mairi Sinclair who was enthusiastic about each day, who knew exactly where she was going in life, who fretted about her restrictions but found a way around them nevertheless.

She removed her nightgown and began to dress, irritated with herself, Logan Harrison, and life in general. James was not going to be happy, but like it or not, he was going to have to drive her to the newspaper.

"I'll not leave you," James said, opening the carriage door.

"Allan is here. You don't have to stay."

"It's the middle of the night. I'll not leave you."

"Very well," she said, "but you're not going to sit out here. It's too cold. Come with me."

After she unlocked the door, he followed her inside, where she led him to her father's office.

"You can stay here," she said. "It's warmer than sitting outside in the carriage."

He nodded and settled behind her father's desk.

Work had always been a panacea. She'd always found comfort in the pressroom, being able to immerse herself in a story, a broadsheet, or reading through the submissions to the paper.

Tonight, however, she roamed through the room, feeling the cold of the night that even the lit brazier in the corner couldn't dispel.

She loved the look of the *Edinburgh Gazette*. She loved that it had been founded thirty years earlier, that it bore the Sinclair name on its masthead. It was created from thoughts converted to words, and printed using metal on paper. Each issue took her breath away.

Somehow, however, the paper wasn't enough. When had that happened? When a certain tall and broad man had crossed her path, grinning at her until her heart stuttered?

She missed him.

Dear God, she missed arguing with him, touching him, anticipating his kiss, his comments, his stubbornness.

What was she going to do?

Work—that was all she had left.

Allan slept above. Could he hear her? Would he come to see what the noise was and why the lamps had been lit?

Perhaps he would keep James company.

Still clad in her cloak, she removed her gloves, wandering from the shelves along the walls to the massive press in the middle of the room. Allan had taken advantage of her absence and cleaned the plates and the mechanism. Her fingers trailed along the metal, feeling no trace of oil or ink.

She would need to talk to him in the morning, ensure that he knew she welcomed him into the family, another person to whom she owed an apology or an explanation.

She should just print an announcement and distribute it like a broadside:

To the whole of Edinburgh, I'm sorry.

For daring to be more than just a woman. For wanting to be treated like a man, or at least with the same respect. For having dreams beyond my sex and my station. For being rash and improvident. For allowing a charming smile to lull me into being fascinated by a man.

She should concentrate on the next issue of the paper. From her pocket she withdrew those submissions she'd read at home. There were enough to fill six columns, at least. She'd let other writers talk for her during this edition, and next edition she'd make the announcement about the *Gazette*.

Would she lose all their subscribers?

Her sources might disappear completely. Would they be as reluctant to talk to her as they'd been after her broadside about Logan?

Perhaps she should tell them that she'd been with him one night, his mistress for an evening, his paramour for a certain number of hours. Knowing the high esteem in which the inhabitants of Edinburgh held their provost, perhaps it would elevate her standing.

After removing her cloak, she hung it on a peg near the

door. Walking to the typesetting area, she stared at the rows of letters and phrases. These, too, had been cleaned. She placed the papers where she could read them, began with the first column, the movements of her fingers learned from when she was a girl, standing in front of her father and taught how to see the type in reverse.

The first article was one on the Scottish Society for the Prevention of Cruelty to Animals, and how each Scot should become involved in their campaigns.

She saw something out of the corner of her eye and glanced in that direction, thinking it might be James or a querulous Allan, coming to ask why she was at the paper in the middle of the night. Neither man appeared.

Turning back to her typesetting, she focused on her task, but not for long. The light in the hall was too bright to be a lamp. She smelled it before her conscious mind could accept its presence: fire.

Fire was their greatest enemy. Not only did they store newsprint on the second floor, but vats of ether used to clean the type were kept in the back along with other chemicals needed to run the press.

James was in the room closest to the storeroom.

She threw down the type and ran toward him, only to barrel into him as he was coming out of the office.

"Allan's upstairs!"

James thrust her in the direction of the building entrance and raced up the stairs.

She stood there for a moment, then ran into the pressroom, grabbing the buckets of sand they kept there for just this purpose. One she emptied in the hall before the pressroom. A second she poured around the press, hoping it might keep the fire from it. The press and type were the most valuable items in the whole building.

She could hear the fire now. How strange that she'd

never realized fire had a voice. It grumbled like a querulous Robert, creeping ever closer.

Logan hadn't told his driver to go past the paper on his way home. But he hadn't told the man to go straight home, either, so he was amused to note that they were nearing the Sinclair Printing Company. Evidently, his behavior of the last week had formed a habit.

He wasn't certain he wanted to see the building.

She hadn't yet returned, and her absence was eating at him. Mairi had never struck him as a coward, however. Sooner or later she would have to return to Edinburgh, and when she did, he was going to start courting her in earnest.

As they passed the building, Logan pushed the grate aside, calling for his driver to halt the carriage. A flickering yellow light beyond the windows confused him. Just as he realized what he was seeing, the sound of a woman's shout skittered down his spine.

He opened the carriage door and began to run.

Chapter 27

"**A**llan! James!"

Mairi shouted for both of them but no one answered.

She headed for the stairs, only to encounter a wall. A living, breathing wall in the form of Logan Harrison.

"What are you doing here?" she asked, a question he didn't answer.

"Come on," he said, pulling her arm.

She jerked away, prepared to argue with him. She never got the chance. The High and Mighty Lord Provost simply picked her up and slung her over his shoulder, leaving the newspaper offices and depositing her on the opposite side of the street.

She pulled away from him, staring at his face, limned in the light from the fire.

"Allan and James are inside," she said. "I can't just leave them."

"I'll go and find them," he said. He took off his greatcoat and wrapped it around her. It settled heavily on her shoulders, smelling of his scent, something about it reminding her of forests and winter.

Since the coat swamped her, she grabbed at it with both hands.

"You stay here," he said.

She had never liked being given orders, and tonight was no exception. As if he could hear her thoughts, he bent down and pressed his lips against her forehead.

"Please, Mairi."

"Allan lives above the paper," she said. "And James went to find him."

"I'll go look, but you need to stay here where I know you'll be safe," he said.

The fire made him a god, a living embodiment of all those Highlanders of old. His eyes hardened, his mouth firmed, and there was something in his expression that silenced her.

He didn't stand on a barren hillside, looking out over a glen of battle hardened men. Yet even though this was the nineteenth century, not the middle ages, and the setting was different, it didn't matter.

Anyone who fought him would lose.

Reluctantly, she nodded.

He left her in the next moment, heading back to the building.

Had she been distracted? Had she erred in lighting the lamps? Had something been too close to one of the globes?

Had her coming to the paper caused the deaths of two men? Please, God, no.

The wind carried a billowing cloud of smoke to her and she began to cough.

She went to the carriage, released the brake, and led the restless horses down the street. She soothed them as best she could, but they were still afraid of the fire. James could have calmed them with his voice. Had he escaped? And Allan?

What about Logan? Why hadn't he returned?

The bells of the fire brigade were another sound

added to the noise of the fire. She didn't know how they had gotten word so quickly, but she was grateful nonetheless.

She walked slowly back to the corner, staying on the other side of the street, watching as the crowd gathered. Although this was not a residential area and there were few houses nearby, some proprietors made their homes above their shops, like the Sinclair family had for generations. People came out, dressed in their nightclothes, standing on the street to watch the fire brigade. With any luck, the fire wouldn't spread. If they were really fortunate, some of the building would be salvageable.

From what she saw now, however, they would not be visited by any luck at all. Flames licked out of the third floor windows, smoke pouring from the attic. Because of the combustible nature of the products stored there, the fire had been fed well.

So many people were watching, all of them speaking in low tones as if in deference to the largest blaze they'd ever seen in this part of Edinburgh.

The fire was spectacular.

Billowing clouds of black tarry smoke puffed up from the roof. She clutched Logan's coat around her as the wind made her eyes water and fueled the fire even higher. The smoke was tinged with a curious nutty odor as bits of charred paper floated to the grounds like black snowflakes.

Her heart constricted to a painful ball pressing against her lungs.

Anxiety, guilt, and worry swelled inside her until she could barely breathe. Tears were just below the surface, threatening to flood her.

Her lungs heated and her eyes watered from the smoke. She pressed her face into the collar of Logan's coat, praying for the men inside.

Flames licked from inside the building to beyond the windows and doors, as if the fire had outgrown its cage, stretching its arms outward in a bid for freedom.

The other buildings were in danger now.

Where were the men?

The wind blew her hair off her neck, reminding her that once again she was without a bonnet.

Moving back still farther, she stood with the others on the street. At first, hearing their excited talk, she wanted to correct them, but that was the reporter in her. The woman remained silent, letting them speculate that an act of carelessness had caused the fire, that someone working late had overturned a lamp or a spark had escaped from a pipe.

The building abruptly shuddered. Flames shot through the roof like the hand of God had speared upward through the brick, flexing fiery fingers.

Mairi took another step back, the street trembling beneath her feet as a second explosion followed the first.

Where were the men?

The stench of the fire made Logan cover his nose with his arm. He knew the layout of the building a little from his visits in the past week but not the upper floors. He searched those smoke-filled rooms he passed on the way to the pressroom. There, however, the fire had gained way, so he stepped back from the inferno.

A narrow hallway led to the back. If he went in that direction, would he get trapped? Did the hall lead to the stairs?

Mairi had said that Allan lived above the paper, but where? Did he sleep on the second or the third floor?

He heard shouting above the noise of the fire and left

the room, heading down the hall. At the end of it, almost like an afterthought, was a set of stairs. He climbed slowly, the heat level rising as he did. He heard another shout and raced to the top, where he found two men grappling in the shadows.

At first he thought they were fighting, until he realized James was trying to move a fallen beam. He bent and added his efforts, finally able to free the other man.

"We can still save the press!"

"It's gone," Logan told him.

There was not a damn thing they could do at the moment. Even breathing was getting difficult and the fire seemed louder, as if it were climbing the stairs after them. To his horror, he realized that he was correct. The bottom half of the staircase was engulfed in flames.

Before he had time to reason it out, he jumped from the landing, hitting the wooden floor on his hands and knees. James shouted something, then pushed Allan from the landing before following.

Logan strained to see through the smoke and the black clouds. The fire raced up the stairs. If they didn't leave soon, they were going to be encircled by the flames.

Standing, he gripped James's forearm with one hand and pointed with the other. James grabbed Allan and followed him down the hall.

From the density of the smoke, they were going to play hell getting out of the building. They couldn't afford to get lost or make any mistakes.

He counted the steps back to the doorway where he stood when the explosion had occurred. The faint outline of a window in one of the offices gave him hope.

Suddenly, an explosion shook the building. He stood in the doorway, both hands braced on the frame as the walls shuddered around him.

When the tremors subsided, the fire seemed even louder. Once inside the smoke-filled room, Logan stretched out one hand, finding a desk in front of the window. He knelt atop it, jerking on the window frame.

He'd been taking shallow breaths for the last five minutes, but now he couldn't even do that without coughing. He was getting dizzy, his eyes smarting, his ears overwhelmed by the roar of the flames now at the doorway.

Removing his shoe, he used the heel to shatter the window. He urged James out, and then Allan, before following.

The smoke was plentiful here, too. They staggered to the opposite curb. Logan bent over, hands on his knees, coughing, then threw his head back, taking big gulps of air.

Glass shattered, another window exploding because of the fire.

Mairi breathed the smoky air, fear and horror keeping her still. Her stomach churned, curling her tongue with a sour taste.

She fought back her tears. If they came, they would drown her. Her throat ached and the prayer she murmured was simple. "Please God. Please God. Please God."

Three shadows coalesced on the side of the building then separated to become Logan, James, and Allan.

Mairi grabbed the lapels of the greatcoat and ran toward them, stopping only inches from Logan, prevented from throwing her arms around his neck by the watching spectators. But she couldn't stop herself from examining him, from his shoes to the top of his wind-tossed hair.

His vest was torn and the right sleeve of his shirt was

ripped. His face was covered in soot. He wiped a forearm across his eyes before grinning at her.

"We got him," he said, nodding at Allan.

She turned to James. He, too, was covered in soot, his clothing in even worse shape. His shirt looked as if it had caught on fire before being extinguished.

"Are you injured?" she asked, fingering the burned cuff.

"No, I'm not. Thanks to the provost. A beam fell on Allan and he helped me pull it off."

She walked to stand in front of Allan. She wished the light were better, because it looked like one side of his face was red.

"Are you burned?"

"It'll be fine," he said. His smile was bright in the scarlet night.

She thought he wasn't being entirely truthful, but he wasn't the type to complain. Perhaps he'd be more honest with Fenella.

"You'll take him home," she said, nodding to James.

"I'll not be going anywhere right now," Allan said, turning and staring up at the building. Only the front facade still stood. The brick had crumbled on the side of the building, probably because of the explosion. "We'll need to see what's left."

"Nothing's left," she said, uttering the truth in a dull voice.

Nothing remained of the Sinclair Paper Company, only memories.

Here, Macrath had the idea for his refrigeration machine, the success of which had propelled him toward his dream of creating an empire. Because of his talent and his determination, he'd moved them from this place to their house, to live a life of near luxury.

This building was the source of her comfort when

Macrath had left Edinburgh, and she'd been fueled with a dream of her own. She'd been as determined as her brother to succeed, to be the editor of the *Edinburgh Gazette,* to be respected for her business acumen, her talent in writing, and her nose for a story.

That dream was in ashes, just like the building and all its contents.

There were no historical copies of the paper or drafts of her favorite columns, the broadsides she written by herself and from information she'd obtained on her own. All the research files she'd accumulated were gone.

Some people might remember the sign that hung there indicating that the printing company had been formed more than thirty years ago. Some of them might recall Macrath's name as editor and publisher. Some might even remember seeing her there, laboring at night when most of the world was asleep.

The *Edinburgh Gazette* had died tonight. Everything was gone, from their supplies to their press.

At least she had the notes for future columns safely at home, as well as the names and addresses of all her contacts.

Most of all, everyone had survived. For that she would be eternally thankful.

Mairi was fluttering about, checking on James and Allan, before returning to his side. By the light of the fire she was a sight, garbed in his greatcoat, so large on her that it trailed from her wrists and puddled on the street. Her hair was askew, tears tracking through the soot on her face.

He'd seen her fuss at him, terrified and in pain. He didn't think he'd ever seen her cry, and he wasn't altogether certain he wanted to see the sight again. Her tears twisted his stomach until it was in knots, made his hand shake as he reached out to touch her face.

"Shh," he said, his voice a raspy croak. "It's all right. They're all right."

"You very nearly weren't, any of you. What took you so long?"

She looked too precious at that moment for her scowl to have any effect. He only smiled at her, reached over and patted her cheek again. She turned her head and placed a kiss on his palm, such a tender gesture that he smiled.

Mairi was a woman of great emotion beneath an exterior of competence and bravado. The greater the fuss, the more she hid.

"I'm afraid Allan was all for saving the building," he said.

She peered beyond him to where Allan sat. He waited for her to say something comforting to the man. A promise to rebuild, perhaps. Or a declaration that a simple fire wouldn't stop her. She didn't, however.

Instead, Mairi turned away, staring at the building that held her life's work.

For a few minutes the four of them watched the fire brigade at work. He knew they should move back, just in case another explosion occurred. When he stood, however, his legs nearly buckled.

He gave himself a minute, bent over with his hands on his knees.

Once he was breathing better, he left them, returning to the building and the fire brigade. As large as the fire was, they could use extra help.

Logan strode back to the fire brigade. Allan and James joined him, all of them helping by grabbing the handles of the pump and working it while the other men manned the hoses.

She went to help distribute tea a few kind ladies offered, grateful for the support of neighbors. She answered questions, accepted condolences, and on more than one occasion was brought to tears.

For hours she sat at a safe distance, watching as the fire was slowly extinguished. From this moment on, she knew she would smell smoke and recall this night. The sound of bells would make her remember the fire brigade, the shout of men, the cackling, malevolent laughter of the flames.

When she finally saw Logan, she walked toward him, holding out her cup. He drank the rest of the tea, handing the cup back to her with a smile.

Reaching up, she placed her fingers on his cheek, gently wiping at the soot.

"I should go home," she said.

The fire was finally extinguished: the fire brigade was packing up their equipment. Nothing further could be done.

"You could have died," he said, his tone rough.

"And you as well."

She owed him so many thanks. How could she possibly express everything she felt? She ought to at least try.

"Without you, they would have died," she said. "Thank you for saving them."

"Allan is seeing if there's anything that can be salvaged and James is helping him. You're coming with me."

How very pompous he sounded. Did he realize she didn't have any energy to oppose him? She could barely blink her eyes.

Logan Harrison, Highlander of old and now, startled her by picking her up in his arms and striding toward his carriage.

"People will talk, Logan. Your constituents will be shocked."

"I find that I don't much care," he said.

That comment surprised her so much she remained silent and allowed herself to be abducted.

Chapter 28

Her face was still, her blue eyes swimming with tears. He wanted to protect her from the sight of the ruins of the Sinclair Printing Company.

Let the world think what they would. Let those people standing in the street fascinated by the sight of a destroyed dream turn their heads and see him. Right now, his political ambitions faded beneath a very real need: to comfort her, and to ease her pain however he could.

"I can't go home with you again," she said once they entered his carriage.

He didn't answer.

She closed her eyes and sighed. "You're the most stubborn man."

He bent his head down and kissed her nose.

"Do you want me to promise to leave you alone? I will, if that's what you want. I'll install you in one of the guest rooms, and you'll be a chaste woman in the morning."

She sighed. "That would be best, don't you think?"

"Do you always do what's best?" he asked, knowing she didn't. Mairi was often improvident and rash, but her heart could expand to hold all of Edinburgh and probably Scotland.

"Yes," she said, turning away from him.

He smiled at the lie. She was right, though, he had to give her that. He shouldn't be taking her to his house. He should tell his driver to turn around and go a half mile in the other direction. There, he'd escort her to the door, wait until he was certain she was settled in, then return to his home. He would congratulate himself on his wisdom as well as his restraint.

He wasn't going to do any of those things.

They entered his home from the rear, the first time she'd seen this approach. His garden, draped by night, was much larger than hers. She had the errant wish to see it, wanted to return in the daylight.

Instead, they crept through the back like thieves.

The tip of one finger skimmed along the top of her hand, a gentle guide.

Logan stopped in the shadow of a large tree, now denuded by winter. He grabbed her hand, his fingers resting between her knuckles, a curious pairing and one that was surprisingly intimate.

He wrapped his arms around her. She sighed into his hug, winding her arms around his waist. She still wore his coat. He must be freezing.

Before she had time to voice her concern, he bent his head.

His kiss was deep and terrifying, leading her to a destination she knew only too well. He fisted his hand in her hair. She wrapped her arms around his neck and held on.

He smelled of smoke and fire and death and destruction and life and promise.

"Mairi."

She shivered at the sound of her name. Closing her eyes, she allowed him to sweep her from the garden, inside the house and up the stairs.

Once in his room, he closed the door, shutting out the world.

She should leave. She should remember her reputation and his. She shouldn't be here, wanting more than a kiss.

But she'd been without him for weeks. He was here and she could touch him as she'd wanted for too long.

She grabbed his hand with both of hers, pressing her lips against the base of his thumb.

"I shouldn't be here," she said, dropping his hand to wrap her arms around his waist and press her cheek against his chest. "I should be wise and sensible and demand you take me home."

Leaning back, he tilted up her chin with his hand. "Shall we be neither wise nor sensible tonight? There's a lot to be said for being unwise and rash."

A glow started deep inside, brushing aside her sadness.

She should leave but she didn't want to be anywhere else but here, with him, with his soot-covered face and his reddened eyes. She wanted to tend to him, to care for him, to cradle him in her body, and feel the joy of possessing and being possessed.

"I have no choice," she said, and it was the truth.

Here she would stay because with him she felt safe, protected, and just for tonight, loved.

He should have bathed, washed the soot and stench of fire away, but he didn't want to step away from her for a minute.

Her eyes widened with each garment he unfastened. When he removed her bodice, her hands fluttered in the air but remained at her sides as if she couldn't decide whether to flee or fight him. She did neither, merely stood like a sacrifice, each successive item of clothing causing her to tremble more. Next was the corset cover, he thought it was called, a gauzy thing that only served to veil her.

He wanted her naked beneath him. Or naked above him, it didn't matter. He wanted Mairi naked and joyous, her lips curved in a smile.

Above all, he wanted to banish the look of sadness from her face, offer her passion in exchange for grief.

He unfastened the busk of her corset, separated it by the simple matter of placing his hands beneath it and widening them. Her skin was so hot that he could feel it even with her shift in the way. She was still trembling, and that made him question whether he should hasten the task or slow it further.

He really had no choice. His body urged completion at the same time, strangely enough, his mind sanctioned it as well. He wanted to bring her joy. Have her recall him each day, each hour, for the pleasure he brought her, if nothing else. If she didn't think of their discussions, if she wasn't interested in his arguments, then let her remember his loving.

Let her hunger for him as he did for her.

He got to his knees in front of her. He had never acted this way in front of any woman, but then she was not like any other woman. He reached up and unfastened her skirt, coaxing the button free, then working on the tape of her petticoats. She hadn't worn a stiff hoop, but then she wasn't a doyenne of fashion. Most of the time she didn't wear a bonnet.

"I missed you," he said. "All those days you were away."

She didn't speak, but he didn't expect her to respond. When she was feeling vulnerable, Mairi retreated to silence, a condition otherwise alien to her.

"I thought about all of those things that I would have told you if you were here," he said.

"Council matters?" she asked, a sparkle in her eyes. "To think that I might have overlooked a great source all along."

Her fingertips danced along his cheek, rested beneath his chin in a tender touch.

His heart swelled at the curve of her smile.

He slid her skirts and petticoats over her hips and down her body, taking his time.

She was trembling more now, clasping her hands before her, her gaze on his face. From time to time he would look up to find her eyes intent on him.

"What are you thinking when you look at me that way?" he asked.

Would she answer him?

Surprisingly, she did. "How I feel like a maiden before you," she said. "How you, a braw Highlander, seem from medieval days."

"Do I?"

She nodded. "It's your fault, you know. That first day, in your kilt. Was I supposed to ignore the sight?"

"Or that day you touched my truss," he said.

"Your holster," she said, correcting him with a smile.

He had never known a time like this, torn in two by lust along with amusement. Then there was the tenderness that nearly swamped him and stole his breath.

He bent to unfasten her shoes, slowly unlacing them with the same care he'd taken for her garments. Now, he rolled one stocking over her perfectly formed knee and then down her beautiful leg. She placed her hand on his shoulder as she lifted her foot. He repeated the action with the other leg, both of them silent.

Kneeling there, sitting back on his heels, he studied

her. Clad now only in her shift, she looked like a pagan goddess.

"Let down your hair, Mairi," he said, wanting to complete the picture.

Without questioning why, she did, slowly removing the pins and letting them drop to the floor, while he remained still and silent and in awe of her beauty. When she was done, she threaded her fingers through the mass of her hair until it hung below her shoulders.

"Not a pagan goddess," he said. "But Aphrodite."

"Are you my shell, Logan?"

He would be anything she wanted, anchor, helpmate, or supporter.

She shivered, and he realized she was cold. Standing, he took her hand and led her to the fire. Then he bent and grabbed the hem of her shift, pulling it over her head until she stood there revealed and simply Mairi.

"Do you know how beautiful you are?"

"I've never been called beautiful," she said.

"Then I can only think the world is foolish, and I'm the only wise man alive."

She smiled, shaking her head.

"I want to hold you in my arms all night," he said.

"Please make sure all my garments are in the same room this time," she said.

His grin widened.

"I have no intention of going through your house gathering up my clothing."

He laughed. "I don't remember your doing that," he said. "I seem to recall that was my task."

He pressed himself to her, feeling a tenderness for Mairi that he'd never before felt for another human being. He thought he'd understood passion in his infrequent encounters, but being with Mairi was different. He didn't want her surrender as much as her complicity.

In this, she was his partner, his other half, his separate match that had been missing all these years.

Her breasts were beautiful, full and tipped by eager nipples standing erect like a beacon for his lips. He loved the sound she made when his mouth grazed them, when his tongue licked first the one then the other.

He took her to his bed, placed her on the mattress, covering her not with a sheet but his body. Slowly, he touched her everywhere, anointing her with his mouth, kissing each curve, relishing her moans.

When it was time, he entered her slowly. He paced himself, raising up on his forearms, bending his head to kiss her gently and inhale her gasps.

He wanted to stretch the moments thin, drive her insensate, until she begged him to bring her to fulfillment. Her hands flattened against his shoulders, then clutched him before trailing down his arms.

Her long, slow moan accentuated his next thrust. When he pulled out of her, her legs widened, her hips arched up to keep him nestled there.

She was driving him mad.

But it was a reciprocal madness, because her hands were on his buttocks now, nails digging into his skin. Again and again she arched upward to meet him and subsided reluctantly.

Had she experienced enough to know how wondrous this was? This was a perfect pairing, bliss so exquisite that his vision grayed.

Just when he thought he couldn't take any more, she shivered in his arms, tightening around him, milking him. He came in a gush of release, uttering a prayer of thanksgiving that he had brought her to fulfillment first.

Chapter 29

"**O**h come quick, miss," Abigail said, shaking her shoulder.

Fenella roused slowly. It felt like someone had hung weights from her lashes, because it was very difficult to open her eyes.

She blinked as the maid lit the bedside lamp.

Abigail was fully dressed, if haphazardly so. Her bodice was buttoned incorrectly, and it didn't look as if she'd done more to her hair than simply wrap her night braid around the top of her head.

Fenella raised herself up on her elbow and glanced at the window.

Arrows of pink streaked across a midnight blue horizon.

"What time is it?" she asked, yawning.

Her dream had been so pleasant that it was difficult to surface from the dregs of it.

"It's early, miss, but there's been a tragedy."

Memories of the dream abruptly vanished.

Abigail went to her armoire, withdrew a dress and placed it on the end of Fenella's bed.

She sat on the edge of the mattress, putting her feet on the floor. "A tragedy? What's happened?"

Abigail's face was as still as stone, her lips compressed until they looked bloodless.

"Oh, miss," the maid said softly, "the *Gazette*'s burned down."

She blinked at Abigail, the words not making any sense. "The paper's burned down?"

Abigail nodded. "Gone to rubble, miss. Nothing left of it."

Allan lived above the paper.

"Tell Mairi I'll be right there," she said. Her cousin was going to be disconsolate.

"She's not here, miss. Just the men, looking as if they're half burned."

She was suddenly wide-awake.

Mairi blinked open her eyes to find Logan asleep beside her. In the faint light of a winter's dawn, his lashes were impossibly long; she wanted to test them with her fingertips to see if they were as feathery as they looked.

He opened his eyes, making the transition from sleep to wakefulness with a smile.

She felt her cheeks warm the longer they watched each other. Should she say anything? Thank him for making her feel so wonderful? Chide him for being a barbarian and whisking her away from the scene of destruction to his home?

For a few hours he'd effectively banished all thoughts of the fire from her mind. In doing so, he'd also given her another problem to face. Or perhaps she had this problem ever since meeting him.

What was she going to do about Logan?

The relationship couldn't be allowed to continue. She was no fool. She might become pregnant at any time. There was no guarantee that she was exempt from that state after last night, being loved not once but twice.

They'd bathed together, then loved again, laughing with abandon and delight.

His warm breath brushed her temple. She closed her eyes, wishing to elongate the moment and, at the same time, magically transport herself somewhere else.

Logan had induced conflict and chaos into her life from the beginning.

She rolled away to sit on the edge of the bed.

He stroked a finger down her bare back, inciting her shiver.

"Cold?" he asked.

She shook her head. Susceptible. Yearning. Wanting something that danced out of range from being identified.

"The fire wasn't an accident," she said, looking up. They'd been so frenetic a few hours ago that neither of them had closed the curtains. The world was a flower, and dawn the center of it. Gold stamens radiated from a pink sun. Dots of vermillion and blue speckled the horizon.

She glanced at him when he raised up on one elbow, the sheet falling to expose his chest and more. A line of hair pointed to his crotch, as if to advertise his attributes.

His smile buttressed her resolve to be gone. Otherwise, she'd fall victim to his charm once again.

She'd already been foolish enough.

"What makes you think so?" he asked.

"The letters," she said.

"You think they're connected?"

"I think they might be," she said. "Someone thinks I shouldn't run a paper. What better way to stop me than to burn it down? What better way to punish me than to take away what I love?"

"You can't love a building, Mairi," he said gently.

"You can love an idea, Logan. And the *Gazette* was an

idea. A way of communicating thoughts from one mind to another. A way of spreading news, inciting conversation."

She glanced away, then forced herself to look at him directly. He knew her body. He needed to know her mind.

"I can still see my father standing beside the press, his fingertips stained black from years of setting type. He always wore a half smile as he worked, as if his task gave him joy.

"He was the best reporter I've ever known; the person who taught me the five rules to any story: what, where, when, why, and how."

She stared down at her hands, flexed her fingers as if to find them stained, too.

"I always wondered what he would have thought if he knew that I had taken his place and not Macrath."

"I think he would have been very proud of you and perhaps amazed."

She looked at him. His gaze was direct. He wasn't trying to be charming now, only sincere.

She cleared her throat, determined not to weep.

"But you were there. Why? It was very opportune." Without him, James and Allan might have been lost.

"Because I'd gotten into the habit of checking to see if you'd returned to Edinburgh," he said, rising from the bed with not a care for his nakedness.

She really should have looked away, but the sight was too entrancing. Even his backside was lovely.

"Did you really?"

"I was missing you, you daft woman."

He turned and faced her.

"Do you think I had something to do with the fire, Mairi?" he asked, his face carefully expressionless.

The amusement she felt was welcome. "No, Logan. You'd be more direct in your criticism."

His answer was to shake his head, go into the bathing chamber and close the door behind him.

She pulled the sheet off the bed and moved around the bedroom, gathering up her smoke-stained clothes. She would miss her cloak, now just one more bit of ash in the building's ruins.

Logan opened the door to the bathing chamber as she was buttoning her bodice. He came and sat beside her on the bed, still naked, still supremely unconcerned about it.

She smiled at the evidence of his confidence. Although, if she looked as good as he did, she'd probably want to strut around without clothes, too.

His chest was well defined. Her fingers had played down the center of it, parting his hair there and tracing around his nipples. She'd felt each muscle and trailed her hand down lower, causing him to gasp.

What kind of woman was she to want to remove her clothes and join him in the bed again?

She pushed that thought away, looking around for her reticule. Was that gone, too?

"I have to go to the paper," she said. "I need to see it for myself in the light." She sighed. That was one task she didn't want to do, but it couldn't be left for anyone else.

After that, she had to find a way to let Macrath know. She really should tell him in person; that sort of news shouldn't be delivered in a letter.

"I'll go with you," he said, standing.

"Not like that." She sent a quick glance in his direction.

He only smiled at her, his eyes intent on her face. "No, not like this," he said.

Before she could speak, say something inane or foolish, something that didn't mirror what she felt, he came to her, placed his hands on her shoulders and smiled down into her face.

"It's going to be all right, Mairi."

How did he know? How did he know that she was suddenly unsure, uncertain, and too close to tears?

She should tell him that she didn't want him to accompany her, that it wasn't necessary, that she could cope well on her own. But that would be a lie because she wasn't at all sure she could be strong right now.

He pulled her into his arms and kissed her, silencing her thoughts by giving her a rainbow. The explosion of color behind her lids was matched by the taste of him. She melted into the kiss, brushing the tip of her tongue against his.

Passion had another dimension to it, a tenderness that made her want to slow him down. He wrapped his arms around her, and she sighed into his embrace, feeling her heart expand.

She wanted him again, just as she had last night, just as she would later. She wanted to talk to him, tell him her secrets, hear his. She wanted to ask his opinion, argue with him, and attempt to change his mind.

She wanted him with her, a friend dearer than anyone, a companion of her heart.

The kiss went deeper and she moaned.

He answered with a growl, pulling her closer until she could feel every contour and ridge, every muscle and bone, as if their two bodies were fused together.

His hand was in her hair; her hands around his neck as she stood on tiptoe.

Just as quickly as she was dressed, she was naked again.

Fenella flew down the stairs, hesitating at the bottom. Where were they? The parlor? The kitchen? The stable?

"They're in the kitchen, miss," Abigail said, following her at a slower pace. "Mr. Robert is looking them over."

Robert? What skill did Robert have? The physician must be called this minute. They must have something for pain. Cool water, she remembered, could take away the fire of a burn. She remembered a recipe her mother had made for a poultice.

Pushing open the door, she nearly sagged to the floor on seeing Allan sitting at the table. Robert was examining his hands, and as she watched, he turned her beloved's face to the lamplight.

"Does it burn?"

"It stings more," Allan said. "I was just too close to the fire."

"Stubborn arse," James said. "Begging your pardon, miss," he added, glancing over at her. "But if it hadn't been for the provost, the fool would have died."

Going to Allan's side, Fenella placed her hand on his shoulder, trying not to gasp aloud at the condition of his clothing. What wasn't burned was tinged yellowish brown. James's clothes looked as bad.

"What happened?" she asked, her voice trembling.

"A fire," James said. "It began in the storeroom, I think."

"Or the pressroom," Allan said.

James shook his head. "Mairi was in there. She would have noticed something."

"How did it start?" Fenella asked.

Each man shook his head.

Fire had always been something they feared, especially when living above the paper. They were all careful to check up on each other. Was the stove banked? Had the chemicals they used been put safely away? She couldn't imagine either Allan or Mairi being lax in that task.

"Is there much damage?"

"It's gone," Allan said, staring down at his hands. "All of it. The whole building."

She turned away, began to make tea, helping Abigail with the chore to keep from throwing herself into Allan's arms or sobbing in relief. He was in one piece and other than the redness of his face didn't look injured. James looked to be untouched as well.

"What about Mairi?" she asked, ashamed that she hadn't asked before now. "How is she? Where is she?"

"She was well the last time we saw her," James said, glancing at the other servants.

Cook was making breakfast and two of the maids were bustling about arranging plates and silverware. If they were sleepy from being awakened before dawn, they didn't look it. Or perhaps the excitement of the news of the fire had simply burned away their fatigue.

What was James not saying?

"Let's have tea in the parlor," she said, "and give Cook room to work."

She glanced at Abigail, who nodded.

A few minutes later, after helping Abigail with the tea tray, she entered the parlor.

When Allan joined her, she touched him on the arm, wishing she could find something comforting to say to him. How many hours had he complained about the press, trying to make it work better? How many modifications had he made? She'd listened because it was Allan, but anyone could see his pride in his job.

Robert entered the room, mumbling something under his breath. Another complaint, no doubt, which was normal for the older man. With the paper gone, he would have more to grouse about, more warnings to issue, more about which to grumble.

She wished there was a way to meet with James and Allan without Robert in attendance, but if there was, she didn't know it. Biting back her impatience, she watched the men settle into comfortable places. James and Robert took opposite ends of the settee, while Alian sat in one of the chairs.

When he coughed, she frowned.

"A lingering effect of the smoke," he said. "Nothing to worry about."

She wanted to put her hands on him, make sure he was well, and examine him from tiptoe to the top of his head. Only then would she feel reassured.

He could have died. That thought kept running through her mind.

After they were served, she dismissed Abigail, sat on the chair across from Allan and faced the men.

"Now, what's all this about Mairi? Where is she?"

Neither James nor Allan would look at her.

That was fine. She'd be as patient as Job. She'd never before considered whether she was calm in a crisis, but up until now she'd acquitted herself well. She might wish to scream and cry but she hadn't.

Although Robert was glowering at them all, he didn't speak. James was looking at the carpet as if he'd never seen the pattern of flowers on it. Allan was smiling at her over his teacup but he wasn't forthcoming with information, either.

"Where is Mairi?" she asked, when it was obvious that even patience wasn't going to make them talk. "You said she wasn't injured. Then where is she? Still at the paper?"

When only silence answered her, she placed her cup back on the tray and frowned at all of them.

"Someone will tell me what's going on this very minute."

She heard the running footsteps before it occurred to her that she'd forgotten someone else in the household—Ellice.

The girl entered the room, dressed only in her wrapper, her hair still in curlers. Her face was gray, her eyes wild.

"Mairi," she said breathlessly. "There was a fire. Is Mairi all right?"

Fenella thought to send her back to her room, except there was a light in Ellice's eyes that hinted the girl wouldn't be amenable to being banished.

Fenella turned back to the men.

"He took her," Allan said. "Marched off with her in his arms."

She didn't even have to ask about whom he was speaking. Only one person would have been able to take Mairi away.

Oh dear, this was not the kind of education Ellice should have about Edinburgh. But it was too late to send her away now.

"Logan Harrison," Allan said. "Like a ravening beast he was."

"He saved your life," James reminded him.

"And then stole Mairi."

Her cousin's virtue was in great danger of being publicly flogged.

"She's been at his house," she said, glancing at the mantel clock, "for how long?"

Abigail entered the room, and Fenella didn't dismiss her. If the whole of Edinburgh was going to hear this tale—which they probably would—what did it matter if every member of the household knew?

"Two hours at least," James said. "We stayed behind to see if there was anything that could be salvaged." He punctuated that comment with a shake of his head.

Robert, who had been uncharacteristically silent until now, said, "Fornicators, all of you. The house is filled with fornicators."

He turned his glance on Abigail, who was standing in the doorway. "Don't think I don't know what you do on your half-day off, girl." He glanced at James, frowning. "Or you," he said, turning his gaze on Fenella. "You and Allan thinking the world doesn't know what you're up to. Gadding about all hours of the night. In my day, women weren't wicked, amoral creatures."

Robert scowled at each one of them in turn, holding his gaze on Fenella the longest. Only Ellice was exempt from his rage, and that was because the girl had only been in Edinburgh two days.

Shame should have oozed from every pore, but she caught Allan's eye and noted the twinkle in it. Although she wasn't fond of being part of Robert's tirade, she wasn't as embarrassed as she should have been.

Was that how Mairi was feeling right now?

"We're going to be married," Allan said, looking at Robert.

She didn't care if she scandalized Robert or not, she stood and went to sit on the arm of Allan's chair, placing her hand on his shoulder. She simply needed to touch him.

Robert frowned. She wasn't surprised that his disposition didn't change. In the three years he'd been living with them, he hadn't approved of much.

"She'll ruin herself," Robert said, "and dance as she's doing it."

Unfortunately, she agreed with that comment. Mairi was being reckless. She'd often done things that weren't lady-like, like walking through Edinburgh alone on her quest to obtain information or working at all hours of the day and night at the paper. Her cousin had never, however, acted as shocking as she had since meeting Logan Harrison.

"Something must be done to save her," she said. Before it was too late.

Chapter 30

Logan finished dressing, a circumstance made unusual by Mairi's interested observation. He'd never dressed in front of anyone before, at least as an adult. The circumstance was oddly companionable, almost domestic.

When he was done, he presented himself to her. She nodded in approval, stood and kissed him.

Long minutes later she pulled back, shaking her head, her lips curved in a smile. "It's best if you don't touch me, I think. Stay over there," she added, pointing to the other side of the room.

He smiled at her, holding his hands up.

"Thank you," she said. "For coming with me to the paper. I would appreciate your companionship."

"Sometimes, a difficult chore can be shared," he said, wanting to take away the sadness in her eyes.

He'd never before felt hurt because of someone else's pain. To be around Mairi was to teach him not only about her but himself.

Love was a curious emotion, one that was unexpected and startling. He wanted to do things for her, take away those tasks that disturbed her, make the world an easier place. He wanted to shield her, or if he couldn't do that, extend his arms around her and support her when she was afraid or uncertain. Above all, he wanted her to know she was not alone.

Did she feel the same?

Another thing he learned—he was capable of being a coward.

He stood toe-to-toe with any number of argumentative individuals. He fought back when people tried to intimidate him. Yet he was curiously loath to ask Mairi what she felt for him.

Sometimes it was necessary to simply follow a course without a compass. When the time came, a man must do what he thought was right. He was going to ask her to be his wife, because as unplanned, ill-timed, and inconvenient it was, he'd fallen in love and he wanted her in his life. Now, tonight, tomorrow, and for a future stretching out as far as he could see.

If she refused him, he'd simply plead his case. If she rejected him, he'd merely convince her.

He wanted to know what she thought. He wanted to share his ideas with her. He wanted to ask her opinion and give her his. He wanted, in a way he'd never once considered with another woman, to combine their lives to form a partnership.

He went to get his case, because he'd go straight from the paper to his office. He was going to be late, a rarity for him. Thomas would have to cope with this change and others he was about to implement.

"Will you be leaving again?" he asked. A question uttered in an offhand manner. Would she realize how important the answer was to him?

Running for Parliament was not as important as his personal life, a decision that had been festering for a matter of weeks. Ever since meeting a certain firebrand with flashing blue eyes who occupied most of his thoughts.

He glanced over at her, curious why she hadn't answered and about to lay the verbal groundwork so she wouldn't suddenly be surprised by his declaration. He didn't get the chance. She moaned, then pressed her hand against her mouth.

"What is it?" he asked.

"There's a carriage parking in front of your house," she said. "I'm afraid you're about to be visited by my family."

He walked to the window and watched as James wound the reins around the brake, then descended from the driver's seat. The carriage door opened and Allan emerged, followed by an older gentleman Logan didn't know. Fenella was next and then Ellice, the girl he'd met at Drumvagen.

"Dear God," she said, "what are we going to do?"

"Go down and meet them," he said, realizing that his chance had come and gone. What he'd wanted to do on his own time had suddenly been foisted on him. "Appear before them in our virtue and our vice. Let them harangue us. There's nothing more we can do."

"You don't look the least upset," she said, her voice filled with panic.

"Why should I be upset?"

"Because they're all there," she said. "All of them. I'll never be able to look any of them in the face again."

He didn't bother hiding his smile. "I'm afraid my servants will be like your family. No doubt they're tittering behind their hands now and will be whenever they see me in the future."

He could, perhaps, dismiss all of them as of today and start anew with a fresh crop. But he had an affinity for Rutherford and felt a genuine fondness for Mrs. Landers.

It wasn't their fault he'd been an idiot. Not by bringing Mairi home or by loving her, but in not seeing her back to her house in time to prevent her family from descending on them.

But it wasn't the catastrophe Mairi thought. In fact, the circumstances might prove to be very advantageous indeed.

When the knock came, he answered the door.

Mrs. Lander's mouth was open in an O of surprise.

Had she thought he'd ignore the knock? Or had she expected him to be attired in his bedclothes? He wasn't going to tell her he preferred to sleep naked. Or was she, perhaps, not expecting to see Mairi standing by the window, both hands pressed against the glass as if she would bodily stop the repercussions they were about to experience?

The devil, as they say, was about to be paid his due.

"We have guests," he said to Mrs. Landers.

She nodded.

"Offer them breakfast. If not that, definitely tea and coffee. Tell them we'll be down shortly."

"Yes, sir," she said with only a quick backward glance at Mairi.

"Shall we go?" he asked, turning to Mairi.

She nodded, her face pale, her lips nearly bloodless. Surprise or horror had rendered Mairi Sinclair mute.

"**W**hat do you mean she's not here?" Macrath asked.

Abigail's eyes were wide, her face as white as the snow that blanketed Edinburgh this morning.

"Sir, Miss Sinclair is not here."

"Tell Robert I'm here, then," he said, entering the house and putting his hat and gloves on the chest in the foyer.

The maid stepped back, wringing her hands.

"Oh, sir, he's not here, either."

What was going on?

He'd left Drumvagen at dawn, the journey cold and taking longer than normal because of the snowfall. He was in no mood to be greeted with a mystery.

"Fenella?" he asked. "Ellice?"

She shook her head.

"Nobody's here, sir. Nobody but Cook, the other maids, and me."

"Where is everyone?"

Her eyes darted from the left to the right and back again, lighting on anything but him.

"Where is everyone?" he asked once more.

Virginia said he frightened people sometimes with his look, so he deliberately softened his voice and pasted a smile on his lips.

"I can't say, sir. Don't make me."

The maid stared down at the floor, her complexion turning rosy. If he frightened her, he was sorry for it, but he had to know what was going on.

"Tell me and quickly."

"There's been a fire, sir. A grievous thing, truly. The *Gazette* has burned down. I'm not the one who should be telling you, Mr. Sinclair, seeing as how you're the owner and all."

It took a moment for the words to register.

"Mairi? She's all right?"

She nodded hurriedly. "Everyone is fine, sir, although James looks a little worse for wear, and Allan has a slight burn on his cheek."

"Is that where everyone is? At the paper?"

She shook her head. "No, sir, they've gone off to prevent another tragedy."

He grabbed his hat, began to button his coat, and picked up his gloves. Evidently, his journey wasn't finished.

"Where are they?" he said, striving for patience and failing miserably.

She grabbed her apron, twisting it in her hands.

Then she told him the whole of it.

In a matter of minutes Macrath's carriage was outside the Lord Provost's home, parked behind the one he'd purchased for Mairi a few years earlier.

Taking a moment to appreciate the brick edifice belonging to Harrison, he tried to collect himself.

He hadn't heard anything damaging about the man. On the contrary, the whole of Edinburgh seemed to love him. Other than Mairi's broadside, he was never lampooned in any of the papers, and he was generally well thought of, not an occurrence that happened often in the political arena.

When Logan visited Drumvagen he'd found himself liking the man. The provost's political instincts were astute, and he was intelligent as well as ambitious. Plus, there was a light in his eyes when he looked at Mairi that reminded Macrath of what he felt for Virginia.

If Mairi's feelings for the provost were the same, he would suggest an alternative to scandal. If she was just engaging in lust for the sake of being shocking, that was another matter entirely.

He dismounted from the carriage, calmed himself, and climbed the steps. He could hear the commotion inside before using the knocker.

A scant second before the door opened he considered turning around and heading back to the carriage, letting Mairi sort out her own life. But the door was opened by a white-haired man who squinted fiercely at him.

"And who might you be?"

"Are they all here?" Macrath asked, staring beyond him. "You're one of them?"

"I am, for good or ill."

He couldn't see anyone, but he could certainly hear them. Fenella, Ellice, and above all the female voices, Mairi. Another booming voice rang out, one he recognized as Harrison's. Did he really want to enter the fray?

Unfortunately, he had no other choice.

The meeting in Logan's parlor was all very civilized, painfully so.

After the initial shouting, everyone settled down. Voices were no longer raised. Instead, they all stared at each other as if waiting for explanations. Mairi wanted to know why they'd descended on Logan's home. Her family evidently wanted to know why she was still here.

The situation was exacerbated when the majordomo announced yet another visitor.

Seeing Macrath enter the room, she clutched a pillow from the settee to her stomach and sat abruptly.

He nodded to her and that was all the greeting she got. He raised his hand, lowering it slowly, a silent command that each member of her family oddly obeyed. They took their places around the room, some on the settee next to her, some on the adjoining brown velvet chairs.

Mrs. Landers provided refreshments, as if this was a convivial occasion and all of them had been expected to arrive barely after dawn. Logan's majordomo, on the other hand, wore the same expression as Robert, as if he smelled something particularly fetid and was prevented only by good manners from commenting on it.

No doubt both of them would be commenting before the morning was over.

Fenella poured tea while Ellice offered the biscuits provided by Mrs. Landers. Even though both Allan and James frowned at her, they each took their share. Robert just sat in a chair and scowled.

Macrath and Logan nodded to each other. At Drumvagen they'd spoken at length about politics, Macrath's inventions, and the future of Edinburgh. This meeting was necessarily strained. Her brother was protective to a fault and wouldn't care if Logan was the Lord Provost or the Lord Dog Catcher.

Logan no doubt felt challenged by the arrival of her entire household.

Each man waved off food and beverages. Nor could she eat anything with her stomach in knots. Besides, this was most definitely not a social situation.

"My sister has been here all night?" Macrath asked pleasantly.

Logan nodded, glanced at her, then focused his attention on Macrath.

"And not the first time, either," Macrath added.

She looked at her brother. He wasn't being tactful, a hint that he wasn't feeling as amenable as he appeared.

She closed her eyes, stifling a moan.

Macrath had a temper that he kept banked. This situation, however, might compel him to forget the restraint he normally practiced.

She certainly didn't want him to strike Logan, but what he did next was even worse.

"I think we both know what needs to be done," Macrath said. "The honorable thing, of course."

Logan nodded, just once, acceptance without a word spoken.

He couldn't be serious.

"No. Macrath," she said, shaking her head. "You're

not going to make an honorable woman out of me, not if it means being forced into marriage. I've never heard of something as barbaric."

"Barbaric?" he asked.

"It's ridiculous to have to marry simply because my family found me in flagrante delicto, as it were."

"You're supposed to report the news, Mairi," her brother said. "Not be the news."

Fenella and Ellice each looked transfixed, while Allan and James pretended an interest in the scenery from the front window. Robert's curled lip and narrowed eyes revealed his disgust of the proceedings. She didn't know if the older man was more revolted by her remaining at Logan's home all night or her refusal to consider herself compromised.

"You don't know, Macrath, but there was a fire. There is no more *Gazette*."

Macrath came to stand in front of her. "I know, Mairi. You can build again if you want to."

She shook her head. "Not if I were married," she said. "Not if my first duty was to be a wife."

"Do I have any say in this?" Logan asked.

Macrath glanced over his shoulder. "Of course," he said.

"I'd like to talk to Mairi. In private."

"Fine, talk to her. I wish you well."

Macrath motioned to the rest of them, and one by one they left the room. No doubt they would congregate in the hall listening.

"You aren't leaving me alone with him?" Mairi asked.

"I believe the entire situation is because you were alone with him, Mairi. Of your own accord."

She sighed.

Once Macrath and the others had left the room, she

turned to Logan. "You needn't sacrifice yourself, Logan. My family will eventually forget about this."

"Will they?"

She nodded.

He smiled before walking away and serving himself coffee and a scone. How very polite they were being. She wanted to shout or scream or stomp her feet to express her frustration and embarrassment.

Every single member of her household knew what she'd been doing the night before. Allan, who before today had been her loyal employee, was a future member of her family. Somehow, having him witness this debacle was even more humiliating.

Logan didn't speak, seemingly content to watch her as he sat on the opposite chair, arranging his cup and plate on the table beside him.

She'd never known anyone who could be as calm while inciting violence in others. Very well, violence in her. She wanted to pummel the man. Or kick him in the shins. Or trip him as he walked. At the same time, she wanted to kiss him senseless and wrap her arms around his neck as they went through the rest of their lives.

If she married him, her life would never be peaceful again.

How could he throw her into such a state so easily? How could he run riot over her emotions? How could he do this to her by not saying a word?

"It's an idiotic notion," she said.

He bent one eyebrow at her and continued chewing.

"I'm not sure I even like you. How can I contemplate living with you the rest of my life?"

He took a sip of his coffee, then placed the cup back on the table.

"I think you like me," he said, his lips curving. "I think you proved that last night."

Her cheeks warmed.

"Nevertheless, this is not a grand scandal," she said. "No one knows but the people in this house. There's no need for heroic gestures to save me. I'm perfectly able to save myself."

"Then your answer is no?"

"Most emphatically no."

How dare he sit there looking at her with his beautiful green eyes, stirring his coffee so silently that she couldn't even hear the clink of the spoon against the cup. There was no sound in the room at all. Even his breathing seemed muted.

It should be storming. Thunder should be bellowing from cloud to cloud. Lightning should spear the earth. Instead, it was a snowy December morning and she was absolutely terrified. Perhaps she could blame her trembles on the cold, even though this room was warm from the blazing fire.

"I wouldn't be a good political wife, Logan," she said. "I'm not at all retiring. I'm not conformable." Her laughter held an edge. "I am most definitely not conformable. I want to know the answer to things. I may even invade the council meeting and report on what's happening in Edinburgh."

What was he thinking? Why wouldn't he look at her?

Part of her wanted him to rage at her, try to change her mind. She suddenly realized, watching him, that he would do no such thing.

Logan would never attempt to manipulate her. If she went to him it would be of her own accord. He wouldn't try to convince her; she would have to be certain of her own mind.

Was she that brave?

Her body thrummed at his touch. He drove her to tears.

She wanted to laugh with him and sob against his chest, all violent expressions of emotion that didn't seem to be love.

Love shouldn't be turbulent or troubling.

Words were her stock in trade. At the moment, however, they were diamonds glittering in a field of glass. She couldn't find the right ones.

Standing, she walked to the window. This view was of his garden, no doubt a lovely place in the spring.

"You only want to protect me with marriage," she finally said. "It's not necessary. No one, if they ever hear of this morning, would ever think ill of you, so scandal isn't a consideration."

"For an intelligent woman you're remarkably stupid."

She glanced over her shoulder at him.

He was angry. Angrier than she'd ever seen him. He was very calm, very reasoned, but his eyes were flashing fire and his smile was tight.

He held his cup with a white knuckled hand.

Who was he to be enraged? She was the one who'd been trotted out like a mare ready to be mounted.

"I think you'd better tell Macrath that there will be no marriage," she said. "That way, he'll know it for certain."

She was determined to be polite and calm. Every second that passed was even more difficult to hold onto that resolve.

"Are you saying your brother doesn't trust your word?"

"That's not what I'm saying at all," she said, feeling her temper slip a little. "Only that if you tell him, he'll understand that it isn't just my idea. He'll know we both feel the same."

"But we don't," he said, taking a sip from his cup.

How dare he throw her into confusion with three simple words?

"You didn't suggest marriage, Logan. My brother did."

"Is that what concerns you? Fine. We'll wait an hour or two, send them home, then I'll sweep you up in a romantic embrace and propose marriage."

"The reason would be the same."

"Would it?" he asked. He smiled, an expression that was polite but not the least whit intimate.

She folded her arms, staring down at the carpet.

"You'd better tell your brother," he said. "Because if I speak to him, he'll know the truth."

"And what is that? That you're determined to do the right thing? You're much too honorable for this situation."

"No, I fall under the category of fool," he said, still speaking in an even tone. "For falling in love with a woman too stupid to recognize that fact."

He left the room before she could rally, before she could think of a thing to say. She stared at the closed door, hearing his voice. Still even, still polite, still capable of stirring her to the core.

He loved her?

Why had he suddenly declared himself now?

And why did she suddenly want to cry?

Chapter 31

The carriage ride home was a silent one and uncomfortable as well. Mairi deliberately didn't meet anyone's eyes. She knew what she would see: condemnation as well as surprise.

She had always been level-headed. She'd never been a dreamer or a romantic. Not for her balls or parties or strolls in the park. No, she wrote her articles, solicited information from her sources, set type, and ran the press. Until Fenella had spoken up, she'd no idea she had imposed her schedule on anyone else.

Calvin had been her only frivolity, if she could call him that, but the relationship was short and painful. In the end he had considered her unacceptable and unfeminine in her pursuits.

At least Logan had never thought her unwomanly. She wanted to fan her heated cheeks but didn't wish to call any more attention to herself. No doubt each of the carriage occupants were thinking Calvinlike thoughts.

There she goes, losing her mind. And not just subtly, either. She had an affair. An affair with not just any Edinburgh inhabitant. No, she had to choose the Right Honorable Lord Provost.

Then, to compound the horror of her actions, she turned down a perfectly acceptable proposal of marriage. Just when she would've been saved from her own actions and contemptible character, she refused.

She could hear the words, although not one person spoke in the carriage.

Marriage was too high a price to pay for being foolish.

Oh, and she had been foolish, hadn't she?

She could fight against society's prejudice of her as a woman. She could convince a man who was reluctant to speak with her that it would be in his best interest to do so. She could produce broadsides and sell them, thereby preventing the company from going under financially. She could force herself to stand in front of a group of strangers and speak to them about her life. She could even survive being attacked by a gang of men.

But she had no defense against herself.

Nor had she ever thought she'd need one.

No one had ever told her that she might feel such passion or be helpless when faced with it. They certainly had never told her that she'd call herself twelve times a fool.

What had she done?

She was not a weak woman. Why, then, was she acting that way around a man? Logan smiled at her and her insides warmed. He grinned and she wanted to laugh. He walked away and she had the strangest compulsion to follow him.

In his bed, she'd acted the harlot. How could she disagree about that? She'd nearly dared him to take her on the floor of his library and gloried in the possession.

They were combustible together.

Just like that, memories of this morning were there, so real she could almost feel him inside her. A hot tide swept over her, made her look down, anywhere but at someone.

They would see it on her face. They would know, by her eyes, that she was suddenly overcome.

What had she done?

What did it matter that he'd asked her to marry him in a moment of embarrassment for both of them? Why was that important?

He loved her.

Oh, dear God, he loved her.

What had she said? Something foolish about not being a politician's wife. She didn't care if he was a politician or a ship's captain.

What had she done?

Logan would probably never willingly be in the same room with her after this morning. Had he ever been rejected? Or so publicly?

After all, he was the Right Honorable Lord Provost and Lord Lieutenant of Edinburgh, Highlander of old, braw and strong and too much a champion to lose easily.

A man with a great deal of pride, too much to appear on her doorstep and beg her to hear him out or take his hand in marriage.

No, he'd only agreed to Macrath's outlandish proposal because of circumstances. He felt nothing but a smidgeon of embarrassment, if that, over the situation.

If they'd never been found out, he wouldn't have demanded she marry him. Instead, he would have fed her breakfast, had his driver take her home, and congratulated himself on a night well-spent.

Or maybe she was wrong. Had she really been so foolish to turn her back on Logan Harrison?

Dear God, what had she done?

When they returned home, James stopped the carriage in front of the house.

"I need to speak with you, Mairi," Macrath said.

She truly wanted to escape to her bedroom, but a look from Macrath indicated that it wouldn't be wise to avoid this meeting. She sighed inwardly and went into the parlor, standing in front of the glowing fire.

She heard him entering behind her.

"Say what you have to say and be done with it, Macrath," she said without turning.

"Thank you for joining us," her brother said in response.

She turned to see Robert entering the parlor. Everyone else, however, had evidently been dismissed, because Macrath closed the door, leaving the three of them alone.

She truly wasn't in the mood to be lectured by both of them. Very well, she erred. She'd admit that without reservation. It was altogether likely that she would make stupid mistakes in the future. Perhaps even mistakes involving the Lord Provost.

Would Logan ever seek her out again? Or would he be so offended by her refusal that he avoided her?

She would have to simply learn to get along without him. Granted, he'd been in her life for two months, but before that, she'd never seen him. She'd never sat in a room with him, feeling like the air was charged by his presence. She'd never argued with him, feeling her blood heat from trying to convince him of a point. She hadn't seen him in his kilt, a laughing glint in his eyes daring her. She'd never known what it was like to kiss him, or to be loved by him.

She would probably be known as a fallen woman, but the journey off the pedestal had been glorious.

All she had to do was forget a few things. Like the way he kissed, for example, or the shine of the sun on his hair. Or his eyes glittering with amusement. How he'd laughed, the sound echoing through the room and lodging in her heart. Or his white-toothed smile as he grinned at her.

She would take pains to forget his anger, too, as well

as his heroism and courage. She would not remember the
chill in his eyes or the knife edge in his voice.

"We have something to discuss, you and I," Macrath
was saying to Robert.

"Then you certainly don't need me here," she said,
grabbing her skirts. She would've made it to the door had
her brother not grabbed her elbow and held her there.

"This involves you as well, Mairi."

"Is this truly the best time to discuss finances, Macrath?"

"I'm not discussing finances, Mairi."

He dropped his hand and she turned to face him.
Robert went to sit on the end of the settee, stretching his
feet toward the fire. He often complained, in the winter
months, that each joint felt the crimp of the cold.

Now, however, he didn't utter one word. She looked
from him to Macrath, frowning. Perhaps, after the debacle
of this morning, it was best to keep her mouth shut, at least
until she figured out what Macrath had to say.

"Don't you have something to tell us, Robert?"

The older man tilted his head back, staring at Macrath,
the point of his beard making his face appear long and
narrow. A smile would have softened his appearance, but
Robert rarely found amusement in life.

"Your father was nearly a saint," Robert said. "I never
thought to say this, but it's glad I am that he hasn't lived to
see the day when his children turned against all he thought
dear."

He extended a bony forefinger in Mairi's direction.
"You have acted the whore with no shame, no regrets."

Before she could comment, he turned to Macrath. "And
you, encouraging her in her sin. She should be punished,
and all you do is accept her willfulness."

"Is that your long-winded way of denying your culpa-
bility?"

Robert stood, drawing himself up so straight he looked as rigid as one of the iron poles of the ornamental fence in front of the house.

"You set the fire?" Mairi asked, stunned.

"I did not. I most assuredly did not."

"No," Macrath said. "You might not have set the fire, but you wrote incendiary letters. Or are you going to deny that, too?"

Robert dragged a hand down his beard until it pointed toward the floor.

Macrath folded his arms in front of his chest, looking as sympathetic as a wall.

Did he really believe that Robert had done such a thing? Granted, he was a fire and brimstone kind of man, but she couldn't see Robert using the words that had been written in the letter.

"Not only did you write the letters, Robert, but you've tried to make Mairi's life miserable. I asked you to help her, not question the expenditure of every coin."

Robert held his hands out, palms up. "If I erred, Macrath, it was in memory of your father. I knew what he gave up to make the paper profitable."

Mairi had had enough.

"I loved my father with all my heart," she said. "But the *Gazette* was never profitable when he was alive. Macrath didn't make it profitable, either. Whatever contributions you made to it, Robert, were in terms of words like frustration and irritation. I was the one who made the paper profitable. I was the one who worked all those nights alone. I've been the only reporter for weeks and months and years. I even became a hawker when one of them couldn't come to work.

"What did I come home to? Not praise. Not support. Nothing as fine as that. I had to justify every cent I spent. You never said a kind word to me, including anything about my father. If you cared so much for my father, you would have cared a little for his daughter."

Macrath started to speak, and she turned and faced him. "I love you, Macrath. You are my only brother. Yet you treat me like I'm a child. Why not come to me and tell me your suspicions about Robert, rather than confronting him in my place? I don't need to be protected. I don't need to be shielded from the world."

She shook her head, but stopped abruptly when Macrath began to smile.

"Am I amusing to you?"

"I just figured out why you turned down the Lord Provost," he said. "Not because you don't love the man, Mairi, but because of your pride. You won't be married for the sake of shame."

"You don't know what you're talking about, Macrath."

"Which part? That you won't be married? Or that you love the man? Any fool could see that part."

When he was a little boy, Macrath hated to have his face washed. Instead of listening to him fuss, she would simply grab him around the neck and apply washcloth and soap to the dirty bits, holding him firmly when he squirmed. Right now she wished he hadn't grown too big for such treatment. She would've done the same thing, and while she was at it, left the soap in his mouth.

"You're like two donkeys in harness," he said, still smiling.

"I thought you would offer me an apology, Macrath, rather than a smirk. And you," she said, pointing at Robert, "I deserve an apology from you, too, for three years of being an insufferable ass."

When the older man reared back, she almost apologized, but restrained herself. People—men—simply had to understand that she was not going to stand for it anymore.

She was tired of working herself to the bone and receiving absolutely no appreciation for it. The only person who had ever seemed to appreciate her was Logan.

Must she think of him again?

She looked from Macrath to Robert.

"Just tell me why. Why would you do such a thing?"

Robert looked at her. "I thought you would listen to reason, realize how the world perceived you. But you didn't. You were all for going about your business with no care to propriety."

· She wasn't certain if he meant running the newspaper or lusting after Logan. She wasn't going to ask for clarification, either.

"I want you out of my house." She turned to Macrath. "I don't need a keeper. I can keep myself."

Macrath had the good sense to stay quiet and mute his smile. Robert almost started to say something, but she gave him a look that made him think twice before she marched out of the room, leaving the two of them alone.

The next morning Mairi opened her door reluctantly at the knock. She really didn't want to see anyone. What could she say that she hadn't already said? Nothing anyone told her would make her change her mind.

Macrath stood there, looking much as he had when he was a little boy and caught her doing something wrong: part charm and part delight that she, as the older sibling, had erred.

She sighed inwardly and waited for his lecture.

Instead of launching into a speech, however, all he said was, "In view of all that's happened, I'm taking Ellice home."

She didn't offer a comment, such as: the girl hasn't had

a chance to see Edinburgh yet. She'd been a hideous chaperone and she couldn't blame Macrath for whisking the girl away, back to Drumvagen and safety.

"I understand," she said, her voice sounding oddly gray.

She should get dressed and bid them farewell at the door, ensure that Cook supplied them with a basket of treats for their journey. What she wanted to do was go back to bed and put a pillow over her head.

Macrath's eyes were filled with sympathy, an expression she disliked when aimed at her. She looked away.

"I meant the fire, Mairi," he said. "You'll have enough to do finding a new building and getting the *Gazette* up and running."

She nodded. One day she would have to think of that. Tomorrow, perhaps, or when she felt able.

"I've made arrangements with my banker," he said. "All you need do is go to him and tell him what you need."

"A loan, Macrath," she said, her feelings of tenderness balanced by irritation. "That's all. A loan."

"Don't be foolish."

"I'm not being foolish, Macrath," she said. "Allow me a little of your pride. Just a smidgen of it."

"A ten year, noninterest loan, Mairi. If you don't pay me back, I'll send you to debtor's prison."

An unwilling smile tugged at her lips. "You know we don't have those anymore."

He thought for a minute. "I'll assess your wages."

"What wages?"

He frowned at her. "Don't say that you haven't given yourself a salary, Mairi."

"There was never enough money to pay me, Macrath. I was getting to that point when the fire occurred."

"Then you'll just have to take the money, Mairi. If you

want to consider it a loan, then fine. But you deserve the chance to run the *Gazette* as you wish. Besides, you'll need the money for the publishing company."

She shook her head. "You do know how expensive that will be, don't you?"

"It's worth it, even if we only publish Enid and Brianag's book."

He had a point.

"Let me know if there's anything you need." He held her gaze. "Promise you will."

She nodded.

He turned to leave her but hesitated.

"I'm sorry, Mairi," he said. "For my part in all of this."

"I know, Macrath. You do have a tendency, however, to barge in and think about the consequences later."

He laughed. "Virginia would agree," he said.

"I have nothing to fault you for, Macrath. Everything that happened was my doing." She held onto the door, feeling as if it was the only solid thing in her world. She didn't want Macrath to go, but he had his own life at Drumvagen. She had hers, whatever it might turn out to be, here in Edinburgh.

"Not Robert. That was my doing and none of yours."

She nodded. "Very well, not Robert. Will you replace him?"

"Do I need to?" he asked.

Did she need a chaperone? Once she would have enthusiastically told him no, but after the last two months, perhaps she needed to reassess herself. She hadn't been wise or calm or measured or anything else she thought herself to be.

She shook her head, determined never again to be as foolish as she had been.

"About Harrison. I think you love him, Mairi, and love

is such a fleeting and rare thing that it would be a shame not to acknowledge it and act on it."

"What does it matter?" she asked. "I ruined everything. I doubt he'll even want to see me again."

"Don't be foolish. You're mirror images of each other. Come now, haven't you seen it? He's stubborn and so are you. He's filled with pride and so are you. He's also intelligent, passionate, and determined to convince other people. All traits you possess, Mairi."

Macrath smiled, such a sweet and understanding expression that her heart felt as if it had been squeezed. She really was going to weep if he didn't leave, and soon.

"Are you an authority on love, Macrath, just because you married?"

"I'm an authority on love, Mairi, because I almost threw it away, just like you're doing. If Virginia hadn't been as hard-headed as you, I might not be as happy as I am today. Go to him. Tell him you love him. Don't throw away this chance at happiness."

The effort of simply standing there, listening to him, nearly overwhelmed her, and he seemed to sense it, too, because he caught her face between his hands and kissed her on the nose, much as he had as a boy.

"Be happy, Mairi. Do it. I want you happy."

She was not going to let him see her cry. Macrath would be horrified at first and then he'd tease her unmercifully. She looked away, studying the floor intently, trying to salvage a shred of dignity from this moment.

Chapter 32

Mairi sat in the parlor, wondering how much longer she could bear the room. She'd already grown tired of the house. She wanted to be doing something, anything.

She'd made one daylight visit to the site of the building that had once housed the Sinclair Printing Company. Charred timbers and the remains of the staircase lay in a heap in one corner. She thought the grayish lump of metal near the front of the building must be the press. Ash and a black, tarlike substance lay a foot thick everywhere. The acrid stench of smoke and a curious chemical odor hung in the air.

She knew she would remember that smell for the rest of her life and be able to label it. Nothing so easy as Fire or Disaster. It was pain, sharp and persistent.

For almost an hour she stood in the bitter cold, remembering. James and Allan were beside her, silent, as if they were all mourning. Perhaps they were, for something forever gone.

Nothing could be salvaged from the fire, so she hadn't been back. Nor would she ever return again. She didn't even want to rebuild on the site. Too many memories were buried there. No, if she was going to start the Edinburgh

Women's Gazette, she would do so in a new location, not
build on a ruin. She would lease an acceptable building
and start from the beginning.

She stared out the window, transfixed by the snow
piling on the mullions. Edinburgh in December could experience a day of bright sunshine followed by three days
of snow. The snow had been falling for two hours, covering the street in white, making every corner of her world
beautiful for a little while.

She glanced down at the book in her hand. She'd read
the same page three times and had yet to remember anything.

Yesterday she'd sent Abigail out to collect as many
broadsheets published by their competitors as she could.
Blessedly, there wasn't a hint of scandal about the Lord
Provost.

Although news of the *Gazette* fire had been reported in
the other papers, none of them gloated over their demise.
Instead, she'd been pleasantly surprised when several
representatives of competitive papers came to call, each
of them offering their press until she could find another
building. As gratified as she was, she'd turned them down.
Once the Edinburgh Women's Gazette was up and running, she intended to be the best newspaper in Edinburgh,
and she'd feel bad trouncing someone from whom she'd
taken charity.

Robert had left the house, packing his trunk, finding
lodgings in Leith. They hadn't spoken, and when he bid
the rest of the household farewell, she remained in her
room, refusing to see him. She'd taken a great deal of
abuse at Robert's hands. Not only his weekly tirades about
expenses, but his forever muttering dire predictions about
her actions. The letters were almost anticlimactic, demon-
strating exactly what he thought of her.

Although she wasn't certain she believed his protestations of innocence about the fire, or even that the fire had been an accident, she was sure she couldn't trust Robert again.

James occupied himself in duties in the stables. She noted, however, that Abigail took him his meals from time to time, along with a cup of tea and a few biscuits. Not to mention a purloined scone or two.

Were they all guilty of a subterranean life?

Allan had been offered the surprising task of helping out at one of Logan's bookshops. When he announced that he'd taken the position, she couldn't find the words to protest. How could she employ him when there was no paper? With no means to make an income, she couldn't afford his salary.

"The minute the paper is up and running, Mairi, I'll be your pressman."

She had only nodded, wondering when that would be.

She'd also begun to wonder if the fire wasn't a lesson of sorts or punishment for her arrogance. The moments of introspection were coming too frequently, as if someone had given her a stereoscope. Except that the slides she viewed weren't those of famous sights in Rome and Florence but those of her own life.

Each scene was a different example of where she hadn't been the person she'd always thought herself to be. Instead of diligent and conscientious, she'd been intense and dismissive. She recalled times when she wasn't as kind as she could have been, when she was impatient or simply didn't see other people. She heard her voice etched with irritation or boredom.

She'd told herself that she had to make the *Gazette* a success, which had only been an excuse to justify living a solitary life. She'd been hurt and shamed by Calvin's rejection but never admitted it. Looking back, she saw that she'd wrapped all that pain around her in a tight cocoon.

Fenella was right.

Somehow, she'd thought that Fenella wanted the same solitary life. How selfish she'd been, and now she compounded that feeling with envy.

Until meeting Logan, she hadn't known she was lonely. She thought her life was full, rich, and filled with events that propelled her from morning to night to morning again. She woke up energized and excited. She went to sleep grudgingly, knowing she needed her rest but unwilling to lose so many hours.

Yet something had always been missing.

She knew what it was now.

How odd that being refused admittance to the Edinburgh Press Club had changed her life simply by introducing her to Logan. Until that very instant when she'd first seen him, when her eyes locked with his, she'd been content with the existence she created for herself.

Seeing him had changed something, had unlocked a door she hadn't even known existed.

Would she ever be the same again?

She pressed her fingers over her eyes, trying to ease their stinging, a result of nights of fitful sleep.

From the moment she left his house she'd been in pain. She hadn't been able to sleep. She questioned everything in her life, and she was miserable. Worse, she was angry and on the brink of tears most of the time.

The door suddenly opened, and Fenella entered, followed by Abigail, each of them carrying a tray.

"Since you insist on remaining here or in your room," Fenella said, "I've brought lunch to you. We'll sit and eat together."

"I'm truly not hungry," she said.

"Then you can watch me eat," Fenella said, directing Abigail to place her tray directly in front of Mairi. "You can surely have some tea."

Before Mairi could say a word, Fenella thrust a cup into her hands. She took it and remained silent while Fenella poured the tea, then added the sugar she liked.

Maybe she would have a pastie or two. The smell wafting from the platter made her stomach growl in protest.

Fenella didn't bother hiding her smile when Mairi reached for one.

"You've been avoiding me," her cousin said a few minutes later.

Her pastie finished, Mairi reached for a chocolate-covered biscuit. She wasn't hungry so much as fumbling for something to say.

"I wasn't avoiding you," she said. "I just didn't seek you out."

"Or come down for dinner. Or lunch. Or breakfast."

An unwilling smile curved her lips. "Very well, perhaps I was avoiding you."

"Why?"

"Jealousy," she said.

Fenella's eyes widened and she stopped eating. "Of me?"

Mairi nodded.

Fenella put her pastie down on the plate.

"Why would you be jealous of me?" she asked, smiling gently. "You have the same potential for happiness."

"Embarrassment, then."

She sat back and looked at Mairi. "Hasn't that faded?"

"Regrettably, no."

"Are you embarrassed about being caught, Mairi? Or embarrassed for going to Mr. Harrison's home?"

She didn't know how to answer that. She wasn't embarrassed about going with Logan, but all of them descending on his house like hungry locusts was still humiliating.

Her only answer, however, was a shrug.

For a few minutes they didn't speak, the room cocooned by the falling snow.

Fenella dusted off her hands.

"You seem very interested in the idea of fighting for the rights of women, Mairi. Could you not also fight for the right to be a woman?"

She put the half eaten biscuit down. "What does that mean?"

Fenella sighed. "Why can't you love someone and still be yourself? Love doesn't change a woman. It makes life better, Mairi. It doesn't make it worse."

"I wouldn't know."

"Oh, you know," Fenella said. "If you'd allow yourself to. You're in love with Logan, but you won't allow it. Why, Mairi?"

She didn't answer.

"If I didn't know better, I'd think you were afraid. But you've never been afraid of anything." Fenella sat back. "Or am I wrong? Does he frighten you?"

She shook her head.

She felt protected around Logan, as if his size, the power of his personality, shielded her, even from herself. She'd never had anyone to depend on like Logan. Her father had always been too busy. Macrath had been too driven. And Calvin? She almost laughed at the thought of depending on Calvin. He'd been a weak man, terrified of the opinion of others. He would be horrified at her recent actions.

Calvin was a shadow next to Logan.

When would she stop doing that? Measuring other people against Logan wasn't wise. Worse, it made her sorrow even greater, if that were possible.

Fenella drank her tea then put the cup down, eyeing Mairi.

"I think you're in love with him."

"What I feel for Logan Harrison isn't love. Love isn't volatile. I want to shout at him more often than not. I want to march up to him and poke him in the chest with my finger." And then pull his head down for a kiss.

Fenella smiled. "The right man excites you, pushes you, makes you laugh with abandon."

She stared at her cousin.

"Love shouldn't make me want to run from the room and hide my head under a pillow."

Fenella shocked her by laughing.

Mairi frowned at her cousin.

"Love should make me feel warm inside, not as if someone has punched me in the stomach. I shouldn't be trembling at the thought of love. It should make me sigh in contentment, not make me nauseous."

"If you want to feel contentment, get a kitten. Or a puppy," Fenella said. "Feel that way for a pet, not a man."

Fenella shook her head, still smiling. "You're just like him, you know," she said.

Surprised, Mairi gave up all pretense of eating. "Macrath said the same."

"You're both strong-willed people, determined to get your way. You see a goal and you go after it. I think Logan is like that, too. Did you know that he's our youngest Lord Provost?"

"I may have read something about that," Mairi said.

"He's also been very successful in his businesses," she continued. "He has three bookstores."

"Yes, I know," Mairi said.

She glanced at her cousin, to find Fenella's eyes twinkling.

"We're not the same at all," she said. "Besides, he never said a word about the future until Macrath suggested marriage. I'll not force a man to the altar."

She didn't tell her cousin about his declaration of love, even though the words still echoed in her mind.

"Is that what has you in knots?"

Mairi studied her skirt as her fingers pleated the fabric. "I'm human. I have feelings."

"Perhaps he's the same," Fenella said, picking up one of the trays.

Mairi looked up at her.

"Perhaps he was loath to say anything for fear of your reaction. Would you have been receptive to his courtship?"

She stared at Fenella, who smiled at her.

"Oh, Mairi, love is exactly what you described. It's volatile and messy and inconvenient and glorious."

She vanished through the doorway, leaving Mairi to stare after her. Had Fenella always been so direct and she'd never noticed it before? Or had love changed her, as it seemed to change everyone?

As for her, she was almost sick for the loss of Logan and furious because she was. Then she was even more miserable because she realized she'd brought all this unhappiness on herself.

Logan had come up with a half-dozen strategies, all of them worthwhile. He could simply appear everywhere she went until she threw up her hands in exasperation and allowed him to plead his case.

Or he could send her a note for every hour of every day until she begged him not to write her again.

He'd compose a broadside—perhaps write a bad poem to her—have it printed and distribute it around her house, sending a hundred or so to her. Or hang them from the branches of the trees around her house.

He'd take out an ad in one of Edinburgh's papers and confess his love to her for all the good citizens of Edinburgh to read.

He'd stand in front of her house with musicians and serenade her. He'd been told he had a passably good baritone.

He would bring her books he'd liked, editions from his own library. He wasn't a fan of poetry, but perhaps she would like Burns. Every Scot liked Burns.

The problem was that none of those ideas would change Mairi's mind if she were determined that it wasn't going to be changed.

She didn't want his money. Although he hadn't amassed a fortune, his bookshops were doing well. Edinburgh was a city of lawyers, bankers, and politicians, and he catered to each group. Because of the success of his business, he'd always have an occupation to return to should he wish to leave politics.

He suspected that if the costs he had to pay to be a politician became too dear—the loss of privacy and the endless need to always be available—he could walk away from being Lord Provost without much difficulty.

He couldn't walk away from Mairi.

She didn't want his house or his possessions.

She didn't want him.

That was the most difficult thing to accept. How could she forget those moments in his bed? Or those hours when they'd talked and he'd been more honest with her than anyone?

He opened the bottom drawer of his desk, placed his feet on it and settled back in his chair. Weaving his fingers together over his stomach, he stared out the window at the view of the castle.

His classic thinking pose, as Thomas would say.

He had never courted a woman, let alone one like Mairi. Perhaps if he instituted all of his plans, she wouldn't have a chance to say no. She'd be so overwhelmed by his single-minded assault that she'd surrender.

He grinned. When had Mairi ever surrendered?

Thomas entered the room, his arms filled with papers. No doubt a hundred tasks he had to review before the next council meeting.

He smiled at his secretary. "Have I ever taken a holiday, Thomas?"

Thomas deposited the lot on top of his desk, rearranging his face from an instant frown to a more acceptable expression.

"Other than the few days you went to Drumvagen, sir? I don't think so."

"Then I think it's time I do, don't you?"

His secretary straightened, reached out one hand to align a file that had dared to stray from the stack.

"There isn't time now, sir. Perhaps in the spring."

He raised one eyebrow. "What if I disagree? What if I insist on now?"

"Then I would urge you to reconsider, sir. The Tramways Act is about to come up for a vote and your cooperation is needed in the venture. Plus, Sir Douglas Wood is giving a speech next week on the advantages of steam power."

None of which was as important as his personal happiness. He thought it of vital importance that the balance of his life be restored, a balance that had somehow become skewed when he wasn't looking.

"That's all well and good," he said. "But I want some time cleared from my schedule."

"May I ask why, sir?"

No, damn it, you may not. A thought not expressed due to his years of practice at tact.

Was Mairi the only one with whom he'd been completely honest?

"I'm going courting, Thomas," he said. "For a while, I want to be myself and not the Lord Provost."

"Miss Sinclair, sir?"

"Most definitely Miss Sinclair," he said, dropping his feet and sitting up.

"Sir, do you think that's a wise idea?"

"I don't believe being my secretary gives you the right to question my personal life, Thomas." He smiled as he said the words, but they were a slap, nonetheless.

Thomas recognized them as such, straightening from his stance by the desk. His face firmed, his lips thinned, his eyes were flat with hidden thoughts.

"I've been with you ten years, sir," he said. "From the beginning. I helped you win your first election and I was instrumental in your becoming Lord Provost."

Some of that was true, some was grandiose posturing, but he let Thomas have his say.

"Have you given up thought of running for Parliament, sir?"

"Not necessarily," he said, placing both hands on the top of his blotter. Where was Thomas going with this?

"With my guidance, I have no doubt you would win, sir."

Another bit of exaggeration he decided not to challenge.

"Your point being?"

"Sir, she's not suitable."

While he was in council chambers, he was adept at allowing words to wash over him like a fierce northern wind, separating those he wanted to examine in greater detail.

Most people talked twice as much as they needed,

words to convince, cajole, and persuade. Sometimes he paid attention more to how a conversation was initiated in order to make decisions about the speaker. Did he come directly up to his desk? Did he speak down to the floor or address him directly? Did he hurry with his words or give each the weight of gold?

Rarely, however, had he ever heard a comment and felt that the words had a power greater than the speaker had intended.

"She's not suitable?" he asked, his voice giving no hint of his rage.

"No, sir," Thomas said, warming to his subject. "Not like Miss Drummond. The Sinclair woman doesn't come from the proper family, one with advantages."

"You know who her brother is, I take it?" he asked, picking up his pen and examining it as if he'd never seen the instrument before this moment.

Thomas's lips twisted. "But who was her father, sir? And she's not related to the peerage in any way."

"Poor Mairi," he said. "She might as well be a bookseller." He smiled humorlessly.

"Your own background is such, sir, that you need a touch of aristocracy."

He held himself still with an effort.

"And even if you chose someone other than Miss Drummond, sir, I dare say she would comport herself with greater care than Miss Sinclair."

"Explain yourself," he said, leaning back in the chair. "How, exactly, does Miss Sinclair comport herself?"

All these years, he'd respected Thomas's intelligence. Any other man would have figured out by now that he was in trouble and that the best course of action was to simply slip out of the room and start running.

Instead, Thomas prattled on.

"She doesn't do what women should, sir. She doesn't act like a proper woman. She speaks her mind, and publishes drivel. You should know, sir, being the subject of one of her broadsides. She shouldn't be allowed to do what she does. She's not only shocking, sir, but she steps over the boundaries of proper behavior."

"Who set up those boundaries, I wonder?" he asked, his voice still surprisingly calm. The question was similar to Mairi's complaints. Why should she be judged by someone else's criteria?

Thomas didn't have an answer.

"You don't endorse her, then?" he asked, allowing his lips to curve into a smile, almost as if soliciting Thomas's approval was important to him.

Thomas smiled, taking the bait. "She wouldn't make a proper wife, sir."

A glint of an idea burned bright in the back of his mind. Almost as if it were a spark, the beginning of a larger blaze, say a fire that engulfed an entire building.

Logan stood so abruptly that the stack of paperwork on his desk flew to the floor.

"It was you," he said. He rounded the desk and advanced on his secretary.

Thomas finally had a sense of his own danger and backed away, but not fast enough. Logan grabbed him by the lapels and threw him against the wall.

"You're the one who started the fire. Why?"

"I don't know what you're talking about."

He went to Thomas and shook the man. "Why did you do it?"

"I knew you felt something for her," Thomas said. "She was going to ruin your career. I've worked too hard for her to destroy everything."

"So you thought to burn her newspaper down?"

He released Thomas only to throw him against the wall again.

Thomas straightened his jacket, regarding Logan much the same way he might an errant mouse that had found its way into his desk drawer.

"She won't do for you, sir. Not at all. She's already making inquiries into buildings to house the paper. She won't change."

"You could have killed her."

"I didn't know she was working that night," Thomas said.

Logan stared at the man he thought he knew.

"I wouldn't have done it if I'd known she was in there."

"What about the man who lived above the paper? What about him? How far are you willing to go, Thomas, to ensure I'm successful? Murder? One murder? Two? Just what are your limits?"

Thomas drew himself up, his eyes glowing like a fervent monk.

"There are no limits, sir."

He gripped Thomas by one arm and opened the door with the other, shouting for the runner who occupied the bench, waiting for orders.

"Summon the authorities," he told the young man.

He nodded and stood, his Adam's apple bobbing in his neck.

When Thomas made a sound, he glanced at him.

"Did you think I was going to let you go?" he asked. "Because of everything you've done for me? Because of how hard you've worked?" He shook his head. "Power has gone to your head, Thomas. What you did for me was as much for yourself. You liked working for the Lord Provost, having my ear. I can only wonder how you've taken advantage of it."

"I gave you ten years of my life," Thomas said.

"I'd give it back to you if I could, to be quit of you now."

As the authorities took Thomas away, he stood watching, feeling curiously relieved. The man's actions had helped him make a decision, one that had been hovering in the back of his mind for weeks.

He was going to change his life drastically. First, he would obtain some freedom for himself. Next, he would convince Mairi Sinclair that she couldn't live without him.

Of the two goals, he had the thought that the second was going to be more difficult than the first.

Chapter 33

The holidays had come and gone, for which Mairi was grateful. She hadn't felt like traveling to Drumvagen for Christmas or Hogmanay, so she'd remained behind in Edinburgh.

January was here, bringing in a new year, a new start. She was anticipating anything other than the malaise that had marked the last two weeks.

She'd pushed aside her pride and written Logan. Would he call on her? She had something important to tell him.

When he came, she was prepared to confess that she was a fool, that she was desperately in love, and that she couldn't live without him.

Except that he had never answered her note. Nor had he appeared at her doorstep.

What if she'd truly ruined everything?

Should she write him again? Should she beg? If begging was necessary, she would.

Instead, she'd written a letter telling him how she felt, but this one she hadn't posted. She was trying to find the courage.

She could get a new press delivered in three weeks and could replace the type with little difficulty. The problem was the building. She had yet to find the right location for the new Women's Gazette. Even though she'd always thought she knew Edinburgh before, after the last two weeks she was familiar with every inch of the city.

Edinburgh was her home and she had no plans to relocate, but she was considering acquiring land outside the city and constructing her own building, anything but exist in this purgatory of waiting.

Her fingers itched to fly along type. She'd filled pages after pages in her journal with ideas for columns. She'd written the writers who'd contributed to the *Gazette* in the past, urging them to submit articles for the new Women's Gazette when—not if—it became a reality.

In the interim, Mr. McElwee had surprised everyone by announcing that the SLNA had received approval from the council for their march through Edinburgh.

In the middle of January, on a cold, crisp day, she arrived early to the staging area dressed in her new red cloak, a present from Fenella.

A platform had been erected on Princes Street, and banners were already proudly flying. Some of the women were assembling placards. She debated if she should volunteer to carry one as well.

The weather was cooperating, piercing blue skies hinting not at snow but a glimpse of the sun, at least for an hour or two. The cold, however, penetrated to the bones, which meant they wouldn't be attracting a huge audience like a summer event might.

She caught sight of Mrs. MacPherson, startled as the woman raced toward her, her beaming smile turning into a curiously charming giggle.

"We cannot thank you enough, Miss Sinclair," the woman said, enveloping her in a hug. She pulled back and smiled toothily at her. "Thanks to you, the SLNA will get the attention we need, and the causes of women will be advanced a hundredfold."

"I don't understand, Mrs. MacPherson."

The older woman extended a gloved hand toward the hundreds of women beginning to congregate around them.

"This is because of you, Miss Sinclair. The Lord Provost made that clear. Without your efforts to convince him, he would never have agreed to the march."

Suddenly, she wasn't as cold as she'd been a minute earlier.

"The Lord Provost said that?"

"Oh, yes, and that he himself would be here today to laud you in public."

Logan here?

"There he is now."

She knew, even as she turned, that he would be standing there, watching her. She hadn't expected him to be on the platform, hatless as usual, without a scarf wrapped around his throat. Where were his gloves?

Someone spoke to him, and his head tipped back, revealing the column of his throat. Her stomach clenched. Every part of him was magnificent, even the parts that weren't visible.

Her cheeks were going to catch fire. Her ears warmed and she clamped a mental door on the thought that she wished he were wearing a kilt.

He winked at her.

She'd spent the last two weeks in agony and he was winking at her?

He began to speak, his voice easily carrying over the growing crowd. Instead of welcoming the women to the march, he startled her by addressing her personally.

"I own a building," he said. "One I've been meaning to find a use for. I only use a portion of it for Blackwell's and the rest is storage. I'm thinking it would make a fine place for a newspaper. But only to the right tenant, of course."

She could barely breathe, let alone speak, but she made a valiant effort.

"Are you thinking to offer me your building, Lord Provost?"

A murmur in the audience indicated that those who hadn't known who he was certainly did now.

"Aye, lass, I am, for a price."

"What would that be?"

She kept both hands clasped together, conscious of the interested gazes of the women close to her.

"Marriage."

She wished she had some witty remark to say in response. All she could do was watch as he slowly descended from the platform.

"I decided to offer you a bribe, Miss Sinclair."

"Is that so, Lord Provost?"

"Perhaps not a bribe. Perhaps we could call it an exchange. You get a building. I get a wife."

"I wrote you," she said. "You didn't come."

"You wrote me?"

She nodded, deciding to be brave and daring. "I wrote you and asked if you would come to the house."

His face darkened for a fleeting moment.

"I didn't get the letter."

She glanced away.

"What would you have said if I'd come to your house?"

"That I'd try to learn tact, and how to keep silent. That I'd be the very best politician's wife I could be."

His smile made her heart soar.

"That'll not be a problem, lass. I'm retiring from politics."

"You can't do that on my account," she said.

"As much as I'd like you to think I'd sacrifice all I have for you, it's not the reason."

"It isn't?"

He shook his head.

"Then I'm glad. I doubt my tact would have lasted all that long," she said. "I'm very opinionated," she added, wondering if she needed to be so honest.

"I've noticed," he said, his smiling broadening.

"And so are you, Logan Harrison."

"That I am."

"I won't become your shadow, just because you're a man."

To her surprise, the women close to her broke out in applause. Logan turned and grinned at the audience then looked back at her.

"It's part of what I admire about you, Mairi. Your passion and your spirit. I want to know what you think. I want a companion, not a shadow. But I've a feeling it's not going to be all roses and rainbows with us. There'll be enough vinegar to make it interesting."

Anticipation nestled behind her heart. What would life be like with Logan? Joyous. Fascinating. Exciting.

"I'll remind you of what I said before," he said, walking closer. "I love you."

He reached out and touched her cheek, trailing his finger down to her chin.

She pressed both her hands against his coat, not to push him away as much as simply be closer to him.

"I want to start the *Gazette* again, Logan. This time a paper devoted to women. The 'Edinburgh Women's Gazette.' I'll be at the paper every day and sometimes into the night."

"Then wouldn't it be handy if Blackwell's was nearby? When I can, I'll be with you. When you can, you'll be with me."

"It can't be that easy, Logan."

"Aye, lass, it is."

Her heart was too full and her eyes overflowing.

He tucked her to his side and addressed the audience, surprising her once again.

"I know you witnessed a private moment, and that's as it is. You'll know that I love this woman with my whole heart. Enough to make an idiot of myself in front of all of you."

Laughter swept through the women.

"It's entirely possible that you'll be privy to the rest of our courtship and our marriage as well."

How could she possibly refuse him? He stood there, his green eyes blazing, his legs braced apart as if he stood on a hill attired in a kilt, addressing an army he was about to lead into battle.

She fought the sudden urge to press her hands against her bodice to see if the hole in her chest was real or something she only felt. Her heart was crystal and it had shattered, all those tiny shards crashing around her insides as he smiled at her.

Bending his head, he kissed her right there in front of hundreds of women. When he dropped his arms, she reached up and placed her hands around his neck, not wanting the contact broken.

She heard a collective gasp from the audience, but they were going to have to get used to Logan kissing her, and often.

"Heaven help you, Logan Harrison," she said, blinking up at him, "but I love you with my whole heart as well."

"A wise lass you are, Mairi Sinclair."

She heard laughter around them, but she didn't pay it much heed.

She was too busy being kissed.

Author's Notes

A broadside ballad entitled, "Address to Robert Montgomery Esq; Late Lord Provost of the City of Edinburgh," 1758, was my inspiration for Mairi's poem about Logan.

A number of women met discrimination for one reason or another in the nineteenth century and went on to form their own journals and magazines. One of them was the *Women's Journal* (1870-1917), published first by Lucy Stone, then her daughter, Alice Stone Blackwell.

The LNA, or Ladies National Association, existed, and was the first group to be formed and led exclusively by women. The Contagious Diseases Acts, the reasons for which the group was originally formed, were repealed in 1886. The SLNA is the author's fabrication.

The Municipal Franchise act of 1869 applied to English women only. Early in the Parliamentary session of 1881, a member from Glasgow, Dr. Cameron, introduced a bill to ensure that Scottish women had the same rights as English women.

The Lord Provosts of Edinburgh were responsible for many changes and additions to Edinburgh, such as the adoption of, and statue to, Greyfriars Bobby, as well as the renovation of St. Giles Church. I've used some of the previous provosts as models for Logan.

The Edinburgh Press Club wasn't formed until 1939. However, several organizations existed in the nineteenth century that would have hosted popular authors of the day.

In the way that it sometimes occurs, I happened on to the story of Jane Cunningham Croly after *The Witch of Clan Sinclair* was written. In 1868 she was barred from attending a banquet honoring Charles Dickens at the New York Press Club because she was a woman. At the time, she wrote a column for women for the *New York World*.

Mary Louise Booth was the founding editor of *Harper's Bazaar,* originally called *Harper's Bazar,* in 1867.

A suffragette march occurred on Princes Street in Edinburgh in October, 1909, and was well attended by both participants and onlookers. (In 2009 another march celebrated the hundred year anniversary of that historic occasion.) To the best of my knowledge, a march did not occur prior to that time, but if it did, Mairi would have been there.

Want more of Clan Sinclair?
Keep reading for a sneak peek at Ellice's story,

THE VIRGIN OF CLAN SINCLAIR

Chapter 1

Drumvagen, Scotland
May, 1875

His lips skimmed down her throat and hovered at her shoulder.

"I knew you would taste like a sweetmeat."

Lady Pamela shivered.

A teasing smile curved his lips.

Pressing one hand against his chest, she moved back.

He countered by grabbing her hand, turning it, and pressing a tender kiss to her palm.

"You have to leave," she said.

"I am not leaving you until dawn comes, my dearest. Even then, I will have to be pulled from your arms by a host of your servants."

"I've my reputation to consider," she murmured.

He laughed, easing her closer until her cheek was pressed against his shoulder. She held back her sigh with some difficulty, closing her eyes and reveling in the feel of him.

"Banish me, then, lovely. Send me away with a

gesture. Give me the word and I'll leave your cham-
ber, your house, and even your life if you wish it."

How could she possibly send him away? If he left,
he'd take her heart with him, not to mention the glo-
rious pleasure she felt in his arms.

"That woman is the most annoying creature it's ever
been my misfortune to know!"

Ellice turned and stared at her mother.

Enid was advancing on her, determination in every line
of her face.

Quickly, she flipped over a page in her manuscript so
that none of the writing showed. Putting her pen down, she
addressed her mother.

"What has Brianag done now, Mother?"

Enid stopped, narrowed her eyes and pointed at the door.

"That creature!" she said, singling out Brianag with
that one imperial finger. "That abomination! That—
That—That housekeeper!"

Her mother's face was becoming a mottled red, her
mouth pursed up until it resembled a furled rose.

Oh, dear.

Her mother dropped her arm, resuming the march
toward her.

Any moment now she was going to notice the stack of
pages on the surface of the desk and demand to know what
they were.

That would be a disaster of the highest magnitude,
worse than when they were living in London and pretending not to be poor.

Ellice stood, turned and faced her mother, blocking her
view of the manuscript.

"She's done something to upset you. What is it?"

Her mother stopped, frowned at her, and took a deep
breath.

"That vile and despicable creature has insulted you!"

"Me?" That was a surprise.

Her mother nodded. "She bragged about her grand-daughter getting married."

"How is that insulting me?" Ellice asked, genuinely curious.

"She intimated that you would never marry. That you would remain on the shelf. That no man would ever want you. That I could not arrange a marriage for you as swiftly as she had acted the matchmaker for her granddaughter."

The first three points weren't troubling, especially since they were probably true. The last comment, however, had her staring wide-eyed at her mother.

Oh, dear.

Her mother was looking at her with such intensity that Ellice wished she would blink. Finally, Enid nodded just once, a sign that she'd made up her mind about something.

Once determined on an action, her mother never changed course.

Calm. She needed to remain calm, that was all. She wouldn't fidget, which was—as her mother had often told her—a nervous habit, one her sister, Eudora, never had. Nor would it do any good to let her mother know she was terrified. Eudora had always been poised and in command of a situation.

"You're of an age to be married," her mother said, moving through the sitting room, touching objects Ellice had brought from London to give her a bit of comfort in the Scottish countryside. A book Eudora had given to her on her fifteenth birthday. A sketch of her brother, Lawrence, framed in silver. A small porcelain statue, called a Foo dog, that resembled a wrinkly lion more than any dog she'd ever seen.

"You're not a child anymore, Ellice. You need to give some thoughts to a home and family of your own."

She was aware of her own age and circumstances, perhaps a bit more than her mother, who occupied herself with quarreling most of the day.

Because of Macrath's generosity, she and her mother had been given a home at Drumvagen, almost as if they were family in truth, instead of claiming only a tenuous relationship.

Virginia, Macrath's wife, had once been married to Ellice's brother. After Lawrence's death, Virginia had fallen in love with Macrath Sinclair, a Scot who made even Ellice's heart pound occasionally, especially when he looked at Virginia across the room with that certain look in his eyes.

Perhaps it was that look that had sparked her imagination. What would she feel if a man looked at her in that way, or treated her as if there was nothing more important in the world than her?

The problem was—she didn't want just any man for a husband. Where did she go to find another Macrath?

Her mother was still walking through the sitting room, her substantial skirt and train grazing the tables and brushing against the wall.

"Why should I marry?" Ellice asked. "I'm perfectly happy." A bit of a lie but was it necessary to be honest all the time, especially about something so personal?

Her mother drew herself up, shoulders level, hands clasped tightly in front of her. Enid was a short woman, one whose bulk made her appear squared. A small yet disquieting enemy if she wished to be.

"Marriage is a woman's natural state, Ellice."

"You're not married."

"I have mourned your father all these years, child. I do not wish to replace him in my affections."

Not once had she ever heard her mother speak fondly about the late earl. Whenever Enid referred to her long dead husband it was in an irritated tone, as if his demise had been solely to annoy her. Now she was claiming to feel affection for him? Ellice didn't believe it. She was not, however, unwise enough to make that comment.

Enid, Dowager Countess of Barrett, never forgot a slight, even one from her own daughter.

"Is it truly necessary that I marry?" Ellice asked. "Could we not find a small cottage somewhere? Not every woman marries."

"Only if they are desperately poor and without family. Or," she said, eyeing Ellice, "they are of a temperament unsuited to be a wife." She abruptly sank into a chair. "Tell me you haven't done anything to shame the family."

She eyed her mother. Was she supposed to be a child, ignorant of how, exactly, they came to be living at Drumvagen?

If Virginia hadn't bent the rules of society, with her mother's encouragement and collusion, they wouldn't be living in this grand house, each given a lovely suite, and treated like family members.

Perhaps it was best not to pursue that topic of conversation at the moment.

"No," she said. "I haven't done anything to shame the family."

She wanted to—did that count?

"Thank the good Lord and all the saints for that, at least." Enid fanned the air in front of her flushed face.

Should she tell her mother she was still a virgin? Not because she was all that virtuous and proper. The groom she'd met last year had been remarkably handsome, with soft green eyes, a quirk to his lips, and a Scottish accent that made her toes curl.

He'd been new to Drumvagen and hadn't known who she was. He'd kissed her soundly, leaving her to wonder at what she hadn't experienced. He'd gone on to work in Edinburgh, but she remembered him sometimes, and wondered what he might have done if he hadn't heard someone coming.

Society, however, would have skewered her had she done anything shameful. So she was left to view the smoldering looks between all the couples in her life, catch the sight of swollen lips and flushed cheeks and pretend she had no interest in such things.

What a silly notion.

Mairi had been the one to educate her, if only by accident. Macrath's sister was knowledgeable about a whole world of things, one of which was passion. Ellice could tell that from the way she looked at her husband, at the laughter they shared, not to mention Mairi's love of lurid novels.

On one of her visits to Edinburgh, she'd discovered two of Mairi's favorite books, devouring them on quiet afternoons when she was alone in the house, accompanied only by the servants. She learned a great deal from *Memoirs of a Woman of Pleasure* and *Tom Jones*. Coupled with her observations of life in Scotland, she'd gotten a very good education, enough to realize that Drumvagen was teeming with passion.

"Is there any reason I should rush to be married?" she asked. Other than her mother's wish to best Brianag?

"You are not getting any younger. Do you wish to be dependent on Macrath's charity for the rest of your life? A poor sad female reading in the corner of the room, hoping no one notices her?

Well, she did that now. She'd learned to keep silent, retreating into herself. At least she could write her feelings. Every word she'd never spoken, every thought she wasn't supposed to have, went into her manuscript.

Lately she'd had a great many adventures in her imagination, all of them centered around Lady Pamela.

Lady Pamela wouldn't meekly sit back and let someone else plan out her life. She wouldn't acquiesce to a marriage simply to have a place to live. She'd create her own world, with a smile and a promise in her eyes.

Men would drop at her feet.

Her mother stood, brushing down her skirts.

"Eudora would have been married at your age, child. No doubt I would have been a grandmother by now."

"Do you want to be a grandmother?"

To her surprise, her mother seemed to consider the question.

"Once I was in my own establishment, surely. What would truly be preferable is if your husband could defray my expenses so I wouldn't have to use my own money."

Now she was not only supposed to be married, but to be married well? What else did her mother want, a title? She didn't bother to ask. As the Dowager Countess of Barrett, of course she wanted a title for her last remaining child.

Where was she supposed to find a titled bachelor in Scotland? No, if she were going to get married, let him be handsome, gifted with a sense of humor, and that indescribably deliciousness that some men had. She wanted to feel the air charged around him. She needed him to look at her with eyes that smoldered with passion.

"We can afford to stay in Edinburgh for a few months," her mother said. "Long enough to find a husband for you, even if he is a Scot."

The glint of determination in her eyes warned Ellice.

For the next months she would be paraded in front of every available man, given endless lectures on decorum, especially peppered with comments about how her dear, departed sister had been so much better at everything.

Nor would she have a moment to herself. She'd be in her mother's company every hour of every day until she was married.

Why had the housekeeper challenged Enid?

Ellice didn't say a word as her mother sailed out of the room with the same disregard she'd shown entering it.

Suddenly, the suite was too close and confining.

She threw open the window to breathe in the spring air, heavy with the sweet perfume of roses and heather. To her right was the rolling glen beckoning her to come and walk. *Sit here awhile and dream your thoughts on this flat rock.* How often had she done that?

The day was enchanted, like most days at Drumvagen, promising its inhabitants tranquility and joy. Wagons would rumble down the road from the village bringing provisions. People would walk from the house to Macrath's laboratory. The staff would be intent on their tasks, as they were even now. Someone was whistling, and before the day was out she would probably hear someone singing.

If she belonged here, she'd feel blessed. Because she didn't, all this happiness was simply too much.

She felt like she had in London after Eudora's death. Her mother had retreated to her rooms, leaving Ellice to find her way through grief. She couldn't chastise the servants for the occasional laugh or jest. Their joy never touched her, however, and that's what she felt at Drumvagen as if she were in a bubble that prevented her from experiencing the happiness of others.

She wasn't unhappy. She just couldn't borrow someone else's emotions. She couldn't live off Virginia's joy. Even her mother's constant harping at Brianag was to be envied because it was heartfelt and real.

What did she feel?

Anxious and impatient for her life to begin. Not what her mother wanted for her, but what she wanted for herself.

Perhaps that's why her book meant so much to her. She felt every page of it, every paragraph, every word. The love

Lady Pamela experienced for Donald was the love stored away in Ellice's heart, just waiting for the right person. The passion Donald and Lady Pamela knew was hers. The yearning each felt was what sat, impatient and heavy, in her own heart.

She wanted to be away, leaving her suite, Drumvagen, and all of its inhabitants behind.

Mostly, she wanted to be away from who she was. She wanted to be someone more courageous, like Mairi. Mairi didn't chafe under the role circumstance had given her. Instead, she molded life to fit her, like Lady Pamela.

Nor was Mairi the only courageous person she knew. Everyone at Drumvagen was strong-willed and memorable: from Virginia, who had challenged society's rules, to Macrath, who created an empire from an idea, to her mother and Brianag.

She was the only one people ignored. *Oh, yes, Ellice,* people probably said, wrinkling their brows to summon an image of her.

Poor dear girl, she's Enid's daughter, correct? Pity the other one didn't survive. Heard she was a beauty, but this girl?

Brown hair and brown eyes and a completely malleable nature, they would say, describing her. Once, she'd been endlessly chastised for speaking out of turn, for saying what she thought. Years of being castigated had taught her to keep silent.

Taking the manuscript, she tied a string around it to keep all the pages together. It wouldn't do to lose one here or there, not when she'd worked so hard on the book.

Holding it against her chest, she opened the sitting room door, looking both ways. Once she was certain no one was there, she made her way down the corridor to the servants' stairs. She would go and work in the cottage. Virginia had made the place available to her and ever since it had been a sanctuary.

Through her words she'd become someone else, someone memorable and unforgettable, a woman of courage and daring, someone who captivated others, especially a man her equal. She'd have auburn hair and startling green eyes. She'd laugh with abandon and keep every man who looked at her in thrall.

She'd be Lady Pamela.

In the pages of her manuscript, she released every thought that trembled unspoken on her lips, every secret wish, and every torrid desire.

Lady Pamela wouldn't accept marriage to anyone simply because her mother wished it. No, she would be fiercely opposed to such a bloodless union. She would demand a say in her own life.

Virginia had altered her future herself. So had Mairi. Her mother had done the same, which was why they were living in Scotland.

Was she the only weak woman at Drumvagen? She was very much afraid she was.

The distant rumble of thunder warned her. She didn't care. She'd go to the cottage even in the pouring rain and remain there while the windowsills wept and the floor grew muddy.

She skittered to a halt at Macrath's voice, ducking around the corner just as he and a stranger appeared.

"I'm grateful you decided to call," Macrath said. "I've had questions about your father and the original architect for years."

"I've often thought of Drumvagen," the stranger said. "It's featured prominently in my childhood memories, especially the grotto."

She peered around the corner.

A man stood there, his back to her. As tall as Macrath, with black hair to match, he was attired in a dark blue suit. She wished he'd turn so she could see his face. His voice alone was intriguing.

Scottish English varied even within Drumvagen. Brianag's manner of speaking was vastly different from that of the maids. Nor did the maids sound like Jack, Hannah's husband.

This stranger's accent was Scottish in certain words and very English in others.

"Had your father planned to incorporate the entrance into the house?"

"I was hoping he would," the man said. "It's a wondrous place for a boy with an imagination."

"My own son considers the grotto his."

The man laughed. Ellice's toes curled, the first time they'd ever done that at a simple sound. Oh, if he would only turn.

Perhaps he had a misshapen nose. She'd consider a scar to be dashing, but crooked, black teeth would be very off putting.

"I'm surprised we haven't met before now," Macrath said. "With you being Logan's friend and the distance not that far from Edinburgh."

The stranger lived in Edinburgh?

An hour earlier she wouldn't have given the thought an iota of life. An hour earlier, before her mother announced her new plans, Ellice would have pushed aside the notion and laughed at herself.

She might write of a daring, shocking woman, but it was quite another thing to be that person. But was she simply to wait until circumstances happened to her? Was she never to act on her own?

Ellice looked down at herself. This morning she'd worn

a blue dress with bone buttons, white cuffs, and collar. She and her mother had instituted so many economies over the years that it was difficult to relinquish the habit now. The dress was like most of those in her wardrobe, constructed for long wear and serviceability, able to withstand the laundry and fade only a little over time.

Because of the bustle her mother insisted on—after all, just because they lived in Scotland was no reason to be fashion heathens—the dress was a little shorter than it should have been, revealing a glimpse of her ankles. At any other time, she would have been embarrassed to be seen in such old clothing. Right now, however, it was perfect for the plan that was bubbling up in her mind.

The stranger might be persuaded to think her a maid at Drumvagen.

If she waylaid him, would he take her to Edinburgh? She wasn't above begging. Would she need to tell a story? Would he believe she needed to visit a sick mother in the city? Or that she was pining for an errant lover?

If she must, she'd tell a tale, something that wouldn't cast Drumvagen or Macrath into disfavor but would appeal to the stranger's better impulses.

If he had any better impulses.

Perhaps he was a slaver, or a smuggler wishing to purchase Drumvagen for his evil uses. Had he come to scope out the land before leading his flotilla of ships to fire on the great house?

No, Macrath seemed to like him, and Macrath was a good judge of character. Besides, the stranger knew Logan. Any friend of Mairi's husband had to be a decent man.

Clutching the manuscript to her chest, she crept to the front of the house—the better to avoid Brianag—and slipped out the massive double doors.

The minute Ellice saw the carriage, she changed her plans.

The visitor to Drumvagen didn't travel in a normal equipage. Instead, his team of four horses pulled a brougham, a massive carriage similar to a mail coach.

She would not have to flag down his driver after all. She wouldn't have to throw herself on the visitor's mercy. She would not have to grovel.

Instead, she was simply going to hide in the carriage.

To her relief, the driver was nowhere in sight. She neared the carriage with a nonchalant walk, glancing over her shoulder to see if anyone was watching her from Drumvagen.

Virginia was in the Rose Parlor. Brianag was no doubt giving orders to the maids. Sinclair was escorting his visitor around the house, which only left her mother and the children, both of whom she adored. Whenever Alistair saw her, he ran toward her, arms spread wide as he screamed, "Leese!" His sister, Fiona, was only a year old, but she was already beginning to emulate her brother in not only her affection, but her shouts of glee.

But she didn't see any childish face pressed against a windowpane. Nor was her mother standing there admonishing her with a look.

She couldn't hide in the rear of the carriage. Two trunks were stored behind the brougham and secured with a leather flap from the top of the vehicle to the fender.

She could only wonder about Macrath's visitor. Was he a world traveler? Where had the visitor gone before coming here? Was he truly returning to Edinburgh? What if he wasn't? What if he was going to Kinloch Village and from there to America or an even more exotic location? What if he was traveling on to Inverness instead?

She didn't want to get trapped in a city with no funds or friends, but if she returned to her room to get some money from her strongbox, there was every possibility the stranger would leave before she got back.

Worse, she might be seen by Brianag or her mother before she could return to the carriage.

No, she was simply going to assume that what she'd heard was correct. The visitor was returning to Edinburgh. Once in the city, she'd find a conveyance to take her to Mairi's house, where the driver would be paid.

She glanced back at Drumvagen.

The darkness on the horizon, as well as the swelling wind, gave evidence of a fierce storm to come. Drumvagen stood up to the elements well, a house buttressed against all types of weather. The snows of winter melted from the edifice as if in apology for marring the perfect beauty of the twin staircases or four towers. The winds that came off the ocean pressed against the brick and the rows of windows without effect.

Every time Macrath returned to the house, he had the driver stop just before the curved approach and simply stared at his home. Anyone could tell how much he loved Drumvagen and how proud he was of the house he'd finished building.

By leaving, Virginia and Macrath would probably think she'd rejected their kindness. They'd both effortlessly enfolded her into their family. She didn't want to hurt either of them, but her mother wouldn't be stopped.

Either she took this opportunity or she ended up being married to someone her mother chose.

In one of Macrath's carriages, the seat lifted up, revealing a storage area. This carriage was easily the size of Macrath's. Would it also boast a secret compartment?

Entering the carriage, she ducked down beneath the window. The carriage smelled of leather, which was understandable because of the leather seats. But why should it smell of lemons?

To her wholehearted relief there was a compartment beneath the seat. Only she was very sure she wasn't going to fit, not with the bustle her mother insisted she wear. Every morning Ellice tied on the garment that looked like a fish-tail hanging over her backside.

No one at Drumvagen, except her mother, cared if her dresses hung correctly, plumped from the rear.

In order to fit into the compartment she was going to have to remove the hated thing.

She put the manuscript into the compartment, then hurriedly reached beneath her skirts, finding the ties to the bustle and slipping it off. Folding it into as compact a size as she could, she pushed it, too, into the compartment.

In a normal carriage the journey to Edinburgh would take four hours. It was altogether possible they might reach the city in less time in such a vehicle as this.

Ellice entered the compartment, kneeling before wedging herself in sideways. The space smelled of wet boots and horse.

She was more than willing to be a little uncomfortable in the short run. After all, her freedom was at stake.

Telling herself to be as brave as Lady Pamela, she closed the seat on top of her.

In minutes she'd be on her way to Edinburgh. She'd take her own life in her hands and determine her own future.

Along the way, perhaps she'd get to see the stranger's face.

NEW YORK TIMES AND USA TODAY BESTSELLER
KAREN RANNEY

A Scandalous Scot
978-0-06-202779-5

After four long years, Morgan MacCraig has returned home looking for solace. Yet peace is impossible to find with the castle's outspoken new maid trying his patience ... and winning his love.

A Scottish Love
978-0-06-202778-8

Gordon MacDermond has everything he could ever want—except for the one thing he most fervently desires: Shona Imrie, the headstrong beauty he foolishly let slip through his fingers.

A Borrowed Scot
978-0-06-177188-0

Veronica MacLeod knows nothing about the breathtaking, secretive stranger who appears from nowhere. Montgomery, Lord Fairfax, agrees to perform the one act of kindness that can rescue the Scottish beauty from scandal and disgrace—by taking Veronica as his bride.

A Highland Duchess
978-0-06-177184-2

Little does Emma, the Duchess of Herridge, know that the dark and mysterious stranger who bursts into her bedroom to kidnap her is the powerful Earl of Buchane.